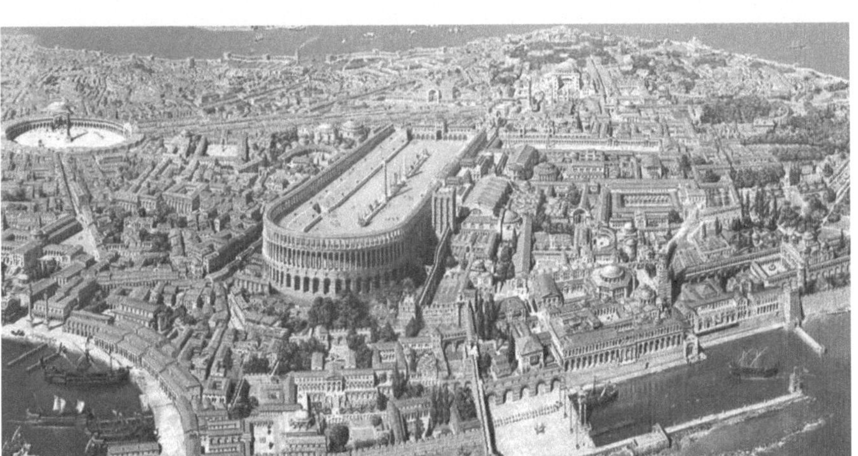

Constantinople and its sea walls, with the Hippodrome, Great Palace and Hagia Sophia in the distance, ca. 10th century, by Antoine Helbert, image source: TheCollector.com

BLUE GREEN

FANS AGAINST THE EMPIRE

A NOVEL

RICHARD WALL

Published by Atlantic Editorial, LLC

Atlantic Beach, Florida

1AtlanticEditorial@gmail.com

Printed in the United States of America

ISBN 979-8-9891419-1-3

Library of Congress Control Number 2023918967

Cover and Typesetting: Stewart A. Williams / stewartwilliamsdesign.com

"You can tell they are mad from their behavior: the chariots have barely set off before they start reporting on what they see. I regard it as a form of madness. They don't see what's been thrown down, they think it's the starting flag, but in reality it's the figure of the Devil flung down from the dizzying heights."

—TERTULLIAN

Acknowledgments

Book cover design and interior layout by Stewart Williams. My thanks to the several readers who reviewed and commented on the first draft and the revised final edition. Their comments were helpful and their support much appreciated. I am grateful for the many sources referenced to establish the historical facts, from the contemporary "Secret History" (ca. 550 C.E.) by Procopius to "A History of the Later Roman Empire, from Arcadius to Irene" (1889) by J.B. Bury. Three additional books were particularly helpful in understanding key aspects of the times and actions: "Circus Factions: Blues and Greens at Rome and Byzantium" (1976) by Alan Cameron; "Among the Thugs: The Experience, and the Seduction, of Crowd Violence" (1992) by Bill Buford; and "The Perfect Servant: Eunuchs and the Social Construction of Gender in Byzantium" (2007) by Katherine M. Ringrose.

Prologue

The Eastern half of the Roman Empire in 531 C.E. was strong and intact, unlike the Western Empire where titular emperors existed at the discretion of German warrior kings. Yet East and West still comprised the Roman Empire, with the East historically richer by far and firmly connected to Greek culture that had held sway since the conquests of Alexander the Great 800 years earlier. In the eastern capital of Constantinople (present day Istanbul, Turkey) Emperor Justinian the Great ruled, dealing with a mounting disruption of society and order: the hundreds-of-years-old clash of the chariot racing fans, sometimes called factions. Beginning in the early days of Rome, chariot racing was highly important in popular culture, with more people witnessing chariot races than gladiatorial events. Chariot races were astonishing competitions that stirred spirited emotions and excitement during the events and were the talk of the majority of the population for days preceding and following them. For hundreds of years, chariot racing fans had four teams they cheered for: the Blues, the Greens, the Reds and the Whites. In the fourth century, Constantinople had become the New Rome, appropriating and expanding the role of chariot racing.

The circus, Circus Maximus in Rome and the Hippodrome in Constantinople, was also the one place where citizens could "petition" their emperor, with requests for more bread, the ouster of abusive ministers and other issues. In Constantinople and other eastern cities, such as Antioch, Alexandria, Ephesus and Thessalonica, the circus was located adjacent to the palace, indicating the direct connection between the emperor, the races and the cult of Nika (victory). Attendees exalted the emperor's divine authority and their loyalty to him as the personification of the victory exhibited in the competition.

In sixth-century Constantinople, the established relationship of loyalty was breaking down, and the clash between the more prominent Blues and Greens had reached an apex of violence and destruction. The entire city and much of the Eastern empire was divided between Blues and Greens – in a manner much more intense and widespread than the importance of sports in today's society. Theater performances were also very popular and similarly divided into competing factions, with Blue and Green pantomimes, actors and supporters. At this time, Emperor Justinian the Great was changing the independent nature of the factions and bringing them under imperial control, a shift that did not sit well with many.

Destructive young male racing fans of Constantinople, what today we would call "hooligans," often rioted after races and theater performances, burning down parts of the city while killing each other, innocent citizens and the imperial troops that tried to control them. Rioting mounted in Emperor Anastasius' reign, once causing him to offer his crown to quell the ongoing disturbances. Justinian's uncle, Emperor Justin, had a difficult time dealing with racing fan riots. When Justinian succeeded him in 529, the tensions and disorders of the Blues and Greens were more pronounced and volatile than ever.

— R.W.

Contents

Wilder Again

Occasionally I wonder about Tedius Afer standing at the foot of my bed, as he is now, but holding a bloody knife or my own pillow he has just murdered me with in my sleep. Every master feels that burden, the constant prospect that your slave will turn on you, no matter how good you've been to him.

I shouldn't think this of Tedius, whose bony-nosed Greek face looked anxious on this morning. But I do sometimes, even though that kind of thing rarely happens. Most likely I would look up to no face at the foot of the bed, Tedius having fled for a chance at a better life, a better master. And I would lose not just an excellent slave but a dear friend – something we do not speak of, nor need to.

"A beautiful morning and still part of it left," he announced, yanking the drapes open like pulling off a scab. He knows I hate that. He was given to me on my 13th birthday, though he was around well before that as a house slave for my family. Far from cutting my throat, Tedius would be more likely to cut someone else's – for me, as he has threatened to do in the past.

"I'm unmoved by your beautiful morning," I mumbled, shading my eyes. "I've been up for two hours doing some work – by soothing candlelight."

He raised a skeptical eyebrow and bumped the bed with his knee. "You have a visitor."

"Surely not so early."

"It's not so early." He extended a sesame roll like a treat to get a dog to sit up. I bared teeth and shook my head no.

He's been at my bed most mornings for 10 years, sometimes when he is worried about me. I used to get angry that he would concern himself with anything other than my sharp-stropped razor, my starched tunic or my calendar for the day, which resides in Tedius' nimble head. I have come to realize that his instincts for worrying have kept me alive on several occasions – another thing we don't speak of, nor need to.

"I am glad you're being so productive, Gaius Galen. But you need to rise for this guest."

"She can wait."

"Not so lucky, Sir. A gentleman from the track: Ammianus Dio Verus awaits in the vestibule. He says Flavius sent him, but I think that's a lie."

"Good God, Tedius! Why didn't you tell me?" I started to look for my underclothing on the floor and he threw them to me, then handed me a beige tunic with crimson trim. He knows my love of good clothes and dresses me with expert taste.

"Your toothpowder and brush are ready, I'll be in to shave you on your call," he said, beginning to eat my roll on the way out to tell my guest, my superior's superior at the Hippodrome and a high subordinate of one of the most important men in Constantinople, that I was thrilled he was there and would join him shortly and with pleasure.

While I cleaned up – deciding to shave myself today – Tedius brought our guest into the large living area of my apartment, seated him and served him spring water. When I came a few moments later, Ammianus was examining a statue of Hermes, over whose extended arm pointing to something in the future I had hung a wineskin the night before.

"Ammianus Dio Verus, thank you for waking me from a horrible dream with not a woman in it," I dipped a slight bow and gestured wide with both arms. "Welcome to my home."

"You should have sent me packing coming to you unannounced,

Gaius Galen," he said with false humility, re-tossing a fold of his indigo toga across his shoulder.

"Nonsense. You actually are not disturbing my sleep, or bad dreams. I've been working out some cost calculations on a new mix for the track surface." This lie brought an amused huff from Ammianus.

He was a fat man, and looked to have sweated his toga under the arm – in December, probably from the exertion of climbing the steps to my second-floor home. He also was a sour man, with a round head that appeared squashed downward, bunching his eyes into pained bulges, his wide nose and small mouth into an unpleasant look piled above a double chin. He worked his lips with distaste, as if he had just swallowed someone else's bile.

I guided him by the elbow to three couches along the wall, offering him the green one and taking the gold brocade one beside it. Tedius said he would get more wood for the fire and took off downstairs, though we both knew there was plenty a few steps away outside on the balcony.

"Flavius has sent you to me, I understand."

"No. That's what I told your imbecile. Why tell a slave the truth?" Ammianus snorted, looked into the large landscape painting of vineyards on the wall then to me with a purpose. "Gaius Galen, this is a completely unofficial visit on very personal business."

I nodded and waited.

"You've done a fine job with Flavius these past years, proving yourself to be a quick learner, competent manager and sly negotiator – as I am sure your morning calculations would bear out." He gave another snort. "Tell me, did you ever think it would go this well for you?"

"Ammianus, I always think it will go well for me – this moment, tomorrow, next year," I said, with confidence and a little sign of boredom to cover my wariness about why he would possibly be here.

With a light smile he said, "I am not interested in your future, it is your past I am here for."

"The past is over."

"That is never so, *Wilder.*"

The name struck me hard, and my chest tightened but I didn't change my expression. He was watching for that and continued before I could think of a decent reply.

"You are well liked at the track, and are all over the place, places you aren't intended to be I have noticed at times," Ammianus' eyes sparkled for his resources. "You are poised to continue moving up in the Green organization, are well respected and apparently trusted."

Still surprised by *Wilder*, I thought I needed to push back. "Will I have to return these compliments in a moment? Because I am happy to do so."

His chins jiggled in a derisive little laugh. "You are also a fool and remain lucky to be alive. You probably started out on the streets by stealing rings from cripples." He made that snort again, a tick I believe. "But it is that part of your past that I want. Do you still have it?"

No! I wanted to shout. But that wouldn't do. In an instant he had overturned the three years I've spent trying to move away from that past, from that nickname.

"You'll have to tell me what you mean, Ammianus," I said, remaining as calm as I could.

Sandals rasped up the stairway, and Tedius entered with wood, adding two logs to the fire and shoving a handful of small branches onto the coals for encouragement. Ammianus had tightened his mouth shut and folded his arms over his chest, slanting an impatient brow toward Tedius.

"Anything you care to tell me, you can say in front of Tedius," I said.

"Then our conversation is over," and he cinched his arms tighter.

"Tedius, leave us," I said. He has a knack for disappearing like a thought and was on the stairs before Ammianus could relax his cocked eyebrow.

"What I mean is, people want your skills with the mob. Green, Blue, it doesn't matter. You were good enough as Wilder, one of those self-installed leaders of the mob, content with mayhem alone. But then, your shift to brilliance," Ammianus said awkwardly, probably unused to giving compliments. "No one has ever done what you did. I know you're completely out of all that now, and how you managed to get from there to here is itself an accomplishment."

Ammianus had thrown my secret at my feet. He knew of my criminal past as a wanton rioter, knew my nickname of Wilder I had earned along with my rank as an informal lieutenant of angry thugs, knew of my extraordinary accomplishment. But I could not admit it, not at this moment.

"You flatter me, Ammianus. May I get you wine for your water?"

His eyelids shuttered to deflect my evasion. "You have an opportunity here, a wholly unique one."

"Who wants to give me this wonderful opportunity?" I asked.

"That detail is not going to come from me," he said. "You will only ever know me, as a representative. I am like an old woman matchmaker."

I saw the resemblance, but did not remark on it. "So, you are not here at the behest of Maximius Clater Nerva, Lord of the Factions?"

"Maximius Clater Nerva, the Emperor's Actionare," he corrected, "doesn't know I am here. He has no part in this ... opportunity, no knowledge whatsoever. You should know that." Ammianus hauled himself to sit upright on the divan.

"Gaius Galen, let's not make this difficult. In the riots three years ago, you worked magic – for yourself, your men and your clients. I want you to work that magic for someone else this time. We see the ire in the streets building again, the disaffection with the emperor, as he – rightfully – moves further to bring the racing teams and their factions under his control. It will need release. Soon. And your reward could be much greater than what you made on your own before." He squeezed out a tight-lipped smile. "On the other hand, I'd hate to see you lose this easy position you have, playing in the dirt, so to speak."

It irritated me that this soft bureaucrat had me immediately on edge and wary, and my instinct was to physically intimidate him, perhaps a slap – remind him that he was in the den of a murderous thug, his bodyguard useless for the moment downstairs. But I could control my instincts much better now than in my destructive days – and I knew he surely would have had me killed for a slap, though the idea was comforting enough to raise my spirits.

"Magic is condemned by the Patriarch as well as by most competing sects," I offered with a generous smile. "I know nothing of any magic, Ammianus."

I caught myself just before admitting to being Wilder and paused. I had made piles of money by figuring out how to direct sections of rioters toward and away from specific properties. I blackmailed owners, offering to try to spare their homes or businesses, and earned rewards from other wealthy people by skillfully turning rioters against properties owned by their competitors or enemies. It was wildly profitable and even more intoxicating. But it's not something I could go back to. One cannot live through such dangers twice. I was lucky before, and I am different now.

"I don't have that magic you speak of. And I don't want it."

He looked at me like he knew something I did not. "Well, some offers are not to be refused," he said while clapping his hands once, softly. "This, unfortunately, is one of those. Hardly an offer, really."

"Of course it is an *offer*," I scoffed and stood to prompt a close to our meeting. "Ammianus Dio, are you certain you desire no wine before you leave?"

"No wine, even if it were from the hopelessly inaccurate vineyard in your painting." He rose and nodded at the cheap replication of a masterpiece on the wall. "I see this news has startled you – brought out the uncivil hothead I am looking for. This is a good start, Gaius Galen. A start of an important relationship." Ammianus closed with me, his blubbering belly slightly grazing my flat stomach as he leaned in and kissed my right cheek, rather sweetly. He backed away and patted both my shoulders, giving me a *There's my boy* smile. "We will be in touch."

"I look forward to that," I responded, my tone ambiguous, my skin crawling from his contact. "I will walk you down."

"No need," and he made a piercing whistle with his little mouth. "My ass will do."

He was at the top of the stairs when his slave appeared, a bruising Isaurian as rugged looking as the Taurus Mountains he was from.

"My street escort," Ammianus explained. "Only a mad man crosses an Isaurian, and it would take several to dent this one's skull," and he gave that skull a rap with fleshy knuckles. "Now, Phocas," he ordered, and down the stairs they went, Phocas leading.

I turned back from the stairs and there was Tedius, standing in the archway to the dining area. He tossed me a sesame roll and looked down the stairs, the lower door just closing shut.

"I was talking to Phocas a few moments ago," said Tedius. "Joked that he would piss in the man's pomegranate juice every morning if he didn't think the master would like the taste."

"So, you came up the back stairs and heard it all, I assume." I took a bite out of the roll, the taste of thyme a pleasant surprise.

"Yes, Master. I'm afraid I did." Tedius narrowed his eyes and winced his mighty nose. "This is not good, for you or Wilder, I fear."

"No, not good." I took another bite. I watched a few sesame seeds sprinkle my Persian rug, then looked at Tedius, a step nearer now to better nag me.

"Not good for tomorrow, either," he said, picking up some seeds, cutting his glance up a couple of times. "Should we call it off? It could likely be reckless, now."

"No, certainly not." I half laughed. "This makes tomorrow even more interesting, I think. He'll probably have me watched – seems to have been watching me for some time."

My slave frowned at me.

"Tedius? Can you bring me some pomegranate juice, with no urine?" I asked to lighten him up.

"That I will."

Fetching the juice, more rolls and two apples, he sat on the carpet and we planned. That always soothed Tedius. We both needed a little calming.

Tomorrow was already a big day, and Ammianus' uncovering my secret identity along with the threat of extortion was not going to ruin my desire to entertain lovely Messalina in grand, reckless fashion: women were not allowed at the races. Tedius and I went through the planned mid-race rendezvous with her and the seating arrangements.

My friend Atakam, an imposing Hun and Roman Army officer, was accompanying us to help it all go off smoothly – or, as he had said, to enjoy the resulting trouble.

Tedius had been worried already about tomorrow but was now even more concerned after Ammianus' revelation.

"He's got you, Wilder," said Tedius, biting into an apple while eyeing me. "He probably also knows about your careful erasure of past low-life connections, the upward path to esteem with all the right decisions, and token gestures to regain the respectability due your family."

Tedius was getting himself all worked up, and I needed to calm him with my blind optimism. "So what if he knows my past? I am not happy he appears to – and I will definitely try to find out how he did – but if I lose my job at the Hippodrome playing in the dirt as he put it, I will survive. And Tedius, it's most likely that nothing will come of our visitor's offer."

He shook his head. "He seemed sure of himself to me. And to the heart of it, Gaius Galen, we couldn't survive that again."

"We?"

"Of course, *We*," he said, pointing the apple at me. "It is impossible that I would not be with you, as before and now – in everything – toothpowder, helping engage Messalina for you in this crazy scheme tomorrow, keeping your finances in order and your father at bay."

"You are a true friend, Tedius, as well as an outstanding slave!" I shoved his shoulder a bit and took his apple. "What would I do without you?"

"What would happen if you were forced back into the rioting, as he intends – I bet he has his marks already set." Tedius' Adam's apple started to wobble, a sign of agitation. "You've developed a taste for respectability and grown soft. You haven't even thrown a punch in almost three years. Yes, you're still strong and relatively young, but you now stroll the streets as a gentleman, not a fighter. What would you do?" he asked with worry.

"I would become Wilder!" I said, my mouth watering for that old taste for mayhem.

He nodded slowly. "Yes, you would ... and you know what that would bring back."

Tedius had recognized the downside before I did. I took a bite of his apple and handed it back to him.

Hippodrome Imposters

I've been a pagan, an orthodox Christian, a monophysite, an Arian and a Jew, but I always come back to my true religion here: I am a Green.

"Green wins – again and again!" I shouted along with half of the Hippodrome, the Green fans at least 35,000 strong and roaring over the losing Blues. Our Constantius was first and Diosophone second, Blues lost and humiliated on the final lap. Up from the crowd here and there flew pigeons, a message with the race results tied to the leg on its way to a betting shop in the city or across the Bosphorus Strait in the Asian suburbs.

Eighty-two thousand men below me and one Messalina beside, lightly pressing against me as she delighted with the gleeful chariot racing fans, her luscious bounce constrained and unseen yet vibrating my being. Her bosom bound as tight as a charioteer wraps his reins around his chest, Messalina had paved over the curves of her hips and breasts with layers of cloth, adding extra belly wraps for pudgy detail. She was made up to be a he, Semacus, who accompanied Atakam and me.

Over the Greens' jubilation and hyena taunting of the Blues rained a near invisible cloud of dust from my track mix, pulverized into the air by 48 horses and 12 chariots through seven laps, dusting all, Blue and Green, winner and loser, senator and slave, alike.

This chilly day of December races was well viewed from the railing of the top row where we stood in the Green section. Up here Atakam and I could talk more freely and explain things to Messalina. The Hippodrome shimmied from the rhythmic stomping of the victorious Greens. Shaped like a massive elongated ark with curved bow pointing south to the nearby shore, the shaking arena seemed ready to launch downhill into the Propontis Sea.

Messalina pointed across the track to an ornate, enclosed viewing box and asked, "Is that where Emperor Justinian and Empress Theodora are, watching the races?"

"Yes, from the Kathisma. But they probably watch their subjects around them more than the races," Atakam answered. "Many come hoping to see the crowd tangle with the emperor, yelling for relief from taxes and even hissing and stamping their feet at the emperor himself. In these times of growing discontent, people are beginning to think that the bear keeper – " and he nodded his head to the Kathisma – "might well be devoured by the beast he tries to control. And everyone here who backs a color would love to see that sight – much more than any race."

"I always thought the idea of chariot fans posing a danger to the emperor was fanciful bragging," said Messalina, taking in the raucous spectators. "But here among them, I feel a force barely contained. I don't know how to describe it. Is it the same in Rome?"

"Not the same," Atakam answered. "The people's attachment to the colors is more intense here and volatile. Our Hippodrome is smaller than Rome's Circus Maximus, but in our New Rome, we have better drivers, better horses, better fans, better riots."

"I despise rioters," she said with disgust. "Their destruction and violence have nothing to do with these athletes' accomplishments."

"Sounds as if you have some personal experience with that," Atakam said to her in a joking manner, for the two had struck up a liking for each other after just meeting not an hour ago.

"I do, and it's not something I wish to talk about," and she turned away to look at the Kathisma, where vigilant fanners worked to keep most of the track dust out.

Learning that I was technically a despised person by this woman I very much wanted to like me chased this enjoyable moment of Green victory out of mind and replaced it with a vivid recollection of Ammianus kissing my cheek. I chased that image away by looking at Messalina, hidden underneath Semacus.

Her lovely face was disguised as if in a recent fight, with artful makeup of bruises, a couple of healing cuts with dried blood (lamb's), a bandage across the top of her left eye and forehead, and the look of dirt and sun from daily toil roughing her skin. Pantalooned and heavy-booted like a northern barbarian, Semacus in her peasant's field coat blended in with the hundreds of other such coats around us. On this cold race day her green knitted scarf marked her allegiance and was worn high across her mouth to hide the pure female sex of her sensuous lips. Being right next to her, I couldn't even see that she was a woman – but certainly sensed it.

She has begged me for three months to bring her to the Hippodrome – in violation of law, God's command and my own common sense, which has been called meager. She wanted to experience how everyone in the city and the empire got so worked up about the 70 race days a year given to this entertainment, some days crammed with as many as 24 races. It was heaven for race fans and most everyone in the city, but a devilish mystery for the minority of others who could not understand how a color on a chariot going around a track could mean so much to so many.

Now Messalina was taken with my Constantinople Greens, stomping slightly herself and raising her rough-gloved hands to the sky, as triumphant as the veteran fans around her watching the emperor hand the laurel wreath of victory to Constantius.

She leaned in to speak to me behind her hand, "Thank you for bringing me, Gaius." She pressed her hip against my thigh, and I had to keep myself from pulling down her scarf and kissing her. I hadn't felt that leap of heart in ages.

I distracted myself from that by telling her a little about the spina area that split the track down the middle. This dividing island was decorated with fabulous statues and other treasures brought from around the world. I told her a little about the serpent column, the Egyptian obelisk and the colossal statue of Hercules. Atakam pointed out the huge eagle with holes in its outstretched wings that directed shafts of light to the ground marking time like a sundial.

While the track was clearing for the next race, insults flew back and forth among the Greens and Blues. Many were religious-based chants to paint the other side as heretics, a favorite Hippodrome game. It was no game for the emperor but a serious, often bloody series of challenges to herd the competing Christian sects into one under imperial imprimatur – all the while attempting to terminate the still considerable draw of paganism, and tolerating in some fashion the Jews, who disdained Christ more than did the pagans, which was an accepting group always willing to bring another god into their tent.

The Blues roared out that Greens were all monophysites:

Deranged with their one-natured Christ,
All God and no man cannot be right!

"How do so many know to chant this at once?" Messalina asked me.

"See that fellow down there with his back to the track, raising up his hands as if leading a choir?" She nodded. "He's a professional claquer, as they are called. He and others coordinate the calls, which are familiar to all Blues. The Greens should respond – and look, see the Green claquers standing up?"

She saw them exhort their fellows, and the Greens yelled out a practiced chant that Blues were all Arians, slandering God by denying that his son Jesus is divine.

The Blues responded, getting in the final word, for this moment:

We're Blues not Jews and love our Christ!
Man and God in equal measure,
Chalcedon orthodox forever!

The stands cheered as one to this appropriate embrace of the imperial-established orthodoxy, which I adhered to myself these days in the 531st year after Christ's birth. Though the crowd was hardly united in orthodoxy, it would not do for the monophysites, Jews, Arians, Nestorians, Donatists, Manicheans, pagans and worse to malign their emperor's chosen religion, even though it was well known that Empress Theodora was a monophysite. Sharing the imperial bed with her orthodox husband was not so strange an arrangement. Every family had its share of heretics.

Just as Atakam said it was time to reposition to the seats Tedius was holding for us, the Blues' wheeled pipe organ started up a spastic march. A parade of 12 actors garishly dressed in shades of pink ran out from a gate in the spina to tease and dance around the track crewmen bucketing horse manure.

Messalina tugged at my tunic and in her husky Semacus voice pleaded, "Can't we stay? Remember, I want to see the entertainers as much as the races."

"On the impossible chance that your sister might be one of them?" I asked.

"Yes, anything's possible," she said. "I'm here with you, aren't I?"

Atakam said to her, "We'll be in a better place for you to see the entertainments between the 12th and 13th races, which promises to have the best dancers and acrobats today. And we'll be in a less contentious area than this Green section. Those Blue actors could really rile the Greens around us," he said, glancing at a group of Greens nearby that began hurling curses at the Blue players. "The only thing perhaps more contentious between the colors than chariot racing is their theater favorites."

Messalina understood this well. She had told me she feared for her actress sister's safety, though she hadn't known where she was in years. The Blue and Green troupes of theater actors and staff were not often molested themselves, but their supporters were keen on hurting each other, unleashing chaos and mayhem after theater contests as fully as after chariot races. During Constantinople's Brytae festival in 501, Greens smuggled in swords and knives in flower bouquets and began slaughtering Blues. Three thousand or more died that day. I had personally always looked down on theater rioters and never joined with them.

Atakam led us down, a grimace complaining that his left leg was not yet up to striding down stadium stairs. He took them rather slowly, impatiently blocking a man from entering the aisle as we neared the bottom, raking us along past others with a commanding hand. With every limping step, every glance my way he reminded me that he did not like this idea of escorting a banned woman around the Hippodrome, showing me his dour side that seems wrong for a Hun.

At ground level beneath the benches, the smell of grilled sausage partially won the battle with horse manure, the smell of the Hippodrome that flavors both ignominious defeat and glorious victory – our "Nika," one of many holdovers from the days when our gods were many and concepts like victory were worshiped almost as dearly.

In line to buy us three pork sausages in discs of unleavened bread with some pickled olives, I looked over to my odd pair, a frowning White Hun standing six feet tall and a five-foot-three lump of bumpkin underneath a leather cloak that covered like a tired hide. One would never make the tall one out to be a philosophizing gentleman, nor the small lump to be a Syrian beauty and repentant prostitute in Constantinople six months from Antioch. And no one who knew me would ever guess that in three months of trying, I had not been able to bed this gorgeous, newly chaste Messalina. Hadn't even come close.

Atakam had downed his sausage and bread in three massive bites and moved us along underneath the stands to our next spot. We dodged laughing partisans with their blue and green capes, silly hats, painted faces and waving pennants.

Not all were so gay. Some roamed wolfish, sniffing for trouble and garbed in Hunnish fashion, the rebellious style favored by young toughs, which I used to mimic myself. Atakam visibly bristled when he passed a group of such men, whether Blue or Green, and thumped the illegal weapon hidden under his tunic, a subtle warning that he would be glad for a chance to use it on them.

These types of ravenous color supporters were a minority, but certainly a force for all to reckon with. The hierarchy of the Green support, and similarly for the Blue's, in this city of about 800,000 sorted out something like this. There were roughly 300,000 Green enthusiasts for their theater and chariot teams who sang drunkenly and harmlessly in the street on their way home. About 2,000 were employees of the Green faction organization – people like me and others who carried out a variety of functions. Two hundred or so were neighborhood captains – selected by the local Green fans to carry out directives of the organized faction. There were about 1,000 Green destroyers – the Green thugs, unofficial and uncontrolled. They often fell in behind street leaders, like my former self, who had earned their positions through bravado and recklessness. These last two Blue and Green groups roamed in what was becoming known as the "murder hours," from just before sunset to sunrise, spreading their fear with robbery, assault, murder and brawling with other faction toughs, the city prefect and imperial guards, or anyone who looked at them. They terrorized everyone else – and that is exactly what we did when we "took the city" as we liked to call an unchecked rampage.

As we moved to pass one clutch of four Green toughs coming toward us, their leader Lukos, a slouching man I knew well, halted his group and hailed me.

"I see you're with your barbarian friend, Gaius Galen, but who's this troll with him?"

Lukos reached out to lift Messalina's hood, but Atakam shoved him away before he touched her. Lukos stumbled backward, and in the instant it took to right himself, Atakam had one hand clamped on Lukos' shoulder and the other pointing a short blade inches from his eye.

"Gaius Galen's barbarian friend says keep your hands to yourself," Atakam said, throwing a threatening look sideways to the three others, which held them in check, fearful a move would cost Lukos his eye. "I say imposter Huns should be exterminated," he said, backing away from Lukos. "What do you think, Gaius Galen?"

"Leave him," I answered. "Atakam is no barbarian, Lukos, he's an officer in the Roman Army."

He did not reply to me but glared at Atakam, who removed Messalina to a safer distance, keeping his eye on the other three. I moved closer to Lukos, who used to rampage with me, and quietly said I would be in touch with him soon; we might have business again.

Lukos said, "His reaction wasn't necessary, I was just curious. I actually came to tell you you're being watched."

"Who?" I asked, smiling as if in another conversation to cover my question.

Lukos kept an eye on Atakam, saying, "Three men. I first saw you when you headed up to the top rail, and saw them follow you most of the way up, crammed themselves into a row and kept an eye on you. When you three came down here, so did they."

"Are they still here?"

"Ugly fellow back there with a ring in his ear half way up." He rubbed his chest where Atakam pushed him hard. "Tell that Hun he's lucky, for now."

"You might be the lucky one, not Atakam. But thanks, Lukos."

I caught up to Atakam and Messalina. By her side I said, "Welcome to the races, my peasant friend," and clapped my hand on her shoulder as I would a man's. "I hope that wasn't too upsetting."

Her Semacus voice startled me with, "I'm not the helpless whore you think I am." She strode ahead, waving her half-eaten sausage at me to pick up my pace.

Atakam caught my eye and grinned; the skirmish with Lukos must have lightened his mood. When I first met Atakam four weeks back, it was also at the races, outside after the last of the day. And it also involved a tangle with a group of Greens that had him on his back, kicking his recently injured leg, still bandaged and re-bloodied by their boots. Proud Atakam was cursing them in three languages, as their daggers and short swords pinned him down. That time I saved him, by throwing one off, disarming another and appealing as a fellow Green to their sense of fairness in a fight. Atakam had now half paid me back protecting Messalina's identity.

That I was being watched added some menace to the outing, and I was a little surprised that I enjoyed it – welcomed it. Was it Ammianus trying to rattle me? There was only one way to find out. I did as Semacus had bid and picked up my pace, hoping the ugly fellow with the earring was coming along behind.

— 3 —

The Cult of Nika

While we moved under the stands to be near the Kathisma where the dancers and acrobats would be the best, I saw the three men following us. I quietly told Atakam.

He looked at me like I was stupid. "Yes, since before we were at the top rail," he said. "I also saw your slow-moving friend Lukos watching them and us. That's what you wanted me here for."

He was right about the stupid. These were things I would have been aware of in my former days. I needed to sharpen up.

We were at the southern end where the ground sloped downward toward the sea and where the Hippodrome's level circuit rested on arches that raised it above the ground. The roadbed of this curved end of the track stood 15 feet above us.

This was the spot the superstitious placed their curse tablets under the dirt, where the summoned spirits could rise straight up and into the intended victim as he slowed at this 180-degree turn. My hooded pleasure bent to pick up one of the lead tablets that held an etched message. Reading aloud in her Semacus voice, she related it was desired that demons find succor in the belly of the Blues' Polynices, son of his mother Galatea, doubling him over in vomitus pain in the 20th race. It was not necessary that he die, only that he lose.

"Why is his mother mentioned?" she asked, feeling the weight of the tablet.

18

"So the demon won't pick the wrong Polynices," explained Atakam. "I suppose they're not too smart."

"Neither are Huns, I hear." Messalina's hood shook at this unholy nonsense as she replaced the curse tablet. Atakam feigned worry, saying the demons had her scent now.

Back up in the stands, the crowd and excitement thickened as the mid-race break was ending before race #12. Blue and Green garments of every variety flowed in a colorful stream around us. Some said that Blue represented the sky or the sea, and Green represented earth and the spring of new beginnings. And Red was fire and White air. Reds and Whites raced but as supporting teams of the Blues and Greens, which ruled supreme throughout the empire – and had since the early days of Rome.

Atakam was in neither color, wearing dusty, brown road clothes; Semacus was in similarly dingy countryside brown. I was also dressed somewhat plainly for me but wore the finest pair of Green boots in the city: coal-black leather with Green chariot wheels aside the ankles, gold whips slashing up the side of the boot shaft, cracking sparks of green and silver. Earlier Atakam had said they looked like something an 8-year-old boy would like, with Messalina laughing in agreement.

We climbed up 20 rows, where three men rose to give us their seats by the aisle, a pre-arrangement with Tedius and two of his friends, who thanked me with subtle glances for a day of racing I had paid for.

"These would be excellent seats for my parents when they watch you free me at Founders Day next month," said Tedius with a grin.

"Best not to push too hard, Tedius," I said. When he passed in front of me, I whispered, "We're being watched. About eight rows down, ring in his ear, black and green coat."

"I only hope for the best – for you, of course, Gaius Galen," he said in reply to the other conversation, winking that he understood about being watched.

Once seated Messalina told me she was impressed that I might make Tedius a freedman. "I'm sure he deserves it. I know what it's like to be kept."

Perhaps enthused by the hypothetical freeing of my slave, her left foot tapped on mine with nervous excitement.

"Not the boots, remember?"

Her Semacus grunted, "Sorry."

As part of the re-opening after the break, we performed a chant to the health of the emperor, Greens and Blues singing praises together in ceremonial response. Everyone stood and cheered toward the Kathisma to Emperor Justinian, because this was why we were here. This was why there was a chariot racing track attached to the emperor's palace, to praise him and thus God almighty. The races, the Colors, the fans were part of the cult of Nika, of victory that surrounded the emperor. These were not just races but ritual, or so they were intended.

This race was a *biga* with two horses per chariot instead of the four of a *quadriga*. It was not a paired run with team strategy but every driver of each Color out for himself. The 12 chariots were spread across the starting line at the north end in their starting gates called *prisons*, which were all catapulted open at once.

"They're off!" yelled thousands, the obvious a common cry at the Hippodrome. The 12 chariots advanced in their starting alignment, not able to pass until they reached the chalked line 150 paces from the starting gates. There began the chaos of horses and chariots heaving forward, holding back, whatever the driver's strategy required with the general goal to be at the inside of the wide track to cut the distance of the laps. The Hippodrome was a continuous roar – a howl of primal desire that broke over the city as if it might topple the multitude of crosses that crowned every house from the tip of the peninsula to the Theodosian Walls to the west.

This roar always both agitated me and settled my core, the sheer concentrated focus of so many on noble victory – over anything, even a different Color – was humbling. To most priests in this holy city the same roar was a cry from Lucifer, our bishops grudgingly allowing us the sinful entertainments of the races and theater. They were the only things some of us had. And as long as we primarily only bashed each other, the emperors tolerated the sport and the occasional fan rioting afterward.

Messalina's left foot danced on my boot again. I gently moved it away, reluctant to deny any touch. She had questions. Atakam and I tried not to be too obvious as we versed her on elements of the race.

"Who are those men riding around on horseback?" she asked.

"Scouts surveying the action in front and behind and reporting back to their charioteer," Atakam told her. "See how the reins are wrapped around the driver's torso? That allows him to turn his body to signal his horses left or right, easing forward means faster and a lean back means slower."

"Why not hold the reins in their hands?" she asked.

"They can be wrenched free, costing a race, even a life. The dagger is strapped to his chest so he can cut himself free if thrown, rather than be dragged to death."

A scuffle broke out, eight rows below us. It was one of Tedius' friends fighting with one of the men tailing us. Two nearby officials came over to roughly take both out. One down. Tedius' doing: he was just too good to set free.

After the race – unusual because it was won by a White – the Greens' motley pack of dancing dogs, always a crowd pleaser, performed in front of our section of the stands. Atakam and Semacus had great fun enjoying their tricks and antics.

As the dogs danced to their exit, the Blue and Green organs together blew shrill notes closer to a scream than music. From gates all around the stadium, men, animals and the apparatus of the wild animal hunters, called *venatores*, took to the track to replace the other entertainments. This game of animal evading was a much subdued variety of men actually fighting wild beasts, which Emperor Anastasius banned some 30 years ago.

Instead of an armored hunter fighting to kill the beast before it killed him, he now taunted the animal – from above it on a narrow platform, or vaulting over it using a long pole, or ducking into a barrel with holes in it. In front of us, a bear on a long chain so it couldn't assault spectators plowed the barrel 20 feet across the track, once almost turning fast enough to bite the hunter's hand when he pulled the fur on the bear's back. Thus had our Roman bloodlust been softened by Christianity: we might see a bear eat a hand, but not a whole man.

Messalina's foot assaulted my boot again, her glove pointing to a gate in the spina from whence sprang a troupe of Blue pantomimes. Each of these was beloved by their Blues. The fans, mostly Blues, cheered them on as each actor struck a well-recognized signature gesture, such as Leo playing his famous eerie monk begging for alms. Lute and flute players ran onto the track and began a popular melody that quieted the crowd, suddenly polite so we could try to hear.

The pantomimes were all dressed as women today, all wearing their inscrutable masks, all virtually worshipped by their fans, who were entranced and ignited by their low taste, sexual suggestions, and allusion to current events and personalities. Because of their tremendous ability to inflame violent passion in their followers, they are sometimes banned from performing, as they were for years after the Brytae festival incident.

Messalina was half standing, almost leaning on the elderly man in front of her and absorbing the pantomimes' every move. In fluid motions aligned to the melody playing, each pantomime dove backward onto a blue canvas circle held tight by six men wearing horse heads.

Messalina poked her face to my ear, holding both sides of her hood tight against her head. "My sister Arbella could be working for one of these men."

I told her, leaning in as an excuse to press a little closer, "We didn't see her earlier in the faction staging area for actors, so she is most likely not here. I haven't found out much yet, but I am very hopeful. My Tedius rarely fails at what he seeks to discover."

I sometimes wondered if Messalina's hope I might be able to find her sister because of my faction involvement was the real reason she continued to show interest in me. The two sisters were separated when sold by their degenerate mother right after their father died. Arbella went to a slaver at age 12 and Messalina to a sophisticated brothel at the same time, at age 14. She was in that trade for seven years, quite successfully, and was now all-too successfully repenting, motivated by her deep faith, her desire to put herself in a position to free her sister and her underlying longing to lead a normal life. She idolized

Empress Theodora who herself had repented from a life of acting and prostitution, and now was very active in the rehabilitation of others.

Pantomimes flew through the air, flung up by the canvas holders, landing softly and tossed up again, a foursome peaking in time to the popular song. Each made appropriate gestures for the lyrics, one swooning to "*he woos me*," the next hugging himself at "*he loves me*." At the end of the song each pantomime was wrapped up in his canvas like a cocoon and carried back into the spina gate. Even many Greens expressed their approval.

We did not finish watching the 13th race, as was our plan. Because four laps into it came a *shipwreck* at the meta turning post near us, the kind of deathly pileup of chariots whose aftermath resembled the wreck of a ship on rocks – the epitome of chariot racing entertainment for the more vulgar among the enthusiasts.

But the sudden violence of flying bodies and a blood-spewing horse's broken leg forced a full-throated woman's scream from our Semacus. The noise of the crowd covered up her scream except to those nearby, causing several heads to turn from the great crash.

"Was it her first time?" yelled out a wit.

While I hesitated an instant to look at the crash, which had gathered a Red chariot and two more Greens, Atakam quickly pulled Messalina by her arm over my lap, into the aisle and headed away. Eight rows down, the man with the earring stepped into the aisle to stop them, but was leveled by a screaming man who flew through the air to ram him out of the way and onto a pile of spectators. It was Tedius. The third man following us was about to step out to block me as I rushed down, but reconsidered and stopped to let me pass. I did, after I punched him in the face and shoved him backwards.

Atakam and Messalina were gone under the stands before I was down to row 10. Everyone else kept their eyes on the shipwreck. There was much talk of it at taverns that night, and a little about a woman being smuggled into the stands.

When I reached the walkway under the stands, Tedius caught up to me, pointing over a wall to a fur cap moving fast outside the stadium. "There Sir, there's your Hun and whore."

"She's not anymore," I snapped, surprising myself with this defensiveness.

"Certainly not, Gaius Galen; not anymore," agreed Tedius. "We'll catch up. His limp has returned after his run down the stairs."

In a few minutes we were beside Atakam and Messalina, still hooded as Semacus. She was crying. "For the horses," she explained, wiping at her eyes, "and the drivers."

We trotted along between the Hippodrome and the wall of the Great Palace, organ music flaring up, the action stopped as the crews had begun clearing the track. Atakam wondered aloud if they would be using the Gate of Death today and that he might be missing it. Messalina gripped his arm and pushed him onward; Tedius and I followed, to our pre-arranged rendezvous.

We snaked along a tight lane of two-story brick and wood buildings with storefronts at ground level and apartments above. In most places where there was a gap in between buildings were temporary hovels of the city's most wretched beings. Two rotten boards and a scrap of old sail was a home – to a family of four, freshly ruined from the country-side and in great Constantinople for free bread, begging and likely an unmerciful death. *Istan polis* they would say in Greek, *I go to the city*, no need to say which city, it was The city. And once here, they clung to it, like the scores of souls stacked up against the very walls of the Great Palace, a warren of poverty and filth that made a rabbit hole grand. The emperor loves all his people, even these city mites, who mostly feed on imperial scraps. And as long as he could keep them out of his house, they might help keep others out of it as well.

A few streets downhill from the Hippodrome was the litter with four men to carry it and Messalina's friend covered in a double cloak and looking worried. The two women stepped into the litter, the four men manned their handles, and Atakam, Tedius and I accompanied the litter on its journey to the hillside home where Messalina and her friend lived with other former prostitutes chosen to be saved and reconstituted by their new mother. This was Sister Flacilla, who ran Holy Mary's Refuge for the Wayward as her personal charity, the same calling as Empress Theodora's.

It was a long, quiet walk save for the outbursts from the Hippo-drome that continued to serenade the city. As I walked like a foot-man for a noble lady, I thought of how Messalina was risking being expelled from the Refuge if she was caught. Her story was that she and her friend had met me at a choral recital. We arrived at the large old home. Colorful cloths hung from upper floor windows where the women lived. The house was located three street tiers above the Gold-en Horn, the bay that narrowed at this central part of our peninsular city.

The men set the litter down, and out stepped Messalina's friend looking straight at me as her hand trailed inside to fetch not Semacus but Messalina. Her lush brown hair fell down her shoulders, her head covered in a yellow silk scarf with painted peacocks on it pinned to-gether at her neck, a sculpture of veined marble. Her face was curves and smoothness with no sharp angles. Her skin was now cleaned but unadorned with rouge or such effects and more radiant for it. From her chin to her green and grey flecked eyes that were always searching, she had the slightly toothsome look of a very beautiful chipmunk. Lips like graceful wings flew her smile at me, her teasing expression asking that question she knew the answer to: *Do you want me?*

She and her friend safely inside, we walked away, her unspoken question heating me up with thoughts of how I wanted her. We had only gone one block when another face suddenly chilled me: that of the man I had punched during our escape. His right eye swelling to a squint, he gave me a wicked grin from the back of a horse galloping away down the side street.

There was no way to catch him on foot. My stomach churned, knowing I might have just delivered Messalina to Ammianus.

Riches From Riots

The three of us discussed the implications of being followed, "Semacus" likely discovered. Tedius and Atakam refrained from openly faulting me for taking Messalina to the races, but their demeanor couldn't hide it.

Atakam took his leave, and Tedius and I walked uphill from Messalina's home to The Mese, the main street of Constantinople. The most beautiful and expensive of everything was found along The Mese, sprawling townhomes, elegant jewelry, storefronts displaying dazzling carpets, and colonnaded buildings of powerful commercial interests. With marble arcades on either side, The Mese presented a walk among the grand statues of the world, pilfered by the thousands at the order of Emperor Constantine to adorn his namesake city, founded 200 years ago when he turned the modest town of Byzantium into New Rome.

The trinity of the Great Palace, Hippodrome and nearby Hagia Sophia were the iconic images of Constantinople, but our statutes most impressed the population on a daily basis. Besides those taken from Luxor, Delphi, Rome and such were statues of the famous people of our city – patriarchs, senators, wealthy eunuchs, pantomimes and conquering generals, who gained the emperor's consent to erect monuments of themselves to ensure they were remembered after death and possibly respected before.

Music from a lyre fell to the street from above us, mixing with the laughter and voices of people on their rooftops, where smoking braziers and an orange sunset warmed them as they shifted from their day's business to their evening's pleasure. We dodged carts and wagons, not allowed on city streets until evening, as Tedius led us to Mithridates Street, where my friend Monaxius lived in a rickety, five story insulae tenement, living in one of the many apartments with his wife and two daughters.

A monk was standing like a starving sentry beside Monaxius' door. He was tall, wore a filthy brown robe, had a corona of wild, black curly hair and a fearful look that he threw everywhere – to a board in the floor, his hands, my knee. Tedius purposefully ignored him and knocked on the door with his foot. Monaxius Caelius soon opened it and embraced me.

The two-inch streak of white in his dark hair was the first thing one noticed about Monaxius, who had a confident face undermined by a sharp chin that jutted out like an old man's.

"Gaius! It's so good to see you," he pushed me back to arm's length. "Excellent, you look excellent! Now, we need to hurry to a wedding ceremony I am performing."

"Manichean," whispered the monk.

"Is this man right, Monaxius?"

"Yes. We're all God's children. Must get my things." He went inside, waving us in.

It was a large apartment for a tenement like this, and second floor was a nice premium. His two girls, 3 and 5, hung behind their mother.

"Hello, Annia. How are you and your darlings here?" I asked, hugging her and putting my hand on the 5-year-old's head.

"He's handsome, Mother," said little 5 year old.

"Yes, Martha, he is," Annia answered. "He's been your father's friend since they were just about your age. But Gaius Galen doesn't come to see us enough, particularly since he left his family."

I forced a smile. "True, I haven't seen you enough, and I must change that."

Monaxius came from a small room off the living area and escorted us to the door, blowing kisses to his girls and wife.

"Brother Zazo, take us to the wedding party," Monaxius said, giving the monk a gentle push out of his mumbling trance.

Tedius asked him quietly, "Isn't it punishable by death to be a Manichean, Sir?"

"Possibly, I don't keep up with laws passed against these or those heretics," said Monaxius.

We left the tenement, winter's early night falling, few glimmers of light at the windows, candles and lamp oil being luxuries for many city dwellers. As we walked, I asked Monaxius about this monk two strides ahead and still mumbling.

Zazo had been roaming in the "wilderness" for two years, a common test of monks, though Zazo's wilderness was the not-so-wild outskirts of the city. Monaxius ran across him about a month ago, at a crossroads in a thunderstorm. Zazo had an epiphany, regaining some of his lost mind and agreeing to help find business for Monaxius, who had been making money as an independent man of God, ministering to just about anyone. This included the Manicheans whose house we soon arrived at.

"How do I look?" asked Monaxius, hair shooting out from under the red Manichean ceremonial hat that was too small for him.

"I'm reminded of the saying: *Even if the gospel flowed from the mouth of a dead dog, it would be holy and pure.* You look holy, Monaxius," I told him. "Go marry those two heretics so we can have more to burn in the Hippodrome someday."

Manicheans were roundly disliked, in part because they held that Christ has not one, not two but three natures! In the ongoing fervor to define Jesus, I believe we may continue splitting him apart until there is nothing left.

Tedius and I retired to the dining room of an inn a couple of blocks away where Monaxius would join us. From our table on the second-floor we had a view of the Propontis Sea that floated the wealth of the Mediterranean world to Constantinople.

After a while, a commotion arose at the entrance from the stairs, and there was Monaxius trying to assure the upset proprietor that

Brother Zazo was reputable. Wandering hermits and monks were no good for anyone's business, as many of them scared people off begging or stealing things. At least the bad ones did. On the other hand, the truly ascetic monks and holy men who ministered to the needy while depriving themselves of comforts were highly regarded, often more so than a famous charioteer or pantomime. I could tell Zazo was not one of those so revered.

Moving to the stairs I said to him, "Brother Zazo, I have personal things to discuss with my friend. Would you wait for us outside? I will bring you wine and a fine meal – and I am sure you will find someone in need of ministering in the street."

"I will, Gaius Galen Licinius," Zazo replied. "Monaxius tells me you two are like brothers, something I understand well."

His exit down the stairs brought a thankful nod from the proprietor. At our table, I offered a toast to the newly wed Manicheans, which appeared to upset some nearby diners more than Zazo had.

"Quiet down, Gaius Galen," hissed Monaxius. "I married them because marriage is forbidden among Manicheans, and none of their holy men would do it."

"You mean you served two heretics of heretics? And they paid you? You are extraordinarily sly," and I lifted my goblet to him.

Monaxius sipped at his and asked, "What do you want to talk to me about, Gaius? Tedius was completely unhelpful in this regard early this morning."

"My master is leaning toward trouble," Tedius told Monaxius. "If I may, Sir?" Tedius asked, and I indicated I didn't care. "He has been approached to reignite his past, your past."

"The riots?" Monaxius asked, now taking a full swallow.

"Yes," I answered. "Though I have no details. My anonymous client's representative spoke to me about this just yesterday, making it more an announcement than a request."

"Who?" asked Monaxius.

"Ammianus."

"Your employer who assists Maximius Clater Nerva?"

"Yes, but he says Nerva knows nothing about it."

Monaxius leaned back in his chair and propped his right arm against the stone window ledge. White stars over the sea sparkled behind his head, filled with thought. After a moment he asked with interest, "Gaius, are you considering this? That was three years ago – and you and I have moved past that phase, into respectability, or certainly you have." He paused a moment and looked sharply into my eyes, "Are you capable of that? That was another life altogether. Maybe you can smash open doors and torch a market stall, but can you cut a stranger? Still?"

His questions hung without my response, because our dinner was approaching – a large platter with a baked mackerel and asparagus moved toward our table, the small boy carrying it over his head barely visible. Two serving men took it from him and placed it in front of us, with three kinds of bread, relishes, a dish of peas in cream sauce and more wine. I led us in an orthodox prayer – before Monaxius might offer some heretical blessing. Then Monaxius surprised both of us.

"I could use another plunder of cash, though," he said, taking a bite of fish. "Being an independent priest is not working, and I've been making more money doing legal work, wills and contracts for people who can't afford a real lawyer. But the windfall we earned three years ago is dwindling. And I confess, at times I miss the action."

Tedius stared in disbelief at him, then said, "I am surprised, Sir, that you would be ready for this again. All three of us are lucky to have lived through all that rioting, putting ourselves in the midst of it like insane directors."

"I could be," answered my former partner in crime.

Tedius shook his head and took out his frustration on the fish. He was too organized and cautious to ever enjoy our rioting. Monaxius and I had begun to veer into that sort of raucous entertainment around age 11, running with a pack of others, commandeering docked fishing vessels at night, ganging up on drunk monks and the like. In fact, it was encouraged by our fathers, particularly mine – not the bad deeds but becoming part of a cohort, growing from boy to man in the group dynamics of a military nature. Spoiled rich kids, with a taste and knack for violence.

It was natural for us to step into the Blue vs. Green drama that animated the city – the empire – and I had been thrust in that direction by my father, in a fashion. Monaxius and I had been fervent Green supporters since we were 6, learning the names of drivers and horses, keeping up with the results of race days that caused an odd mix of joy and disappointment – except on those rare occasions when either Greens or Blues won every race, in which case it was total ecstasy or total misery.

We began to make our place, a lowly one due to our age, among the unruly Green partisans. A year or so later, Tedius was given to me by my father, and so we dragged him along with us. We ran with the Greens, did everything in the name of the Greens. Like other young toughs of the circus Colors, we emulated Huns, who scared us Greeks as well as Goths, Persians, Gauls, Romans, everyone. They lived with abandon and seemed intent on disobeying all authority. We admired that, and lived it – in the anonymous safety of a riot ignited by chariot team supporters.

It grabbed me first, the intoxicating effect of losing oneself to the intense power of a crowd. Monaxius also fell to that sensation, like taking a mind-altering potion. We looked forward to the races, usually able to do some street rampaging afterward, but it was the full-blown rioting of an unstoppable crowd we most hoped for. And when we got it, it got us.

By 16 I was a true terror, the most fearless (or stupidest) among our gang of 30 or 40, many of them older than Monaxius and me. When I led us to overrun an imperial armory and we stole a catapult siege weapon known as a "Wild Ass" along with many other weapons, my gang dubbed me *Wilder*. We later sold the Wild Ass to pirates. I was soon acknowledged as the leader of our gang, also due in part to the grave injury that felled the previous leader.

There were perhaps 20-30 of these individual gangs, each with a leadership of sorts. Often a Color's gangs joined together for greater numbers and destructive force – and when everything aligned just right (or just wrong), these many gangs joined together as a crazed crowd that swept you along like a herd of animals. You knew anything could happen to you – even death – but felt at the same time that in this stampeding crowd you were invulnerable.

"We could be Crassus again," said Monaxius, daintily touching his napkin to his mouth like an aristocrat. Tedius moaned.

"Oh, be quiet," Monaxius shushed. "You benefited yourself, Tedius."

Marcus Licinius Crassus, an ambitious Roman now dead for some 600 years, would rush his slave firefighting crew to a burning building and offer the owner a fraction of its worth. In old Rome there were no organized fire brigades as our guildsmen now provide. The owner could refuse and watch helplessly as Crassus' fire brigade let his building burn down, likely catching others nearby afire. Or the owner could get some of its worth from selling it to Crassus, whose fire brigade would then save their master's new property.

Our transformation from average street brawlers to manipulators was, without doubt, the most fantastic and proudest achievement of my life – and the unique skill Ammianus was now after. I had come up with a plan like Crassus' but through the faction riots, not fires. Monaxius and I organized our team of not firefighters but fire starters and trained them, a conglomeration of beggars, lazy students, volatile monks, street criminals, low-brow actors, and washed-up claquers from the Hippodrome.

Our first client was a wine distributor. With a small mob five streets away and ravaging its way in his direction, the merchant was dumbfounded with gratefulness at my offer to deflect the mob for a fee. We pulled off a skit of sorts, creating a rival force of rioters that turned the mob away from the back doors of the warehouse, aided by planting two wagonloads of the merchant's wine a street over that one of my men "found" and related to the mob, leading them off like kittens to cream. Alcohol is an excellent riot accelerant.

We refined our methods and learned how to augment my normal gang with these trained auxiliaries. And we had good success when five days of rioting broke out again soon after, earning fees for several destructions and some commissions for protection, though not all succeeded. Still, Monaxius and I made out like imperial tax farmers with a haul of money. We called each other "Crassus" for a good while afterward.

"Gaius, we can do this again," said Monaxius with a big grin. "The emperor has continued to strip away the powers of the cities, diluting their garrisons and his own urban imperial units like the old Praetorian Guard, both skilled in containing the occasional riots that broke out over food prices, faction squabbles or political tumult. Those forces now keep Huns from sacking Constantinople, Vandals from raiding our Mediterranean shipping, Persians from taking our eastern provinces. Since we last owned the streets, it has gotten even easier, Gaius. Tedius would come along, in spite of his long face right now."

"I go where my Master wants me to go," answered Tedius. "But what I want is not relevant."

"Well said – and a fine play at irrelevance, which we know you are not," I said. "But I am not settled on this, as persuasive as my friend wishes to be."

This lifted Tedius' spirits, his eyes showing hope. He and Monaxius looked at me from opposite sides of the table and the issue. I could go either way.

Something tugged at my sleeve, the serving boy who delivered our dinner.

"Sir, your monk friend in the street looks to be in some trouble," he said. "I thought you might want to know."

"He's not my monk, but his," I said, pointing to Monaxius. "But thank you, my boy," and I gave him a small folding knife, telling him to keep sharp.

Monaxius rose. "Let's see what he's gotten into, Gaius. Tedius can pay the bill and join us."

"What do I care about Zazo?" I asked slowly rising.

"Brother Zazo has his practical side; he could have 40 foaming-mad monks at the palace gates by dawn tomorrow. You may soon be very thankful to have some violent monks around. Let's go, we need to conserve this asset – just in case," said Monaxius, giving me a teasing smile.

5

Brother Zazo Recruits Jacob the Jew

When we reached the street, we saw Brother Zazo surrounded by five fellows. Whether they were threatening or just talking, we couldn't tell.

Monaxius called out, "Zazo! Do you need our assistance here?"

He shook his head, doubled in size by his frizzy hair, and motioned us over with an all-is-well assurance.

"I have a friend – five of them – sent by the Lord," said the tall monk pointing to the short man at his side. "This is Jacob."

"We thought to take his habit, rough him up a bit for trying to convert us," said Jacob through a coarse black beard trimmed straight as an imperial hedge. "But he talked us out of it."

"Zazo would convert that cat over there if he could," Monaxius said, returning Jacob's tone of humor. "You should be honored, not threaten to beat him."

Monaxius closed on the half circle of men around Zazo and stopped a foot from Jacob. Three of the others with him were of medium size and obviously strong. The fourth was a large, brawny man with a patch of scorched-smooth skin where his right eyebrow should have been. Three of them wore pendants with the star of David. I moved to the side of the building a few feet behind Zazo, leaning my palm against the mildewed stone. Tedius, who had arrived with a fish dinner wrapped in a palm leaf and a small skin of wine, stepped to the other side of Monaxius and put down the food. The cat Monaxius had mentioned slinked out of a shadow to try to claim it, so Tedius picked it back up.

Brother Zazo swept a look around landing it on me. "God has sent these men to me, but for you, Gaius Galen. Jacob is well known, in some circles, as Jacob the Jew."

"I haven't heard the name," I said.

"Show him, Jacob," said Zazo, "Green!"

Jacob grinned, and he and his four men pulled out Green wool caps and put them on. Each covered a fist with his palm, looking ready to fight.

"Now Blue!" said Zazo.

The five turned their caps inside out and put them back on, suddenly Blues all. The big one seemed to be getting excited and looked at Zazo as if ready to lay into him. I moved Zazo aside to stand in front of the big one and pulled the end of my green scarf out from under my cloak.

"We are ready," I said, coolly staring at the excited one, dropping my hands to my sides in the universal fighting signal of, *Come try me.*

Zazo's hand squeezed my shoulder as he stepped beside me. "Gaius Galen, these men are ready to fight with you, not against you."

"Why do you think I need them?" I asked.

"Just as these men were walking over to me," said Zazo, "an idea came to me – perhaps from an angel – that Gaius Galen would need these men."

He smiled as if that was it. "Go on," I said. "I'm not impressed with angelic whisperings. Give me facts."

Zazo related that while he was recommending Christianity to them after seeing their pendants, two of them turned their hats inside out showing the bi-colors. He asked if one was Jacob the Jew. Jacob said he was, and Zazo wanted to know more. Jacob and his associates were all sailmakers, in business down by the commercial docks next to the Harbor of Theodosius. Twice rioting partisans running wild after a day of races burned his shop badly, and several others around his. First, Greens did it, smashing Jacob's nose that gave it the curious bend it had. A year later, Blues burnt him out and murdered Jacob's apprentice as the man tried to save a new sail that he dragged out of the fire they had thrown it in.

"But he did not get very far," Jacob said, taking over Zazo's narrative. "About 10 of them wrapped my apprentice – my wife's younger brother – in the burning sail and watched him die. So did I, as the Blue devils restrained and taunted me."

He dropped his wool cap, blue side out, and ground it under his foot.

"From that day forward, myself and some fellow sailmakers took our revenge whenever riots started," Jacob continued. "We would put on blue hats and stalk careless Blue rioters – and they are all careless – separating two or three from their pack, beating them senseless and worse. Greens got the same," he said, tightening his left eye as he stared at me. "The violent colored ones are sorely hated by honest merchants, craftsmen and little people who get crushed in their destruction. I know many who'd like to see all of the violent Blue and Green backers dead."

"And have you killed, Jacob?" I asked.

"Yes we have, a few – but it's not our intention, we just want to serve them back some pain. Blues and Greens, it doesn't matter to us."

"At least you're fair," I said, "and no better than either yourself."

Jacob nodded heavily; this wasn't a new thought for him. I gave him a commiserating look, then turned to the monk. "And Zazo, why do you think I need to know this, know these men?"

"As I said, a message came to me just before Jacob did," Zazo held his palms up like a praying pagan. "The message did not say why or when, it just said Monaxius' friend Gaius needs Jacob the Jew."

He politely pointed to his leaf-wrapped mackerel, moved over to it and began devouring it in a manner that sent the hopeful cat under a nearby bench.

I turned to the band of Jews. "Well Jacob, and you fine fellows who follow him, it may be that someday I would be happy to have you with me. Brother Zazo may actually be right in that, though how I do not know."

I reached out my hand to Jacob, who shook it sincerely, as did the other four in turn. "You know, I converted to Judaism myself at age 16, was circumcised too at the time. I can show you," and began to pull up my tunic.

"No need to show us," said Jacob holding up his hand.

"Are you still a Jew?" asked his big man.

"No, Chalcedonian orthodox, currently," I said. "We're similar, you're Blue and Green; I've been Jewish and Christian – pagan too, for that matter. Should the occasion arise, we will talk about turning Blue to Green and Green to Blue. Until then, farewell. Come Tedius, time to go home. I will see you again soon Monaxius, and most likely you as well Brother Zazo."

"Fine mackerel and wine, Gaius Galen. Thank you," said Zazo, shaking a piece of fish at me in thanks before tossing it to the cat.

"Send Tedius to me, should you have any news," called Monaxius.

I nodded that I would. Tedius and I wound our way mostly along back streets, their uneven stones challenging our ankles.

He told me as we walked that earlier before the races when he went to see if Monaxius could meet with me later, he had hinted to him about the reason. "The monk was nearby and may have heard, so it was likely no angel that informed him of your need," said Tedius.

"No, you are no angel. But I appreciate your honesty."

"I don't trust him," said Tedius, "or this dark street." He looked behind us several times as we walked, concern for thieves and still being followed on his mind.

I stopped us, deciding in that instant on my next step. "I don't trust this situation I seem to be falling into so quickly. I will meet with Ammianus again," I said. "If he speaks for powerful people, which he probably does, and I turn down his offer, his clients should want me dead so I will not spread tales after they've set their fires by some other's hand. Tedius, go to Ammianus' house now, and alert his servants that I wish to speak to him as soon as possible tomorrow. Say it is urgent."

"Yes, Sir. Are you considering refusal?" he asked, hope in his question.

"I don't know what to think. But I will know after I speak to him."

A nod and Tedius was trotting off, smiling, I am sure. I moved on in silence except for the few conversations muffled behind doors I passed, and my boots crunching across the stone. I exaggerated that sound with each step, to announce that someone dangerous or dumb was passing through, and it would be fine with him if some fool tried to determine which he was.

I didn't get much sleep, my mind keeping me up trying to determine if I could be dangerous again – and whether it was more stupid for me to try that or to turn down Ammianus. One of his servants came not long after sunrise to tell me when and where Ammianus would meet me.

It was midday when I arrived for the meeting at a tattered building that looked one gust of wind away from tumbling into a pile of rotten timbers. His man Phocas was stationed outside and nodded to me to enter. Inside was a luxurious dining establishment, a secret place where imperial elites could relax in comfort. Ammianus was in a private room, wearing a masculine gold necklace that hung wide on his shoulders and across his chest. He snapped and a servant soon entered to pour wine for me. A plate of cheese, smoked meats and bread was on the table.

"Thank you for seeing me with such short notice," I said.

He frowned a little and rolled a finger around for me to get on with it. For an instant I thought to deviate from my plan and tell him the truth – that I was happy with my new life, liked being responsible and even respected for my work, and just as importantly that though I truly had grown past the joy I used to find in the violence of the crowd, I feared that once I was pulled back into it, the addictive thrill would grip me again. But I resisted and stuck with my plan.

"I am flattered that you think I am the man to help your client in this endeavor of his, and I wanted to talk to you about two important things," I said. Ammianus cast his frog-eyed glance to the ceiling impatiently. "First, it is not possible to time this kind of thing, to prepare for it as if it will fall on such and such a day, week or even month. Since

Emperor Anastasius' time, the disorders of the factions have grown more frequent, with flare ups routine in Justin's reign and even more so now in Justinian's. But you can't count on it and time it."

"You can, in fact, count on some part of the city being rampaged at least once every few months," he said, plopping a slice of meat into his mouth. "And when the next riots erupt, you will be ready, and do what I say. Just as you did three years ago on your own. There is no difference, and you know this. You were prepared before, and you can be now as well."

"You don't understand the difficult details of how this works and –"

"– I don't need to, that's why I have you," Ammianus cut in.

"You assume too much."

"And you too little. Make your point; I have important things to do," he said. I could tell my approach wasn't going to work. But I continued.

"I'm going to be honest with you. I was, once, able to re-direct parts of a mob," I admitted. "In truth, we were incredibly lucky. In our first effort we successfully protected a wine merchant, but we quickly learned that deflecting a mob from destruction was much harder than directing one to it. Before the next riot opportunity, I had found several clients eager for us to destroy their competitor, be it commercial, political or just someone they hated. Over the course of five days of off-and-on rioting, we successfully destroyed most of the targeted properties. But of the properties I proposed to protect as the crowd approached, we saved only half. Not very good results."

Ammianus looked down at his folded hands on the table and nodded for a moment. "That's good enough for me – and my client," he said. "And you might be pleased to know that we are interested more in striking than defending – though if I told you to protect a beggars' camp you would do it. Gaius Galen, I am surprised that it has taken only two days for you to come to me, purporting to be no good at what I need. Humility doesn't come easy for you, does it?" He couldn't help sneering at me.

"You are right about my humility but wrong about my involvement. I decline your offer, and will not intercede in any troubles that may inflict the city in the future."

Ammianus was impassive for a long moment, then startled me by standing quickly with an angry little shove to get the table out of the way of his rising gut.

"Here is a gift for you," he said, "a second chance – we don't get them often in life. Stop this rebellion against me, stick to your task. I won't ask you again."

"You won't even tell me who I might be working for," I said. "Rebelling against you might just save my life – you could be leading me into treason!"

"Then it would be your only path to live." A thought seemed to grab him. "You don't think you're capable any longer, do you *Wilder*? Not the fearless idiot you used to be. I see it on your face. And so will the mob, and you fear that it will devour you for your weakness."

"My weakness? I *miss* the mob, the mayhem, the danger. Clearly, you don't understand me," I said, suppressing the desire to stab the cheese knife into his neck.

"I don't need to. I need to please my patron, and you need to please yours – me in this instance. We know it is how the world works, how we all get what we want."

This simple admission unexpectedly deflated the tension in the roles we were playing. There were no self-made men, only dreamers believed such. We all lived in webs of patronage, and I considered how he himself must be entangled.

"You are right, Ammianus," and I smiled to him. "We each must choose our patrons – and in turn our clients who depend on us – carefully. I have given you my choice."

He calmly nodded, saying, "It is not a wise one, my friend."

Peril was in the way he said *friend*. And he said nothing more. He could have threatened to oust me from my Green position at the Hippodrome, or threatened to go to my father, or to have me killed. These were not necessary to say, though. He only shrugged when I waved a two fingered salute to him and turned to leave – almost bumping into Phocas, who was standing a few feet behind me with his sword drawn.

6

We Can All Be Turned

I left Ammianus to go see my immediate superior Flavius, who had sent word late yesterday for me to meet him this afternoon. A drizzle of rain with the promise of snow seemed to bring the dark clouds that hung over us all morning down into the streets. I pulled up the hood of my cape and walked bent forward, same as the people moving busily about me with a purpose. Sometimes, just not getting lost in the tangle of winding lanes, alleyways and poorly remembered shortcuts was purpose enough, made more difficult today by thinking of what I had to ask Flavius.

I wound my way between a huge block of horse stalls and the courtyard and banquet hall of the Blues, its river stone walls freshly painted the ultramarine-blue of the faction. The wide steps of the hall and portico were thick with out-of-town visitors gawking to be inside the Hippodrome stable area, where they hoped to catch a glimpse of a charioteer, maybe the young whip Philippus from Berytus.

The Greens' clubhouse complex was next door, and both were regularly populated with their partisans. These men all considered themselves racing experts, who stuck their noses into everyone's work, calling to Maculous' handler that the steed would do better with a loser bridle, or critiquing the mix of feed for the horses after tasting a bite – which is better than the zealots who followed a horse during its exercise so they could smell its droppings for the same purpose.

I soon faced the large half-circle glass window over Flavius' desk as he related to me the details of my folly at the race track yesterday, which was the purpose of his summons. He was oddly calm. I suspected he had taken some potion. Looking from notes on a piece of paper, he cataloged the Lukos incident with Atakam, the curse tablet picked up by Semacus, who the reporting spy suspected was a woman, and the punch I threw to help us escape the stands after the scream. While he wondered aloud at my reckless disregard of my position and how it might taint him, I considered the side wall's brightly colored mosaic of Porphyrius the infamous whale (not the famous charioteer who raced yesterday) about to ram another fishing ship. I felt like the vessel.

"Gaius Galen, I got wind of this report on you, my subordinate, that was going straight to Ammianus, bypassing me," said Flavius, shaking his head in disappointment at either me or Ammianus or both. "Of course, he got the report anyway – and doesn't know I have these notes from it. But why would he keep this from me? Why would he have you under surveillance?"

"Because he doesn't trust me? But he didn't get his money's worth from his spy, because there was no woman with Atakam and me, that was his friend Semacus," I said to stall a moment. Some of his assistants were working in his large office pretending not to listen, and I wanted no one to hear the rest of our conversation.

"Come Flavius, let's move our conversation to a more appropriate setting." He understood I wanted privacy, and we began to make our way to one of many rooms for meeting and business that surrounded the other side of the open courtyard from Flavius' office. As we walked, I told him I knew why Ammianus set a spy on me, said again the report was wrong because there was no woman (I needed to keep her out of this if possible), and said I had a question for him as well. He nodded and remained quiet as he digested my words into a worried look. Like Tedius, he was a natural worrier. Even if I had secretly brought a woman to the track, that was nothing compared to the secret he and I shared – or had.

Flavius, who manages the physical track of the Hippodrome, is a

Lombard, I believe, or some other kind of German. Names are tricky. A Frank or Lombard might have the three-name string of Roman heritage, not know a word of Latin but speak Greek as most of us did in the East, and be a Roman citizen. Yet Flavius was always insecure about not being Greek or Roman, and worried that prejudices against Germans might result in a Greek taking his job one day. He had reason for concern. Where the Western emperors are titular heads kept like children these days – a case of too many Germans involved in too much for too long – that is not the case in the Eastern Empire.

A little over 100 years ago, the emperor expelled the Germans who lived among us from Constantinople. Their leader Gainas began moving his Gothic army out of town, but when citizens saw his soldiers beating an old woman praying by the city gates, they closed those gates on the last of Gainas' army, trapping inside thousands of troops, who fled for sanctuary to an Arian church. But the citizens were so angry with pent up dislike of the Germans that they removed the church roof and hurled stones on them and set the church on fire, killing all. Or so it is said.

Perhaps he had that image on his mind as we sat down at a table in a small meeting room off the stables. An attendant brought us a bowl of radishes and water before leaving. Flavius bit into a radish, a piece of it falling into his frightful orange beard distracting me while we spoke.

"Ammianus came to me two days ago to tell me he knows of my background and tried to force me to resurrect it for the benefit of an unnamed client," I said. "Did you tell him? Has he turned you?"

"What? No, Gaius Galen! I, I swear on God's ... on his soul I have told no one, no one," Flavius sputtered, full into panic. "Why, why would I do that? It is the same as cutting my own throat!"

How I turned from being a hell-bent rioter to becoming a respected member of the Green administrative faction was by bribing Flavius. Tedius had come up with the plan that an excellent place for me to hide from my past would be in the midst of the teams I fought for in the streets, using my father's close ties in imperial business as a leg up over others seeking such desired employment. And he had learned that this Flavius fellow was both in a position to hire me and in a dangerous spiral of gambling debts about to ruin him. We made a deal and a pact of secrecy, because if that got out, both of us would be dead or wish we were – Flavius for his bad judgment, me because rioters were considered vermin by most of these hard-working faction employees. It had gone well for us both for three years. And at this moment, I realized I still wanted to trust him.

"Is it naive of me to believe you in this Flavius? I want to. Is it possible you slipped up in speaking to someone else about me, rather than directly telling Ammianus?"

"That would be the same thing," he said, pulling his beard down and making a slashing move with his other hand across his throat – thankfully knocking out the piece of radish. "Gaius, I have told no one anything about you or our arrangement. But oh God, what now?" And he covered his face with both hands, hiding from this new misery.

After a few seconds, he spoke into his hands, "I don't know anything about why he went to you – but I fear it means he knows about our involvement." He dropped his hands from his face. "As for the woman, I don't care about that, though I know you can certainly be that foolish. It's Ammianus I'm worried about. Did you say anything to him about me when he visited you?"

"Not a breath. You're my friend, Flavius, aren't you?" He shrugged a big shoulder. "I saw Ammianus not two hours ago, and I declined his offer."

"Not a wise thing to do, Gaius Galen," he said.

"That was his response as well."

"Ammianus is not a man to trifle with. Your position here is the least of your worries," said Flavius.

I gave him a brief rundown of my conversations with Ammianus. When I was finished, he swallowed a bite of radish, and this thought: "Suddenly I am blindly involved in some deep scheme of Ammianus' involving your dark skills, which I have overlooked to help you – yes, with pay, but I still helped you at great risk to me. It is not good to get between Ammianus and anything, now you are that *anything* and

I am in between." His hands went up in despair. "Surely, he knows our secret – and surely, I'm done, my position gone. My debtors will crush me without this income."

He rested his chin pitifully on the table. Whatever potion that might have had him calm a moment ago was not strong enough for this new woe I had brought on him. He lifted his head and distractedly rolled a radish over with his finger looking for bad spots, the room's air rich with the aroma of barley and sweet hay from the feeding troughs of the stables outside.

Flavius and I were at home here in the complex, as were so many others who were part of the family of the track – indeed track people tended to intermarry and many of them were related. Drivers, grooms, trainers and faction officials frequently came about their positions through family members in the trade. Flavius and I were unusual in that we did not, and we shared a bond of sorts for that.

"You are my patron in helping me turn my life around," I told him. "You didn't have to do that. I would do nothing to jeopardize you."

"I know that, Gaius." He smiled at me, genuinely. "I know you mean well by me."

"Bear in mind that nothing has happened yet, Flavius – may never happen."

He bounced a laugh of disbelief off the table. "Would Ammianus dare to broach the subject were he not already empowered?"

I wanted to calm him. Tactically, it would be bad to have Flavius against me. Personally, I was in his debt, for it was largely the kind heart of this otherwise ruthless German administrator that had allowed for my slow climb back to respectability. Suspicions about my background slipped out after a while at the track, though at a low-key level that went nowhere. Still, I had to work hard to gain the trust of many of these people, which I believe was only possible through Flavius' active support.

"Friend Flavius, you have my word that I will protect you any way I can." He didn't look comforted. "I had no idea any of this was coming, and have tried to deal with it as best I can. Perhaps it would have been best for me not to tell you this at all. But I could not leave you in the dark. You've helped me immensely, and I will eternally repay that favor."

"I have found that being in the dark is never better, in the long term," he said. "It may seem to be just a matter between you and Ammianus, but I could be crushed as well."

He haphazardly threw his last radish out the window. A horse thanked him.

"See, Flavius? We all love you, even the horses. And we're all going to be fine, trust me."

"Unfounded optimism is worse than being in the dark, often followed by a funeral." Flavius raised an orange eyebrow to me and added, "If you are dragged back into rioting for profit, you could well be ruined here at the track, Gaius Galen. You know that."

"I do. I don't want to lose that, or the rest of the life I've rebuilt. I still have choices."

He gave a pitying little laugh, stood and put a hand on my shoulder. "Choose wisely while you still have the chance. And trust no one, except for Tedius perhaps."

I nodded slowly. He had just told me not to trust him, knowing we can all be turned.

I walked back to my common work space near Flavius' office, entering the open receiving area, a semicircular space created by 50 feet of curtains hanging from ceiling to floor, presenting a curved wall of blue and green cloth, embroidered with racing chariots. Here clerks received dirt and sand vendors from various parts of the empire, ushering them to the appropriate person behind the curtains, including myself.

I am the Green faction's sand representative to Flavius, charged with getting as much Green-procured sand and dirt into the track mix as possible. My Blue counterpart Gildo, a Moor moved up to the Hippodrome from the Carthage track, did the same. Lots of people wanted their dirt under the hooves of their beloved teams, and they were free with bribes to be in that sacred ground. Wooden holding pens covered half the floor, perhaps 30 of them, standing two feet high and subdivided into numerous cubes large enough to accommodate a tin bucket, its colored handle marking it Blue or Green earth, candidates for the mix.

Then there were the people who wanted to be part of the sand mix – add in the ashes of some recently departed, or fluids and tissue from the still living. For instance, last week I spoke to a gentleman from Sicily who offered to ship in soil burnt in an ancient siege of Syracuse, which would have the dried blood of several of his patrons mixed in it. The sum he offered me was insulting, and I dismissed him, fairly sure he would return again with a better offer.

To get my thoughts off the import of my two earlier meetings, I did a little work, approving a few bill payments and addressing other paperwork. After about an hour, my assistant John, who did most of my work for me, entered agitated but glad to see me.

"Tedius has sent word that if anyone sees you, to tell you that you must go at once to the home of your friend Monaxius," said John. "The message arrived about half an hour ago, and I've been looking for you. I'll get you a horse from the stables. You must go now!"

In a short time, I arrived leaning back on a black Arabian walking as fast as he could down the steep hill to Monaxius' tenement building. A young boy came flying out of the building, yelling, "Gaius Galen, Gaius Galen! Tedius has sent me to help you!"

I gave him my horse's reins to hold and ran up the stairs and into the open door of the apartment, hearing her sobs before I saw Annia sitting on a bench holding her youngest daughter. She looked up at me, eyes bleary slits of pain.

"They took Martha," the terror in her face showed to me but not to Elissa the 3 year old in her arms. "She'll come back though, won't she, Gaius Galen?" asked Annia for Elissa's benefit.

"Of course, she will," I said, and moved to touch Elissa's shoulder but was stopped by the piercing look Annia gave me. She glanced over to Tedius who was standing lookout by the window.

"Monaxius is trying to find her," Tedius said. "And he will." He smiled weakly at Annia.

"I must go help him," came from the couch across the room.

Brother Zazo was trying to pull himself up, his bloody right arm was in a crude bandage ripped from the bottom of his robe. He made it upright in pain.

"It's my fault, my fault," said Zazo, breaking into sobs that hurt his bleeding arm.

"We were at the fountain two streets away, pausing to watch raindrops hit the pool. Three men turned me, hit me, sliced my arm with a knife and pushed me into the fountain." He looked up as if we might not believe him. "I tried to get out of the fountain but was kicked back in. And they were gone."

"It's not your fault, Brother Zazo," said Annia, with genuine kindness that switched to instant disgust when she turned to me. "It's Gaius'."

7

Following My Slave's Lead

Annia, always so pleasant and warm with me, turned her back, shielding Elissa as if I would try to pull the other child from her arms, too.

"Annia, I'm sorry this has happened, and you're right. It is my fault."

"So, some powerful man is pushing you to pick back up where you two had left off three years ago," said Annia. "Monaxius told me this last night when he returned from dinner with you. He said you were ready to do it – and worse, that he felt obligated to be with you."

She nearly choked on *you*. I was not surprised Monaxius had apparently told her I was the one eager to return to our criminality. I couldn't tell her, not in this moment, that her husband was the one who really wanted to be Crassus again.

"Yes, he is too good of a friend to me," I said instead, unsure of what to say or do. I felt weakened and inadequate. I felt like giving up, something I always knew was an option before in my wilding days: when things got difficult, I could simply walk away to save myself. I owed no one anything. But in this moment, once again my slave pushed me in the right direction.

"Something isn't right, Gaius Galen," said Tedius, rubbing his sharp chin. "When I last saw you this morning, you were headed to speak with Ammianus and not sure of what you would do. That you are here and Martha isn't must mean you declined his offer. Is that correct?"

"Yes, I declined. I tried to reason with him, but he is determined," I said, appreciation welling in me for this man who has saved me so many times from my bad decisions, who has never let me give up in building this better life.

"You thought he would threaten you for rejecting him," Tedius said. "And you were prepared to deal with that. But he went for a softer, more effective target we didn't expect: Martha."

"I had no idea, Annia. No idea or I would not have declined."

Through trembling lips she asked, "You told him no?"

"I didn't want to go back to that – I don't want to be that anymore. And I did not want to jeopardize your husband." I didn't want to add anything else until I could get things straight with Monaxius about what he'd told her. Tedius stepped back a little, giving me the slightest nod of approval that only I saw, that only I could understand. I took control.

"Tedius, you stay here with Annia and Elissa. Tell your boy outside to take my horse to your father. Send a note with the boy telling your father we need four stout men here at once to guard Annia and her daughter. I'm sure my father's household will not miss four men. When they are here, send Zazo to my physician to be mended."

I turned to Annia, assuring her, "I have to start things in motion immediately to show Ammianus he has touched the wrong child and the wrong man. I will be back as soon as I can. You will be safe here with these men and your neighbors. You can trust me, Annia." I hugged her and Elissa and indicated for Tedius to follow me.

Just as we stepped outside the doorway, two women came rushing down the hall calling Annia's name and flew past us to comfort their friend and her daughter.

"What do you have in mind, Gaius Galen?" Tedius asked.

"My first thought is to kill Ammianus. But what I will do is agree to do his bidding – I see no other choice. He has me, but I won't squirm. I will threaten his life if Martha is not returned. Threats won't nudge him, we need leverage. See what you can come up with – he has a son, I know. I will make contact with his house now, give my warning and then we can follow it up with weight. Brother Zazo will be hot for revenge and has friends who can help. Keep him close by after his wound is treated. I have others in mind. I will be back here as soon as I can."

"I think that is a good plan, Sir," he said. "The leader in you is returning."

"Once your slave pushes you forward, it is difficult not to lead. It was a good push, Tedius." This touched him, and me as well. "I'll be back here as soon as possible."

Wet, cold, angry and uncertain, I headed off. Even if I got Martha back – and I would – surely Messalina would be next. Then who? Elissa, Annia, Monaxius, Tedius' wife? I had to do what Ammianus wants. When this ruin settled and the current danger was past, I would settle up with Ammianus. That alone was motivation enough for me, and there was more than just me to consider. Three years ago, I don't think I would have worried over these people. I was too stupid, too full of myself, too fearless. And that's what I needed now, that rash of fearlessness.

The rain had become sleet, then rain again. I walked fast and hard with a purpose. Soon, I was at the gate of Ammianus' stables behind his large house with its beautiful view out to sea.

I pounded as hard as I could on the wooden entrance door set in the larger metal gate, my knife's hilt amplifying the knock.

"*I Want Phocas Now! I Want Phocas Now!!!*" I shouted up into the rain. A rock came over the stone wall from the right of the gate, followed by an unintelligible curse and another rock that missed me. "*Phocas Now!*" I replied and pounded the door repeatedly. A slat opened, probably the rock thrower, asking who the hell I was.

"I am the last man you will ever see if you don't open this door and get me Phocas. Tell him Gaius Galen Licinius has come to lick the boots of Ammianus – in the rain. And he needs to do it *Now!*"

The slat was shut, with a curse in Aramaic. A few moments later, Phocas came through the door, dressed in a tiger-patterned sleeping gown a boy might wear, soaking up the rain.

The Isaurian held out his hand; I shook it and gave the professional nod slaves share when on master errands. Phocas smirked his amusement, rain drops disappearing into his moustache. "How may I serve you, Gaius Galen Licinius?" he asked, giving me a bow no slave would give to another.

"I have business with Ammianus, pressing business, he will find. This is what you must tell him now. The girl Martha will be in her mother's arms this morning. If not, Ammianus will not live to eat his midday meal. I would burn half the city to singe one of his nose hairs, so help me God, I will!"

Phocas looked impassively at me.

"I have 30 men in the neighborhood around this compound," I continued, "with more arriving, and we will set it ablaze before a single prefect's guard catches a whiff of smoke – he knows my fire-starting skills! I have three assassins whose goal at my signal is an arrow or knife in the eye of Ammianus. One is working in his home right now."

I paused to catch my breath because I was talking in excited bursts, as the insane in the streets often do. Phocas nodded as if we were negotiating a reasonable price for a loaf of bread.

"If the girl is returned," I said, "I will do everything that Ammianus tells me to do. We will be back in business and I will dutifully finish that business as he wishes. But if the girl is not returned, or if she is harmed in any way, his life is done – and I don't care if it costs me mine. The girl is to be returned to the fountain where she was abducted. Tell your men who release her to beware and clear out fast, for there is one group I cannot control and I know they wish to chew on Ammianus' eyelids, but they'll settle for those who do his bidding in this affair."

My nostrils flared pulling in air. Each word I forced out. I was tensed and cocked to spring on him at the slightest provocation. Phocas was calmly observing me, with some agreement, or so I thought, and this eased the tension in me some.

"Are you able to repeat what I have said, Phocas?"

"Everything – except for the excited breathing," and he cackled at my lack of control.

I nodded my approval of his forwardness, and said, "Good. And Phocas, do it quickly. Once some of these men are roused, I may not be able to hold them back."

He went back through the wooden door. I turned and sprinted like an Olympian into the night, and into the safety of my 30 imaginary men.

At about midnight four country boys from Macedonia – young men heavily armed, who worked for my father – stood shoulder to shoulder blocking the door to Monaxius' apartment. Three others in the stairwell had stopped me until they learned who I was.

Monaxius was still out searching. One of Tedius' boys he had gathered from the building to help us had found the anxious father and told him we were protecting Annia and Elissa. They were being comforted by her friends in the bedroom, and her sister was also there. Zazo, whose arm was professionally bandaged, gathered with Tedius and I around a candle on a small table in the sitting room.

"Brother Zazo, are you with me?" I formally asked. "Will you run with Tedius, Monaxius and me? Fight with us? We start by going after the one who has Martha."

He frowned two thick black eyebrows together. "The Lord will make it right," he said, pulling an Arabian knife from his bandage then hiding it back inside.

I set a leather purse of silver coins on the table. "This is to hire men, men like you. Can you have a dozen for me by dawn?"

The left side of his mouth made a half smile as he pushed the purse back to me.

"I will have 20 men in two hours – if we are to go after the one who has taken Martha from me."

"Good. All I need right now is for the people inside Ammianus' home and stable complex to know our men are watching them. Maybe throw a torch on the stable roof, minor harassments, that sort of thing. But these men of yours can't be monks roaming about, they must blend in as normal people if they are even seen."

"I understand," Zazo said gravely. "In two hours, I will be there with *normal* men."

I pushed the purse back to him, saying, "Brother Zazo, I do not take your allegiance to me lightly. I understand you want revenge for

Martha and will take no pay for that."

His black eyebrows separated, releasing a few frown lines.

"But your men have no such desire. This coin is my goodwill, and right now, I know your men would respond well to this gesture."

His left hand, still with a little blood on the back, gathered up the purse, he nodded his thanks and off he went.

"Tedius, how are you holding up?"

"Not as well as you, I think," he said. "It is a strange comfort, Gaius Galen, to see you rise to the occasion, collected and conniving. That is good."

"I almost went at Phocas, while yelling about burning Ammianus' nose hair. But I think he even has sympathy for us."

"He probably would have killed you," said Tedius dryly. "Any sympathy he may have means nothing. Phocas will not go against Ammianus."

"He won't need to." I told Tedius of my bluff of the men, which Zazo was now going to produce. "But we need more to leverage Ammianus. What about his 12-year-old son? He will be locked up in the house today as Ammianus determines what to do. How can we get to him, trade the boy for the girl?"

"Ammianus will return the girl without that need, Gaius Galen. I am sure of it," Tedius said. "I have been checking on him since his first visit, and he is afraid of you, which he has told his steward, as my source reports." He flashed a proud look and continued. "The boy, Honorius, has a playmate of 11, the son of a lawyer a couple of blocks away. I can go to Ammianus' gate with a note stating the friend will not be able to play with Ammianus' son until Martha is returned."

"Do it. Take a couple of these Macedonian fellows with you," I said and tore off a piece of bread a comforting neighbor of Annia had brought and handed it to Tedius. "I'll be at the fountain to receive Martha."

"And who will go with you to the fountain – you won't go alone, correct?" asked Tedius with concern.

"I'm going to wake up Lukos and a few of his fellows. Then I'll pay a visit to Jacob the Jew. The sail-making district is near Ammianus' house. We have maybe four hours before dawn, so we better get moving."

Tedius pointed to a pile of dry clothes on a chair, rugged pants, a thick wool jacket, and an oiled canvas cloak with floppy hood.

"They're Monaxius' clothes," he said. "Annia set them out for you: she knew you would be soaked."

I smiled in relief that she might not hate me completely. I changed on the spot, the dryness giving me strength. I buckled a short sword around my waist that was hidden by the cloak.

"Master, once we get the girl back – or once we don't – what is the next step?"

"We will get the girl back. But if not, we burn Ammianus' house down."

"And then he surely harms the girl or worse. Is that so smart a plan?" he asked.

"If we don't get the girl, we see what Monaxius wants us to do. But let's get the girl." I poked a piece of bread in my mouth, parted the Macedonian doormen and left in a trot.

8

The Accord of St. Euphemia

Snowflakes fell instead of rain as I made my way to Lukos' rat hole in the loft of a wretched warehouse where human vermin slept all over the lower floor. I pushed open Lukos' door. Two dank rooms, one slit of a window, six bodies asleep on straw mats, and Lukos on a cot, snoring thunder from a drunken night.

"Lukos," I whispered while shaking him. "Time to get up. Your mother has your favorite breakfast ready."

He snorted, I grabbed his chin and squeezed tight. His eyes opened. "Gaius?"

"Sshh. Come with me outside."

On the catwalk overlooking the sleeping bodies around the warehouse below, I flipped him a half gold solidus that he caught.

"What's – what are you doing here?" he asked, looking at the halved coin and rubbing his disordered blonde head. "You are welcome here with this, but what do I do for it?"

"Wake up three of those slugs asleep here, arm yourselves and come with me."

He gave me a challenging look.

"I have an urgent need for a menace like you. And this gold is just a token. You and I stand to make more of these – more than we did three years ago."

He rubbed hard at his crotch – God knows what pests might thrive there – and was finally awake enough to ask, "Blues?"

"No, kidnappers. I need your help, Lukos, this moment."

I knew he would like the idea of being needed. He asked, "And your Hun, why not get his help?"

"He's too civilized, not as vicious as you boys. I need your fire."

"Yours is dying, eh?"

"I'll be dead by noon if you don't come help me now." I pulled back my cloak to show the sword. "Morning may break with my blood on this fresh snow."

"You said three of my boys, I'm bringing all six," he said. "Where and when?"

"In an hour, no later. At the fountain next to the Church of St. Euphemia."

He nodded. "We'll be there."

The sailmakers' area was just to the north of the Jewish Gate in the defensive wall at the Harbor of Theodosius. An early riser outside his door pointed out Jacob's shop and home.

Jacob answered his door, looked down at my cloak where the sword pushed it out a little and asked, "So soon, Gaius Galen?"

"A surprising need."

"It will only be me," Jacob said. "I will not put my men in risk until I have seen how you act. You talk well, but that's not enough."

He slipped off his nightshirt moving through his shop toward his living quarters, where a young girl about Martha's age was at the curtain, watching her father and the stranger. He stroked her hair and kissed her cheek, went inside and was back out in a moment. On his way out the shop door he grabbed a three-foot iron rod with a leather grip.

"Wouldn't a sword be better?" I asked as we walked on.

"My rod and my knife are all I need. If a Jew gets caught carrying a sword, he will not get off like a Roman or Christian might." We walked silently for a moment until, like Lukos, he asked, "Blues?"

"Not Blues, not Greens." I told him the story as we made our way through dark, narrow streets. A few blocks from the fountain, Jacob insisted on taking a different route himself.

"I'll be able to see if they're leaving men in reserve for an attack," he said, then answered my worried look with, "Don't doubt me, I'll be right there with you. You just tell your friends that the short fellow with the golden tassel on his hat is with you." Jacob jogged off down an alley.

Thickening snow had whitened the fountain by St. Euphemia clean and pure. The small plaza around it was empty. The leafless treetops in the adjacent church's garden were barely visible. Dawn would be slow and weak.

Lukos and three men approached from the east. He looked like death with an escort, all wearing black capes, thankfully without any green. I was about to ask Lukos about the six he promised when three more black capes came from around the garden. The capes were Lukos' idea. Members of a leading team in riots often wore similar clothing to identify themselves to followers, but capes struck me as excessive. I told them of Jacob nearby, then positioned them: three in the garden, Lukos and I at the fountain, and three across the way at the street corner. I wanted numbers visible.

Lukos and I talked quietly of this current affair and of my future needs, which would be a little different from our past days. After a short time, we heard horses coming down the street next to the church. A carriage accompanied by four riders stopped at the plaza. A dark-skinned man jumped from the driver's bench. The four riders dismounted and the five of them approached Lukos and me, glancing at the others in the garden and at the corner.

"Are you with Gaius Galen Licinius?" asked the dark-skinned one, a Libyan I think.

"Yes. I am he, here to retrieve a child Ammianus found here just last evening. Do you have her?"

He waved his hand to the carriage. A woman in a fur coat climbed down, helping out a smaller bundle of fur. Martha was under the fur. I pushed my hood off my head, and when she saw me, she bolted from the woman's hand and ran to me. I clutched her and asked if she was alright.

"Uh huh, but I'm scared," she said, smiling weakly. She looked up at me with teary eyes and said, "They hurt Brother Zazo. Is he alright?"

"He's fine, but more hurt that they pulled you from him. He and your family will be happy to see you."

I gently transferred her over to Lukos, who was dumbstruck by a 5-year-old girl clutching his thighs, her head against his stomach, sobbing some. He held his arms up at first, then brought one, then the other down around Martha's shoulders. He patted her back as he'd seen mother's pat their babies to burp them.

The Libyan eyeballed Lukos' men, who had stepped forward a bit, one was snickering at Lukos hugging Martha. "I am glad we could reunite you with the girl," said the Libyan.

"As am I," I returned. "We'll take her safely home, and I'll remove my men from the home of Phocas' master."

The Libyan nodded and turned to go back to the carriage but bumped into Jacob, leaning on his iron rod like a cripple.

"A small coin, Sir, for a worthy man?" he asked, holding out a hand.

The Libyan pushed his hand away and strode back to the carriage. Jacob watched the men mount and turn to leave, saying to us, "Six more mounted a block ahead of them and five more on the other side of the church." He spit on the street. "Defensive, just in case, I would say."

He went straight toward Lukos but started talking to Martha. "My child, you are safe now. You can go home. A little adventure, that's all."

He stroked her hair, as I had seen him stroke his daughter's earlier. "My name is Jacob," he said to Martha then smiled at Lukos and patted his shoulder as a welcome protector.

I sent Jacob to tell Brother Zazo to end his presence around Ammianus' house. Eight men walked in a clump, a girl among them – at my side holding my hand, leaning into my short sword as it swung with my steps. People were beginning to move about, kitchen chimneys sending smoke up into the falling snow. Strange light, or lack of it, made it seem like evening. Martha squeezed my hand tight, whispering, "I feel safe with you now, Gaius Galen."

I squeezed her hand back. "You are safe, Martha. We are going home."

Guilt wrenched through me for dragging this innocent thing into danger. She could have been a corpse in that carriage. I could have made the wrong call pressuring Ammianus – or one of Lukos' still-drunk boys could have attacked the Libyan, bringing on her slaughter. It could have been the end. It was an end, I realized, squeezing Martha's hand again. My life was no longer my own.

A half block from Martha's building, I recognized standing outside the boy Tedius had engaged as a lookout earlier – and he recognized us, yelling out, "Martha! You're back!" He ran up the hill to us, hugged Martha and said, "We knew Gaius Galen would get you back. Tedius promised your mother and father he would."

"Did he? Well, Tedius is most always right, and there was never a chance I wouldn't bring Martha back," I lied, perhaps to soothe the children and myself.

The boy, Pawah, who was from an Egyptian family that lived in the building, took Martha's hand from me and led us up to her home. It was full of people, instantly joyed to see her. Monaxius was back and Atakam was with him – had been from early on helping him hunt for Martha in the streets after Tedius had someone rouse Atakam to help us out. The seven Macedonians had been given the family table as a gesture of thanks and were eating a simple breakfast of porridge and bread. The others stood around talking and eating bread and dried oranges. Tedius, Annia, her friends and sister, the girls, Lukos and his six filled the kitchen area. When Brother Zazo walked in from his vigil at Ammianus' house, Martha jumped at him, kissing his bandage all over. The tall one broke into silent tears at the intensity of their reunion.

Soon the Macedonian strongmen left – heartily thanked – followed by Annia's friends, Lukos and his men, and Pawah. Atakam was going to leave, but Monaxius asked him not to, saying, "You stayed with us looking for our daughter, for which I am grateful and honored. I ask that you stay with us now. We can use your advice, can't we Gaius."

"Yes, we can," I said, glad that Atakam had answered Tedius' call and come to help. "Brother Zazo, will you take the girls to their room while the adults talk over a few things? You and I will speak later."

After their departure, I told the others there would be no second chance to get out of this, and that I would do Ammianus' bidding. Monaxius and Annia insisted they were with me in this, and all agreed that there was no other choice. The first step would be this afternoon, when Annia and the two girls would go with Annia's sister and her husband in his fishing boat to the Asian side across the Bosphorus, then travel to a second cousin who had a farm 10 miles inland and would help. Annia and the girls would stay there until this was all over.

I emphasized that we needed to be as secretive as possible about this and everything. We all needed to keep our eyes open and mouths shut, for spies and informants were rampant in Constantinople, and not only imperial spies but private spies gathering information for leverage on any number of people.

"It would not take a spy to know I am great friends with Monaxius and to go after his daughter to force my agreement," I said. "But we can't rule out informants among or near us." This brought an awkward exchange of glances. I offered as assurance, "I trust you all, but let's be careful who we each trust, and keep quiet about any of this situation."

Monaxius, Lukos and I had networks of our own, and Tedius seemed to have a slave connection to every household in the Eastern Empire, offering an underground river of knowledge. So, we might be able to stay a step ahead of Ammianus and his secret client.

Monaxius wondered if Ammianus might be pretending to act for a client and was really acting for himself.

"When I told him I wouldn't do his bidding, he warned of the bonds of patronage that none are free from," I related. "He wields power over actors and athletes, but his client undoubtedly has more power, the type of man – or men – who might want to turn a riot into a revolt. Perhaps Ammianus is as unsure as us right now, and is himself afraid."

"As we all should be," said Monaxius. "A little street rioting might be the least dangerous thing we face. But we do need to start building our team.”

“We have a good start with Zazo, Jacob and Lukos.” Atakam almost choked on the idea of Lukos’ involvement; the two had glowered at each other when Lukos walked in earlier. I needed to stop that. “Lukos is actually a good man, Atakam, though a bad sort of man as well. We need him, and Monaxius and I have others from the past we can use. Let’s aim for having a team of about 30 identified and purchased in two weeks.”

“And isn’t there one more thing to consider, Gaius Galen?” asked Annia. “Your Messalina, I have heard about? She must be in danger as well.”

“You are right, Messalina is becoming ... an influence on me,” I said, hiding my worry. “But she’s no more powerful an influence than darling Martha, or more powerful than you, Annia, or than Monaxius – my personal rescuer in numerous tight spots in life. When you told Elissa just a few hours ago that it was my fault Martha was taken, I was deeply ashamed.” Annia smiled sweetly and shook her head *no*. “I will get you all through this, so help me God. I don’t know exactly how or when. But I know why.”

Atakam rose from the pink child’s stool he was sitting on, pulled his knife from its sheath and handed it to me.

“Here’s a leader I can follow. I think he has some Hun in him after all, this *Wilder* – and a bit of a soft heart too,” he said, pinching my cheek.

Tedius and I walked home. He knew I didn’t want to talk, though that didn’t stop him from trying a couple of times. My mind was filled with worry about how to get us all out of this situation in one piece. Responsibility was something of a foreign weight for me: a pressure born of caring for others more than myself. For the first time ever, I think I truly regretted my past. It seemed much more dangerous to me now than it was living through it, propelled and near overcome by the thrill of it all.

Setting up the details in the task before me would not be so difficult, particularly with Tedius’ help. Reacting to the unknowns that would come up was most troubling for me, partly because I used to look forward to such surprises. Not now. Ammianus was the biggest unknown – and as we turned the corner, damned if he wasn't at the stairway entrance to my apartment! Not his fleshy self, but Phocas. The man who had mocked me in his tiger sleeping gown just a few hours before now removed his metal half-helmet in deference, offering a slight bow.

"Honorable Gaius Galen Licinius, my Master sends his good wishes, along with this," and he indicated a large wrapped rectangle of something behind him. "And this," the Isaurian gave Tedius a wax-sealed, folded papyrus. "Good day to you," he said, adding in an undertone that wasn't part of his official message, "And I am glad your friend's child is back with her mother." He paused to fix his helmet on his head just so, then trod off through the quiet street, his mammoth furry boots squeaking crunched snow.

Tedius and I looked at each other, a little shocked at Ammianus' immediate contact. Tedius led the way up the stairs, carrying the package. It was a beautiful, and expensive, landscape painting of a vineyard. The papyrus, an invitation to me for a banquet tomorrow evening at the home of a wealthy senator known for his lavish parties. A note at the bottom said:

You must bring your race fan, Messalina. I can't wait to meet her, Ammianus

"I *must* bring her?"

Tedius tossed the invitation on a table. "He's already testing your recent commitment to do as he instructs," he said.

"He's also bragging. I think I am beginning to know how Ammianus thinks. Go see Flacilla now, Tedius. Tell her about the invitation and ask her if I can come by later today to ask her permission."

"You will usher Messalina into Ammianus' presence?" he asked.

"Would you rather us try to get her back, as we had to do with Martha? Do you think that will work twice? Now off with you, as I instruct." Sometimes I am not sure if I crack authority to remind me or him that he is my slave.

While he was gone, I tried to decide which of the bad options I might follow. Should I be honest and tell Messalina she was being watched by a dangerous man who had already kidnapped a child to extort me to re-enter the faction rioting she despised? Or should I lie and hide it all from her?

Warning her seemed like the right thing to do, even if that turned her against me. But wouldn't she still be in danger, whether she knew the truth or not? And this whole thing might never come about – a prospect I did not want to abandon.

9

Party of Conspirators

Tedius returned, relating Sister Flacilla's agreement to meet me later and Messalina's delight at going to a senator's party. Tedius would find and deliver a suitable gift to our host, Quintus Cornelius Alban, while I took a gift of jewelry to Sister Flacilla to serve two purposes: to accentuate Messalina's beauty as an emissary for Flacilla's good works and as a contribution to the same by selling the jewelry afterward to buy medicine to heal the miserable. I would sell Ammianus' painting gift to cover the jewelry, maybe turning a profit. I wanted nothing from him around me.

After buying the jewelry, I visited Sister Flacilla, who was more interested in the goodwill Messalina might spread for her cause in Quintus Cornelius' constellation of rich stars than the proceeds of jewelry, which she humbly accepted nonetheless. No one knew just how much of her once-considerable wealth she still had from her dead husband, who had plundered assets from two eastern provinces as an imperial governor. Flacilla poured money into the city's bottomless pit of poverty, while also turning their fine home into a collegial refuge where prostitutes could prove themselves to her, and she worked to find suitable matches for the newly polished women, an endeavor believed to have stemmed from her husband's rumored death in a brothel.

"Only because I trust Messalina am I allowing her to go," Flacilla told me. "Guide her safely, but don't try to be her protector, even if she is disrespected. If you do this tonight, it can only help your cause," she said, her still beautiful eyes flaring encouragement while she cascaded the gold and pearl necklace into one palm then the other.

I left her with the promise that I would.

The next evening, with Messalina across from me in the carriage, my knee touching hers as we bounced along, I was caught off guard by the wave of affection for her that came over me. Was it heightened by guilt because I was about to lie to her?

"The necklace looks even more beautiful around your neck," I said to steady myself.

"Thank you, Gaius Galen. This will buy hope, the hope I see in the eyes of a broken man I give a bag of walnuts, or a sick mother receiving a wet nurse's milk for her weak infant. Did you know the gold chain is in a Syrian weave? We braided our hair in this same way when we were girls, Arbella and I." She fingered the chain at her clavicle.

"I told the jeweler I needed a stunning cross for a Syrian beauty."

"I think of Arbella always," she said. Messalina talked of how she and Arbella were separated by her mother. It was a story she had told me before but I didn't stop her: I could listen to her talk of mathematics with pleasure.

Her father was an Antioch seller of charcoal, her mother a drunken wastrel – always had been as far as Messalina could remember. After her father died from a ruptured lung, being poor, female and beautiful was a curse that cost the sisters their freedom. Her mother sold Arbella to a slaver and she immediately disappeared. Messalina, no doubt the more beautiful of the two, was sold to an exclusive house of love by her mother, her new guardians cultivating her to be a companion for their well-bred, wealthy clients. The last time Messalina saw her mother was in the street, her beggar's cup jangling at Messalina. She didn't recognize her own daughter, then 16.

"Why did your father marry her, Messalina?" I asked with gentleness, for she was upset by these memories.

"She was a prostitute and he fell in love with her, determined he could help her be the good woman she said she wanted to be."

Messalina's eyes, moist and blinking, showed her vulnerability and trust in me. I caught her first tear on my finger.

"I don't want to be like my mother, I want to be a good Christian woman. Sister Flacilla came into my life almost at the moment I had fled my former one. She is the mother I always wanted." We leaned into each other for a hug we both needed. "Now you know my secret fear, Gaius Galen, being like my mother. You can share yours with me anytime."

"What a serious way to start a party," I said.

"It's a good way to start, Gaius. It's a good way," and she kissed the cross on her necklace, a luminous pearl where Christ's head would be. The offer for me to share my secret with her threatened to undo me, for it was time for my lie.

"Messalina, the man who invited me here, Ammianus who is my high superior at the track, suspects you were at the races with me the other day," I said, swallowing a little. "It is a matter between him and me, though I believe he might bring it up to you. He likes to make his employees squirm."

"How does he know this, Gaius? Did he see me under those bandages and disguise?"

"He had someone watching us, I am told. You were not seen, but you were heard," I reminded.

"Just because Semacus screamed a little at the shipwreck – yes, in a high-pitched voice – does not make him Messalina. Have you admitted it?" she asked, getting a little perturbed. I shook my head no. "Then I was not there and I will not know what this person might be talking about should he bring it up."

"I wanted to prepare you, Messalina, as I got you into this and I – "

" – You did no such thing," she huffed, cutting me off. "You only humored me after I begged you to take me. I'll not give you up to this man, Gaius Galen. I am not that type of woman. I know how to hold a secret – and handle this Ammianus."

She probably could: she was surely handling me, and the affection for her warmed me (along with guilt from lying to her).

We were silent for a while, and she cooled down. She let her knee stay in touch with mine as we turned onto the private road that snaked around the hillside and through the several homes and assorted buildings for slave quarters, private bakery and such that made up the complex Quintus Cornelius Alban called home.

"You see the soldiers stationed everywhere?" I asked.

She nodded.

"Look at the emblem on their breastplates, the orange *QCA* in the mouth of the red roaring lion's head: they are Quintus Cornelius Alban's private army. Legally forbidden, but the emperor turns a blind eye to the armed retainers some of the wealthiest have to protect themselves."

Crassus once said that you're not truly wealthy unless you can afford your own army. Quintus Cornelius Alban did not have the Roman legions Crassus had purchased (and led to ruin and his own death), but he was almost rich enough, being a direct descendant of the famous clan of the Cornelii that was keenly involved in the Western Empire's former glory. I gestured to the house we were approaching.

"This is one of the homes of the Cornelii that was in Rome some 200 years ago. Emperor Constantine dismantled the house stone by stone and rebuilt it here – or so goes the legend," I said.

I did not say that some think Quintus Cornelius Alban has more reason to be emperor than Justinian, the Macedonian peasant who currently occupies the palace. I thought this might be the reason Ammianus had invited me here, to give me a hint of our client as a reward for me agreeing to help Ammianus serve him. As Messalina eyed the complex and soldiers, I wondered at my stupidity in bringing her here, closer to the man who might use her against me. Tedius thought my decision to bring her was a terrible one, though he didn't say so. Becoming closer to Messalina by the moment, our knees holding contact, I wished I hadn't brought her but also was glad I had.

As our carriage neared the entrance, Messalina primped at the stiffened cotton collar of her yellow quarter jacket. Three layers of sheer cloth, each a different shade of rose petal pink, were alluringly draped and pinned to fit her lovely form and flowed down to her ankles.

Our turn. Tedius opened the door, I climbed out first and tried to maintain my composure as Messalina's peachy bottom backed down the carriage steps, my hand a useless suggestion on her elbow. She turned, kissed me quickly on the cheek and placed her forearm on mine.

"Gaius, your face is red. Should I have gotten out first?" she asked, glancing down quickly at the front of my toga. She almost laughed but said, "Come Sir, the evening is ours."

In curve toed slippers lacquered pink, Messalina glided amongst the flowers strewn from the drive to the entrance. She tightened her grip on my arm at the sight of a massive, angry dog five feet tall snarling at us – from the mural that filled the four walls of the sizeable vestibule. The scene was a dark wood in rainy Britain, a Druid priest with barbaric blue skin strained to hold the Mastiff back on a chain.

The double doors flung open and a real Druid – 6 feet and more – stood blue skinned and snarling before us.

"Welcome, Gaius Galen Licinius and the beautiful Messalina of Antioch," the blue one thus announced us, opening his arms wide and smiling just as big. "Ravenia will guide you to your pleasures."

A lovely, slender woman offered Messalina her hand and led her, leading me. I looked over my shoulder to see the Druid shut the doors so he could startle the next arrivals.

Messalina whispered to me, "Should I ask her? She must be a professional dancer the way she glides."

"No. Let Tedius dig among the slaves and servants," I said, and she nodded. "He will not fail to find your trail to Arbella – if there is one to find."

There would be no difficulty finding entertainers here. They seemed to outnumber the guests. A group of barrel-chested black Africans wearing long white wigs moved through the central hall, proffering silver trays to guests so they could choose delicacies – hot prawns peeking out of pastry puffs, smoked snails dusted with crushed pistachios. The marble hall was huge and decorated with luxurious cloth hangings, paintings and fantastic mosaics in the floor. Oil lamps and aimed mirrors cast wavering light in every direction. Two smaller halls flanked this larger one, with shallow pools of violet water joining them to the main one.

We wandered about, sampling treats, engaging with some people, attracting looks. We entered the open-air heart of the home, and I stopped to talk to two fellows I knew from my father, both imperial lawyers, their wives dripping jewelry and disdain from bored faces. After our introductions, Drusilla said to her friend Cassandra, "Someone told me this Syrian is one of those repentant whores it is so fashionable to take up as a project and re-purpose for honest mothering." Her eyes sliding under emerald-colored lids looked over Messalina. Drusilla lightly pushed away a puff of her hair, crisped out like a blond cloud restrained by a net of purple thread holding small diamonds. "She is pretty, I suppose. Birthing should be no problem after her extensive preparations."

Her husband raised his eyebrows at me to indicate this was how his wife was. I followed my orders from Sister Flacilla and said nothing but pursed my lips at Drusilla, who was watching for my reaction from the corner of her eye.

"It is my honor to be one of Sister Flacilla's 'projects' – and God's," said Messalina, who stepped closer to Drusilla while planting her wine goblet on the tray of a passing servant. "I am her emissary tonight, a quiet one. It is so lucky for me that prostitutes are fashionable in this peculiar way. I can't tell you how tiresome it is to baby all the men who come to us for understanding and affection."

"Not for sex?" Drusilla sneered.

"Yes, but I am happy that your man comes to you for that." Messalina quickly smiled to the husband, then bowed to Drusilla. "I do not want to make anyone uncomfortable, especially my betters," she said, extending her hand behind her to me. I took it. "Please Gaius Galen, show me the singer from my home country I heard earlier in the smaller dining hall."

Drusilla's husband winked his approval to me as Messalina turned us away. I put my arm around her shoulder as we moved through the thicket of servants and guests.

"I couldn't admire you more, Messalina." I stopped us and faced her. "Your restraint is remarkable. I wish mine were half as strong."

"Gaius, that was not difficult. This," and she squeezed my hand, "is much more so, resisting you."

She released my hand, opened it and brushed my palm with her ruby fingernails. She lifted my palm to her mouth and kissed it, looking into my eyes through my spread fingers. All so fast, my mind a mess, my heart wanting to be hers. As she guided me blushing at her side, it struck me that this could be the finest moment in my life. Was I in love, finally? That made me laugh.

"Do I amuse you?" she teased, offering part of her come-on look.

"Oh yes."

Before I could make a complete fool of myself by kissing her neck right below her left ear (one of my fantasized obsessions lately), I spied four servants coming toward us, our host's son behind them.

"Gaius Galen, so good to see you again," he put a firm hand on my shoulder. "My father sends his appreciation for your presence and for the thoughtful gift you sent."

Rufus Cornelius Alban, youngest of three sons and one I had a youthful acquaintance with, smiled at me then took in Messalina with pleasure. About 30 with an air of benign superiority, wearing a 4-inch band of blazing gold on his forearm worth more than my home, Rufus Cornelius had made an effort to single me out, certainly beyond what my status deserved.

"Your father's kind invitation is the true gift," I said.

"Your gift reflects your good taste, as does this," and he held out his upturned hand. Messalina responded placing hers within.

"Sir, I am humbled to be here," she said. "Thank you, from me and from my sponsor Sister Flacilla."

Rufus' eyes ate her up.

"Messalina from Antioch," I managed as an introduction – rather than shove him backwards away from her as I wanted to do.

"Yes, I know – a lot of people here know this, now. Word travels like light at times."

"Extraordinary banquet," I complimented. "I was hoping to see Ammianus, who graciously arranged for our invitation."

"Yes, that's one of the reasons my father wanted me to seek you out. Father is in a private dining hall with guests on senatorial business and asked me to welcome you. Ammianus was called away to deal with some crisis of a theater riot in Prusa. Something about actors being caught up in a melee of supporters."

"Then my appreciation falls to you, Rufus Cornelius, and to your father." I bowed a little, while thinking that Ammianus wasn't involved in any such affair. Like a good matchmaker, he'd put us together and stepped aside. And now here I was, probably talking to the son of my "client."

"Gaius the Younger, how is your father Gaius Galen Licinius? Are there still pagan temples left for him to convert to churches?" Rufus asked.

"I am certain of it. In truth, I do not see my father often."

"I know, quite a rift I understand. But this is not my business," Rufus took a heavy breath, his head slightly nodding. "I know how difficult it can be to be the proper son. But tell me Gaius Galen, how did you know my young sister would love the bridle you sent? The silver work is excellent, I have never seen another like it."

He seemed truly pleased. A bull's eye for Tedius.

"Yes, supple leather with the bright colors of southwestern Hispania. I have seen young Quinta and her attendants many times at the Green stables – and the Blue's, for she is color blind when it comes to horses," I said, making a mental note that Quinta might make an excellent hostage if need be. "She has a fine eye for the best. Each time I have seen those cheerful blue eyes of hers light up for a horse, it was a Spanish breed. I have a good man who found this bridle. I am very pleased she likes it."

"She loves it. Very thoughtful of you, Gaius Galen." His hand on my shoulder again.

"He is often thoughtful, Rufus Cornelius," said Messalina. "As are you to host me, here among the flower of Constantinople." She lowered her head and looked up to him.

"Think nothing of it, my dear. We have known Flacilla long before she was a self-made sister," said Rufus with a knowing smile. "She stayed with us one night when wine had dulled her husband into a stupor. But do not relate that to her, an old upsetting memory that belongs to a different woman."

"Of course, Sir. I am an expert at keeping secrets," assured Messalina. "She spoke highly of your father."

Rufus' servants were stirring that it was time to make other calls.

"I met Sister Flacilla for the first time just today," I said, needing to get in my pitch before he left. "I convinced her that Messalina would be safe among rogues like you and me." Thank God Rufus laughed. "I gave Flacilla my word of safe keeping, and tomorrow I will give her a donation for her good works."

"Ah, this one is indeed a good work," his eyes slathered Messalina. "But Gaius Galen, may I join you in making a donation to Sister Flacilla's cause? I am sure Father will add to mine."

"She will be doubly honored. You are most gracious, Rufus Cornelius," I said.

An elderly servant clasped his hands together to indicate an end.

"Thank you both for coming tonight," Rufus said. "Should you need anything, send for old Cincinnatus here. And Cincinnatus, spread word among the servants for their masters to also consider supporting Sister Flacilla."

Rufus began to turn to leave but stopped, saying, "Messalina, if I may, I hope you attain the reform you are seeking. And perhaps you might bring along Gaius the Younger here. He has a few rough edges still."

"Bold, Rufus Cornelius, bold," I returned. "But that's what makes people like you and me so dangerous, eh?"

"Ha! Always at the surface, Gaius. Ammianus will be pleased to know. Enjoy, young lovers," and Rufus with his four plowmen in front split through the crowd of guests.

Watching them away, I was convinced I had just met my client's son, or why else would Ammianus be pleased to know anything about me as he suggested?

Messalina had her eye on me, and it wasn't a lover's look.

"That's a strange expression," I said to try to end it.

"It was a strange thing to say – by both of you – talking of being dangerous people and Rufus saying that would please Ammianus, the man who thought he knew who I was," Messalina replied, about to fold her arms, a defensive set I wanted to avoid. I extended my hand.

"Come, it's almost time for our seating in the third dining room." My hand was alone for the moments she didn't budge.

"Only if you tell me what that was about," and she did fold her arms.

"Youthful bravado and a dig at my subservience to Ammianus," I managed. "Rufus and I followed different crowds, which uhm … crossed at times."

She took my hand, tensed a doubtful brow and followed.

10

Scorpus, Glory of the Roaring Circus

Our progress was delayed several times by people stopping us to talk. Rufus' highly visible approval of us unlocked a gate. We were an interesting couple. Me, the disobedient son of the well-known Gaius Galen Licinius, on the arm of a chaste Antiochian prostitute, who was nothing less than radiant in a home-made gown she wore to more effect than the array of the latest fashions on display.

We dined in the smaller triclinium through 10 courses, punctuated by speeches from Rufus' brother Aetius, this room's host, and numerous toasts. As the lights dimmed, a languid song floated over us like approaching sleep, Messalina's head resting in the curve of my side stretched out on our couch. Our personal attendant whispered to us about the cottages up the hill ready for our pleasure. I shook my head no. Messalina smiled warmly and gave me a pinch at the same time, perhaps as a consolation.

"You are maddening, my love," and I kissed the top of her head.

"I was your *dove* earlier. Did you misspeak?"

"Yes," I said. "You were my *love* earlier, as well."

She hugged into me. This night had streaked us along as a shooting star across the sky: unnoticed at first, then unmistakable, then determined in its direction.

We moved about as one for another hour, talking to others,

listening to singers in the peristyle. We were nearing time to leave, and when I returned from the wondrous latrine – where I was entertained by a bald fellow performing magic tricks as I pissed into a hole ringed with sliver – Messalina was laughing with a loud man with a beard braided below his chin, an inch-long silver trident tied at the end of each braid. It was Scorpus, one of the most popular Green charioteers in the empire, his wooly beard and tridents famous and featured on dolls of his likeness fondled by girls, women, boys and men. He was laughing as he grabbed at sparks ascending from the fire each time the attendant threw in a branch.

"Scorpus, it is an honor to see you," I said and bowed my head slightly to his celebrity, for otherwise he was a mere freedman and former slave, though an incredibly rich and famous one.

He slapped a hand on my shoulder, no care for the ashes on my white toga. "I've seen you at the track – our Green Sandman. This one, she tells me, is yours. That so?" He ticked his head toward Messalina, who was close to the brazier and wrapped in a bear skin draped on her by an attendant.

"Tonight, she is mine," I said. "I have sworn to return her as pure as I received her from Sister Flacilla." Scorpus beamed at her, saying to me, "Well, you better get her away from me then!" Another laugh, a man who loves his own jokes. But I sensed truth in his good nature.

He looked to Messalina and announced, "A bear hug for the adorable bear by the fire," and he quickly had her in his arms trying to squeeze the honey out of her. She was giggling, putting her chin to her chest to keep him from sneaking a peck on her neck – my neck!

As I stepped toward them, he released her. "Alright, alright. You don't know Scorpus and his odd ways. I see a jealous man. In fact, I am jealous of you, having this charming beauty all to yourself. I've been waiting for my chance to pounce on you two, but you had her kissing your palm, then stuck to your side after dinner."

He bowed slow and low to me – Scorpus, who can't walk down a street without being mobbed and showered with attention. A lithe, strong man with quick reactions, sharp still at age 35, he was a beloved driver to all but the most bilious Blue partisans. He was a natural clown, always playing to the crowd. I once saw him stick his whip in his mouth to make a quick salute to a group of four elderly Green fans just before he careened his chariot on one wheel in a wild redirect across a Red's path on a final lap for the win. That reckless salute to those old fans at that moment could have killed him – and the Hippodrome knew it, yelling his name to heaven for five minutes in appreciation.

"How did you know she kissed my palm?" I asked.

"Gossips and spies. This place is filled with both." He turned halfway to Messalina, "Gaius Galen, will you and this lovely do me the honor of attending another party with me?" He gestured to the fire brazier and said, "This one is dying, the attendants are putting in branches, not logs. Here is wood on fire, there is water on fire. Here they let people like Messalina and I in as novelties – we might as well dance a number for Quintus! There, the dancers who performed here are the guests. There are men like me, charioteers and others of the track you will know."

"Where is this?" I asked.

"On the bay of the Golden Horn aboard two triremes – new replicas of the old war ships, one Blue ship and one Green, redesigned to accommodate drinking, eating, dancing, music and fun. If you come, Gaius Galen, I promise not to hug this beautiful bear again."

"We will come, but only if you *do* hug this bear again," said Messalina, stepping from the fire to my side.

"Excellent! – because I've already alerted your man Tedius that his master and lady will be my guests. A wrestler friend of mine will escort you to the landing," Scorpus said. He removed a silver trident from his beard and put it carefully in Messalina's hand. "I will collect the hug later," he said, looking to me for approval, which I nodded.

The wrestler was a copy of Scorpus with a similar laugh we heard from below as he joked with Tedius and the carriage driver during the ride. But Messalina was next to me on the leather seat, my hands were caressing her shoulders as we kissed, she checking my hands with a dropped elbow, skillfully defining her boundaries. How could a prostitute be so good at this?

We rode through a crisp chill with a lick of salt air as we arrived at a commercial wharf, its lot filled this night with carriages, town chariots, litters and a swarm of slaves attending the transports and relaxing while their masters played on the bay. Our wrestler escorted us to a gate in the high wall that ringed the city's shores to repel attackers. Four young men rowed us to the triremes.

These war ships, about 40 yards long and narrow, were built for speed and ramming, angry eyes painted on either side of the pointed bow. The ships were lashed together, with gangplanks attaching them, as if in battle boarding mode.

From the top deck, Scorpus looked down at us. "Ha ha! Come aboard, my night sailors!"

There were perhaps 100 people milling about on the ships, loose and unfettered by the stuffiness of Quintus' affair, superb though it was. This party's purpose was fun, where famous Blues and Greens displayed only playful rivalry, a scene that might shock some of their more rabid partisans.

Scorpus claimed his hug as soon as Messalina stood on deck. Then said, "Come. Meet my friends."

Before we took a step, one met us.

"Scorpus, Glory of the Roaring Circus, or so your foolish fans call you, who do you have here?" asked a man of about 35, distinguished and urbane.

"Typhos!" Messalina shrilled, pressing her hands together as if a prayer had been answered. The man struck a dramatic pose of folded arms, thrust out chin, cocky smile and confident look to the side that said, *Yes, I am incredible.*

Messalina cooed, "Oh my goodness, the famous Typhos on Top."

"Exactly," he said, his signature pose falling away. "And you, my dear, you can dismiss your servant here in the chalked toga."

"This is my friend, Gaius Galen Licinius."

"Her protector this evening," I added. "An honor to meet you, Sir."

"Honored myself – but can you leave us? I need to get to know this charming thing." One of his eyebrows went up like a battle flag.

Messalina answered by pulling my hand around her waist and leaning her head on my shoulder. "What about this pose, Typhos? Ever seen it before?" she asked.

"That's my girl!" Scorpus said loudly. "Taking an actual man over one who can play the part of a sobbing woman from the heart."

The four of us talked and drank, Messalina getting close to giddy, likely from the wine and the attention of two famous men. Typhos was actually warm and friendly. He and Scorpus shared a good-natured rivalry of celebrity, and of being worshiped. After one moving performance, Typhos was given a townhouse in Athens from a rich, swooning matron. Scorpus had his own island populated by camels 10 leagues south of us, granted to him by a nobleman when Scorpus had the most wins several years back.

They also spoke about how tiresome it could be to strike that Typhos on Top pose, bellow that Scorpus laugh at a fan's request. Both traveled with bodyguards and knew that pleasing fans was important for their continued popularity. Typhos described what he had heard about the theater riot in Prusa that Ammianus was allegedly seeing to. The quarrel started in the audience before the acting competition was over, for most performances were matches of sorts between Blue and Green actors. The fight suddenly spilled onto the stage, where three Green youths stabbed a Blue lead actor and his assistant. Typhos was shaken by this violence to a fellow theater professional, but quickly put such seriousness aside.

"Enough about myself and this horse sniffer, what about yourselves? Tell, tell, tell."

Scorpus took over the answer. "I rescued these two from Quintus Cornelius' dull party. Messalina is one of Sister Flacilla's girls in the redemption program."

"Oh God," moaned Typhos, pressing the back of his hand to his forehead.

"Yes, and this is Gaius Galen. Have you heard of his father Gaius Galen Licinius the architect?"

"Perhaps. Has he given me a building?"

"He may have given you a church," said Scorpus, "not that you would ever go there."

"You malign me, Sir. I am a – what is it I am supposed to be? – a loyal Chalcedonian orthodox, by God's mercy," and Typhos made a hash of crossing himself, ending with a finger stuck in his nose. Messalina gasped and giggled at the same time.

With a pondering look and a finger moving to his chin, Typhos said, "I think I have read this trashy novel before, and before and before. Young aristocrat, handsome and spoiled, falls madly in love with a prostitute with a big heart and a tragic background. Of course, it will never work out – but what do you know? – it does work out. Joy, joy! Tell me, there are pirates involved somehow, right?" he asked with a perfect look of question. He was good.

"I think you would be the pirate, if I would only leave," I said.

"Scorpus, where do you get these people?" Typhos asked. "They seem to follow you from alleys like stray pets."

"Natural charm, and my eye for the unusual, the savory souls who make life entertaining."

"And worthwhile."

"Yes, Typhos, worthwhile," agreed Scorpus. His eyes swept around our little circle before peering into his wine goblet. He bolted upright as if he'd seen a scorpion in it, then hurled the goblet into the Golden Horn.

"How did that get empty? I need more wine. Come," and he gathered Messalina and I with an arm on each of us. "Let me show you around. Join us, Typhos?"

"I think not. I have to pee over the side and need to find a slave to hold onto me." He winked at Messalina and thrust out his Typhos on Top chin.

Scorpus walked us up one side and down the other of the trireme. These racing professionals talked shop, like Hierax, charioteer of the Blues, showing Julian of the Greens a hand crossover technique with the reins. I did know some people from the track, all employees of individual factions, not from Ammianus' world of imperial overseers.

True to Scorpus' word, the water was on fire – whenever they squirted out a stream of naphtha from the bow of the ship, using a bellows contraption with a nozzle and a burning wick. They played with this semi-secret, imperial weapon for all of Constantinople to see.

Scorpus introduced us to sportsmen, trainers, dancers, musicians and a few eunuchs, some in imperial service, some affiliated with private houses. We crossed the gangplank to the Blue trireme, where acrobats swung from mast ropes to tumble and twist in perfect style on their way into the water, one catching a flaming torch tossed to him mid-flight. Scorpus assured Messalina they would be fished out.

Seated at a round table with a warming brazier in the middle we settled into a lively conversation, folks from the theater and the Hippodrome sharing their good time with us. Messalina was in her element, her wine goblet waving about as an extension of her expressions, nearing drunkenness, yet composed.

"Do you men know who this Messalina is?" asked the actress Chara, touching the arm of Messalina sitting next to her.

Scorpus informed us, again, that she was one of Sister Flacilla's projects.

"Before that," Chara said. "She was a prostitute, but not a base screwing animal like Messalina, the long-gone wife of Emperor Claudius." She turned to Messalina and asked, "You never coupled with 24 men in one day, did you dear?" Messalina said she had not.

"She was the most prized companion in Antioch – for this," Chara put a long red fingernail to Messalina's heart. "The loftiest of men called on her – prefects, admirals, bishops, sculptors and even a King I've been told. Isn't that right, little one?" Messalina nodded yes.

"They came for her heart, for her comfort, her companionship." Chara smiled to Messalina, who shook her head to cease this praise. "Oh, I'm sure she rutted, I'm sure she pleased their manliness, but they always left their hearts with this one." Chara stood up, goblet held high. "To Love – what we all want, what we all need, and what the fortunate find."

Everyone at the table stood and drank to Love, most looking to Messalina and me.

"Bravo!" said Scorpus clapping. "Love, trust, companionship, so good of you. And some men do need that." He gave a mocking shrug. "While some men like me need ... great sex! Let's say Chara asked your advice on that, Messalina. What would you tell her?"

Messalina looked as if she wasn't sure she would answer. Then said, "First, know your horse. Does he like a treat of apples or oats? Does he finish strong or does he merely start strong?" she asked this looking at Scorpus, which brought a table laugh. "Second, delay and reward, delay and reward. Third, make love like you want to get pregnant – passionately with the heat and urgent desire necessary to conceive. Finally, don't conceive, so don't forget the crocodile dung beforehand!" and she patted herself below her belly.

Scorpus made a face of distaste. "I thought only peasants still did that. It doesn't really work, does it?"

"The kind we used did," said Messalina. "It wasn't just the dung, but other substances included in the mix specially made for our house by a respected witch. It was invisible, odorless and I never once got pregnant."

"Maybe you're barren," offered Scorpus.

"And maybe you are an ass, charioteer," she hurled this at him hard, surprising us all. She reached over Chara between them and took Scorpus' wine goblet as her own. She was hot.

"Let's talk about your sex now," she challenged. "Tell me Scorpus, is it true what some of the local girls I live with say about your prediliction for orally enjoying your women? Don't you men *still* consider this debasing yourself to the weaker sex?"

The table was silent and attentive as she drank from his goblet, then put it back in front of him, sloshing a bit over the rim.

"We hear you have a different woman visit you early each race day," she gave an incredulous look for the benefit of the table. "We hear from one among our group that you like to flavor that beard with your woman's wetness."

Scorpus was about to speak, but she stopped him – "We hear that you then take your perfumed face to seek the approval of your horses!"

The table laughed lowly and rumbled with crosstalk.

"What are you mumbling about? Some of you know this already," said Scorpus with irritation, then adopted a calmer tone. "Since I have been experimenting with this strategy, I have won more often than last year. And did you know, Messalina, that my lead horse likes the scent of Syrian women more than all others? Makes him fly like an eagle."

The two locked eyes. Messalina stood, still looking at Scorpus as she moved behind his chair. She put her hands on his shoulders pinning him there with some force. He didn't move.

"I could have told you that," and she bent down to peck a kiss into his beard. "We are the best," she said as she slid her hands from his shoulders down to his wrists, slowly.

Everyone at the table – and none more than I – felt her breasts pressing into Scorpus' back. This, I thought, was Messalina of the House of Eros, the one I never got.

She patted his wrists, slowly rose and said softly, "Best in many things, dear Scorpus."

He was up in a flash, pouring from his goblet into Messalina's and handed it to her.

"Friends of the track and theater, do we keep this pair among us?" Scorpus asked the table.

"*Yes!*" they all said, saluting goblets to the stars before drinking them empty.

The tension had reanimated the group, and the talk continued, a good bit about sex. After a while the table began to break up; some were anxious to leave after word reached us of an outbreak of violence in the city, a disorder of faction fans south of The Mese. Two buildings were on fire, and the city prefect's guards were tangling with the partisans.

Hierax cursed his unruly Blue fans and the Greens alike as scum. Most of the drivers did not approve of the mayhem caused by such destroyers like my former self, who used their Color affiliation as an excuse to go off. With such talk going on around me, I felt like an intruder, the weight of Ammianus' task hanging heavy over me, knowing these good people – and Messalina – would hate me for it.

Unhinged by Chrysanthos

Our evening had rolled past midnight. Messalina and I sat in two deck chairs under thick woolen blankets. We held hands under the covers, admiring Constantinople. We could make out the city's seven hills (one was hardly a hill) – same as old Rome. The site of New Rome here was partially chosen for that reason by Constantine when he created the world's first Christian city. Constantine was a great man who did great things, and if he had to boil his wife in her bath and murder an untrustworthy son along the way, so it was.

Some lights were still on at the Palace of Blachernae, Empress Theodora's building project, which sat atop the sixth hill. The noise of our floating party had died down considerably, and Messalina rested her head on my shoulder. A moment later a hand clamped down on my other one.

"Don't worry about me, love birds. I'm fine," said Scorpus, patting us both. "It's beautiful. I see this from my home in the Sycae suburb every night. That's partly why I prefer to live across the Horn over here, where they allowed the wild Celts to settle. I'm sure you saw the Druid tonight at Quintus' entrance. He's a Celt and lives near me, though this is the first time I have seen him painted blue."

Scorpus rubbed my shoulder absently, probably confusing it with Messalina's.

"It's an odd place, Constantinople," he said, the normal bombast in his voice replaced by the introspective drag of drunkenness. "It's like a giant tit, you know – excuse me, Messalina – it's like a giant breast. The bountiful breast of Europe jutting out into the Bosphorus."

"You've put much thought into this, haven't you, Scorpus," said Messalina.

"I do wonder at the city's good fortune at times and mine. I could be killed in any race, and Constantinople could die as well, if not for our protective wall that has repelled Huns, Germans, Goths and Slavs who have bounced off it and turned west to assault the poor old teat of Rome instead. Attila himself turned his multitude away from the Theodosian Walls, the bribe of gold and 3,000 pounds of pepper helped, but it was our wall that stopped him short."

Scorpus made his listing way in front of us. "What I really want is this woman, but since I am not able to have her – though who knows if I really tried – I wish to honor her. Messalina, I heard that Rufus Cornelius made your sister and her Home for Has Been Whores an offering. Do you think she would want a stud?" He cocked his head to the side, imitating Typhus on Top, poorly.

Messalina laughed. "I am sure she could find some use for you, perhaps in the garden – or can you plaster? We need to re-plaster the upstairs rooms."

"Studs do not plaster. The stud I am speaking of is an Arabian stallion I am putting up for auction in two days." He pulled one of the remaining silver tridents from his beard and gave it to Messalina. "Give this to Sister Flacilla and tell her I will reclaim it after the auction when I bring her the proceeds from my stallion. This is my offering."

He was entirely serious, for the first time since I met him.

"We are blessed by your generosity," she answered, holding the trident tight. "You must come to our house of worthy has-beens, and we will shower you with love – not the physical kind, of course. How would you like to dine with 20 fine young ladies?"

As Scorpus grinned at the prospect, I looked beyond him and saw a ghost from my past standing at the stern of the ship not too far away. I had seen several eunuchs on the two ships tonight, but not him. I rose from my chair.

"You two excuse me for a moment, I must talk to someone." Messalina cast a questioning look my way that I did not answer.

As I approached the stern, a gust of north wind blew my cloak open, as if to uncover me at this moment. Chrysanthos turned to greet me, his arms spreading for an embrace we entered immediately. He smelled heavenly, perfumed in bliss. I hugged him deeply, my eyes suddenly swimming in tears of happiness mingled with anxiety. He patted my back and pulled away, his face two feet from mine.

"You have grown well into manhood, Gaius. Yet I easily recognize the boy of 10 I saw so long ago."

"And in you, Chrysanthos, the handsomeness I always recall is now richer with dignity." I released his shoulders and stepped back. "You look as wise as Moses, but without a beard." I didn't know the emotion filling me but smiled, trapping a pair of tears on the ridge of my cheek. He wiped them away with a finger weighted by an emerald ring, then tousled my hair, just as he did when I was 10.

"I would never have expected to see you here among men as coarse as Scorpus," I said.

"But I love Scorpus – I love all these people, most all of them." Chrysanthos laughed, impossibly perfect teeth brightening his smile a magnitude. "Besides, I furnish horses for many of the teams. I have a string of stables in Cappadocia. But you must know that from the track."

"You know where I am? I didn't think you would," I said, a reflexive smile showing my pleasure.

"I have always known where you are, Gaius, even when you were *Wilder.*" The lift of his greying eyebrow said that he knew much. I felt ashamed before this man.

But not a man, and not a woman: a eunuch, the third gender intentionally constructed to serve. Boys' bodies prevented from reaching manhood, filling out instead with female attributes of smooth skin, fat deposits in hips and thighs, and high-pitched voice, plus the adopted mannerisms of the tribe of eunuchs that existed in another world within Constantinople. Chrysanthos' face was somewhat

Persian with a strong, contoured chin and a mouth fit for either sex. But the eyes, so dark, so kind, were shaded by lashes Messalina would be proud of. I had become lost in those eyes as a boy, looking up to this man I considered to be better than any man I knew then.

"But I also know you no longer prefer Wilder," he said, squeezing my arm and smiling in approval.

"No, not now – and never to you, Chrysanthos. I am not Wilder." Just saying the name to him embarrassed me for every stupid, violent thing I had ever done. "I am just trying to be Gaius Galen Licinius."

"Your father's name. But you are nothing like him."

"I am The Younger, yes. But it is not my choice to be so subordinated. We do not speak."

He laughed warmly. "He and I don't speak either, these days. But associates of my master Tribonian have dealings with him."

Tribonian, the quaestor who compiled the Roman laws into Justinian's Codex, was one of the emperor's most trusted advisors. Chrysanthos was in a high circle of power.

"I am humbled before you, Chrysanthos – the student proud of his mentor, who no doubt had a hand in the famous Codex." In respect I touched the side of his head, long hair falling in curls tied with golden threads. I pulled my hand away. "Proud of you for that, and for leaving me whole."

"I am also *whole*, Gaius. But I understand you," he said, showing no offense. "I have always wondered that you might have misunderstood my part in our drama, and glad to learn now you did not. I could not share everything with my 10-year-old charge, of course. But I did not share your father's desire, either."

He paused for my reaction, spotting the shallow, rapid breathing I hid poorly trying to staunch the terrible memories rising within me. "Within the first day or two, I knew it was wrong for you. I stalled with your father, I kept you longer on purpose. I could have told him on the second day, instead I told him after the second week – to protect you from him. But I have to admit that the threat itself worked, perhaps too well. It seemed to set you on the path to becoming Wilder."

I recalled being in the garden at his knee, adoring him, so completely different from my father, wishing he would take me as his son. Now 13 years later, here I stood rigid staring into his face. I couldn't stop, couldn't move mind or muscle.

"Gaius –" I think he grabbed my shoulder – "Gaius, my boy, come out of those old times," he spoke this softly but with urgency. I couldn't really see him, overcome with the sickening sensation of my father wanting to maim me. Was I 10 again? Was I Wilder? Who was I?

He raised his voice from the whisper to announce out loud, "Now is the time to introduce me to this dream wandering toward us from the night," and he turned me around with a tight hold on my neck.

I faced Messalina approaching with Scorpus. They were smiling, I was floundering. Into my ear so only I could hear Chrysanthos breathed, "Gaius, rise out of that moment and be in this one!" And he pinched me hard.

"Oww!" I hissed and rubbed my neck. It felt like he'd pulled out a tendon.

"What a sight, an old eunuch bullying a strapping young man," said Scorpus. I felt I was coming around. Chrysanthos sensed it, too, and gave my neck a pat.

"Yes, Scorpus. An aged eunuch is a dangerous thing, to be sure. It is good to see you," and the two clasped together, Scorpus wobbling Chrysanthos with him. I re-entered the present in time to take Messalina's elbow and held onto it like a rope thrown to a drowning man.

"Chrysanthos, steward of the Quaestor Tribonian, I present Messalina of Antioch," I said – though I got it backwards. I nudged her ahead of me.

"Your Excellence, I am so pleased to meet you," she said and started to get down on the deck, but he stopped her with a tug of her hand. "No, my dear, we are not in court but on a floating clubhouse for spoiled athletes."

He said the last to Scorpus, then offered his cheek to Messalina, which she kissed.

"That's better. You are with Gaius, I understand. He has told me nothing of you in our brief moments together, recalling old times, eh Gaius?"

He moved on quickly without waiting for my reply. "I was his mentor for a brief while. How long ago, Gaius?" Again he answered himself, knowing it best I stayed quiet. "Thirteen years it's been." He paused, then glancing to shore said, "In truth, I must leave in a moment, and Gaius and I have one thing more to discuss, briefly."

Scorpus' mouth hung dully open, not sure what to do.

"So, some other time perhaps we can talk again, Messalina," Chrysanthos moved quickly to kiss her hand. She knew she was dismissed. Scorpus needed help even closing his mouth, so Chrysanthos turned him in the opposite direction and gave him a little push, sending the pair under way toward their deck chairs.

"Gaius, are you alright? You were stricken with panic there for a moment," said Chrysanthos, looking at me seriously, caringly.

I offered an excuse. "Chrysanthos, I have fallen in love tonight, and it has unhinged me."

He put his arm around my shoulder. "I am joyed for you; I can already see that her beauty begins from within. And I know that love can make a man do many things, but it does not cause the hole you've just fallen into."

"Seeing you, I think, pushed me in."

"That, I can believe. Such a scare does not ever leave one. I know many eunuchs whose feelings toward their parents who forced them into their altered life are often dark and unsettling – forever. I believe seeing me for the first time in years brought something of that terror back to you." He released me and we turned away from the stern. "Gaius, I want to see you again. I didn't know I would see you tonight, but now I am concerned about you. Will you agree to that?" I nodded I would. "Good. I will be in touch. But should you need me sooner, have Tedius come to my home and speak to this man," and he gave me a card with the name of *Herulian*.

He smiled and began to walk off, tiny bells at the top of his slippers faintly tinkling a three-note chime.

"It was good to see you," I called.

He turned his head mid-stride. "Was it?" Then walked on.

It was a good question, causing a wave of nausea to come over me as I imagined my father about to sever my testicles himself.

I took a moment to calm down, then gathered Messalina to take our leave. Scorpus gathered himself and would not hear of us leaving without an escort of six armed horsemen. The disorders of Blues and Greens in the streets had not yet been subdued.

The horses' shod hooves clopping stone and the horsemen's jangling swords seemed unnaturally loud, and I could hardly think. With Messalina on the seat with me, tired and content, holding onto my arm, I wondered why I endangered her showing her to Rufus Cornelius. I wondered how could I have slipped so fast into that daze with Chrysanthos.

Messalina stirred next to me and constricted my arm. "Gaius, you're not trying anything," she said, a sleepy jest of disappointment.

"Oh, but I am," and I kissed the top of her head. "I'm trying to think of only you." She sighed a little laugh and snuggled in closer. But Chrysanthos wouldn't leave my mind.

There's the younger Chrysanthos brushing his hair while talking to me at the foot of his bed before I retired to mine. There I am in the garden of his wealthy employer, the man's 13-year-old daughter holding me tearfully like an injured bird, telling me how sorry she was for me. There's Chrysanthos talking to my father on the first day he dropped off his 10-year-old son to become a eunuch. Almost becoming a eunuch had affected me in many ways – and tonight, it had kicked me once again.

We arrived at Messalina's home and entered the greeting room, where Sister Flacilla stood in a magenta robe, her expression buzzing caution. She kissed Messalina's head, where I had a few moments earlier, and sent her on her way. Sister Flacilla folded her arms over her chest and relaxed.

"You have done well, Gaius Galen – late, but well. Your host Scorpus sent timely word of your delay." She smiled warmly. "Good night," and she followed Messalina out of the room.

I told the leader of our guard we would make our own way now and thanked them. He protested: his scout had reported that the disturbance was between where we were and my home. Scorpus would want him to escort us home.

"The woman is no longer here, Captain. And you may tell Scorpus that I don't need you to tuck me into bed, though I appreciate his concern."

The captain laughed. "I will honor your request, with reluctance. Godspeed to you."

The smoke was getting stronger in the air, as our driver took larger avenues, trying to avoid the small, dark streets where troublemakers liked to roam. When we reached the wide avenue of The Mese I had the driver stop. You could hear the commotion of yelling and fire, and mounted soldiers were heading down two streets off The Mese's south side. I told the driver to hurry to the Church of 40 Martyrs also to the south. When we arrived, several buildings away you could see a hot orange light reaching toward the sky. I got out.

"Tedius, your knife," I held out my hand for it.

"What for? You should get back in the carriage, Gaius Galen."

"Give me your knife." He tossed it down sheathed in leather. I tied my green silk handkerchief around my neck. Tedius jumped down and grabbed me.

"No, Gaius Galen, please, no. You can't do this!" he said as I wedged his knife under my belt. "Why on this lovely night for you and Messalina?"

"I saw an old friend tonight – remember Chrysanthos?" I snatched Tedius' ugly hat from his head in his moment of speechlessness and put it on. "Of course you do. I began to break down within a minute of speaking to him."

"And you think this will help? – you know it won't. Master, stay," he was pleading, but knowing I would not listen at the same time.

"Don't even think of following me, Tedius." And as I was running away, his cry of, "Come back! Come back!" faded with my distance.

I cut down a tight alley and caught a glimpse of someone wearing blue running past on a cross path. I followed him, sprinting as I pulled out Tedius' knife. He was slow, I was fast, speeded by an old excitement. As I overtook him, I was ready to come down with the knife, but turned the blade to the side at the last instant and crushed the handle of the knife into his ear. He fell, I ran. I came out on a wider street all lit up by a burning building, a fire brigade was on the spot, forming bucket lines. Someone was throwing rocks at them, so the rioters were near and not yet relinquishing control.

I was off, down the street from the fire where the main gangs must have gone. Flames behind me lit up building fronts as I ran past them, breathing hard, heart pounding, head reeling, knife a part of my fist. I passed two bodies, one had to be dead from losing all the blood now slicking his patch of street, the other moaning for help. "Good luck," I bid him as I bolted past.

Ahead was a group of men, maybe 60 of them, moving fast. Shouts rose up, and their movement almost stopped. They had destroyed someone or something. There came a roar from them, and I ran toward the tumult screaming an old favorite, *I Die Green Tonight!*"

12

From Shy Boy to Street Fighter

I've been a pagan, an orthodox Christian, a monophysite, an Arian and a Jew. But last night I took communion with the Greens again – being *Wilder* in the streets, fighting with soldiers, getting my head kicked, setting a building on fire, all of it a blur of crazy action. Now safely in my bed and exhausted, I know I have passed my test: I am back in the action I left three years ago. It felt as if I had never left – except for my slower step. And I suppose I hadn't.

At one point last night, I was in love, sailing along with Messalina in our dreamy trireme. Then came Chrysanthos, re-igniting a 13-year-old trauma that changed my life. In the carriage before dropping her off, I was completely confused, weakened by the forced recollection of facing my almost-eunuch past. Even with Messalina in my arms, I knew that the smoke and skyglow of nearby flames were signals that this was the time to test myself. Why not see at this moment whether or not I could run with them? Better to find out now than when it really counted.

Once again, an encounter with Chrysanthos was the catalyst. For it was in reaction to my experience with him as a 10 year old that pushed me toward violence: Father wanted me to be less timid and weak, but what I became was far beyond what he wanted. That time it took a couple of years for me to turn into a committed hellion; last night, it took maybe 5 minutes.

Imagine being a moody boy and your father decides that you are unfit to be a man and would do better as a eunuch. He took my testicles in his hand, pinched them out like a pair of grapes and showed me where the cut would be made – not to remove them, just make them useless in atrophy. He was the paterfamilias who ruled his family, and Mother's objections were useless. In the old traditions, which Father adhered to in most things, he could have killed me and would have suffered no ill because pater could do anything he wanted in his family. Same principle for an emperor and his people.

He has maintained, when he would speak about it, that it was only an attempt to scare me into becoming more manly and less shy, an out-of-date practice but not a dead one. But I have learned that Father is greedier than he is honest. Good eunuchs could make extraordinary connections – like Chrysanthos – that could have benefited him through me. Though it was illegal to neuter a pre-puberty boy and make a eunuch of him within the Roman Empire, it happened. There is good trade in importing eunuchs from other regions, because these odd fellows are in high demand, at court, in government and in the homes and enterprises of fine families. I was a thoughtful boy, and Father was, and still is, an unfeeling brute. I truly believe he would have enjoyed seeing my testicles pickled in a jar on his library shelf.

However much I hate to admit it, his plan worked, though not as he intended. The idea that he would even threaten such a thing turned my quiet moodiness into relentless anger against Gaius Galen Licinius the Elder. I was motivated to make him sorry he ever considered it. I took to destroying things because I could not bring myself to destroy him (I have thought seriously about it on several occasions). He lectured and punished. I ignored and went further – rebelling against the Orthodox religion he had us all embrace.

I've been a pagan. I announced it at dinner one night when I was 12. Father sputtered rage, slapped me senseless and locked me in my room for a week. Didn't matter; I was happy to have found this way to disturb him.

Even as a younger Christian boy, I often admired Hellene gods doing fanciful things, Olympian snobs acting out their petulant rivalries at humanity's expense. It seemed to me an easier thing to have hundreds of gods who really didn't care a fig for you, than to have the one God who knew everything you did – even thought – and punished you accordingly. I thought maybe it was that God who sent me to be neutered.

The old gods only cared about what you gave them. Without the sacrifice, you were nothing to them, and I found comfort in that. The god of rust, the god of the doorstep and mighty Optimus Jupiter himself all wanted their due of sacrifices and convoluted prayers you had to recite exactly, or do it all over from the beginning. To entertain myself and irritate father, I took a full plunge into Hellenism, now fashionably called paganism to associate it with barbarians. I think this bothered my father so much because he made most of his wealth as an architect contracting with the imperial government to convert pagan temples into churches. Christianity continued to grow, pagans continued to dwindle, even having to hide their religion as Christians in old Rome had to do. Their temples were remarkably easy to convert to churches. Basically, you turned them inside out: temples were outdoor oriented places, churches are indoor oriented. So my conversion in the pagan direction was particularly odious to Father.

In spite of the joy that brought me, this was becoming a truly turbulent time in my life. As I leaned into paganism, I also leaned into becoming a delinquent – with Monaxius next to me. We both took youth military training. Boxing, wrestling, bow and arrow, javelin, short sword, sling – put anything in our hands, or nothing, and we could do serious damage. Together we took the aggression of these skills to the streets. The Colors provided a ready outlet and plenty of companions to push us further along. As I fell deeper into the worst of the Green supporters, it angered my father more and more, which only spurred me onward.

I remained Green but not pagan. All the taunting and accusations of the rival Color supporters being heretics of some sort or another began to trouble me. Once I opened up the jar of who really is God/gods and what does He/they want of me, I began to flounder. Instead of becoming a eunuch, I was becoming a petty criminal bent on hurting my father any way I could. But was being a pagan a smart thing to do?

Over the next four years as I grew into a bigger, stronger young man of some renown in the streets, I flopped between religions. The two forms of rebellion seemed to go together. I dropped paganism and adopted the monophysite version of Christianity, which irritated Father but not as much as paganism had. Monophysites believe that Christ was a God, pure as his Father, not part man and part God, but one divine being somewhat incorporating both.

About a year later, I took to Arianism. This version of Christianity, popular with Germans and Huns, holds that Jesus is the Son of God and subordinate to God his father. Christ was a secondary god, similar to Gothic demigods. It's amazing how such differences of interpretation cause so much anxiety. But humans like to control their gods, no matter what they say about it being the other way around.

Coming home with such notions – as well as cuts, bruises and loot from rioting – drove father near to madness.

My turning to Judaism made him sick, seemed to knock even the meanness out of him for a while. I was circumcised at 16, which was a testament to either my resolve, confusion or foolishness. Cutting part of my penis off added to my reputation as a crazy fellow who would do anything. I almost made Tedius become a Jew with me. I'm glad I didn't – as was he – and I soon wished I hadn't made the change. I found this religion to be too demanding and I preferred an easier faith. I also found that being a Jew ultimately harmed my reputation among my Green cohorts.

So I returned full circle to being an orthodox Christian again, and am one now.

Proper orthodoxy was decided once and for all (or so they hope) at the Council of Chalcedon about 80 years ago. One side of battling bishops got the best of the other and declared that Christ and God are one, though with two separate natures, God and human, equal and comingled. Christ is *homoousios* "of the same nature" as God, and not *homoiousios* "of a similar nature" with God. That iota of difference – the Greek letter *i* replacing an *o* – separated us from the heretics.

I was not alone in confusion over the correct religion, as the competing faiths pushed and pulled us all. Though while most settled here or there, I never really have. And I know many others haven't as well. For me, it was easier to stick with a racing team Color than with a religion.

I might become a Persian fire worshipper next, but I could never become a Blue. While it was accepted for the professional athletes like Scorpus to change Colors, it wasn't easy for us hopeless fanatics. I've known some killed for that switch. I remain a Green, and through my several religious shifts, I had never doubted that whatever form of faith I had moved from or to, God blessed my Greenness.

Dawn was nearing when I finally fell dead asleep, the last 12 hours having over stimulated me with the lifting of love, resurrected fears of eunuch transformation and a rebirth of street fighting. I wrapped myself in a sheet and left my bedroom, finding Monaxius and Atakam at the dining table.

"I suppose that happened to your eye last night," said Atakam of my black and yellow eye socket, my forehead was scraped and bloody from some fellow's boot grinding my head onto cobblestone.

I nodded that it had.

"Tedius will be upset," said Monaxius.

"Tedius is always upset," I said. "Where is he? And what are you doing here?"

"After you ran to join your frolicking Greens, he came to me, wanted me to go with him to save you from yourself," said Atakam, giving more attention to cracking open a walnut than to me. "I refused."

"So did I," said Monaxius. "You would either come back or not. And if not, we would look for your broken or dead body in the street. We're your friends, not your mother."

Atakam put his shelled walnut in front of me saying, "Eat up; you look horrible. Here, have some pomegranate juice," he offered me his. "Tedius went to see Sister Flacilla an hour ago after she sent word for him to come to her. You had already dragged yourself back here and had been asleep for a while. We came over just as he was leaving."

"Why did you join them, Gaius – and how did it go?" asked Monaxius.

"Why? I was addled by seeing Chrysanthos last night, who – "

"– Chrysanthos! Oh, my God," from Monaxius.

I nodded. "Jolting, yes. I almost collapsed and fell off a trireme from the powerful emotions that enveloped me: it felt like a 13-year-old demon screaming to escape from my soul. Later, on the way home we were near a Green disturbance. I was confused – I also fell in love last night, which was also disorienting – and I thought the stars had aligned for me to join the fracas so I could see at that moment if I still had it."

"Did you?" Monaxius asked with keen interest.

I smiled proudly at my friend and drank some juice. "I do, and I wish you had been there with me to enjoy it."

"Enjoyed it? I don't understand this attraction you had – have again! – to rioting," said Atakam.

"You've spoken to me of your thrills from battle," I said. "It's very similar, I am sure."

"But we're organized," he scoffed.

"As are we, in our own way." I turned to Monaxius and continued.

"I found them, about 70 Greens, younger men mostly. It took a little while for me to get in the feel of it again, but the cycle of anger growing into a rage that increases the anger returned soon enough. I got my bearings and recognized the usual groups of degree, from the unsure come-alongs to the true destroyers. But this bunch lacked organization, and the few who seemed to be leaders were vacillating. The whole affair was on the verge of collapsing for want of initiative. I started yelling: *Who do these bastards think they are to herd the mighty Greens like cows!* I encouraged others to yell insults at the prefect's troops blocking the street ahead of us. I got three men to help me push over a cistern of water next to an inn, the chaotic crash and water rushing down the street invigorated them, and others began to smash things up, windows, carts, stalls, owners protecting their property.

"The yelling from the crowd grew in proportion to the growing noise from smashing things. And the crowd grew, pulling in more people as the mob showed its strength. I felt the energy shoot up – and so did they, becoming bolder as they allowed the anger to fire in them. *Why is that wooden shed not on fire?* I yelled at two men near me, and they instantly ran to make it so, with others joining them. I was doing things, I was filling the void with actions, and they responded to it, to me. I saw hyper excited types heeding my calls, and looking to me. They wanted a leader, some structure.

"At a crucial moment when the mounted soldiers came up to block the progress we were now making, I stepped to the front, picked up a broken brick and stopped – and so did those behind me. I was breathing like a madman and looking around for cowards who wouldn't join me. I bellowed for them to follow me, threw my brick and hit a mounted soldier, then ran at the soldiers screaming, *Fear the Greens!* The mounts broke as I and about 100 rabid Greens were just about to reach them, shouting hellfire, throwing rocks – and the most demented of us running faster to try to slash at horses and soldiers' legs with knives and whatever they could find. The 15 or so mounts galloped away uphill, doing considerable damage to their 30 infantrymen behind them trying to get out of the way. I turned them, Monaxius. I turned them – the Greens and the mounts."

He nodded approval.

"We laughed at the fleeing soldiers. The crowd stalled with this battle won, and took to breaking anything breakable, looting shops, beating up some men in their houses and guzzling stolen wine. I was having fun in a game of throwing torches into second floor windows, when some fellows jumped me from behind and did this to my head, throwing in a round of group kicks as I lied helpless. I'm sure it was revenge directed by one of the erstwhile Green leaders I had shown up. They were content to let me bleed on the street, and I to let them move on."

Monaxius was excited by the tale, his eyebrows pleased and arched.

Atakam nodded a soldier's respect to me and said, "I can't follow you in this, Gaius Galen, you know that. My life is as a Roman officer and I want to keep that. Though I wish I could see you lead your legions, I'll have to just wish you luck."

"I understand." Then to Monaxius I said, "We can do this again, brother. We can lead. I just hope we can pull back out of it after we've fulfilled our duties to Ammianus. The thrill is still in me – in us. I felt that old feeling of invincibility taking over me again like a powerful potion."

"I can see it," said Monaxius. "You must be careful of it, Gaius."

13

Monks, Actors & Criminals

"Estrilda – I found Estrilda!" Tedius fairly yelled out as he crossed the crowded room, thick with Greens and the vapor of pent-up friction that often fills this local club near my home. A few turned their eyes to Tedius as a possible irritant to rub against. He quietly sat down with Monaxius and me, meeting here to assess our progress in team building. He had always been fond of Estrilda, a statuesque blonde now about 24 years old with enough body to completely absorb Tedius, which I believed was his wish.

This Green tavern, one of many in the city – no fewer than Blue haunts – was an unofficial lair where all types of Green elements gathered. In the back left corner near the kitchen, smoking from rancid oil, a pack of fellows about 18 talked loudly and looked for trouble. These were some of the firebrands who roamed the streets intent on nothing but mischief, like Lukos' men, like me at their age.

At the opposite end of the spectrum were the three shopkeepers at the bar, talking up the merits of drivers like Fortunatas or Alexander, discussing chariot composition, training strategies, all sorts of minutiae about racing. These men were sport fans and certainly Greens. They'd get drunk, sing Green songs well past midnight, but at the end of their race day they returned to families, accounts and the business of living.

Next to them at the counter, and sometimes joining in their discussion, were two Green neighborhood captains. These were elected, in a fashion, by the fans in the local area. One was a man named Boniface. Like me, he was a member of the Green organization and an imperial employee. Boniface was an organizer who gathered with local area partisans to dispense news and desires of the organization, and to carry news from the streets back to the organization. You can bet Boniface knew who the 18 year olds were, and they him. They coexisted, however uncomfortably, as Greens, one an administrator, the others liable to burn your shop to the ground or break your brother's jaw.

Tedius, Monaxius and I had been out gathering our team. With his daughters and Annia safely in the countryside, Monaxius was excited about the prospects of gain and marshalling men in the streets again. He had culled in half Brother Zazo's 20 men who had tormented Ammianus' house, eliminating the mentally unstable and the hopelessly lazy. Zazo said he could get more – and of better quality.

"Where did you find Estrilda?" I asked Tedius of his good luck.

"In the Gothic Quarter outside a hide market." He sighed into his wine and water. "She's still amazing – and interested. She and her husband, Adalwolf, have been back in Constantinople from a mercenary adventure in Spain. She has four friends she wants to bring along." Where some women would venture into a riot on the fringes looking for looted goods, Estrilda liked to be in the vanguard, the first over an estate wall.

We added up our tallies. Monaxius had Zazo's 10 plus seven more. Tedius had Estrilda and company; 12 beggars who were cunning survivors; and eight ruined farmers from Cappadocia who had come to Constantinople to appeal their eviction from their own land by a ruthless governor's agent and having failed in that effort, they turned to theft, or as they put it, working the soils of the great city. I had Jacob and his four; Lukos and his six, which he said would soon be 10; and nine "students" I knew, who were easily outraged and ready to smash things whenever an opportunity arose – especially one that paid. That was a total of 68, well beyond our target number. And I had a promising interview later with a disgruntled claquer, who was recently rolled out of his job by new blood from Alexandria. If Ammianus' need for us didn't occur soon, we would lose some men and have to rebuild. But Ammianus understood this and said he would be quick with more money as needed.

The singing of a sword drawn from its metal scabbard silenced the room. One of the young toughs had drawn on a shopkeeper.

"Why are you rolling your eyes at my beard, old man?" The kid challenged in a woozy sway. "It's better than your face fur. Arm yourself!"

"Stop this at once!" came a command from the door. "Instead of killing one of my fans, let Scorpus buy you a drink, young swordsman," and he pulled a silver trident from his beard and tossed it to the youth. When he lowered his sword to catch it, the shopkeeper hit him hard in the face. The lad dropped the trident as he buckled to the floor.

"Thanks!" said the shopkeeper scooping up the trident. He raised his cup: "To Scorpus, master of the whip, master of the shits," and he drank down his wine, then bounded over to hug Scorpus.

Three bodyguards pulled him off. Scorpus made his way to our table, others' hands touching at his boar skin cloak as if it were the robe of the emperor. One of Scorpus' other bodyguards had a word with the proprietor who announced that Scorpus would remain for a short session with his fans if they would leave him in peace for a few moments. The fans left off quickly and the room buzzed with excited talk.

Tedius quickly rose and pulled his stool out for Scorpus who took it.

"I like this man of yours, Gaius Galen? I saw him two days ago at Sister Flacilla's when I arrived with five workmen and a wagonload of plastering tools and materials to fix up the second floor of her Refuge, as Messalina had suggested at the party."

Tedius jumped in to relate, "This charioteer soon had a blob of plaster hardened on his toe, and had women laughing and running from him in their bedrooms – and even Sister Flacilla giggling and fending off his advances as he came after her with a trowel, saying he wanted to touch up a few spots."

"I bet she would be a game one, if she forgot she was a Sister, of sorts," said Scorpus. He glanced at his bodyguards and the three tightened around our table, providing privacy.

"Your housecleaner told me you were here," Scorpus said to me. "Not much time, word of my presence is spreading in the street and a crowd will be here soon. I'll deal with them. Your Messalina mentioned to me a name while I was making a mess of their hallway: Ammianus."

Scorpus leaned close to the table. "This Ammianus, I know him as the Actionare's man. But he is more, I am told. Much more." He looked around. "We are hearing rumblings, credible enough that my fellow drivers are beginning to pay attention."

In seriousness, Scorpus was a different man from the one I knew at the party. He continued.

"I am not sure what your involvement is with this man, only that Messalina said Rufus Cornelius Alban mentioned him in a peculiar fashion to you the other night. She knows nothing about him, and I didn't tell her more."

Scorpus wanted me to speak. I didn't. He leaned back a little and pulled at his beard.

"You're right to keep quiet, I probably wouldn't tell me either." Now came the big laugh as he confiscated my goblet and emptied it. "I like you Gaius and your Messalina. I came to warn you about your link to Ammianus. He is dangerous, and you need to watch yourself carefully with him." He sat up straight and signaled his bodyguards. "Now to my adoring fans."

"Stranger than hell," said Monaxius under his breath as Scorpus left us. The charioteer embraced the young tough he had yelled at, who had pulled himself up off the floor. Scorpus called for, "the best wine in this stinking hole – but it is a Green stinking hole, thank God!"

He made the young man and the shopkeeper drink together – with him at a large table the proprietor had cleared away. The door was choking with people trying to pry their way in, the news of Scorpus gracing the lowly Green Corner Tavern ignited the neighborhood.

He answered several questions, arm wrestled one fellow, playfully flipped a green hat off another's head, and grabbed a piece of dried meat out of the hand of another and ate it. The young man with the sore jaw and the shopkeeper who caused it shared looks of disbelief that this was happening and toasted their good fortune. Scorpus' bodyguards formed the people into a line so they could file past to touch his arm and wish him well. "For five minutes only!" his guard yelled out.

Thirty minutes later, the line was twice as long, and Scorpus had to beg a retreat. His bodyguards cleared his exit, made easy by those grateful for the famous man's humility and generosity with his fans. His beard now shy of the dozen tridents, his belt gone as a souvenir, he gave his cloak to the proprietor on the way out, sailing it to him from the door like a flying boar over the counter.

We joined him briefly in the street, and I thanked him for making the effort to advise me and having to deal with his fans. He hoisted himself onto a sturdy farm horse.

"This is a good horse for the city sometimes," he rubbed the beast's neck. "It is good for me to be among my people," and he spread his arms to include the many fans standing around listening to us. "Besides, everyone in that room, in this neighborhood now, knows that Scorpus is a friend of Gaius Galen Licinius. That can be of assistance." He turned his horse to leave, calling over his shoulder, "Most of the time!" His laughter and his plow horse cut through his admirers filling the street. Flower petals rained down on him from a balcony overhanging the street.

Sunset was upon us when Monaxius and I reached the school in the far west part of the city, a watchtower on the Wall of Theodosius rising above the one-story structure that sprawled along the side of the defensive wall. Soldiers were talking about 30 feet above us on top of the wall. The watchtower rose another 60 or so feet above that. Beyond this wall to the west were two others, and a trench of water between this one and the next.

Inside the school, we walked toward the music of a piper. On a small auditorium stage facing 50 empty seats were four young women going through a seductive dance routine.

"No, no, Marsa you're not trying to lure a horse," chastised a thin man who gestured exuberantly with his hand. That must be Bargas.

"When you roll your shoulder and look back, your eyes should be almost shut, as if you're drowsy," he instructed. "You must tell them – the drooling men in the audience who want to sink their teeth into your rump – tell them with your eyes you are ready for bed, in this one look. Again piper, and just you Marsa."

"I have heard this voice before in the Hippodrome," I said loudly to announce our presence. "A voice that rang out like a church bell and commanded more attention."

Bargas smiled at me. The piper cut off his tune and the four girls took the opportunity to head offstage to get water.

"Gaius Galen Licinius?" he asked.

"Yes. And you are Bargas, correct?"

"At your service, possibly," he turned his head half toward the stage and called out to the missing dancers, "Short break girls, short break." He put a hand on my shoulder and leaned in to say, "It really must be a short break if I am to have them ready next week. With luck, the college of glassmakers will be too drunk to notice anything but their bushes, which we will flash them once. It is the best part of their routine." He shook his head.

"I understand you are no longer burdened by your duties in the Hippodrome." His hand slid from my shoulder and he nodded. "You have fallen far rather quickly. Ammianus' doing, I am told."

"Come, walk with me along the wall and we can talk freely," Bargas suggested.

We followed the curving narrow street beneath the great wall, passing a boy loading firewood into a basket the soldiers hauled up. I introduced Bargas to Monaxius, and then asked if he might want to employ some of his skills as a claquer for some private events.

"That depends. Depends on the money and the nature of the events," Bargas said with a challenging look. "I do not perform at birthday parties, Gaius Galen Licinius the Younger, your full name

I am told."

"I assure you the money will be very good, and the event extraordinarily exciting, more so than a race." Bargas poked his tongue against his thin cheek, waiting for more. "And I will need three other claquers, perhaps some of your colleagues given the boot by Ammianus."

An escaping donkey ran toward us in the narrow street, a boy and a girl chasing after it with a tether. We flattened against Theodosius' wall to let them pass.

Bargas brushed possible donkey hairs from his toga and continued. "Replaced as a group, with a whole crew from Alexandria. Men, Ammianus told us, who were more attuned to new styles, more effective, more loyal to the emperor."

"You and your brothers were bucking orders from the Actionare's men," said Monaxius, "confronting the imperial mandator between races with real grievances from the people."

"And isn't that what the people want, defiance when called for?" he asked with a dose of indignation. "In these new times, the Hippodrome has become an imperial game, infected with the Blue and Green diseased faction elements that were once confined to the theater. And those argumentative lunatics have changed the sport's experience – have nearly destroyed it."

"But not yet," I said, picking up his anger. "These theater flies hardly know a trace horse from a lead, happily ignorant of the nuances of this great sport in our blood since the Hittite days 2,000 years ago. Circling chariots are a mere diversion for many from the theater, who are intent only on conflict. Monaxius and I were racing purists but we did engage in the extreme street fighting ways also. And it seems we will be forced back into that realm."

"I have been told you are a student of the circus and not just a common brawler, *Wilder*. And now I see for myself," said Bargas. "What do you make of these times when the violence crackles routinely through the city?" He narrowed his eyes at me straining in the darker twilight shadowed by the western wall, and I sensed my answer could determine his to my request for his assistance.

Three or four bats flew fitfully over our heads. I pointed to them.

"See how they appear to fly randomly here and there as if they are lost and agitated?" I asked. "They are not; they are feeding on insects in this weak light. This imperial consolidation of entertainments from the longstanding private organizations is separating the performers and their factions from the common people. Some are flying around as aimlessly as bats seem to, but they are testing the sky in these new times, I believe, testing the limits. The majority of those backing their Color are unsure and waiting. This is happening as the imperial ability to control its own house has faded, allowing this great city to burst into flames with regularity. More bats will join those out now," I said, pointing overhead. "They will become even braver, as we've seen so far in Justinian's reign and in his uncle's before."

Bargas nodded. "Exactly why my cohorts and I bridled against Ammianus and the Actionare. These bats, as you put it, are untamed. They skirmish out of control now. The faction leaders know it. And fear it." He was half right, I thought, and half just plain angry about changes that forced him out.

Bargas turned us back toward the school. After a moment of silence, he said, "I think I am with you, assuming the money is suitable for the task. And I can bring more than the three others, if you like."

"Might be a good idea, Gaius," said Monaxius.

"Now," said Bargas with a widening smile of thin lips, "just what is it I may have agreed to help you with? Surely you men are too old to be rioting," and he laughed – until he saw me bite my lower lip and exchange a look with Monaxius.

"Bargas, have you ever been in a riot before?" I asked, taking hold of his arm as we walked. "They can be very entertaining."

"Exhilarating, to be sure," offered Monaxius, taking Bargas' other arm. "And highly profitable."

"I'm intrigued. But do you have to hold me down to tell me?"

Monaxius and I released his arms, and with bats above seeming to follow us, we told him what he would be getting into. He was fascinated, and a little scared.

On our way home, Monaxius asked me when I was going to tell

Bargas he would actually be helping Ammianus.

"Never. Bargas, us, even Ammianus – we are all being manipulated. At least Bargas has a choice to join or not."

14

Theater Eruption

Messalina was very nervous, fidgeting with a seam in her lavender gown. "What if she doesn't want to see me?" she worried. We were standing by the fountains of the Great Nymphaeum sanctuary originally built to honor the pagan nymphs, a place still highly regarded by many Christians. Across the square was the entrance to the theater, where she would soon rejoin her sister Arbella.

Tedius and Sister Flacilla had quietly worked together on this, combining their connections and luck to find Arbella and arrange this meeting on her final day of performances in Constantinople. The secretive pair sprung it on us this morning. Messalina was beside herself with joy and appreciation for her sponsor and me, for Tedius told her I was behind it all, though I knew nothing of it.

"She always thought I was father's favorite. I wonder if she still resents it?" Messalina fretted.

"Your sister will be delighted," Atakam advised. "Calm yourself, child."

She rebuked him for his child remark with a little kick to the Hun's injured leg. "Can't you go back to your army yet?"

He grumbled impressively, and looked impressive in his crimson cloak clasped by the silver pin of the Illyrian Army depicting a soldier heaving a long spear.

"He is a fellow enthusiast of the theater," I said.

"Not these Blue and Green competitions for the vulgar," he countered, rubbing his leg. "Give me Aristophanes anytime over this sop."

"I wanted him to come," I told Messalina. "These places can be dangerous – the large outdoor theaters that hold 20,000 are bad enough but these smaller indoor affairs are completely unpredictable."

"Prusa two weeks ago, two actors murdered on stage in a brawl of Blue and Green *theater enthusiasts*," sneered Atakam.

"I still enjoy this entertainment for the vulgar, as Lord Hun calls us," said Messalina. "The pantomimes are my favorite, the elaborate gestures and dance saying all."

"None of that tonight," Atakam said. "Banned once again – all pantomime acts temporarily forbidden in the Eastern Empire. Their objective with these performances crafted of base emotions is to gain the loudest acceptance to win the competition for the – what color is your sister slaving for – Blue? Green?"

She didn't answer but began moving toward the theater. At the back entrance several armed guards scowled at us, but the note Sister Flacilla had given us from Kyros got us inside.

Tedius approached, putting his hand out to Messalina. "Come with me. Arbella should be changing soon and you can see her then." He led us backstage.

We were completely ignored by the scores of performers and stage hands running around. A young man almost knocked over Atakam, pushing him aside as he flew by trailing a long dress and swinging a blonde wig as he ran. A dozen beauties clothed entirely in different colored ostrich feathers, but each wearing Green slippers, paraded by like a line of chicks. And an ample display of faction guards, pooled from Green and Blue to protect the emperor's investment in talent, watched us all.

We went down a dim hallway, Tedius ducking into a doorway and waving us in. The room had several long tables with mirrors, face paints and such. Women were dressing, undressing, chattering and calling out to costumers.

Arbella was at the end of the second table. I could tell it must be her, the resemblance to Messalina was striking: the same hair, brown eyes, high and full cheeks as Messalina – then I noticed, not exactly like her sister.

Messalina ran to her, Arbella catching her sister's face in her makeup mirror and spinning around with open arms. "Oh my dear, Messalina!" They hugged and cried.

"Arbella, I never hoped to see you again – oh goodness!" Messalina gasped just as she had pulled back to admire her.

Arbella's hand went up to her face and traced a scar that arced from the left side of her nose to her mid jawline.

"If you had been two minutes later, you would not have seen it," said Arbella smiling to comfort her sister. "I'm very good at hiding it. Watch me, Sister, while I get ready to assist Kyros, my master and leader of our troupe."

Arbella pulled up a stool next to her, and the two fell into conversation for the first time in seven years. Arbella was a little shorter than Messalina, with the body of an athletic dancer. I faded out of their way to stand with Atakam and Tedius taking in the flesh, the costumes and the camaraderie. They appeared to not even notice us. Atakam nodded to indicate a voluptuous woman trying to fit her bosom into a much too small, zebra-striped halter, which must have been the point of the costume.

"Should I offer to help?" he whispered to me. But a dancer beat him to it and helped cage the zebra breasts. "I should transfer to this duty."

The sisters made the scar disappear ("a gift" from her first owner was all Arbella would tell Messalina) while talking and laughing. Their reunion was interrupted by a man who strutted into the dressing room like a rooster, making clear these were his hens, even the male ones. Conversations died down.

"Nay my darlings, continue. Big finale in 10, not time to panic yet, but always time to think Victory! This pack of Green actors we're up against couldn't rouse a tear at a funeral," said the man, wearing a beggar's costume that was so realistic it probably had lice jumping around in it.

"Ah, how sweet! My Arbella and her sister together at last!" the beggar (Kyros, of course) swooped over and had Messalina's hand against his lips in an instant. "Welcome, Messalina, to your sister's home, her family," and the beggar swept his hand around the room with the grace of a prince.

"And I see you brought gawkers – we love gawkers, don't we ladies?"

The room agreed, the zebra woman saying, "I like the one in red," and she winked at Atakam.

"You're lovely Messalina – almost as lovely as our Arbella," Kyros dipped his head to her. "Is the one next to the Hun in red yours? I love that Greek look with the dirty blonde hair."

I smiled appreciatively and called out, "Gaius Galen Licinius at your command, most generous Host. Thank you for allowing us this brief union of sisters. And thank you for caring so well for Arbella."

"Well, I try," and he put a hand on the shoulder of each sister. "Gentlemen, your man Tedius there has your seats. I don't always get to do these smaller performances. I hope you enjoy as we take the pyramis cake, our final skit certain to put us over the top."

"Cake and the bonus money!" shouted someone.

"Yes, the bonus money is tasty too. Tighten up ladies," said Kyros, giving the three of us a raggedy beggar's bow. Messalina and Arbella talked intensely until another actress took Arbella by the hand to go, the sisters having one last hug and kiss. They would meet here together again after the finale.

We took our seats (Tedius was off stage and could see us from behind a gap in the curtain). Messalina excitedly related that at the dressing table, they had hurriedly discussed her plan to buy Arbella from Kyros with the money she had accumulated over her years of professional companioning. The money was safely in Sister Flacilla's hands.

We caught the last part of the Greens' closing skit, which was hilarious, actually. Atakam laughed out loud several times and punched me in the shoulder to further his enjoyment. The actors portrayed a scene that had been talked about in the city for the last week, the sacking of the chamberlain's head chef after the Vandal foreign minister dinner guest threw up climbing into his carriage to leave. Messalina loved it, but in deference to Kyros and Arbella, she didn't join us Greens rhythmically chanting our enthusiasm.

Out came Kyros and the other Blue actors and dancers, with Arbella singing in the background for two skits and playing small roles in two others, each also about recent rumors. But the last skit was the best – written just that morning about a juicy tidbit of gossip. Kyros' beggar related the strange behavior of a certain litter that remarkably resembled the one often used by the wife, Santolia, of an austere imperial admiral. This was not-so-subtle code for Antonia, the fast friend of the Empress Theodora, who had a lurid reputation still suitable to her past as an actress. The "admiral" was Antonia's real-life husband General Belisarius. The beggar had observed the litter picking up a youthful officer.

"The good officer must have been helping the lady adjust the springs of her litter seating," said the beggar, "because there was such a lurching of that litter that the bearers almost dropped it twice." Roars of laughter, but undercut by some hisses. The beggar said the litter's heavy curtain opened and the young officer got out, with a kiss on the top of his head from a flushed Santolia.

The hissing grew louder.

"And it was so touching," announced Kyros' beggar, "that the lady tossed the young man a pair of men's undergarments she generously donated to him for his help with the cushions."

Laughter, chanting, hissing, arguments and movement started everywhere around us all at once.

"I serve under Belisarius and will not have his wife so maligned," yelled out a drunken soldier who threw a clay wine cup at the beggar but missed. "You'll not slander General Belisarius!"

"I'll slander everyone in the city," called back Kyros. "And if that's as good as you can aim, heaven help Belisarius!"

The insult brought laughter before shoving, yelling and blows broke out in the audience. A column of faction guards quickly rushed onstage from the wings and locked shields in front of Kyros, Arbella and others in the troupe. Another cup thrown from the audience shattered against a shield.

The head judge in the low box just in front of the stage stood up with a Blue placard and proclaimed, "Tonight's contest goes to the Blues on the strength of this rousing final performance. Hail Blues! The Theater is closing – now!" And with that, the judges exited below via a trap door.

Tedius was motioning to us frantically. Atakam pulled Messalina to his side, swirled his crimson cloak over her and drew his dagger. I got behind them and we moved toward Tedius then on to the back stage door. Kyros yelled to the guards to let us pass. I heard a scream from the auditorium behind us that sounded to me like a stabbing, then another bloody scream.

The actors, stagehands and attendants adhered to a somewhat orderly evacuation. Eight wagons out back loaded up Green and Blue actors, mounted guards ready to speed off. Infantrymen stationed nearby marched into the area to protect the talent.

A torch arced through the sky and landed on the roof of the wagon Arbella and Kyros were climbing into. "Hurry up Arbella. Wave farewell to your sister; you'll see her again soon. We're off to Smyrna, a little sooner than planned," cried out Kyros, blowing a kiss to Messalina at my side.

Arbella looked distraught, matching the anxiety of her sister, who waved pathetically. A mounted soldier raked the burning torch off the wagon's canvas top right as it thundered off, escorts bracketing the wagons front and back. We watched the remaining guards begin to grind into the reckless rabble that had come around from the front of the theater.

"Let's go," said Atakam, taking Messalina from my side and putting her under his red wrap again. "It'll take them a moment to realize they have no chance against these guards, and by then we can be at our carriage."

He strode off like the fearless Illyrian commander he was but with a disgusted look. He wove us through those streaming out of the theater, fights erupting as small groups of Greens and Blues went at each other, sometimes joining together to push back against the prefect's troops that arrived and were effectively sweeping them away.

We were about halfway to the carriage when Messalina pulled

herself out from under Atakam's red cloak draped over her shoulder and stopped.

"I'm not worried about my safety, but about Arbella's and the others'," she said. "Should we follow to make sure they are safe?"

"They are well protected, and we couldn't catch up to them anyway," said Atakam, scowling at the partisans scuffling around us. "The faction troops will guard their theatrical assets. We are in more danger than your sister."

"I don't need your protection, Lord Hun! And I'll decide how to help my sister. I don't even know why you are here – wrapping me up like a baby in your mighty soldier's costume!"

"The only reason I am here is to protect you – at his request," yelled out Atakam pointing to me. I had never heard him yell before. "And you don't know what you're talking about!"

In the midst of the bedlam around us, Messalina and Atakam fairly squared off in confrontation. I was momentarily stunned, but Tedius immediately stepped between them.

"We are friends, here for the same reason," he said in a calming tone. "Messalina has seen her sister for the first time in ages – and then saw her chased off by a mob. It was an unsettling goodbye, and she's understandably upset."

Messalina's chest heaving in excited breathing visibly relaxed.

"He is only trying to help you, Messalina, and Gaius Galen." Tedius was silent for a couple of moments, the faces of the antagonists softening some. "I will escort Messalina to the carriage, if my master and Centurion Atakam will cover us along the way." Without waiting for approval, he gently took Messalina's arm and led her off toward the carriage.

In silence we followed them at a short distance, the pockets of commotion disappearing as we got further from the theater. Atakam was disturbed and with a violent shake of his head broke our silence.

"You see this?" he said to me in an angry, hushed tone, grabbing at the pin holding his cloak. "You know what I had to do to earn this? This simple pin – different from the thousands of others like it for this tiny sliver of ruby here on the javelin's tip – indicates assassin training and experience that enables me to kill you and any of your street kind in an instant. An interesting detail is that when I am angered, I don't really care who I kill!"

He released his pin and continued walking. "I go into this den of simpletons to help you and I embarrass my commander and comrades by wearing this sacred pin. Same with the Hippodrome the other day," he said with a hand flourish worthy of Kyros. "I wasn't wearing any official markings that day, but do you think I am not an army officer when my uniform is off?"

"I appreciate your help in both instances, Atakam." I touched his shoulder, but he pulled away. "You are more friend than perhaps I deserve."

"It's not easy sometimes – and her comments certainly don't help," and with the dagger he still held, he pointed at her ahead of us.

"I know, I know. She's also complicating my life – in good and bad ways."

"Such are women." He touched my shoulder in understanding.

After a minute of silent walking, I asked him, "What did you mean when you said that you don't care who you kill?"

"Once before, in a run of deep despair and deeper drunkenness, I killed a good friend of mine." He looked away down an alley as if he might see him.

"It was not really my fault, they all told me, for my friend had unwisely followed up a curse at me by drawing his sword. He was also very drunk." The Hun looked at me squarely, unashamed of the tear on his left cheek. "It was the worst moment of my life, and near destroyed me for hating myself."

"I too have come close to killing people I like – and still may yet," I said.

"Yes, you are in a difficult position. But you know, you should beware of me. I might lose control again. You should beware of me, Gaius." His eyes held a dull truthfulness.

"Believe me, I will my friend. I will."

"And I'll beware of you, too," he said. "You may get me in some real trouble, yet – and not these minor irritations I'm complaining about."

"I probably will, if you stay around me long enough."

15

Sneaking Back Home

The first day of the New Year, the 532nd since the birth of our Lord Jesus, was a ceremonial affirmation of Him, our empire, and Emperor Justinian and Empress Theodora who led it. The day was cold but bright and sunny, with stupendous banks of blazing white clouds seeming to race each other, presenting an entertaining sky above the earthly show in the streets.

The city turned out to honor this heritage, every person in his or her finest garments. Even the riff-raff from the countryside filling the city to escape crushing times at home played roles by carrying imported palm branches to line the route. Every balcony was decked in garland and brightly colored banners. The streets had been swept by an army of prefect workers, and perfumed sawdust spread on the processional route down The Mese from the Golden Gate at the western Theodosian Wall to the Great Palace.

And on raised stands along the route were competing choirs of Blues and Greens, singing hymnal praise to the imperial couple that interceded for us all with God and Christ. Church leaders and the Patriarch of Constantinople followed Justinian & Theodora's massive rolling stage – not in front but behind the couple, as the Eastern Roman emperors had for decades steadily pushed the church into their train, unlike in Rome.

The choirs of Blues and Greens hit their musical marks and together rang in the New Year praising to heaven Emperor Justinian, with precision counterpart singing that sounded of unity. It was high ceremony all around, with easily a thousand imperial employees and Excubitor and Scholarian troops parading in show like so many dolls on horseback. Those in the Blue and Green choirs all wore ceremonial swords to indicate they would draw them as one to protect their emperor. For the most part, these were not the hard partisans. Still, Lukos was singing out there somewhere like a Green church choirboy. He always fancied his voice, and even destructive partisans like him supported the church and emperor. And this day Lukos was happy to sing Justinian's praises to God. The next day found him in a different mood.

He was not the best of students in Bargas' school auditorium, where the first class of our team was gathered to learn some acting and stage direction, not things Lukos took to. We had two sessions of about 30 men each. This first day was an introduction to each other, as well as to Bargas, myself, Monaxius, Tedius, Brother Zazo and Lukos, the street leaders they would look to for direction. We needed some of our men to appear like they hated each other for the sake of deception. Monaxius told them that when the moment came for concerted action, the sight of two men following a leader together, who were at blows just moments before, is a powerful attraction.

Another lesson was how to suddenly organize behind one or more leaders at the right sign, presenting to others in the chaos a section of ordered determination. It displayed purpose and spontaneous cohesion that draws others to follow you. Just about all people in a riot actually want someone to lead them into trouble and to lead them out of it. Monaxius, Lukos and I showed them how to bring in others around you, invite them in subtle ways and direct ways to join your strength. The group takes you in, but it expects loyalty. We practiced joining together but also dispersing when signaled, to break up the group when it drew attention of the troops. We practiced picking up speed as a group as a way to excite those joining you, raise the tension – and it can save your life too.

Our recruits learned that every crowd is restrained to some degree until it is not. It's a collection of normal people who have joined together to do what is not normally done, like smashing a person's cart or face. Then, these normal people can't go back; they belong. There aren't many moments like this in a person's life, when civilization ceases to exist for them.

Bargas was quite interested in the insights us old hands had into the mob, and told me that against his better judgment, he was beginning to look forward to it. For two full days we trained our troops. Bargas viciously barked out orders alternated by kind-hearted encouragements. The favorite part for everyone was the gold solidus coins Tedius handed out. Ammianus was handling that part of the affair very well. We used some of his money to situate Monaxius' wife and daughters outside of town to keep them out of Ammianus' reach, we hoped.

About every three nights, marauding Green and Blue youth gangs were taking to the streets smashing and burning things and robbing anyone slow or stupid enough to not stay out of their way. This gang violence usually came in waves of flare ups, then was gone for months at a time. In the past weeks, it was not receding, and some feared that the growing frequency was becoming permanent.

When Blue met Green, one of two things could happen. It might be a loud and larger version of two men squaring off who really didn't want to fight but wanted to appear as fighters, with lots of bluster, some blows landed and cuts inflicted before the Blues and Greens disengaged. Or they could be awfully bloody, when the leaders were in true belligerent mood and did not want to back down, or when the crowd reached its apex of rage and exploded in violence. Those were bloody and unpredictable.

Rarely did the two sides fight to the end. Most of the time the two gangs bounced off each other to spin away in another direction, inflicting destruction in disorganized retreat. Quite a few marauders were usually arrested, and some of these were quietly reclaimed by their wealthy fathers. Though they were a minority of the participants, faction rioting was a game for many well-off young men who could afford to steal and destroy and have their father save their skin, as mine had done for me on two occasions. Even so, the murder hour was dangerous, and death took many a pater's son, something I always wondered that mine might have hoped for.

I woke on the 4th of January to angry voices on the stairs. I flung my door open and called out, "Tedius, what is the cause of this hissing argument on my stairway? You and your guest come up immediately."

I heard his sandals and a pair of boots pound up the stairs. The boots held an unpleasant sight, Timasius, a stout slave from my old household. That meant my father had sent him. A message from Father was an ugly way to start a day, and Timasius' lack of natural beauty didn't help. A former German warrior captured by our troops many years ago and enslaved, his long white-gold hair was tied into a tail behind a horsey face. Father's favorite German strongman was my least favorite.

"Timasius, so good to see you – and so early!" I joked. "It must be important business to argue on my stairs with Tedius. May I invite you to breakfast with me?"

His eyes puzzled over this invitation, and he gave me a sweeping bow, "Gaius Galen Licinius the Younger, a pleasure to see you again, though I know you seldom like to see me."

"Fairly said, Timasius. Tedius, some broth and bread for me and whatever Timasius wishes. We'll dine on the balcony as soon as I dress," and I turned to go do that.

Tedius' Adam's apple was all agitated as he served his fellow slave a boiled egg and honey-roll, nervous about what he knew was coming from their angry discussion on the stairs. I looked at Tedius as I spoke to Timasius.

"I venture that you have arrived to inform us that my father is ending, suspending or pretending to cease the stipend he has thus far allowed me so I might stay clear of him and the rest of the family. Is that so, Timasius?" I asked with a smile.

"That is so," he said. "But there is more. You are summoned to meet with your father, Gaius Galen Licinius the Elder."

"I am familiar with his name, Timasius, and you were instructed to deliver this exact message." He nodded that he was. "Does this summons have an appointed time?"

"No, my Lord." He glanced at his boiled egg.

"Yes, yes, go ahead and eat."

Tedius stepped in.

"Gaius Galen, the removal of the stipend is a threat at the moment," he looked to Timasius, who affirmed this by raising a half smile. "The audience will determine the final decision in that regard and also whether or not you can keep this apartment."

"Timasius, you can ferry my answer that I will be delighted to see Father, very soon. He'll not be delayed on my account," I told him, not delighted in the least as a memory flash of Chrysanthos on the trireme shivered through me. "Now, let's finish our breakfast, and you can tell me how things are at the old home."

Timasius offered some small household talk about a reconstruction of the kitchen and a new oven that would keep the fractious Corinthian cook happy for a while. He avoided the loaded topics: Timasius didn't reach age 50 as strong arm of a strong man without being discreet.

After he left, Tedius and I talked it out. Loss of the stipend would not seriously damage me; that stipend was a gesture by my father intended to make me feel bad, and he hadn't expected me to take it. So of course, I did. Expelling me from my home – he owned the entire building – was more a familial signal. The summons? The obvious guess was Ammianus had found another pinch point. I hadn't seen Father for almost three years, and it was a brief, unpleasant visit. I expected nothing less this time.

I told Tedius that I would first talk with his father, Hesiod, who was my father's steward and slave – the intelligent business hand to Timasius' strong arm. Tedius said he would probably be expecting me.

"So how many days have you known of this request, Tedius?"

"One and a half. I found out from my father late, two nights past." He smiled.

"I suppose I should be as faithful to my father as you are to yours, Tedius?"

"Not at all. My father is an honorable man. Yours is of questionable humanity. And after your reaction to seeing Chrysanthos the other night, I thought it best not to bring it up until necessary."

"It's good that your advice is more valuable than your meddling is troublesome."

He shrugged.

It was close to midnight, and the streets were empty save for some drunks and a few bands of soldiers to give the false impression that the city was under control. I had on my stalking shoes I hadn't worn in some time, a form of snuggly fastened outdoor slippers so quiet they made me feel invisible. I walked through the Servant of the Winds tetrapylon, a four-sided gate set in the center of The Mese to mark the crossroads of the great Makros Embolos mall. As I neared my family home, I dropped one street below the mall on the slopping hill and continued on parallel to The Mese.

I was probably 16 when I last tried this, but I easily recognized the arched doorway of the shop of a family of tailors. About halfway down the building from the door, I took the dark stairway down a few steps off the street level. By dim memory, I felt along the wall at eye height until I came to a nail protruding out less than a quarter of an inch. I worked my hands straight down from the nail, feeling along until I found the edges of one stone lose – still, after all these years. I worked at it with fingernails and knife until I had it out, and the key hidden behind it in my hand. I unlocked the old doorway that looked to be cemented shut. I entered, relocked the door from the inside and headed into the secret escape tunnel, slanting uphill toward Father's house.

Rats scampered away as I moved on for about 100 feet until it ended at another door. My key unlocked it and I was at the back of a secondary storeroom in the servants' quarters, not the main house. This is where I wanted to be: a hallway down from Hesiod's office (Tedius had assured me all was as it had been and I would find his father there.)

I slipped down the hallway and saw a hint of yellow light bleed out below Hesiod's door. Of course he was up working. I tried the latch and it lifted, silently. I eased the door open and could make out the steward at his desk, stylus in hand, scratching his head for a thought. The wind from the opened door stirred the lamp flame on his desk.

"It's about time, Domitia," he said without looking up from his work.

"I'm sorry to disappoint you," I said, and he turned quickly.

"Young Gaius! Tedius said you would be coming, but I didn't expect you to sneak in."

I smiled at him and shut the door. "You still have the arrangement with the tailors on Chestnut Street I see," and I held up the key. "And should your Domitia arrive, she can entertain us both."

He stood and stretched out his arms. "Come to me young man. I have missed you."

We embraced. I missed him as well, my staunchest ally, though fairly shackled in how much he could actually help me. As we broke our hug, I saw the architectural drawing he had been working on spread out on his desk.

"That is marvelous," I said. "I've never seen such a dome, it's –"

"– Yes, yes, another dream project that may never be more than this preliminary drawing – for Jerusalem, if you can believe it," he rolled it up, muttering about that city being a hell hole of drunken soldiers and relic-hawkers. He slipped it into a leather tube leaning against his desk, still littered with other drawings, account logs, letters and a miniature portrait of Tedius, his wife and the 10-year-old son she brought to the union, the three as stiff as boards looking off into the distance, as if watching the ship sail away that had left them forlorn on a foreign dock.

"Domitia, eh?"

"Sometimes she rubs my neck after a long day of work, just as my wife used to do, bless her soul," and he looked up to Heaven, offering a small sigh. Tedius had his father's nose, that's certain, but Hesiod wasn't as thin as his son. No matter their looks, their characters were both pure silver.

"Well, if she can rub everything your wife used to, I'm happy for you. Always nice pickings around here, I remember that."

Hesiod smiled at me and gestured that I take the red leather chair beside his desk. He had a comfortable office, with several chairs, a large table for discussions, a lounge for sleeping and cabinets with documents filling every wall.

"Father, of course, is why I am here," I said as I sat. "I wanted to talk with you before I return for my official summons. I thought I saw an extra seriousness in Timasius."

"It is serious, Gaius," he said, looking me in the eye. "Very serious –" the corner of his eye caught something, and he turned his look to the door.

It was half open, my father's balding head of thick gray hair and skin red with anger thrust into the room. He grimaced at me.

"Timasius!" he called out the door into the hall, "Halt the man-hunt for the tunnel intruder. I have found not a man but a boy." This last he said to me with a disgusted look, then slammed the door hard behind him. He fumbled to put a key in the lock and turned it with shaking vengeance. Then turned to me.

16

Dig Him Up!

Father's dark eyes, deeply set in skeletal sockets, tried to burn his rage into me. But all I could see for a moment was how old-man bushy his eyebrows had become and his hair tangling over his large ears like weeds. I went to him, grasping his shoulders and kissing him firmly on his left cheek that was hot with anger. His eyes closed as I stepped back, his head shaking slightly.

"Father, I wanted to visit you tomorrow but wished to get advance word from Hesiod first." Hesiod was stone still.

"So you upset two families to sneak here like a criminal, alarming the whole tailor household, and they alarmed ours that an intruder was on his way." His hands balled and un-balled as he spoke.

I didn't say anything, conserving my strength to remain in control. He looked me over for the first time in three years, with the same contempt he always held in store for me.

"Your mother is frantic that faction murderers are after us – and she is right, because her son has come to call." He turned his back on me to open the door. "Both of you be in my library shortly. Timasius will let you out when you are ready," and he locked the door from the outside.

"Not the best start, young Gaius," Hesiod said, looking around for his shoes.

"He seems milder than before. Is that so?" I asked.

"No. He is more volatile than ever. But now he hides it better – until he is about to lose control and then it's the old him. I am used to it, almost. But don't let his mildness fool you."

Hesiod strapped on his shoes as he talked.

"He is livid with you – and I wouldn't cut my eyes and give him that careless look you're giving me now. Whatever it is you are being blackmailed to do – and Tedius did not give me that detail – it has visited your father. Three days ago a man named Ammianus came to see him. Your father later related to me that this man threatened that if you failed in your work for him, it could mean the ruin of the Licinius family in Constantinople."

Having delivered that lightning bolt, Hesiod rose.

"There's that, and Fulvia is now quite interested in you, ever since your well-gossiped appearance at Quintus Cornelius Alban's party – with the Antioch woman."

"Oh God. I thought Fulvia hated me." Yet another complication.

"That has burned away over these years," said Hesiod. "We need to leave Gaius."

Anxiety tried to gnaw its way out of my stomach as I stepped to the door. I pushed the rising panic back down with a big breath.

Hesiod marched us through the courtyard that separated the servants' quarters and other outbuildings from the main house, drawing glances from servants who had been roused by the tunnel alarm. A couple of them waved to me. We entered through the kitchen building, I admired the fine new oven, then across to the house. At the back off a secondary atrium, Hesiod knocked at the door of the library with his toe, opening the door without waiting for a response.

A fire was roaring in the hearth of the large room, several rugs were spread over the pink marble floor and a gallery of tapestries hung on the walls, which also held diamond-shaped shelves of scrolls and rolled up drawings.

"Sit in that cushioned chair over there, Son, the one where your foul friend Ammianus sat three days ago and threatened me," said Father, sipping some drink from a plain bronze cup and offering me none. Hesiod took his accustomed chair at Father's shoulder where they reviewed business.

"Do you recall from the studies in Athens that I wasted on you the line from one of those playwrights that *If frogs had gods they would look like frogs*?"

"I believe it was dogs, if dogs had gods," I corrected. Hesiod winced.

"Of course you do. Well, that Ammianus is god of the frogs. I can see that hideous face still," he said, looking right through me in the chair. "That smug smile more offensive than his pock-marked jowls. And what he said was even more disgusting."

Here a pause, as he handed his cup to Hesiod, who put it down for him.

"He said that if you did not fulfill your obligations to him, that *I* would be ruined – not you, *I* would be ruined," he pointed to his chest saying this. "He must know you are beyond ruin several times over."

The lines either side of Father's Greek nose carved deep past his frowning mouth to the edge of his jaw. The oval pad of flesh at his chin quivered, a prelude I have seen before, and I reflexively tensed my muscles.

"You fool!" He bounded up, "You ungrateful wretch!" He was in front of me in an instant, a short birch rod in hand thudding against my upheld arms, beating me like a child, which that very rod had done years before. A slap on my right cheek, the rod thrust into my ribs as I protected my face. I grabbed hold of the rod, and he dropped it to flail fists against my head, his onyx ring splitting my scalp.

I cried inside, tearless. But I could not strike him back – an old lesson from Chrysanthos to never stoop to his terms and to maintain my personal dignity as my best defense. Blows crashed against my left temple, ear, throat, cheek, shoulder. Hesiod was frantically saying, "Stop, Master! Stop, Master, I beg you!" then he grabbed at Father's arms.

"Leave me be, slave!" and he smacked Hesiod hard with the back of his hand, knocking the faithful servant back against the desk. Father was on him like a bear, pulling back a fist to drive into Hesiod's trembling face. I caught Father's arm, kicked his legs out from under him landing him on his back, picked up the rod and jammed the end into his throat, pinning him tight. I wouldn't stop him from beating me but I could stop him from beating Hesiod.

He gagged and clutched at the rod with both hands but he couldn't move it away. I was leaning a lot of my weight on it, wanting it to pierce through to the floor but instead I just held him there, pulling energy from his humiliation. His eyes frantically searched about for some escape but avoided mine.

"Enough," I said after a moment, and threw the rod to the fireplace, half of it landing in the flames. I went to Hesiod and helped him stand. I turned to Father, who was sitting up, rubbing his throat and glaring death at me. I sat back in the chair.

"You were saying about Ammianus, the frog god?" I asked with feigned control. I was anything but inside: I felt Father was like a boot sweeping in the sand, trying to erase the respectable person I had worked hard to become, attempting to wipe me out and back under his control. At this instant of internal crumbling, the scent of Fulvia rose from the chair I was in. My wife's unmistakable aroma thickened the moment with a whole other sensory torment.

She had probably been here very recently, this scent from the cushion was her signature aroma, lavender trailing a hint of cedar. Fulvia, interested in me again, Hesiod had said. My mind skipped to Messalina. But I couldn't stay in those thoughts.

"Father, come to your senses, I beg you." I gave him my hand and helped him up, surprised that he let me.

"You should hope that I fulfill my contract with Ammianus," I said. "As for Fulvia, I don't know what you two were plotting here a moment ago, but if she wishes to have words with me now after these years, she may visit me anytime. I believe you know the address."

Hesiod glanced back and forth between Elder and Younger, rightfully uncomfortable between us two insane men. Elder was rubbing his throat, still glaring at me from the desk chair he retreated to, just as I had seen other men settle back after they knew they had lost their fight.

"You will no longer be at that address, I think," said Father, not so sure of his footing now. I had to press.

"You are right to be afraid of me – I don't even know what I might do at any moment. You have caused me upset," I said. "And you are aware of how upset I can become."

"My son, I am not afraid of you. I love you." This was shocking, and Hesiod, standing a little back from Father, gave me a quick look of alarm. "Fulvia and all of us in this house have heard about your affair with the prostitute and your grand impression at Quintus Cornelius Alban's party."

"It's Messalina. And she is a former prostitute and a fine woman."

"Yes, Messalina; I have heard. Quintus has sent me a note of gratitude for the bridle you gave his young daughter." He looked me over for a hint of softness, I thought.

"And so, are you upset that I have resurfaced among your friends and peers?" I asked.

"Yes, I am, I think. It makes me wonder, makes me hope that, that I … might have a son again."

Father's brow smoothed all the way up past his former hairline, his dark eyes softening. Hesiod was frowning beside him, his head shaking a barely perceivable *no*. I remained silent.

Father blurted a short laugh, saying, "It's all that I have ever wanted, a son, my Gaius Galen to follow me, help me, help us build a solid life for us all, for himself," he smiled at me, causing instant doubt.

"Was this before or after you threatened to expose me to the elements and death as a quiet 5 year old? Before or after you threatened your moody son with castration at 10? Before or after you threatened to kill me at age 15 – as you claimed was your right – because the Chrysanthos scare had pushed me too far in the direction you desired and into the Green streets? You're an old Spartan pagan, not an orthodox Christian. I may have to alert your imperial clients, and that could be very bad for business." I immediately thought that was too far, but it was done.

Hesiod tried to step in, saying, "Father and son talking, that is a comfort, a comfort to me. Why, I remember the times – "

"Shut up, Hesiod," scolded Father. He rubbed his throat

purposefully. Mine felt suddenly parched; his fight was returning. "I never hurt you beyond beatings you sorely deserved. But you, *Wilder*, are the murderer in the room. You are the criminal, a spoiled rich boy, leading other criminals in the guise of an imitation Hun. Then you begged your father to pull you from jail, and later when your rationality returned you pleaded for his help in getting the position you now enjoy."

I took this silently, nodding to its truth once, wounded by his words of shame. He sneered at my weakness.

"If it wasn't for the slave I gave to protect you, you wouldn't even be alive! Tedius keeps you functioning. His father has more reason for pride in his son than I do." This made Hesiod shake his head in a clear warning to me. Father went on.

"Are you, Gaius Galen the Younger, going to do what the frog Ammianus says, allowing him to blackmail your father and order him around? Or are you going to stuff that frog's tongue down his throat and protect the honor of your family? Which is it to be: obey me and protect the family or serve Ammianus?"

An extreme blush burned my face, the heat covering me in a sheet. Father was burning up as well.

"Is *Wilder* a true a warrior or just a lowly criminal?" He stood up, and I remained down.

"You wanted to push that rod through my throat, didn't you? But you were too weak. Your normal character, isn't it? I bet Tedius would have done it for you."

Hesiod whispered in Father's ear, I couldn't tell what, but Father pushed him away and walked to the fireplace. He pulled out the rod, one end on fire, embers falling on the carpet as he walked toward me. He held it near my throat at the spot where I had pushed at his before. The heat burnt my chin and singed my whiskers. Then he swung it over my head.

"Here's our murdering Hun" – the flaming rod *whooshed* over my head again – "without his slave to protect him, without his gang of street scum," – *whoosh, whoosh*.

Flames excited by the swinging danced on the rod end he held in front of my face. I could only think about grabbing it but couldn't. I was spent completely. He swung it back and forth inches from my nose.

"Would they follow you if they knew what you did to *your* son?" He touched my hair with the flame and pulled it away, the alarming odor of burning hair smothering any hint of lavender. "Would they, *Wilder*? Remember the night?" – *Whoosh* – "Of course not, you were out for days rioting."

"No!" I managed, and swatted at the rod, which burnt my hand. But it was still under Father's control.

"No they wouldn't follow you? Or no you don't remember the night your son died? Answer me, BOY!" *Whoosh*.

I was up out of the chair and I screamed – a howl of torment, because I suddenly realized that Father was in the same frenzy I often felt in the giddy haze of rioting. I was horrified to see in his crazed eyes and actions that we were the same. I knocked the rod from his hand and moved toward the door to the hall.

"No you don't! Come back, we can pull up his little body and you can love him like you said you did." At the door, my hand lifting the latch …

"Yes, let's go to the church graveyard, right away. We can dig him up, *Wilder*!" he taunted.

I flung the door open and ran, "We can dig him up!" ringing in my ears as I made it to the front entrance, sprinting away from my father, from myself, from my poor dead son. Hearing the commotion, one servant at the front door I knew from the old days saw me coming, took pity and opened the locked vestibule door for me, and I was out in the entryway courtyard area. The night guards had never seen anyone climb the gate to get out and they left me unmolested as I leapt away like a crazed animal down the middle of The Mese and into a maddened night, my mania fused with Father's.

-17-

Land of Golden Eunuchs

I pulled my hood over my head and walked along past midnight, full of visions of Father beating me, yelling to dig up my son, plus the sickening feeling that we probably shared the same emotional defect. I thought of my sweet little boy, Alexios, who would have perished of his disease whether or not I was there on the day he actually died. But Father and Fulvia blamed me and my absence off fighting in the streets for his death.

It is a guilt I have never shaken, however inaccurately laid at my feet, making Father's cry of *We can dig him up!* more damaging than he knew. The incident tore me from my wife and further from Father. It was also the thing that most influenced me to change my course three years ago.

I had been walking in a large circle for about perhaps an hour, failing to process how I was to move forward, when I saw through the dark a boy running toward me. For a spectral instant I thought I might be dreaming my son, but I recognized Pawah, panting as he reached me.

"Gaius Galen! Tedius sent me to find you," he got this out before sucking in gulps of air, "and to give you this."

It was a note from Tedius, who was with his father, Hesiod, trying to calm my father who had demanded my arrest by the Prefect for burglary and disobeying the paterfamilias. Tedius' note said that

Hesiod had related to him the incident and my upset.

"Gaius Galen, my father is worried for your emotional condition from the abuse by your father, who has ordered that I am not to leave my father for the time being or come to your assistance. While I can't help now, someone else may be able to. You are in desperate times under unique pressures, heightened and confused by your recent encounter with Chrysanthos that reopened the terrible wound by your father. And now this taunt to dig up your deceased son. Go with Pawah, and I will be with you when I can."

I unfolded the last of the note to find the card Chrysanthos had given me with the name *Herulian* on it and an address Tedius had written on the back.

Pawah and I stood under a large marble archway commemorating some victory over barbarians, me holding the note in a daze. Pawah put out his hand for me to take. It seemed fitting to follow this Egyptian boy after midnight to see a eunuch who may have some understanding of my emotional turmoil. At least that's what I thought I was doing, though I was sure of nothing but Pawah's sweaty hand.

The Great Palace complex sprawled alongside the Hippodrome and further north of it, and we headed in that direction. To the northwest of the palace was another, much smaller complex of houses and buildings. Yet fine and handsome homes, with quite a few lights on for this late at night.

"We are here. Pawah, are you safe alone out at night?"

"Yes, I am good at being invisible, even with this," and he hefted up his little gut.

"This is for your father," I said, handing the boy what was about two weeks of pay for his father. "This is for you," and I gave him an amount more than worthy of a good boy's late-night errand. "Honor your father, Pawah, as long as he will let you. Good night, faithful son."

"Good night, Sir." He gave me an uncertain smile and added, "I hope you feel better."

So did I.

At the first gate off the street, I handed the sentry the card. He felt the engraved name, looked at it carefully, then ushered me into his sentry box and bade me sit on the one stool while a runner sprinted the card to the big house. After a short while, a handsome young man in a fox-fur coat entered the watch house.

He touched my shoulder with a hand that smelled of fine soap and said, "Gaius Galen, I am Herulian. Come, Chrysanthos is eager to see you soon." He smiled, and it seemed so clearly from the heart that I knew it was true. And truth was what I needed.

The main house was active, with stylishly dressed men coming and going, back into the depths of the house and up the staircases to either side of the main greeting hall. I think they were all eunuchs, with older men, middle aged, young men and some boys not yet at the age of puberty they may never reach. This hall was decorated in gold, from the gold-tinted glass covers of the candles in gold sconces to the walls draped in gold cloth. The color was fitting, as most people in Constantinople called this area the Land of Golden Eunuchs because this area was the famous home of wealthy, highly-placed eunuchs in the service of the emperor.

I followed Herulian down a long hallway and was greeted with nods by cordial eunuchs. I returned their greetings, and absently felt at my tender chin so recently burned. But it did not bother me; this place was calming, as if a medicinal mist were in the air.

Herulian led me into a library where several men were seated at a conference table, two of them did not look like eunuchs but had the full beard and stout shoulders of soldiers. Chrysanthos was talking to them but broke off when he saw me at the curtain.

"Gaius Galen, I will be with you in a moment," and he pointed to a young man at a smaller desk.

This boy and another, both about 16 and developing the wider hips and feminine fat deposits characteristic of eunuchs, took me to a private alcove, seated me on a couch and began to gently take off my clothes. One indicated the hot tub of water at the back of the room and said, "This bath will be soothing." The young men, or young eunuchs, rubbed me down with myrrh oil then bathed me. There was nothing untoward about their touch, even as they cleaned me everywhere.

In fact, I was surprised at how I enjoyed being pampered and was soon in a comfortable robe reclining on a soft pallet of pillows sipping cooled wine with one hand and having the fingernails of my other trimmed then dipped in some solution that was buffed off. Chrysanthos came into the room and sat at my couch.

"You are looking better now, Gaius Galen." He patted my hand. "Was it your father who upset you this time?" he asked, but I sensed he already knew.

"Yes, Chrysanthos, my father," I said, offering a weak smile. "It's taken something out of me, which is unusual."

His expression was doubtful. "I saw you just four days ago, and you had a similar reaction from seeing me for the first time in years, bringing back thoughts of your father's intentions." He reached up to rub the tendon in my neck he had pinched hard in our last encounter. "Perhaps it is becoming usual. Herulian will discern what is affecting you. He already prescribed the bath with lithium salts, suspecting some form of melancholia or mania."

"I'm not being affected by anything but my insane father," I lied, while starting to lean forward thinking to rise up.

"I understand, Gaius Galen, I understand," and Chrysanthos eased me back into my pillows. "How your father affects you may be through identifiable emotional conditions. When did you see him?"

"Within two hours, I would say."

He looked closely into the hair at my scalp line, then at my chin. "And he burned you?"

"Yes."

He examined my burn then touched my chin gently. "This will be fine, no scar. We will talk about all this tomorrow. You need to sleep, don't you?"

"I may need to but I don't want to sleep."

He nodded. "Do you fear demons in your sleep?"

"No. Should I?"

Chrysanthos laughed, the raven's feet at the sides of his eyes deepening with his enjoyment.

"No, and I am glad to hear it. Some with melancholia have such fears. We will give you a calm sleep, my son." He was right: I did have a longing at this moment that I was his son and not my father's. One of the young eunuchs brought a burled chestnut box with silver latch, which Chrysanthos opened, withdrawing a small blue vial.

"It's been a busy night – for both of us," he said, eyeing the liquid contents of the vial. "Evenings are busy times for court eunuchs, because that is when most of the private business of the imperial household takes place. My master Tribonian is frequently involved in late-night consultations with His Imperial Highness, who often declines sleep for much of the night. His eunuchs, both the administrators and those who tend to his body and bed chamber, are more nocturnal than most. In serving Tribonian, I serve our emperor and empress."

His hands gracefully uncorked the vial and carefully poured a small trickle in my wine goblet, stirring it with his finger. I pleased him by drinking deeply.

"Herulian will see you when you awake," said Chrysanthos. "Trust him as you would me. Your father has men out looking to arrest you, so you can't go home yet or to a friend's. You need to stay here, where you are safe. I have to go right now and arrange a breakfast meeting with a senator whom I know is reeling drunk at the moment and will not want to learn that the emperor and my master require him in five hours."

He walked across the room to the curtained front entrance, then turned back. "I am glad you accepted my invitation, Gaius."

I awoke with a distorted sense of time, not certain I was really awake – or alive, for that matter. But shortly after opening my eyes, the door crept open and a wedge of light broke in, illuminating the big bed I was in.

"Good morning, Gaius Galen," said Herulian. "Did you sleep well?" he asked, pulling back a drape from a window to my right.

"Yes, it was undisturbed. How long did I sleep?" I slowly drew myself up somewhat, the pillows I was on as comfortable as sleep itself.

"About a quarter of a day; it will soon be midday," he said and made his way to my bed. I tightened up a little as this eunuch as attractive as many a woman I've been with gave me a wide smile approaching me. He sat on the side and put his hand on my forehead, then took my wrist, pressing to find the pulse. With a small mirror he reflected some of the window light into my eye.

"Do you have a headache?" he asked as he peered into my eyes.

"No." I dropped the vague notion clouded by stubborn sleep that he might be desiring me: he was a physician examining his patient, and happened to be a eunuch.

He redirected the mirror so my cheek was sunlit. "Your color looks good, Gaius Galen." He put the mirror down.

"May I ask, do you feel dark spirited, melancholic? Is that what you felt last night in your upsetting times with your father?"

"No." I reached for the water on the table at the side of my bed. "Last night my father beat me, told me I killed my son – a lie but an upsetting one. Can we close that drape?"

"Let's leave it open," he said. "Did the lie, the beating ignite anxiety and excitement beyond what you could control?" He looked into my eyes and asked, "Like the manic sensations you used to get rioting?"

"What?" I asked in incredulous tone. "I don't know what you are talking about."

"Your man Tedius and I have had a discussion while you slept," Herulian said. "The Egyptian boy, who would not leave our door until I promised to take personal responsibility for you, told me where I could find him. Chrysanthos and I thought melancholia was the cause of your emotional instability. But Tedius – a man who cares for you deeply, Gaius Galen – told me that he thinks he saw the mania that used to take hold of you at times when you were leading others in the streets return the night you saw Chrysanthos again."

I put my face in my hands. I couldn't believe this – any of it: burnt chin, this sanctuary among eunuchs with two of them washing my private places and polishing my nails, Tedius telling my life secrets to a stranger with his name on a fancy card.

"I may have to kill Tedius," I said through my hands, "or sell him at least."

Herulian grabbed my calf tightly; I dropped my hands and glared at him. "That would be the biggest mistake you could make right now, Gaius Galen. We are here to help you – Chrysanthos is worried about you, so are Tedius, your friends and even the boy Pawah."

He let go of my calf with a little laugh and threw me my clothes from a chair.

"Are you any good with a sword?" he asked.

"Are you?"

"Better than you may think. We will practice with wooden ones, work up a good sweat," he said. I swear that for an instant he gave me a version of Messalina's teasing come-on expression, before turning it into a very male look that said he fully intended to hand me my head in sword play.

-18-

Medicated and Underestimated

Herulian did hand me my head – three times smacking his wooden blade against my neck, plus stabbing me several times in my stomach and chest. He would not stop circling and lunging until we were drenched with sweat. This hard, regular physical exertion was part of therapy to break the mania and possible melancholia. Herulian fashioned his special therapy after the works of Aretaeus, a physician practicing in Asia Minor 350 years ago who said melancholia and its frequent non-identical twin mania were affected by the play of events and emotions on the psyche, as well as by imbalanced humors in the body. These might be caused by biological factors (too much of the black bile humor) and psychological factors. The biologic would come on slowly, the psychologic more apt to descend rapidly, like a blow from one's lunatic father or a terrible realization.

"Melancholia usually comes first," said Herulian. "But sometimes the mania does, followed by the melancholia. This may be what is starting to happen with you." He had many medical books in his library that was also a physician's laboratory with vials, bottles of medications, powders and herbs.

Physicians to nobility and wealthy merchants came to Herulian to exchange treatment insights, their clientele seeking the access eunuchs were thought to have as go-betweens with the mysteries of the spiritual, the medical and even the demonic worlds.

Herulian gave me a small dose of "Levity," a medication he said was indispensable among the community of eunuchs, who were not men, knew they would die young (aging accelerates when a man loses his virility), most often had no true family since before they were 12, and were prone to melancholia in all its forms.

"Levity is also well known in fine homes across the city," Herulian boasted. "The mixture I am giving you today recently has been on the tongue of Empress Theodora."

I nodded appreciatively as I stuck out my tongue and took my drops – a moderate dose to see if it made me feel better, which could indicate that melancholia was building in me. It did not take long for me to like Levity. Things seemed funny, and I found amusement and unusual insight in my passing thoughts.

After a while, with my mind unburdened by Levity, I asked, "Herulian, do you eunuchs hump each other, or who do you have sex with? I really don't know." I laughed out loud at how silly I sounded.

"Gaius Galen, that's a common source of much misinformation," he replied. "These things depend on the physical condition of the individual at the time of his alteration, and the quality of his mind and discipline."

"Alteration? You make it sound as if a tunic's hem were being adjusted." That also seemed very funny.

Herulian smiled and crossed his arms as I laughed at myself. He did resemble Messalina – the chestnut hair, the mischievous upward sweep at the corner of his eyes, which unlike hers were a light brown with piercing speckles of translucent blue.

"Some of us," he said, "do not 'hump' anything or anybody. We have lost the drive for passion and sex – and more to the point, have refined and controlled our desires. Desires are naturally weaker than those you full males have, the hot and dry fires that push you forward in life. Eunuchs are like women and children, moist and soft. When we lost the influence of our testicles, we became unbalanced, and without the active influence of testicles that are the source of heat, we are sprung into a third realm of sexuality, straddling the world of man and woman."

"Out of balance? I would certainly say so," I said, pretending to lose my balance. Herulian smirked and said my dose of Levity was too strong.

"But this straddling," I asked, "who do eunuchs straddle?"

"Alright Gaius Galen, if we must. Some eunuchs enjoy women, though not to any reproductive purpose. Still, they can attain the rigid manliness you might think a eunuch could not. And some eunuchs, like some men, prefer men or boys to play with. These are sometimes called *natural eunuchs*. Are we finished with this boyish tittering?"

"Yes – no, we are not finished. You do have a penis, correct?" I shrugged. "I am embarrassed at my ignorance."

He said he did and grabbed at his crouch obscenely.

"But your testicles, were they cut out?"

"No, not mine," he said patiently. "*Cut men*, as they are known, do lose their testicles. Boys who are *double castrated* lose their testicles and penis, and most often become sex objects. But the castration of most eunuchs involves one of two methods. Either a snip through a small hole in the sack and then blocking the blood supply to the testicles, which renders them useless. Or the pre-pubescent boy's scrotum is soaked in hot water, and his testicles are then crushed by hand, which severs them from the body as far as functionality but they remain in the scrotum." He looked kindly at me. "This is how I became a eunuch, at age 11, 'boiled and mashed,' as they say."

I did not laugh at this. But I suddenly wondered and asked, "Are you happy, as a eunuch? Or do you wish you could be a man?"

"Ah, your mind is loose, a good sign that melancholia is not your issue. As for happiness, yes, I am quite happy. Do I wish I were a man? Mostly no, but sometimes yes. The answer is not simple."

Herulian paused for a moment, considering whether he should say something, then said it: "But sometimes I want to have sex with a woman badly, and it is a most pleasurable and secret thought, though it usually passes in a few moments. It is exciting to serve a woman so closely as her physician – feeling for her temperature under her arm, her breast almost in my hand – and want to take her like a man. All the while she's thinking of me as a kind of other woman."

He cocked his head to me. "Now you share a secret of mine, Gaius Galen. Keep it to yourself, please."

I promised that I would. And he clarified other things for me regarding eunuchs, as he worked on his medications. I was surprised to learn that around this house and others were women who mascaraed as eunuchs so they could enjoy the male privileges eunuchs have, like going to a tavern, to the Hippodrome, being free to walk the streets without male escorts or a flock of female attendants.

After more insights into eunuchs – and medicine – I asked, "Is it time for more Levity?"

"You do not need Levity, Gaius Galen, and that is good. It's time for you to go with Agrippa while I tend to some affairs," said Herulian.

Agrippa, a tall, curly-haired fellow with prominent lips and spreading hips, came and led me away from Herulian's medical library. He was a good guide because he was learning as he went along himself, after recently being moved up to training at court. While such powerful eunuchs were the more obvious to all the citizens of Constantinople, Agrippa pointed out that most eunuchs did not attain such lofty status. He told me eunuchs knew that most people thought all of them were shrewish, easily irritated, petty, vindictive, scheming, and quick to become emotional and cry in their dinner plate.

For a thousand years all across the East, eunuchs were made to act as buffers between rulers and others. Eunuchs could be trusted completely – or more completely than anyone else, particularly a person who could benefit from the death of a relative. Agrippa explained that many eunuchs were also schooled in intricate skills, such as high-level finance and investing, and other complex dealings that most men considered to be too unmanly to pursue.

"Such eunuchs are in demand and well paid, which is what I am striving for," said Agrippa. "The other way is not pleasant. Life for a eunuch who doesn't succeed can be bitterly coarse and demeaning. I am lucky to have found here a new family that understands me and loves me. The individuals here are tightly interwoven. And for good or for bad, almost everyone knows everyone else's business. Because true to popular belief, most eunuchs are terrible gossips."

I learned a good bit more that afternoon from Agrippa about the lives of eunuchs, and about him. Chrysanthos had taken him under his wing to get him away from the clutches of his father, who was banking on Agrippa's success after he forced him to become a eunuch in Paphlagonia, a source of prime specimens in the allegedly illegal trade of eunuchs.

"I will never give him one coin from what I earn, never," said Agrippa. "Chrysanthos is my sponsor now and protects me from my father."

"We share that in common, Agrippa: he protected me from mine as well, when I was 10."

"Yes, I know. Herulian has told me your story. These are men we can trust, Gaius Galen."

It was a shock that evening to enter Chrysanthos' library before dinner and see my father chatting with him – and smiling. And when he turned to me, and still smiled, I was at a loss. But I was confident. This night and day spent with my eunuch friends had been restorative, and I looked at Father as I would have at Agrippa's father, which was without respect or fear. Chrysanthos introduced us, Gaius Galen Licinius the Younger to Gaius Galen Licinius the Elder.

"Father, son, here are the rules of this dinner," Chrysanthos informed us with authority, turning to face my father. "No brandishing of burning rods. And no ridiculous accusations that a child whose death came from a fever ravaging the entire city could possibly be the fault of his father who was absent the final day of his beloved son's life."

Chrysanthos pivoted to me. "And Gaius Galen the Younger, there will be no ill words between you two this night. Is that agreeable to you, to you both?"

It was, so we dined, Herulian joining us. Chaperoned by two eunuchs, Father and I got along without confrontation, partly due to Chrysanthos deflecting a couple of risky conversations Father brought up, namely Fulvia versus the whore and Ammianus' visit.

"Do not concern yourself with Ammianus and his threats," Chrysanthos said, waving aside the issue with a flopping wrist, a shared eunuch mannerism I had observed. "And this means you must trust your son, Licinius the Elder – even if he has not always been trustworthy," a dip of his head and a patronizing smile to me on this statement. "He is in a difficult situation with this Ammianus, whom I spoke to today and found to be a reasonable man, himself troubled by others who have considerable leverage on him."

If there were to be sparks, they would fly now. I casually sipped wine; Father bent a wiry eyebrow hair back into place as a distraction. Our two eunuch hosts watched us.

"I suppose I will have to trust my son to save the name of the Licinius family – not to mention the various business contracts that would be taken from me were he to fail at his *work*," said Father, so restrained I wondered that his wine wasn't tainted with Levity.

"You could even be proud of young Gaius Galen," suggested Herulian, as Father fought off a frown at this. "If I were his father, I would be proud because Gaius Galen is a generous, intelligent and crafty man, with a balance of cynicism and wit that is truly enjoyable."

"I have not experienced much of that in my son, but I accept your compliment of him, physician," and Father tipped his goblet to Herulian. "By my own choice," said Father, his eyes sharpening on me, "I toast my son, who does deserve credit for turning his life around, for the most part. And may you do your duty for this Ammianus – whatever it may be – and let us hope that it is sufficient to keep us both from ruin."

We drank to that, Father and I in a bit of a stare-down, which I broke with, "And a toast to Gaius Galen Licinius the Elder: may I not ruin you, ever. Myself, I am not so sure about."

We drank to each other, which I am sure felt as odd to him as it did to me.

The truce dinner ended, and Father departed, with a pat on my back as he left. In Herulian's library we talked about why Chrysanthos had me face my father without warning, and he was very pleased at my reaction, or lack of it.

"You showed great poise, Gaius Galen," said Chrysanthos. "I thought a direct approach to mediate between the two of you was best. You have this Ammianus in common. From what Herulian and I have learned today, your father has some kind of important business connection to Ammianus, but we don't know what that is yet."

"I don't either, but it must be the only reason he agreed to see me, I am certain," I said. "He hopes to earn money from this dinner – or not to lose any. I thank you both for your help with my father and in trying to stabilize me."

Chrysanthos said he had always felt some responsibility for the schism between Father and me, and wanted to help repair it if possible. He was also concerned for my mental stability – from our meeting on the trireme, my leaping into the Green disturbance later and from my frazzled appearance at his door last night. The two had agreed that I would benefit from a drug opposite to Levity known as "Descent." Herulian said he would work with me and the medication tomorrow.

"I've already sent one of my medical assistants to instruct Tedius in its use," said Herulian. "We have a good understanding of it, recently studying its effects on some volatile racing fans, in fact. It appears that –"

"– Never mind the medical trials, Herulian," said Chrysanthos cutting him off. "What we know is this can help a man falling under the grip of mania before it takes control of him, causing feelings of super human ability and a mighty wisdom so keen that others can't see it. You may understand this from your own experience, Gaius Galen."

I showed no emotion. But this talk about my potential mania – and studies on fanatics like my former self – convinced me at that moment that I was right in the different understanding that had crept into my head under the initial influence of Levity.

"I have not experienced such capacity for unseen wisdom before, I assure you, Chrysanthos," I said. "But I do understand what is happening, quite clearly."

I gestured toward Herulian, saying, "Here is a learned practitioner, who has tried to help me today to … stabilize as he put it. And here is the man who once saved me long ago and has come back to do so again," I said, gesturing toward Chrysanthos. "Do you not think I wonder why?"

There was a pause before Herulian answered, "We want to help you, Gaius Galen."

"I know you do. But you also want me to do as Ammianus says I must."

I saw the first unhappy eunuch face of my stay, two of them.

"It did not take super human capacity for me to see that. You gentlemen underestimate me, I fear." I leaned into Chrysanthos and gave him a one-armed hug, still holding my wine goblet. "But I do appreciate your attention and concern."

"Our intentions are well meaning," Chrysanthos said. "And we – I – do want you to do as Ammianus says. From the little I have learned of the man, I sense it is the best way for you to continue to thrive."

"Survive is more accurate – your friends and Messalina, too," Herulian added. "Ammianus does not trifle."

"Nor do eunuchs, I have learned during my visit here – an unexpected, enlightening education I am grateful for," I said. "And for your hospitality, therapies and well-meaning intentions, which I know are genuine."

I put my wine down and hugged Chrysanthos, giving him a kiss on each cheek. I thought I saw moisture in his eyes. Herulian and I also hugged, and when I said I was leaving and went to pull away, he held onto my arms.

"You're staying tonight, surely," he said.

"No, I am returning home. Father has likely lifted his charges against me, and if not, I will handle things as best I can – without the aid of you fine and capable eunuchs."

"Will you consider the medication I have given Tedius, should the mania ascend?" Herulian asked intently. "It can help you."

"I will consider it, yes."

"Will you return again if you feel you need our assistance – or just to visit?" Chrysanthos asked.

"I definitely will."

Herulian released my arms and shook my hand. "If you do, we can engage in our wooden sword play, and I will give you another thrashing."

To his taunting smile I said, "You underestimate me again. Had we been in a real fight, Herulian, I would have easily taken you. You don't know my true capabilities, my friend."

From a hidden pocket in my left sleeve, I pulled out a small kitchen knife and placed it on the seat of a chair. "Your cooks will be looking for this," I said, adding with an apologetic shrug, "I don't like to be unarmed in a strange place, and this is certainly that."

I walked out feeling my dignity fully restored, in the Land of the Golden Eunuchs.

Green Backs to the Emperor

As I walked homeward in the mid evening, a cold northwestern wind out of the Bulgarian forests accompanied me and whistled into broken windows, broken this night apparently from Blue and Green violence. Smoke from fires they had joyfully set filled the air.

When I turned the corner onto my street, Pawah saw me, jumping and waving excitedly at his post. Did the child ever sleep? He tore up the stairs and stood smiling beside Tedius who opened my door for me.

"That is an exquisite fur coat, Gaius Galen. Did you yank it from a eunuch's shoulders?" Tedius asked.

I gave him a slow turn so he could admire it. "A gift, the only one I took of several offered. This given to me by Herulian – you know him – the eunuch you've told about my past! I believe you've joined his team of potion pushers and are to administer some drug to keep me sane from mania! Are my private affairs your public gossip?"

I held up my hand to silence him. I took off the coat, laid it on a chair back and calmly squatted down to take Pawah's hand – the one he had led me to the eunuchs by.

"My good man, will you leave us so you will not be bothered by our discussion?" With a glance of worry to Tedius, he said he would. "Go home, you need your sleep. Thank you for your help, faithful friend," and I nudged him toward the door.

"Pawah, first fetch Monaxius and tell him Master is home," Tedius ordered his young employee, who scrambled down the stairs to escape the unpleasant scene brewing.

"Master, Monaxius has important news. And I will explain my actions with Herulian – a good person who cares for your well-being."

"Odd, that's exactly what he said of you."

"I was … worried talking to my father about your father's attack on you. The prefect's men were looking for you everywhere – and I did not think you would heed my note to seek out Chrysanthos. Then Herulian came. But I would never gossip about your affairs, I swear."

His Adam's apple appeared ready to launch out of his throat, and he was shaking. I couldn't let him explode.

"Tedius, it is alright. Calm yourself," I said, gently patting his arm at a slow pace. "Should I give you some of the Descent?"

He laughed with relief at the joke, which settled him some. And we talked. Tedius said Herulian knew of my riotous past and had brought it up, said Chrysanthos wanted to help me and was going to seek out Ammianus to discover what he could of the situation we were in with him. Herulian had reported that I was something of a wreck when I arrived late last night, and that he and Chrysanthos suspected mental agitation they could help with.

"Gaius Galen, I am sorry to have acquiesced to the truth of Herulian's knowledge of your rioting days, but he was certain of it," Tedius explained. "And I was worried about your condition at times, these new times of pressure, your forced return to the street fighting, and – "

" – The manic agitation I exhibited then and now again," I interrupted (he was working himself up again). "You have served me well, Tedius, in this affair. Tracking me down after my visit with Father and suggesting I see Chrysanthos was appropriate. When I stumble, you manage to always be there to help. Still, it was a shock to hear that from Herulian."

This compliment (truthful) calmed Tedius, as I hoped it might. I related details of my visit to Chrysanthos, including the Levity and the dinner with Father that had gone well. I did believe the two eunuchs wanted to help me, but was also aware of their manipulation.

"Their faith in Herulian's potions, I am not so sure of," I said. "I found the Levity pleasurable, like a form of drunken surety. If appropriate, we may test the other medicine. You do have it, don't you?"

"Oh yes, Herulian's assistant brought it this afternoon and told me about it. I later spoke to a potion seller I trust about it, having him sample this Descent. He said it's also called Donkey Kick, for the donkey milk included but more for the power of the poppies that could stun you into stupor if mis-administered."

"No stupor at the moment, please," and I gave a short laugh. "Donkey Kick, Levity, golden eunuchs, crazed monks, lethal Gothic women – they are all one thing to us now: means to our end. Ways to get us through this situation we are forced into."

"And our situation has changed in the day and a half since I last saw you," Tedius said. He related that Lukos now had 40 men; I was to meet with Ammianus in Flavius' office in the afternoon tomorrow; Messalina had cornered him at the front steps today and nearly beat him with questions about where I was and what I was doing, and was dissatisfied with his answers; and that Monaxius would bring amazing news of events at today's races.

As if on cue, which I believe Tedius is capable of, Monaxius' foot knocked at my door. My old friend with the wild stripe of white in his dark hair entered, with a loaf of olive bread, a jar of current yogurt and a hale greeting.

"Wilder has returned – and apparently with his gonads intact! I think," he tilted his head as if trying to look up my tunic. "How did you escape those eunuchs, my friend? How did you wiggle free from their perfumed grasp?"

I shrugged, and said, "I'll tell you all about it later. First, I hear you have signs of changes."

"Surely your eunuchs told you about the Greens walking out of the Hippodrome, turning their backs on the emperor?"

I shook my head.

"Good God, Gaius! While you were relaxing among the lotus eaters, the factions made a move that may have set us on our course with fate," said Monaxius. "It started out as a normal petition to Emperor Justinian by the Greens then became bizarre."

What he related was indeed strange. It was normal for people to petition the emperor in the Hippodrome, the traditional place where they could address him with their concerns. The discourse was held between a faction's head claquer leading the Greens or Blues whose multitudes often accompanied him in chorus-like chanting. Our emperor does not speak, his mandator does that for him, though emperors past spoke to their subjects. On this occasion the Greens first lauded Justinian as the best of emperors, as usual, then accused him of not protecting them, and brought up some business about fearing a particular oppressor. Monaxius related part of the exchange as he recalled it.

The Green claquer protested that an imperial officer named Calopodius was oppressing them in the quarter of the shoemakers. The mandator said Calopodius was innocent and that the Greens came not to watch the games but to insult Emperor Justinian. When the Greens replied they would take care of Colopodius themselves, the mandator called them Jews, Manicheans and Samaritans and told them to stop bringing curses down on themselves.

"Then more argument," related Monaxius, "heated, between the emperor's man and the Greens, who clamored that Greens could not get justice, claiming that 26 of us had been murdered in the Zeugma section. The Blues joined with Justinian, saying the Greens were the only murderers in the Hippodrome. The Greens pressed the mandator who appeared to lose his temper for the emperor.

'Will you blasphemers never hold your tongue?' the mandator asked.

Greens said, 'If it is your Majesty's pleasure, I shall keep my peace, though against my will, oh thrice august. I know all, but I say nothing. Farewell justice, you are no more! I shall cross over and become a Jew! Better to be a pagan than a Blue, God knows!' After the Blues threw in another insult, the Greens – now many voices with the claquer – cried out, 'Let the bones of the spectators be dug up!'

"They finished the rest of that *Let them be killed* curse and some began walking out of the stands," related Monaxius. "And while that has been done before, what I have never seen was the actions of some of the Blue claquers – the new men from Alexandria – they must have known it was going to happen!"

"What makes you say this?" I asked.

"Many Blues were going to counter the "digging up the bones" call but the lead claquers and others I noticed patted down the response with palms to the ground and heads shaking *No*. This quieted the spattering of Blue chants just before the Greens' leaders stood up all at once, then headed to the exits in complete silence," said Monaxius, pausing to lick yogurt from his spoon. "Many were immediately in step with them. But other Greens had to shake their heads and get a hold of what was happening before joining the exodus."

I looked at my friend, showing doubt. "Are you sure?"

"That's what I saw – probably 25,000 Greens and some others in all," was his certain response. "But why, I do not know. The races continued, though several Green teams seemed to be in commiseration and intentionally did not give it their all." Monaxius rubbed his neck where his woolen tunic collar scratched at him. "The question is: why would those Blues hold their thousands back in silence at that point? Why would they not continue to verbally attack the fleeing Greens, as they had during the mandator's admonitions?"

"I may find out tomorrow afternoon."

"Will you ask a sweet eunuch friend?" Monaxius teased.

"I will ask Ammianus."

In Flavius' office, Ammianus leaned back into Flavius' big desk chair, feet and fat stockinged calves on the desktop, and Flavius was at the window mute as a cloak rack. Ammianus wanted a report of readiness, and I told him we were. He asked about my time at Chrysanthos', what it was like to sleep with a eunuch.

"These barbs you toss about for your amusement do not concern me."

Flavius had to turn to the window so he wouldn't reveal his pleasure at my coolness with our superior. I spent an instant praying for Flavius to make it out of this mess in one piece.

"So, Ammianus, the day approaches, if I am not mistaken." He yawned at me and put an index finger to his lowermost chin. I continued. "We are ready to aide you, as agreed – in spite of your awkward threats to my father, friends, associates and self. I will overlook your lack of upbringing."

"Insults: oh Wilder, how brave," and Ammianus pretended to swallow back fear. "I do not know if the day is coming any more than you do. I must say, you look nothing like your father, which is to your credit. But to the point, yes, be ready. I wanted to see you again to look into your eyes, to judge you."

He smiled, dragged his feet off the desk and sat up. "And besides your usual bravado, I see that you are ready. In your eyes I see it, and my men who spy on you and your *associates* say it is so in the street. This is to your credit, Wilder. And to mine for having selected you."

He laughed smugly. I smiled at his pleasure and gave him another moment to enjoy it.

"Tell me, Ammianus, how did you get the Blues to quiet their own yesterday just as the Greens walked out and showed the Kathisma their backs?"

His smile slid away and the right side of his mouth turned down with distaste. He made it a complete frown, saying, "I do not control the Blues, the Greens or even the lowly Reds." He looked at me, his head tilted. "Where did you get such an idea?"

"Spies. My spies, which you are helping me pay for."

He did not react to my taunt.

"It was a test of your new Blue claquers, was it not?" I suggested. He made a comic face of ignorance. "I have never assumed that you and your client would ever rely just on me and my brigade of street scum." I couldn't let him know Flavius had told me so. "You and your client have others involved, of course. This subtle connivance by the Blues, aware the Greens were going to leave, shows your client's hand at play."

"I don't know who knew what or did what," he said, straightening up as he spoke. "And you, leader of scum, should quit worrying about anything other than performing when so ordered. After this co-ordination, as you suggest took place, the filthy colors took to the streets last night and likely will return tonight."

He raked a pair of scrolls to the floor so he could sit on the edge of Flavius's desk. Flavius moved over to pick them up.

"I think we are through here, Gaius Galen. We are satisfied with your preparedness," and he gave a nod to Flavius, who looked a little surprised to be the *we*.

"Ammianus, who am I working for?" I asked. "It can only help him or them, if I know who they are." I paused and brightened my expression. "And it could help you, help you succeed. I am worried that you have gotten in over your head. Who am I working for?"

For an instant, I thought he was going to tell me. Then a greater fear smothered his apparent moment of weakness.

"No, it would only get you killed and put me in a terrible position of having to replace you in a hurry," he said, slanting mean eyes at me. "Do not press me on this. I would say it is for your safety that you not know – and for his, Flavius'. How many children do you have, Flavius? I forget."

Flavius stuck up three fingers, looking out a dirty window and making no further remark.

"The next time we meet, Gaius Galen, this will all be over. Hence forth, Flavius will speak for me," said Ammianus. Flavius' shoulders sank as he nodded *Yes*. "He will deliver instructions. And you both may trust that I will be monitoring everything closely. Flavius, when I leave give him another payment – and pad it so he does not have to ask for money in the heat of the moment when it might be needed."

Ammianus stood up and walked around the big desk to me and put his arm around my shoulder.

"You will have to trust me, Gaius Galen." A squeeze on my upper arm. "You must trust me, as I must trust you. Don't disappoint," he said in a tone that was close to asking. A weak smile of sincerity cracked the menacing mask he always wore, and a sliver of vulnerability came through.

I nodded blank-faced and stepped out from under his arm.

-20-

Steering a Mob

For a moment – with his heavy arm around my shoulder and anxiety fairly seeping from his pores – I thought if I killed Ammianus this instant, my troubles would end. The idea thrilled and excited me. Was it driven by mania or prudence? They had me doubting myself, and I rejected the thought. As he withdrew his arm, I pulled away from the notion to kill him. Better to just leave him instead. Not because I didn't want to be rid of him, but because I knew he would be replaced quickly by his client, who would want to "replace" dangerous, disloyal me – and likely everyone else around me.

It was a sign of how nervous all of us in my group were that we chose to rarely speak of what we thought we must be involved in: overthrowing Emperor Justinian.

What else could it be? Ammianus was a faithful imperial official, but so were Justinian and his uncle Justin in 518 when they turned against the relatives of the freshly dead Emperor Anastasius with the well-bribed connivance of the Imperial Guards. Justin, an Illyrian peasant who couldn't read or write, was then Count of the Excubitors and had outsmarted the heirs of Anastasius and their supporters – rather his brilliant nephew Justinian who orchestrated that turn of events had. And suddenly it wasn't Anastasius' nephew being lifted on the shield in the Hippodrome as the next emperor, it was Justin.

Chances were great that the deed was about to be repaid, for three nephews of Anastasius were still senators, left alive because they were perceived as weak by Justin and Justinian. That pair of emperors had no problems murdering off others they thought would interfere.

Justinian could easily do that again now or find some other way to punish nobles and senators who had been squawking about his insatiable greed. He wouldn't need Ammianus to involve us in this complicated subterfuge of out-of-control rioters attacking Justinian's enemies. We were in a very bad place, and getting out alive would be difficult. If our rebellious side – and I wanted badly to know for certain who headed our side – lost, we would surely be executed if our role came out.

And it would. Retaliatory cleansings after successful and unsuccessful uprisings alike were always overdone and under scrutinized. If our side won, we would stand a good chance of being executed by our client victor to eliminate the prospect that we might change sides again, as easily as the venerable Porphyrius could bounce back and forth as charioteer for the Greens then Reds then Blues then Greens again. But I was not as accomplished as Porphyrius, and except for Tedius and Monaxius, could count on no one to follow me without filling their fists with gold first.

I spent some time around the Hippodrome to gauge the mood. Tension was evident in the faction buildings and in everyone at the track complex. I spoke to a few, who said the opinion of most was that the hardcore partisans were itching for an opportunity to riot. They believed Justinian's aggressive actions in squeezing wealth from the populace had riled up people more than usual. They saw the remarkable display of the Greens walking out on the emperor the day before as a signal of a massive storm swelling up. And with the inflow of the wretched from the countryside due to economic devastation, the normal bulging of the population with the feast days, and the big races of the Ides of January coming on the 13th, it could be an angry, destructive storm.

My head was pounding with tension that clung to me as I walked home through the streets, where tension also hung in the air and seemed to subdue the people moving about. It smelled of smoldering buildings and some freshly set ablaze – to the north, I judged. Tension appeared as silent apprehension on the faces of people. It weighted down the cold air and pushed it into our bones with dread. The city was wary, but not as wary as I.

It was well dark by the time I got back home, where Monaxius, Tedius and Brother Zazo were cinching up boots and concealing weapons, with Atakam observing. While I was hanging around the track for a few hours after my meeting with Ammianus, Flavius had visited and told Tedius of our first action. Monaxius quickly rallied Zazo who had 30 of his men on hold, ready to direct a turning move on a relatively small mob of Blues that had just started tearing up a neighborhood of monophysite (Coptic) Egyptians by the docks on the Golden Horn. That was the burning I smelled on my way from the track.

"You're almost too late for the party, Wilder," said Monaxius, strapping a short sword to his outer thigh under his cloak. "This is real, we earn our pay. Flavius says a tannery is our target of destruction, obviously someone who has irritated Ammianus' client. Some stupid Blues are bumbling around the neighborhood now. As you and I have previously discussed, Brother Zazo will take the lead. From what Flavius indicates, it is not a large disturbance, at least not yet."

Zazo smiled proudly. "They are ready, Gaius Galen. We brothers have learned our signals and practiced rapid organization to project a sense of spontaneous cohesion to the crowd. I lead by doing, by taking action. My three lieutenants are with our main group at the site already. We are ready to destroy like true faction madmen," and he headed down the stairs, looking as crazy as I ever did.

Tedius handed me a dagger, a padded woolen vest and a dark gray cloak with two deep inner pockets. Two knives were in one pocket, a short whip that doubled as a garrote in the other. It had been three years since I last wore this battle dress, and it felt good.

"And what brings Atakam along?" I asked heading down the stairs. "Isn't he afraid he'll tarnish the good name of Hun mercenaries?"

"I am not coming with you," said Atakam. "I just happened along as they prepared to go – just about without you."

Monaxius shoulder bumped Atakam against the handrail as he moved past him. "No time to talk, slow one. Some of us have to fight."

Zazo was already turning the corner, so we ran to catch up. Zazo stopped to speak with another monk giving him intelligence from the action: the mob was taking its time smashing up the Coptic neighborhood, and the prefect's troops seemed willing to let it happen. No imperial guards were in sight. Zazo broke us into a trot, relating that we needed to hurry to catch up to them.

The six of us running toward trouble caught the eye of those still out on the street, or peering out of cracked-open doors and upper floor windows. I reflexively began to speed up to take the lead, but Monaxius tugged on my cloak to slow me down.

"Let this be Zazo's time, like we discussed," he said. "See if we can trust him and his men. We follow his lead, but take over if he falters."

The monk flipped his hood over his bouncing bush of hair to conceal that distinctive marker of identity a real riot leader would never show, because it would make him easy to identify by authorities later. We were getting close; the sky was brightened by fire, and occasional screams punctuated the high-pitched rumbling of angry cries and crackling flames that sharpened as we neared. A few people ran past us escaping the confusion, one older man shuffling in shock, holding his bloody ear in place.

Zazo took a quick turn into an alley, where about 20 women and children were huddled, likely turned out of their homes. Two of his lieutenants ran up to Zazo, and we stopped next to a young family crying about their father, hoping he was still alive somewhere. We could see a mass of people at the other end of the alley moving down an intersecting street. His lieutenants took off in that direction.

Zazo bent down to give a comforting pat on the head of a little boy shaking with fear. The monk spoke to us in a deep whisper. "The brothers are in the crowd, most toward the front. My scouts have identified the large tannery building and complex further up the street in an unmolested area. We will move the mob to it."

He looked eye-to-eye at the boy and appeared to pull a bronze coin out of the child's ear, showing it to the lad then dropping it in his hand. The boy smiled.

"My brothers will begin to move at my direction. Let's go," and Zazo lead us out of the alley and into the mob, the six of us moving quickly to show purpose.

About 200 people were in the raucous horde at this point, half of them obviously Blues, the rest opportunists enjoying the violence against unseen authority. A row of adjoining wood frame and stucco houses on the left side of the street was catching fire nicely, men running up and throwing wooden chairs, boxes, firewood at the houses to burn them hotter. A grocer's door was wide open and a stream of people ran out, the shelves emptied with efficiency, the interior blaze gaining the second floor. An enterprising clutch of paupers attacked some of those with food, beating them until they gave up their loaves and dried meats. Two fellows were taking a wailing woman down the alley we just left to do her no good.

The mob's progress to nowhere in particular had slowed to a stop. This frequently happened, because people in a mob act like children, easily distracted by anything, causing pockets of rioters to become momentarily preoccupied with specific destructions. About 20 people were throwing stones at a tavern owner at a second-floor window above his establishment's sign with a trim of green indicating his allegiance. A roar went up from the stone throwers when the owner was grabbed by three Blues who had broken in from the back and began beating him.

Behind me a cheer of approval went up as a flame thrust triumphantly skyward after burning free through the roof of a metal smith's shop. When the smith who had escaped and was standing among us cried in grief, three men pounced on him with the stubby cudgels favored by many street thugs, a blood thirsty circle of others forming around the action. A loud crash in a shed three doors down saved the smith's life, as the circled crowd and cudgellers gave up this sport to see what caused the crash, hoping there would be more things or people inside to smash.

A chant from some Blues rose into the chaos and roaring fires:

The city burns Blue to show our might
Burns Blue tonight
Burns Blue tonight!

I was struck in the side of the head by an angry drunk man in a Blue jacket who called me a stinking monophysite. I hit him in the jaw, and there was Tedius stabbing him in the leg, which I kicked for good measure leaving him howling in pain.

Monaxius was 10 feet away battling four young Blues, their clothing and hair in popular Hunnish fashion. Atakam burst through the crowd to Monaxius' side, punching his authentic Hun fist into a Blue face. They screamed mightily that they would baptize the barbarian properly, but they fought poorly: Atakam dodged their sluggish blows, easily downing another with a swift nose-breaking jab. Monaxius and I took out the other two.

"Thanks, loyal Hun. But why are you here?" Monaxius asked.

"I had to see if this Wilder and his people really can fight," he said, grinning to be in the mayhem.

We pressed on, shoving people out of our way to get to the front where Zazo's brothers were.

From overhead it rained terra cotta roof tiles, crashing on the street and a couple of heads as well. The red tiles suddenly stopped, and then it rained three men tossed from the rooftop for defending their homes with their roof tiles. I turned toward the back of the mob and saw armored prefect horsemen clogging the street and holding fast, trying to keep the mob from retreating back in their direction.

The vanguard of the mob, mostly Blues, was momentarily stalled in front of a moderate church positioned so the wide street forked around it on both sides and continued on as two smaller streets. Several people had already committed to the left street, attracting some of the Blues off the steps of the church, deciding to leave it and God in peace.

"*There Is the Devil's Enterprise, There, There!*" yelled out Zazo moving quickly to the right street, pointing to two of his lieutenants rushing up to the tannery main door yelling, "*Burn Him, Burn Him!*"

Zazo, with a couple of other monks by him, smashed a lantern against the door. The fire from the oil flashed bright yellow and completely engulfed the door. The extraordinary flash drew the eyes of the mob, watching as tall Zazo kicked through the magnificent flames trying to break the door down. Two, three, five, six others rushed from the crowd – brothers all, I recognized – toward Zazo, echoing the call to *"Burn Him!"* One kicked at the door alongside Zazo and yelled out over his shoulder, "The tanner cheats and steals from the poor, *He Cheats the Poor!*"

Now there were seven pounding the door, its seasoned wood catching ablaze helped by another ceramic lamp smashing against it, but not delivering the spectacular flames of Zazo's lamp. Probably 10 more of Zazo's brothers not dressed as monks drew in from different parts of the crowd to join those at the door, as angry as a swarm of hornets and agitating with flailing gestures for the entire crowd to *Burn Him!* Four Blues resting on the church steps turned toward the tannery following the attention of the crowd. It appeared that they might be leaders, though lazy or inexperienced ones. The crowd stalled at the church crossroads began to clamber loudly, following the example of the crazed brothers at the door. I could feel the mob pause and I turned with it toward the tannery and began to move.

A man ran out from the side door of the building, one of Zazo's, but he pleaded as if he was the tanner, crying out for Zazo and the others to spare his building, his livelihood. Two of the rioters at the door (also Zazo's men) grabbed him by each arm, while a third kicked him in the stomach, crying out, *"He's a Green. A Greedy Green!"*

The one acting the tanner's role – a very dangerous one – broke away and ran off down the street, two brothers chasing him, the third joining them waving a strip of Green cloth snatched from the fleeing tanner. (All our men carried cloth strips of each color). More people broke out of the crowd and headed toward the tannery, with its promise of valuables to loot and equipment to destroy. Ten, 20 then more ran to join Zazo's action and started hurling paving stones, a flaming torch, an unlucky cat at the building and over the walls to its courtyard, screaming, *"Cheats the Poor, Cheats the Poor!"* Scores of others quickly swelled their ranks, livid with rage at this tanner, none of them really knowing or caring why.

The Blue's apparent ringleader, who had stood back in these moments on the church steps, sought to catch up with the crowd he had lost, calling on the Mighty Blues to burn the tannery to the ground – an objective they were already accomplishing at Zazo's behest. More surged toward the tannery's bolted front doors, and as they took turns throwing themselves and each other against the door, Zazo dropped back to let them take over. They broke the door's hinges from the jam and streamed into the opening.

As the mob rushed into the tannery, breaking what they could while looking for loot, Zazo and his men retreated unnoticed to the church steps. Zazo caught my eye and said, "It is God's will." The 15 or so brothers around him crossed themselves as one.

"And your bright fire, Zazo, what was that?" I asked.

"My will," he said, wiping his forehead with the arm of his robe, which was smoking. "These moths fly to the brightest light. A normal lamp, with a special separate chamber that releases an agent, let us say, that wants to burn all at once. I already have more for you, Gaius Galen," and he slightly bowed his head to me. I should have bowed to him.

In a few moments, all of his men were on the church steps watching the tannery light up in multiple places from within. I motioned for Zazo to follow and I led us all down the dark street to the left of the church. We made a wide circle to the rear of the prefect's mounted troops, who didn't dare to confront the mob at the height of its destruction. Fire brigades, falling in behind the troops on cleared streets, were ready when the time was right to extinguish the burnt offering of the Blues.

Zazo's men melted into the city to head back to their monastery, leaving the six of us to carry on. Atakam marched at Zazo's side in front of us, animated in praise and apparently trying to recruit the monk into the army. But his fuzzy hair shook *no* repeatedly.

"Well, Crassus," said Monaxius with a slap on my back. "We might just follow this brother to the vault."

"A good showing, to be sure," I said. "But he might just as well take us to hell."

This prudent statement was calculated to belie the fact that I was highly excited by the action, wanting nothing more than to go back to the mob so I could at least find the man with the stabbed leg and finish our business.

21

Messalına Knows All

I had a restful sleep that took a while to fall into but it did calm me: no dreams of the rioting or the man with the stabbed leg. My morning began with a positive feeling that this might all work out. Zazo's composure and leadership was beyond what I had expected. He seemed more at home in a mob than a monastery.

But I was allowed not even an hour of this warming optimism. Back-to-back bad news arrived from two messengers.

One was a returned letter Tedius had sent to Kyros and Arbella in Smyrna. The letter was undelivered, and the messenger could not find them. Just after that man left, one of Ammianus' runners delivered a gift of an earthenware jar of currant preserves from a rural province on the other side of the Bosphorus known for this product. A simple note said, *Enjoy the preserves, the specialty of a quiet nearby Asian area. A token reward for a well destroyed tannery.*

Annia, Martha and Elissa, whose temporary hiding place was in that same area, could be enjoying the same kind of preserves. Ammianus obviously knew it. Unpleasant news about two important parties, one's location unknown, one's known. I dreaded telling Messalina and Monaxius.

In the afternoon Monaxius and I met after individually checking on our troops, doling out generous coin to make sure they were ready to follow our instructions and promising more afterward. There was much planning for us to do. Flavius had ordered the placement of our men tomorrow around the Praetorium annex across the Golden Horn where the city Prefect Eudaemon was to hold a hearing on several partisans arrested for murder during the previous two days of disorders. The city was crackling with excitement – and some fear – about what might happen if the hearing ended with executions, which was expected.

As Monaxius and I compared notes while walking briskly toward Sister Flacilla's Refuge, we saw skittish people boarding up their windows and loading carts with belongings to make a dash at twilight when streets were open to their carts.

"Can't blame them. I would be doing the same with Annia and the girls," said Monaxius. When he glanced my way mid stride and saw my tortured expression, he stopped. "What is it? Tell me now!"

"Ammianus sent a present of preserves from the area where Annia's aunt lives, congratulating us on the tannery," I said.

His face flushed pink with anger. He glared at me.

"There's little we can do now, Monaxius." He just started walking at a fast pace, staring down at his feet. I grabbed his arm and stopped him. "I've already dispatched a pair of father's Macedonians to escort them to another place at dark tonight. It might work," I said, with not much conviction. "I wish I had never pulled you back into this, Monaxius."

He looked up, tired. "I brought my family into this, Gaius. I'll not blame you." He managed a weak smile and slapped my back with strength. "Will you send Ammianus a return message for me?"

"Of course. I will deliver a message to the Devil for you – always."

"Tell him that his threats spur me, and us I hope – "

" – Us, my friend, us," I assured instantly.

"Tell him his threats spur me to surpass his expectations, to fight for him as I would for my daughters' lives: one and the same now." He had a sudden look of terrible pain and took two fistfuls of hair as if to yank himself bald. But he held onto his head like this without moving.

"It is the same with me, Monaxius," I said. "I fight for Annia, Martha and Elissa just as I fight for Messalina, her sister, my mother, even

Tedius' wife, who was threatened by a man at the market just this morning. Let go of that head and give me your hand, my friend, my Hephaestion."

Monaxius released his hair and gathered himself. "Hephaestion? And you are Alexander the Great? Delusional, yet here is your Hephaestion's hand, Wilder," we held each other's hands in a tight bond face to face in the street, squeezing hard.

"We've something real to fight for, no matter who Ammianus' client is," I said. "My client is you and your family."

"And you are my client and my patron, even if you are the opposite of great Alexander." He smiled and hugged me. Three men standing nearby laughed at us. We exchanged a glance about going after them, but left them alone.

We moved onward, our fatigue evaporated by anger. We hoped Annia and the girls could be secretly moved to a small farm owned by a friend of Annia's aunt, a prearranged backup plan we had wisely made. But neither of us really believed Ammianus would not find them. We walked fast, and I followed Monaxius as he skillfully slithered us through the crowded streets.

Two nights of intermittent rioting had everyone on edge and in a hurry. The action thus far had been random flare-ups of ultra partisans that sucked parts of the populace into their action, like the wandering mob at the tannery yesterday, which showed the skill of Ammianus' spies and his own decisiveness. But the hearing at the Praetorium annex would attract many similar troublemakers, as well as others interested in seeing which way the wind would blow, in case they needed to get out in front of it. Blues and Greens were both possibly on the execution block after the serious hearing due to the loss of life caused by rioting.

As we approached, Sister Flacilla appeared mildly disturbed, standing in the back of a wagon in front of the Refuge directing deliverymen bringing in water, food, candles, oil, medicine. She was also directing her slaves, servants and repenting waywards out of the Refuge bearing valuables and documents to safer places.

"Expecting the worst, Sister?" I asked loudly to draw her attention.

"Whenever Wilder is around, that is the best policy," she said, giving a sarcastic smile that held some warmth for me.

"We always prepare, here – beginning with the soul. And how is yours today, Gaius Galen?"

"My soul is well, and we thank you. I wish to present my best and strongest friend, Sister: Monaxius."

He nodded with lowered head then looked up to her. "An honor to meet you, Sister Flacilla. I have heard your name many times – always spoken with reverence by many of the poor I have served," Monaxius said with a respectful smile.

"Good of you to say, young man. And you must be a strong friend indeed, to stay with this man," she said with seriousness, then turned to me. "Messalina will be happy to see you, Gaius Galen. She's in the basement putting in order the extra salves and bandages we are taking in." She added darkly, "The fires seem to be flaring higher and brighter each night. We have already tended to many injured in these senseless orgies of destruction." Her look lightened as she shooed me away with both hands, "Go to her, Gaius Galen. Go on."

She turned and barked a sharp order to a porter who had dropped an armload of firewood. Monaxius nodded for me to go and bent down to pick up firewood. He knew the message I had for Messalina and left me to it.

When I asked for Messalina inside, one of her companions happily led me to the basement, calling me "Gaius" as if we were old friends, cheerily saying Messalina would be pleased to see me. We entered a large room with smaller rooms cut into the rock at the sides. Three torches both illuminated and clouded the room. Every woman stopped work to watch me enter. Messalina stood up from bending over a low shelf and beamed a big smile. She took a breath, gathered her wrap around her shoulders tightly and came to me.

When she stepped into my outstretched arms and pressed the side of her face to my chest, a dozen former whores cooed, echoing our contentment. They approvingly watched us hold each other. I stroked Messalina's soft hair and breathed in her scent and love for me.

"I love you," I whispered in her ear, lightly kissing the lobe. It was the most honest thought of my life, and I was powerless not to say it. This we shared in a dank basement that smelled of mildew, pungent potions and smoke, with young women respectfully murmuring for the simple goodness of our embrace. It was a drowsy moment before I realized that Messalina had spoken the words back to me, and I hugged her tighter for it. She pulled her head from my chest, looking to her huddle of friends.

"Back to work, girls. We've much to do, but I need to speak a moment with Gaius Galen," she said.

"Of course," answered one of the older ones. "Ladies, let's move to the other storeroom."

"Continue here, my sisters," said Messalina. "We only need to talk, and we feel comfortable with you around us," and looking into my eyes added, "Don't we."

I nodded and took Messalina a few steps into one of the smaller side rooms, half-filled with large amphorae of olive oil. There was no drape or door, and I was caught off guard as she pinned me against a rock wall and kissed me intensely, then broke off to give me quick kisses and tiny bites as if to consume me. After a moment, we broke away from the passion, accompanied by laughter from the main room.

"They're jealous. They all want you, but you're mine, aren't you?" She looked so happy, because she knew the answer. I merely parroted it: *yes*.

I could hardly believe we had first really spoken our love only a moment ago. The last time I saw her she was upset with me. In the time between, I had faced so much and it was weighing heavily on me. Yet Messalina was always on my mind. I had quickly grown to need that badly, for many reasons. And her smile, so happy to see me, distinctly told me she did as well.

"You're not Fulvia's, are you?" she asked, dipping her head to kiss my hand and turning her eyes up to me. "You're not going back to her and the family, are you?"

"No, my love. No." My heart raced at *Fulvia*. "I was going to tell you about her –my former wife."

"Hush, Gaius. Hush," she dropped my hand and came up to kiss my neck lightly. A kiss here, a stroke of her fingernails there, she played me this way as she surprised me with this topic.

"Fulvia, the former wife, mother of your deceased child," and she pulled back to look me in the eye. "I am so sorry for your loss. So sorry," and she stroked my cheek. I was going wherever she led.

"Hush, my love. You would have told me, I know. I know you rejected her, years ago. You seem surprised I know, but don't you think a resourceful woman like myself, living among confidants whose trade is knowing every secret a man ever had, would not arm herself with knowledge of the one she was after?"

She put a finger to my lips to silence me, though I wasn't sure I could have spoken at that moment anyway.

"Oh, I know all there is to know about Gaius Galen Licinius – the younger and older. I would not have gotten in that carriage with you to go to a senator's party without knowing exactly what I might be getting into. So hush, Wilder, hush. And listen. Can I kiss you as I talk?" she asked, but was kissing my arm without my answer.

"I have spoken with several women who still work in your home, your father's home, where Fulvia still lives, with her memories, I suppose, and the money of your father in all his patriarchal prerogative. But I am not concerned about your past. I am concerned about your future. Can I say, our future? But no talking from you. Just take your kisses," and she continued with them, the other arm now. I heard one of the waywards in the main room describing things to the others.

"I am bold, and always have been," she said with pride. "Do I flatter myself that we might have a future? Shake your head. Good, I think we might also. You are in deep trouble, aren't you? Come, come, shake the head. I thought so, I know so. I have spoken with a gentleman lately, one who is also concerned for you, Herulian. He is a lovely man, or close enough. He is concerned. Are you taking his medicine now? Shake it, yes or no. No, alright. Is there a way out for you and your gang of street thugs? It's okay, don't protest. Shake the head, your handsome head, is there a way out? Good. Are you in danger? Are you in danger? – this is no time to play tough. Of course you are. Ammianus is a dangerous man, isn't he?"

"He is, Messalina," I broke in quickly, "and I came here to see you, of course, but also to tell you that he has moved your sister."

"Moved her? But where? When?" She stiffened upright: my arm would not receive more kisses today.

"Tedius tried to contact her and Kyros in Smyrna. They are gone, and we don't know where to, yet."

Messalina looked worried but was still well in control. This stronger side I had seen before, and it was full to the fore now.

"It is Ammianus," I said, "telling me that you are leverage to ensure that I do his bidding. He has located Annia and Monaxius' girls as well, signaling both of these things to me today. But he has withheld the biggest threat he can make to me, until a moment when he really needs it: you."

She wasn't frightened, but tightened her resolve instead.

"What can I do, Gaius?"

"What can we do?" came a voice from the other room. "We can help, we want to help our Gaius," said another. "She loves you so much. And we're all worried about you." The roomful of her friends agreed.

Messalina smiled and shook her head. "I don't believe you women," she said in a loud voice for them. "You will know all, in time," and she turned me around so her back was to the doorway and the listeners outside.

"I'm here for you, Gaius," said Messalina, her hand stroking my bicep. "They are too. I've shared you with them, just as we share everything with each other, support each other. We all want you to be careful."

"So you can come back for her," said one from the other room.

I held Messalina close, maybe squeezing too hard. "I will be careful, I will be crafty, I will do my very best to please Ammianus. We have decided this is the best way for any of us to make it through this."

"And this," she broke in, speaking into my chest. "This what? Say it."

"Rebellion," I whispered. "That's my fear, though I don't know for certain."

"It would seem," she whispered back. "I ask that you keep in touch. And to be as careful – and as cunning – as you can possibly be. I know you can be cunning but I am not sure about being careful."

"It may come to nothing, Messalina. Nothing at all, except a lot of worry," I breathed lightly into her ear, goosebumps chilling her delicious neck. "We just don't know – none of us in the city, I think."

After a brief silence she shifted so we were side by side, I moved my arm to her shoulder and walked us out to the large storeroom.

"Goodbye, ladies. We will meet again." I bowed low, turning to exchange a glance with each woman.

"Come back, Gaius Galen, when you have more time to spend with us," said a grinning blonde girl of about 17.

"I would have kissed more than your arm, Gaius, much more," said a pale Gallic woman.

"Messalina needs you. She needs you to come back," said another.

Messalina stood beside one of the burning torches holding herself, her eyebrows raised, her head shaking that she did need me. I kissed her forehead, caressed her shoulders and left her, enjoying the excited encouragements of the happy women who immediately surrounded her as I turned down the shadowy hallway.

22

Two Un-Hanged Men

On this sunny afternoon almost void of wind, many of the city's less reputable citizens were heading to the Praetorium annex in Sycae, having made their way across the Golden Horn for what promised to be an execution of partisans by the city Prefect Eudaemon, who was also the governor of the city, the leader of the Senate and one of the most powerful men in the empire. The Praetorium proper was in the center of Constantinople, the annex across the Horn was where executions generally took place.

My commanders Zazo, Bargas, Jacob, Lukos and Monaxius approached from different directions and feathered their gangs of about 15 men each into the throngs moving toward the Praetorium annex not far from the shore. Eleven men arrested in rioting two nights before had been moved over here at dawn from the Praetorium's jail. Eudaemon had sentenced seven of the men to death. These executions drew the crowds from the city sensing – hoping for – trouble.

I had about 20 men with me, including Estrilda who easily dressed and acted like a man. Zazo and his men would join me among the crowd there; Jacob, Lukos and Monaxius held back not too far away. Flavius had said there were no specific targets to protect or attack and our orders were to be there and be ready until we heard more from him. He was there somewhere monitoring events.

The crowd's excitement and undercurrent of malice enticed me. I felt like an organic part of the ill will toward order that pushed all these troublemakers along, but I fought to stay out of it and stay in control.

Every few minutes, a boy would tug at my cloak and relay a message from one of my lieutenants. These boys, 11 of them, were our messengers: fast, street-smart, almost invisible, cheap, and under the direction of Pawah, the Egyptian boy who had become a favorite of Tedius. We did not use them in our foray to destroy the tannery because Monaxius and I wanted to make sure Zazo and his men were reliable before we opened up the boy messengers to a possible disaster there. We needed them here. They had been training with us for a couple of weeks and knew our leaders' faces and many of the other street soldiers', as well as the black enamel pin in all our various hats. These boys would try to pick us out among hundreds of others.

We reached the Praetorium annex, which was a rectangular, two-story fortress-like structure with high walls and few windows. A crowd of some 1,000, with more flowing in by the minute, pressed up against the wood-rail barriers in front of the mounted prefect guards on the east side, where a raised wooden platform with chopping blocks and gallows was attached to the building by a walkway to the second story. On the annex's flat roof stood about 40 archers, arrows notched, bows held down. Every horseman, bowman and guardsman tried to hide their nervousness. But the crowd sensed it. I spotted Zazo kneeling underneath the back corner of the platform, apparently unnoticed by the mounted soldiers in front of him facing us.

Eudaemon, bearing the contempt of authority, walked boldly from the annex to the execution platform, accompanied by a dozen guardsmen. The crowd's voice, thick with crosstalk, died down as Eudaemon raised his arms to quiet their noise.

"Citizens of Constantinople," he called out, "seven men have been found guilty of inciting riots and personally killing or directing the killing of innocent people yesterday."

"No one's innocent!" yelled someone, sending a ripple of laughter through the crowd.

"These men, certainly not," said Prefect Eudaemon, and he swung the drooping right sleeve of his ermine-trimmed robe toward the seven men filing onto the platform under guard. Each one wore some form of Green or Blue marking.

"These disorders have grown too dangerous, too frequent, and the people of the city want order. The death of these men will help us achieve that," said Eudaemon.

One fellow at the head of the crowd used a stick to prick the nostril of a horse in front of the scaffolding, causing it to rear up and throw its rider. The crowd flexed like a muscle, ready to strike something, anything.

Eudaemon paused for a moment, then called out, "Executioners, dispense the emperor's justice!"

As jailers tied down four men on chopping blocks, a big man in the crowd wearing a green jacket hurled a rock at the executioner. The crowd instinctively stepped forward, but was stopped by the cry of the rock thrower who had an arrow in his shoulder – instantly the man next to him was felled by another archer. The crowd grumbled but froze, each man calculating if he would draw the next arrow by a sudden movement. Eudaemon smiled.

Then he nodded, and four heads toppled into baskets, the corpses jerking and giving up their blood. The crowd both cheered and moaned, and Eudaemon was quick to point downward again. Nooses were tightened around the necks of the three men left, two Greens and a Blue, positioned under the gallows beam that could accommodate five hangings. The crowd sucked in its breath as one when the executioner pulled the lever to drop the floor – and was dumbfounded when the far end of the beam came crashing down to the platform with the three men tied to it having dropped through the gallows floor. Two of them were standing on the ground, the third closer to the fixed end and higher up strangling to death, his feet kicking just inches above life.

The crowd cheered to raise the Devil – all of us except Brother Zazo who raced to the dangling man, saw that his neck was snapped, then cut the hangman's ropes on the living two, the nooses still around their necks. He put an arm around each of the dazed men and called out to everyone, "*God Has Saved These Men! Praise God,*

Praise Justinian His Servant – And Praise the Blues and the Greens Together – Together!"

He lifted up the stunned men's hands as if they had just tied in a wrestling match, as several of his brothers rushed to him. Eudaemon and guards were sprinting up the ramp to the safety of the annex's second floor, the horsemen were already under attack, and a captured spear was hurled into an archer on the roof, then another. The archers took out a few men but began to flee from the side of the roof out of sight.

Zazo was running away from the back of the gallows with a Blue and a Green under each arm, his fellow brothers circled around them like a turtle shell, joined by some of Lukos' men. The young toughs in the crowd gleefully had their hidden weapons out and were thrashing into the horsemen backed up against the platform.

I shoved and squeezed to the back of the scaffolding and headed after Zazo and his prizes, my group of men following me. Behind us over the shouting, screams and din of the wilding came, *"Praise God, Greens and Blues Saved. Greens and Blues Saved!"* This building chant was belted out as the crowd turned into a mob and set about to destroy the Praetorium annex. I caught up to Zazo as he reached the nearby monastery of St. Conon, three of his bothers pounding on the door.

"Zazo, that was brilliant!" I said.

He turned to me grinning, a froth of saliva at the corner of his mouth. "The brothers of St. Conon will help us shelter these lambs God has saved." He looked sharply at me, "We cannot abandon these men, Gaius Galen – ever."

The door opened, some quick explanations were made and we were welcomed in. Zazo, his un-hanged men, a few of his brothers and I entered, leaving our others outside the door that slammed shut. Some from the crowd had also left the annex to follow the saved men. In the quiet, tiled hall that opened into a gloomy sanctuary, Zazo got on his knees and kissed the feet of the Abbot of St. Conon.

"We will not bring destruction on you, Father," said Zazo between toe kisses. He looked up to me. "We will flee now. To where, Gaius Galen?"

Before I could think, the abbot said, "Go to the church of St. Laurentius on the other side of the Golden Horn almost directly across from us here. They will shelter you, and the two miracles in your arms. Go, quickly. Brother John will take you across."

Ten of us went with Zazo and the two un-hanged men, still wearing their nooses. From the middle of the bay we watched hundreds from the crowd run down to the shore after us, just in front of mounted prefect men bearing down on them.

I have never seen Flavius more excited than he was the next day when I met him at a section of the Green stalls next to the Hippodrome – hands flying around as he talked, making gestures I suppose only another Lombard could comprehend.

"I could kiss Zazo – and I think Ammianus wants to do more than that! Leave it to a crazy monk to declare a broken beam an act of God," said Flavius. "And you and your men yesterday, rowing the spared ones across the Golden Horn with prefect men in pursuit, plus hundreds of fanatic fools following in anything that floated. My God, what a sight!"

"You saw that?" I asked in a calm tone, hoping he would follow my example.

"Yes. Ammianus would have had me on your shoulders, he was so nervous that you might back out." Flavius' green eyes jumped around as he said, "Back out? Hell no, not my Wilder!"

"We were lucky to get that jump," I said. "Zazo and his prizes are still there. Since they arrived yesterday afternoon, no one has come in or gone out, except for my little messengers. Zazo and about 12 of his men are still inside, and he's sent word that the two men are willing to do whatever he asks them to."

Flavius was calming down some, and the horse in the stall responded by relaxing his black ears half back.

"Why does Ammianus think they are so important?" I asked.

"What I speculate – because Ammianus doesn't trust me with any more than I relate to you – is that his clients see an opportunity to use both factions now," he said, flaring his caterpillar eyebrows. "Before the botched hanging and Zazo linking them together, I think Ammianus' clients were going to try to bring the Greens into their camp by sending you and other groups we have – not near as effective as your fighters, of course – against Blue targets, playing on Justinian's favoritism to the Blues."

"That's overstated and has declined since he took the throne," I pointed out.

"Yes, but these rock-headed partisans never forget a slight. The idea of Blue and Green together? Ammianus was instantly intrigued with that. After a couple of hours, he got back to me with your new orders: you are to spread your men out to every street corner, tavern and race club in the city to subtly or directly talk up the idea of Blue and Green together. The sentiment is already there, and we need it to swell, I have been told. And you are to help."

"They want to promote them being together? This madness could be their own undoing!"

"Maybe it's not so mad, Gaius Galen," he said, with what passed as a sly look for Flavius. "I made the same observation to Ammianus. He explained that something similar happened at the beginning of the reign of Justinian's uncle Justin, when the Greens and the Blues jointly asked for various favors of the new emperor, whose claim to the throne was tenuous. The prospect of the factions uniting was so alarming that before the last race, Justin had granted the favors – more races, new pantomimes, that sort of thing. The Greens and Blues danced in the streets that night surprised at their success, and torched a few buildings in celebration. So it's not crazy, Gaius."

"I know that story," I said. "But Ammianus can't make Greens and Blues dance together. I'm not sure I can stomach that."

"You're not like that now, we both know that. You don't really give a damn what Color wins a race day. And just consider: Blue and Green together, in this city, that's pure power." Flavius looked sure that he had me and this new situation pegged.

"You think Ammianus' client was trying to get the Greens behind his cause, which must be rebellion –"

"– I don't hear that word, don't hear it!" Flavius cupped his ears.

"Don't hear it, and you stop saying it!"

"Alright, alright, I understand," I assured, holding up my hands. "So, where one faction would have been a big force behind the client's 'cause,' both factions would be an unstoppable one?" I thought it through for a quick moment. "It would! No one can withstand both factions, perhaps no man and no army."

Flavius smiled and said, "Imagine that, the old dimwitted Lombard, sharper of mind than sly, educated Wilder."

Very happy with himself, Flavius stepped around the back end of the horse and kicked into a pile of straw striking wood. "That's for Zazo, a box of money and valuables in thanks for his fast thinking."

"Nothing for me?"

"Talk to your assistant John, he's got a box for you," said Flavius with a generous grin. "You're going to be a rich man."

"If, if I live through this," and I grinned back at him sarcastically. We walked out of the barn, an arm around each other's shoulder, unwilling partners in Ammianus' schemes.

A little later Lukos almost vomited when I told him what he and his boys were going to have to do – said he'd rather lose a hand than shake a Blue's. But with some reasoning, wine and coins, he saw it our way, or Ammianus'. This was pivotal because Lukos was still one of them and closest to the core of unruly Green supporters. Monaxius, Tedius and I had our contacts in that crowd, but as formers rather than currents, we didn't carry Lukos' weight.

Jacob was fine with it, having long considered Blues and Greens equally pestilent. He and his men would stick to the Jewish sectors and those of other marginalized minorities to do their persuading.

Bargas thought it was humorous and fitting. "They're almost exactly alike – and both dumb as oxen, at least the young Hunnish ones who live to destroy."

I shared my bonus fee with our men to motivate them and told them that we wouldn't be the only ones working this. While we were in the streets trying to deflect events, others in Ammianus' purse were working the faction authorities, the wealthy businessmen, the rungs of society that could touch power, from bishops to senators. I wanted our men to find some comfort in knowing we weren't alone in this rebellion. And there was no doubt in anyone's mind, even the dimmest in Lukos' pack of curs, that this was our fools' errand.

Word of the Blue and Green hanged men's miraculous escape and their protection in the Church of St. Laurentius had reached every ear in Constantinople. So had the refrain of *Blue and Green Together.* Lukos was surprised that the idea was already being talked about among some of the Green street crawlers he knew.

Brother Zazo was now a mystical hero, as admired as an ascetic sage who lives on a pillar for years to show his loyalty to God. The failed hanging, instantly stamped as God's will by Zazo, was a tonic to the masses – a taste of real power validated by each additional moment the prefect and emperor hesitated to remove the Blue and Green from the Church of St. Laurentius.

But Blues and Greens together? Everything in my world – in the world – was upside down now. Yet, that was my charge, our charge. Just about the entire empire loved the sport of chariot racing, but it was the teams we lived for – a difference that could turn an appreciation into a fanaticism. Belonging to one or the other was the key – belonging to anything was important to every man, woman, slave or priest. Blue and Green and Red and White – varied shades of the same sport fanatic – were a power of belonging a wise emperor should be wary of.

But I believe Flavius had it right: if there was ever a time for a usurper to tap into this innate force more powerful than an army of Huns, this was it. Not in 700 years had the factions been gathered in the fist of an emperor as Justinian had been doing, pulling the administration, the funding, the very reins and drivers themselves into his hand. Now charioteers, theater actors, dancing dogs and acrobats were Green or Blue employees of the emperor. This consolidation was very distasteful to the proud sportsmen and their adoring, addled followers. Maybe now was the time for that power splintered by the Colors to come together. Nothing lasts forever.

What Tedius and I encountered in one Green faction clubhouse in the western part of the city bore this out. We entered at dusk, a popular Green song just ending. As Tedius went to get us wine, and I took a seat at one of the big tables, a familiar Blue song started up by a small group of Blues at a table across the rooms. For Blues to be there at all was remarkable; for them to be singing was astounding.

A man across from me, eyes glassy from ale, body weaving on the bench, saw my surprise and said, "Yes, those are Blues singing, here in the Lark's Tongue Tavern where the only Blue welcomed used to be a dead one."

"Not even then!" clarified his friend next to him.

"I'm hearing talk of those two lucky dogs who broke the prefect's gallows bringing Blue and Green together. But I'll not have any of that," I said, looking menace at the clutch of Blues.

"That older one among the Blues – ever heard of Porphyrius?" asked the man, a merchant of sorts it appeared from the quality of his clothes.

I looked closer. "My God, it is! He hasn't been a Green for some time, and he's here?"

"Just a few moments ago, old Porphyrius had this place as silent as a church when he was telling us about how he led the Green rioters in Antioch in 507 and ruled the city for days against Blues and imperial troops. Now *Blue* Porphyrius just stood up there and told us that a righteous chariot fan – Blue, Green, purple, black – was worth three soldiers any day."

"Old Porphyrius!" said his friend. "Here, telling a tale of rebellion. Said it was one of the proudest moments of his life – and he's had some fine ones. A man doesn't get four statues along the spina for nothing."

Tedius put a cup of wine in front of me and was about to sit down, but I held up my hand to stop him and drank my cup of wine in one draught.

"Better bring back a pitcher," I said, watching the Blues who had finished their song. "These men here are telling me some strange tales, and I'm going to need more wine to believe them. I can't imagine Blues and Greens in love with each other in the Hippodrome tomorrow for the Ides races."

23

Beware the Ides of January

"Zazo dolls and Zazo curse tablets!" yelled a merchant shaking a doll over his basket of lead tablets at his stand outside the Hippodrome. "The Tall One has blessed these tablets, they cannot fail!" he promised, shaking the little Zazo, a clay man in a monk's robe crowned by a frizz of blackened cotton.

Atakam gave me a puzzled look.

"No, he hasn't blessed them," I said. "But he is going to be here. He slipped out of St. Laurentius late last night and should already be here staying out of sight in my work area."

Atakam nodded, eying a group of young men all wearing hangman's nooses around their necks. Many people wore this sign, some nooses Blue, some Green, some dyed both colors.

I was proud that behind me scattered among the race fans flowing to the Hippodrome, were more than 200 men following my lieutenants and me. We'd swelled our ranks with some recruits that would remain outside to be ready if and when needed. This race day on the Ides of January (the 13th) promised to be memorable – on the track and in the stands.

I wore my official uniform of amber tunic and green leather breastplate as the Green Master of the Track, doing double duty as Ammianus' plant directing my 200. But directing them to what, I didn't know, only that we were to support the unity of Blues and Greens.

Atakam walked beside me, dressed in ragged clothes. He said he wanted to stand with me as a friend, at least until events might compromise his fidelity. He was a settling force, and I needed that being jittery at the prospect of things going very wrong, apprehensive of what sort of chaos might be kicked up today. It was almost like old times, taking those first steps into what could be wild destruction. Or death.

Atakam and I entered by the faction employee entrance. All my men, including Pawah and his runners, had entrance tokens Flavius provided. Of all of my trusted regulars, only Estrilda remained outside, unhappy but competent to direct the auxiliary poor she had rounded up from around the Great Palace, her offered coins a windfall for them. Atakam followed me to my work desk, where my assistant John had all the documentation about the track dirt's composition laid out for me to inspect. With Flavius' (and Ammianus') approval, he had been doing every aspect of my job for the past few days, sending me updates. On a bench against the wall, Brother Zazo woke up from a quick nap. I clasped his hand as he sat up, then thanked him for his actions yesterday.

He was groggy from lack of sleep and seemed as strange and touched as the day I met him at Monaxius' front door.

"Who is with the Blue and the Green hanged men?" I asked.

"My best men and the holy fathers of St. Laurentius. More of my brothers are hidden in the crowd outside around the prefect's men."

Zazo, hooded and stooped to remain unnoticed, came with Atakam and me to my normal spot at the big opening under the east stands where the dirt scattering wagons and track crews were stationed. During the official opening of the Ides of January races, we all praised Emperor Justinian mightily – as loud and fervently as ever, almost like nothing was different. But it felt different. I could see some of my fellow workers felt it too, looking warily up into the stands.

Bargas and his men were shadowing the claquers of the Blue section, while Monaxius and company hung around the nearby Green section, the Kathisma across the track. Jacob's, Lukos' and

Tedius' groups floated around the small Red and White sectors and the non-factional open sections, where all Colors and the colorless mixed. Our runner boys wore yellow scarfs and had little whips with long yellow strips of fabric they could flick into the air when near one of our commanders so we could see where each other were. Sometimes. My heart thumped against my green breastplate.

At the end of the third race, Bargas got a callout going in the Blue section, weak at first but it caught attention. "We ask our most august emperor to honor God's sign and have mercy on the Blue prisoner and the Green prisoner! *Pardon the Blue, Pardon the Green!*"

His ex-claquer cronies planted in the crowd took it up, as did the other 30 or so of his men. Jacob's men were nearby and joined in, then many in the Blue section were on their feet, calling out to the Kathisma, "*Pardon the Blue, Pardon the Green, to Please God and Man!*"

A Green claquer took it up, with Monaxius and his men joining immediately, "*Pardon the Blue, Pardon the Green, to Please God and Man!*"

The Greens were up, their fanatics shaking billowing green sleeves like Huns wore toward the Kathisma in the face of their emperor. Justinian held up his hand for silence – three times before the chanting tapered off, aided by the starter rushing the beginning of the fourth race.

This race was a thriller and had everyone on their feet for the final two laps. Green's Felix took the lead, aided by a blocking Red driver, but Pyramus of the Blues got an amazing reserve of speed from his horses and pulled aside. The entire last lap was wheel to wheel, with the two pulled well ahead of other chariots. Every man in the Hippodrome was screaming out something, jumping up and down, beating on each other in frenzy – and Pyramus took the finish line by a nose. The Greens drooped, the Blues were dancing on air and shouting, "*Pyramus, Pyramus, Pyramus, All Hail!*"

At the first dip in the accolades, with Pyramus yet to circle around to the Kathisma to receive his victor's laurel crown, Bargas directed all of his men to yell, "*Pardon the Blue, Pardon the Green, to Please God and Man!*"

Others picked it up, the Blues now yelling at Emperor Justinian with angry voices and twisted faces, *"Pardon the Blue, Pardon the Green, to Please God and Man!"*

The Green section echoed the call. One section's callout clashed over the other's same phrase, but within a moment, the practiced crowd allowed one strain to become dominant as Blue and Green voices merged into one phrase that roared with a powerful echo that set the timing. This confluence impressed the fans with a new power, and they chanted louder.

A column of white-uniformed Excubitors double timed out of the side of the lower Kathisma and ringed the bottom of the imperial box three soldiers deep. Justinian above on the top level held up his hand again to silence the crowd, but Blue and Green would not relent, and the entire Hippodrome was now with them. The mandator stepped to his heightened stand and held up both hands to silence the crowd. It took a full minute for the crowd to give their emperor respectful silence, the Empress Theodora shaking her head in privileged disgust at the misbehaving children, though once a fervent Green herself, as her father had been the Green bear keeper.

"Your petition has been heard – the first time," chastised the mandator, looking to the Blue section then the Green. "Your emperor has heard your plea. Today he gives you races! Be seated you Blues, be seated you Greens."

As he was speaking, a force of 50 Excubitors, with spears held in front of them and more soldiers with swords behind them, moved to the front row of the Blue stands, forcing partisans on their feet in front of them to sit on their benches.

"Enjoy your drivers," cried the mandator. "This Raceday of the Ides is yours to enjoy!"

Most in that part of the Blue section sat down, though they probably could have gobbled up the Excubitors. A pipe organ played a happy tune as the stands grumbled with 80,000 unhappy men glaring at the Kathisma. I'm sure that thousands of partisans had felt to check the weapons secreted on them. Only the pipe organ and two dozen singers weakly filled the air with inappropriate merriment.

Senators and important men in private boxes looked nervous. A few snuck out, leaving servants and subordinates in their places so as not to offend the emperor with their empty box. I saw that Quintus Cornelius Alban remained in his, acting as if nothing were out of place. And maybe it wasn't, if he was the force behind Ammianus.

"You must continue to press this, the Blue and Green release," said Flavius, who had snuck right up on me. "Have them push it, all of your men. Push it!"

I glanced at the Kathisma and faced Flavius. "It's treason Ammianus is ordering, Flavius."

"I asked you not to say that, Gaius, but I think you are right," said Flavius, his face tensed with foreboding. "We have no choice. We will be killed within minutes if we do not perform. Ammianus' enforcers are targeting us both this moment – and your lieutenants. We must push."

He laid a friendly hand on my shoulder and retreated back to the staging area, where grooms were calming horses and drivers tightening reins around their torsos as they began to file out for the next race. I sent boys to tell Lukos, Tedius and Jacob to move to the Blue and Green sections near the sphendone curve. These two sections of about 20,000 total, with faction leaders, administrators and a good number of the violent hotheads, usually led the others in the Hippodrome.

Scorpus won the premier race of the day, number 13, and it was a close one. The Greens roared his glory, and he grinned big behind his beard, apparently successfully perfumed. When the cheering began to die down after Scorpus received the laurel wreath with the Green streamer from Justinian, Monaxius' men and Green claquers started up again, *"Pardon the Green, Pardon the Blue!"*

The call quickly spread from there around the track for a few moments until Emperor Justinian stood up and held out his arms, palms upturned. He moved them up and down as if gauging the weight of the chant that was rolling around him. Then he sat back down, pointedly saying nothing, trusting his authority to be enough.

The crowd's chant began to dwindle and dutifully disappeared, their loyalty confused between their newfound might and their age-old allegiances. From our position to the side of the crew area's entrance at track level, Atakam, Zazo and I watched through eight more races, the Hippodrome simmering in uncertainty, chants for Justinian to pardon the Blue and Green rising and falling but not catching on. A runner brought word of Bargas in trouble.

"Atakam and Zazo, let's go!" I said, sensing this might be the right time for Zazo. Bargas and three of his men met us at track level when we reached the Blue section.

"They're stopping," said a flustered Bargas, "these arrogant up-starts from Alexandria think it is the perfect time to show their might. The lead man told me he'll take the Blues where he wants, not where Ammianus wants."

I had our boy whip up his yellow streamer, and four others licked into the air; all my men were close by. More than nervous in my of-ficial Green outfit, I headed up the stands into a sea of ultramarine Blue, with Bargas, Zazo and Atakam behind, and others hopefully following. I went right up to the lead claquer.

"Friend, we are under the same master, Ammianus, and you will continue to push for pardon."

"I'll do nothing of the sort," said the Alexandrian, a dandy wear-ing more rings than the empress. "It is the people who lead, as I direct them. Besides," he said pointing to Bargas, "he sends this old has been of the circus to watch over us." He rolled a haughty Alexandrian sneer at me.

"Too bad," I said, and popped my fist in his sneering face. I got on top of him and pounded as much of him as couldn't squirm away from me, then went after his second in command. Jacob was sud-denly next to me, laying into another Blue with a short hickory rod. I didn't know where Atakam was but I heard a scream from some-one followed by Atakam's delighted cackling. Monaxius and his men were running up the stairs toward us. The Blue claquer I had pum-meled tried to scramble away on the bench, but I pulled him to me in a headlock. All around me Blues were puzzling whether to enjoy our fight or help their claquer held by a Green – an abomination they wouldn't tolerate for more than a dazed moment.

I saw Zazo two rows below in the aisle, and called him, "Now Zazo, come now!"

A few big steps and he was at my side standing on the bench. "Behold You Blues, Brother Zazo has come to cheer you on!" I yelled.

Zazo whipped back his hood and stood tall. Shouts of, "Zazo! It's Zazo!" came from all around.

"Long Live the Humane Blues and Greens!" yelled Zazo, with others repeating it.

Our united presence of me, Atakam, Monaxius, Lukos, Tedius, Jacob and all their men was obvious and puzzling for Blues and nearby Greens watching. But it was Zazo who held them. The drivers on the track, the imperial guards, every eye in the Kathisma and in the Hippodrome was focused on the tall monk with the crown of black hair. He started with deep voice and gestured with arms for all to join him.

"Blue and Green Together! Blue and Green Together! Blue and Green Together!"

Bargas and the Alexandrian with bloody lips were yelling the same furiously. The Blue and Green sections joined like schooled choirboys, the idea of what they were saying gaining their animation. *"Blue and Green Together!"* came from most every mouth that wasn't in the Kathisma. The sound shook the Hippodrome and rumbled through the foundation of the Great Palace attached to it.

Zazo continued to lead the call, accepting people who rushed up to hug him, to touch this holy monk who must have God's ear. *"Blue and Green Together!"* he yelled out, face lifted to Heaven, inciting the 80,000 around him.

24

Blue and Green Together!

A long with this uprising in the stands, there was a chariot race going on – number 23 of the day. The drivers had been rushed to the gate for a hasty start, but after the normal quick opening dash, they were slowing down approaching the pivotal first turn. Every driver slowed his horses to watch a scene they had never before viewed: the crowd was completely ignoring the racers. Instead, they were encouraging themselves with, *Blue and Green Together!* It wasn't letting up.

The Green driver Teres trotted to the first meta turning post in front and looked around at other drivers slowed to a walk, looking into the stands of screaming fans. Taking the 180-degree turn at a crawl, Teres veered his chariot over to the stands and stopped. This caught the fans' attention and the volume in the Hippodrome got louder than before, with the undisciplined cheering of every man screaming approval of Teres' halt.

Quickly along the track other drivers stopped their teams – Orpheus, Julian and Philippus of the Greens, Fuscus, Meander, Crescens and Romanus of the Blues, and two Reds and Whites each. Teres jumped into the stands from the rail of his chariot and was smothered by fans. Philippus threw his whip into the Green section, then his helmet, then himself. Four other charioteers climbed up into the stands to become spectators rather than the spectacle.

A ripple of shouts and laughter from the Blue section and the pointing of fingers turned attention to the Kathisma, which was emptying of emperor and empress, mandator, high officials, wealthy guests and foreign emissaries. Excubitors were guarding the rear as these exalted leaders walked briskly – but not running – back to the palace. The laughter built as the fans viewed the strange scene they had brought about: their emperor fleeing, halted races, drivers in the stands. And they laughed at their power. Giddy, shocked, delighted, the Hippodrome continued to cry out, *"Blue and Green Together!"*

I don't think any of us knew what that chant might actually mean, except that *together* appeared to have doubled the factions' power – maybe tripled it. This was a wild thing coursing through the fans, now feeling invincible, like a band of rioters about to go off in a frenzy.

The circus was a ship of state seized by pirates. As *"Blue and Green Together!"* rang its surreal promise, it felt as if the huge Hippodrome with its curved bow of the sphendone was our ark, about to slide downhill to the waters of the Propontis, leaving Constantinople and the authority of the Roman Empire in our wake.

A strong hand clamped my shoulder. "Listen to your people, Gaius Galen, and enjoy this moment," said Atakam with a grim face. "What follows we cannot know, but most likely it will not be good. It's time for me to shed these beggar rags and return to my unit. I have learned it is moving out of Thrace, probably to here."

"I understand, Atakam," I said. "If I make it through this, we will meet again someday."

"I hope our meeting will not be in the streets as adversaries," he said. "Be careful, Gaius." He walked down the stadium stairs, the only calm man in the Hippodrome as he abandoned ship.

Amidst the shouting, laughing and chanting, faction leaders gathered together where the Green and Blue sections met. These were official faction leaders and men like myself under them in imperial employment, as well as partisan bosses in the city who marshaled the local neighborhood and club fans. Blues and Greens greeted one another, some cautiously, some gladly. The lead claquers of both groups gravitated to this growing band of 200 or so. Out of this odd and very liquid coalition of prominent Green and Blue fans, faction professionals and many ultra Blue and Green rowdies (I was pleased to see Lukos aggressively inserting himself among these) came a quick agreement to work together, at least for a while. But for what beyond the release of the two hanged men, they were not sure.

One prominent Green put his hand on the back of a Blue and declared, "We do what we want! We Greens and we Blues, we are the city! We have the power, the power of these racing fans, of most every living soul in Constantinople!"

The gathering cheered, men hopping up and down as if it were already a reality and each was a prefect of his own province. Some more wise and less excitable men threw caution on these grandiose designs of power, saying that they would first have to live through the imperial counterattack, and many likely wouldn't. They calmed the feverish ones down somewhat and agreed to try to make the most of this opportunity.

And they agreed on a watchword that would stand for this new movement: "Nika," the traditional Greek call of "victory" – over a rival driver, an army, an evil, a ruler. Like a secret club of excited boys, they also decided on a name for their new united faction, the Green-Blues – with a remarkable lack of fussing over which color would be first.

The 200 with the help of the professional claquers started up a new call over the chaotic noise of the Hippodrome, "*The Green-Blues Are One – Nika! The Green-Blues Are One – Nika!*" The stadium soon rang with one voice, "*The Green-Blues Are One – Nika!*" This was quickly shortened to just, "*Nika! Nika! Nika!*" The track was full of fans who had abandoned the accepted rituals of the Hippodrome, just as Emperor Justinian had abandoned the Kathisma. The Green-Blues wanted their feet in the emperor's dirt (my dirt), eyes looking toward his palace connected to the Hippodrome they now commanded. The Great Palace did not appear nearly as formidable as it had an hour ago.

Men climbed into chariots to play driver, climbed up the Serpent Column in the spina area, several falling off. Others hacked at the stone relief face of Emperor Theodosius at the base of the Egyptian obelisk. Horse trainers and grooms ventured out with other faction workers to protect and claim the 48 horses, somewhat dazed by the fans on their track and spooked by their attention, because many fans felt that the opportunity to stroke a famous horse was akin to communing with a dead saint.

One group of a dozen Greens was pulling Julian's chariot freed from its horses toward the north gate. The golden dolphins in the spina that marked laps were haphazardly leaping up and down, as men played with them like excited children. A pipe organ cried out under unskilled hands, and was then smashed and destroyed, wheezing pained notes in death. An unchained bear ran out from the crew area underneath the stands, where partisans were helping themselves to racing gear, whips, the colored tunics of drivers, some even riding out on horses. The bear charged at laughing men shocking them to silence, then pulled back, soon gaining a passageway to escape the stadium and the pandemonium of men wilder than beasts.

A blast of military horns did nothing to quiet the riotous Hippodrome. The dual column of mounted Scholarian guards fronting about 100 prefect police entering from the north gate caused only a momentary hesitation in the crowd. Then multitudes from the stands joined their Blue and Green brothers on the track to happily attack the soldiers. A tune of *"Nika! Nika! Nika!"* pulsed on as thousands pushed into the Scholarian column, toppling horses and killing soldiers. The soldiers killed and wounded many before dissolving into death or fleeing, but the mob seemed to feel none of that pain, and *"Nika! Nika! Nika!"* rang on.

I could see my men in clumps here and there, because they were the only relatively subdued ones around, except for Lukos' boys who were whooping it up in the spirit of this overwhelming moment and their natural proclivities to chaos. The others were standing aside, watching – it struck me – what I had helped cause by throwing Zazo to the crowd like a carcass to starved jackals just at the right moment. Blue and Green together, a bellicose force of half crazed men I had created! My mind was spinning with the intensity popping all around me. I looked up to the afternoon sun straight into the damaging light. And in that instant, I was certain the 80,000 would follow me, Wilder.

But Monaxius grabbed my arm forcefully, and I was suddenly following him, thankful to be pulled back to earth. My former rioting partner recognized that I had left it at that moment.

Tedius, Monaxius, Jacob, Bargas, Zazo and I huddled together in the Blue section. Many people had left the stadium by now, most trying to get to their homes and either flee or shut themselves in well and tight. The jubilation in the Hippodrome would soon spill into the city, where it would become fire, destruction and more death. How it would be turned to the rebellion we suspected, none of us gathered around knew.

"That's where this must go, isn't it?" asked Jacob, rubbing at a cut on his lip and looking to me to answer.

"I honestly don't know," I said, showing more calm than I actually had at that instant. I turned to look at my lieutenants, Lukos now joining us holding up a Scholarian's short sword as a trophy.

"You've done well, each of you, and your men. I am proud of you all," I said, holding back a sentimental whimper that almost broke through. I was touched and humbled, where a moment before I had soared unassailable. I felt out of control, like I was playing a role I wasn't sure of. I bulled through.

"The word I have received from Flavius is that we follow for the moment – whatever may occur and wherever it may go. We shall separate somewhat, each of you guiding your unit but close enough to band together for maximum effect and protection, if needed."

All six were leaning in to absorb what I said over the cacophony of the still sizable crowd, looking to me with fear in check yet still in their eyes, looking to me to lead them through this. I surveyed the Hippodrome calmly, though my mind was about to explode from the unending verse of *"Nika! Nika! Nika!"* trampling through it.

"But no, let's change those plans. No following, we'll lead," I said, struck with the brilliance of my idea. "Zazo and Lukos, take your men to St. Laurentius as quickly as possible and remove the hanged men. I am sure part of this mob will be heading that way once they think of it, so we need to get them out now – and Flavius, Ammianus, they don't need not know that at the moment."

Lukos flipped his Scholarian sword and offered it handle first to Zazo, who thanked him and made it disappear inside his robe. Then Zazo pulled out a small bag, and as he loosened the string around the bag a pigeon poked its head out and flew off.

"It belongs to the brothers of St. Laurentius," said Zazo, watching the bird disappear in the fading light. "This is the signal to take the men through the church's secret tunnels to a small shrine beyond the ring of prefect troops. It has been well planned and will not fail, as we have discussed, Gaius Galen."

"Excellent, Zazo. Our two miracle men will be the next focal point for the partisans *and* the emperor," I said. "Let's win that race. Go now!"

Lukos was outwardly happy to be going to a focal point, and he grabbed Zazo's sleeve and started to pull him away, breaking into a run in a few steps, about 20 of his and Zazo's men tearing off with them. The other five lieutenants watched them run off, looking serious as if they might not see them again.

"It will be a fractious night, I am certain," I said. "Alert your men. As events die down in the early morning – and they will due to cold, exhaustion and a better imperial showing than those hapless Scholarians have offered – try to get your men some rest in shifts."

I rose from the bench to break us up. Monaxius thumped his right fist over his heart and gave me a hard nod of affirmation. Each of the others did the same before moving off to spread out with their men into the crowd.

Tedius was the last to salute me in the same manner, adding, "We're all behind you, Master – even as you change the plan you have been given. Try not to mess us up." His smile feigning a joke did not fool me, nor did he want it to.

25

Burnt to Hell

The Golden Horn, usually a dark trench at night between the lights of Constantinople and the suburbs, was lit from the lanterns of 40 boats bobbing at anchor offshore from the Church of St. Laurentius. Some were prefect vessels, some Blue and Green partisans, each watching the other and the church. Zazo, Lukos and their men were all standing with me as we paused on the city's second hill to look down on the torches of the troops that surrounded St. Laurentius. But to no use. The Blue hanged man, Ovidius, and the Green one, Nikias, were standing with us, snuck out of the church earlier by Zazo through a tunnel missed by the prefect men, who did find two others and had them staked out.

Thousands from the Hippodrome had arrived at St. Laurentius to free the now-sacred pair, but were in a standoff with the prefect troops. Before we moved on to my house, I sent Pawah to tell Flavius only that we had removed the hanged men from St. Laurentius. These men were huge assets we could use to possibly influence Ammianus, the emperor and the mob. We continued through the streets. The more prosperous the neighborhood, the quieter it was, with doors and windows shuttered and locked, residents in hiding or already gone. Boats were ferrying citizens of these areas and their belongings across the Bosphorus to the safer Asian suburbs. Other pockets and neighborhoods were boisterous and ramping up for whatever was coming.

We secreted Ovidius and Nikias to a storage room in the basement of my apartment's building. Since Father owned the building and stored work things in the basement, I had it to myself including lock and key. I put several of our men on guard in the basement and others patrolling the surrounding blocks for prefect men or partisans. An hour or so later, a runner brought news that the mob had scattered the prefect guards at St. Laurentius, discovered the hanged men were missing, and in frustration moved to the Praetorium, releasing every prisoner from its jail. Reinforced by these freed criminals and howling with *Nika!*, the mob appeared to be headed back toward the Hippodrome.

That's where we headed, directing my different squadrons to filter in from the north and south. We soon blended in with the mob, about 2,000 and swelling, which was stalled at the Augusteum, the old center plaza of Byzantium. The great church Hagia Sophia was to the northeast, the Senate directly to the east, and just below that the Chalke Gate, the ceremonial entrance to the Great Palace on its northeastern end. The superb Baths of Zeuxippus, almost contiguous to the Hippodrome, were on the Augusteum's south side. Here gathered together was the symbolic essence of empire. And here, Pawah, panting and worried, found me.

"I told Flavius about moving the hanged men from the church. He was not happy at all, and said to tell you so. He also said to get the mob away from the palace," said Pawah, who looked down at his feet hesitating before reluctantly adding, "The German also said to burn down Hagia Sophia so it looks like the rioters did it. But protecting the palace is of most importance."

To my look of disbelief, he shook his head that it was true. I wondered why on three counts and asked the boy about two of them. "Why burn the church, and why would he trust you with that message?"

"Because he will kill my mother if I ever say a word about this!" he blurted out, followed by a wounded gasp and fast tears. "Told me which of our kitchen knives his murderer would use! I don't know the other why, I don't know about the church …"

I held him to me and stroked his head as he cried, telling him nothing would happen to his mother, I would be sure of that, thinking how horrible I was to endanger this boy and his mother – everyone.

Looking up a side street, I could see the church of holy wisdom, ground level lamp lights gleaming weakly off its gold dome in the night, its high windows dull and blank. Why burn this holy place, I wondered – and why protect the Great Palace? Were we not rebelling against Justinian? Or was it not the time yet? But I had no time to analyze these puzzling orders, only to act. We would try to push them away from the palace and to the Senate as a better target. I would burn Hagia Sophia myself, if possible, pushed by the fear that Pawah's mother would be killed if I didn't. Not mentioning Hagia Sophia, I sent runners to the others with instructions to push the mob away from the palace and toward the Senate.

Pawah had pulled himself together, so I sent him to tell Estrilda, who had been rounding up the poor who lived against the south wall on the opposite side of the palace, to bring those destitute souls to the Chalke Gate. The mob was already headed across the Augusteum plaza to that magnificent gate of spectacle, where the emperor publicly came and went to the choreographed praises of his subjects. A contingent of imperial guards were already placed there.

One man in the crowd heaved a spear into the huge wooden door behind three successive iron gates. The crowd cheered and advanced toward the open area in front of the first gate. Archers popped up on the roof and downed at least 10, forcing the mob to move back away.

Bargas shocked me by running to the buffer space cleared by the arrows, turned his back to the archers, and yelled out to the hesitating mob, "Of course they expect us here! On to the Senate!"

He headed in that direction, and about 20 of his men enthusiastically followed. Many from the mob eyeballed the archers and were about to follow, when a big fellow snatched the shield from an imperial soldier, held it over his head and ran screaming back toward the gate.

The mob overpowered the guards, wresting shields from soldiers and grabbing benches, planks, tables to hold overhead as they rushed toward the Chalke's outermost iron gate. Arrows thwacked into these makeshift shields from above, some finding flesh underneath. Torches were flung against the great wooden doors, and a brigade of more benches and tables rushed to the gate. A few men with bows in the mob downed imperial archers on the roof, more of the mob rushed forward, at least two pressed to death into the iron gates. A squad of 50 nervous soldiers charged into the Augusteum from the north and turned to push into the Chalke attackers from their rear. The mob swallowed them up in short order.

A great roar of bloodlust strengthened the mob, now concentrated like a spear point at the Chalke Gate, with thousands more behind in the Augusteum plaza and more coming from The Mese, where fires erupted and buildings were being looted. An improvised team of oxen with shed roofs and boards lashed onto their backs were whipped furiously to the first iron gate and pushed it down. Hundreds of crazed men ran on to the next iron gates, oblivious to the glorious gold detail in them and the purple marble columns. Another round of fresh archers volleyed into these attackers from the roof, creating a small gap cluttered with bodies, many of them writhing in pain.

"*No!*" yelled out a dirty blond man at the head of 200 or so running from along the side of the palace toward the Chalke Gate. "*Nooo!*" and he pulled from behind his back a double-edged long sword and hacked at a man shaking the iron gate, crumpling him. A back swing took off the arm of a second man at the gate. The crowd froze, confused and awed. In an instant, scores of ragged men and some women ran to the side of the swordsman.

"*Come My Beggars, Save Your Emperor to Save Yourselves!*" he ordered, swinging wildly and moving to challenge the mob, his back to the iron gate. More beggars crammed behind him as they ran up in increasing numbers.

It was Estrilda, leading the beggars she had been cultivating the whole time the Hippodrome was boiling over. They were hers now, aided by whatever she had spent to bribe them but they obviously followed her for more than money. The crowd was momentarily stunned to inaction, a horde of beggars coming at them, holding out their dirty palms as they did for alms on the streets.

"If you kill the emperor, you must take care of us!" called out one. "*Help us, help us!*" rose up from the group, Estrilda swinging her sword before her, leading them on. This was a moment when I needed to lead, and with an idea that just sprang into my head, I told Tedius beside me to wait for me to act, then push hard for the Senate and get all our people to do the same. I ran to one of the beggars right behind Estrilda, grabbed him by the throat and started shaking him – then suddenly stopped.

"*Ahhggg, Lepers, He's a Leper!*" I yelled. Everyone gasped – rioting toughs at the front of the crowd and imperial archers on the roof.

"*His Skin – It Comes Off in My Hand!*" I held them out as if leprosy was dripping off them. "*Lepers, Lepers! Don't Touch Them!*" and I fell to my knees wailing, my hands held in the air.

"*Leave Them! To the Senate! To the Senate!*" yelled Tedius. From nearby Monaxius cried out, "*We're Already Inside. No Archers, No Lepers – to the Senate!*" I stood and saw dozens of men, some I knew to be ours, head off for the Senate just around the side of the palace. Estrilda pushed the leper beggars onward as before and the mob melted away before them not daring a touch, a breath. But not without a few tiles, rocks and a couple of spears thrown into the crowd of supposed lepers, the beggars paying a price for their loyalty to Estrilda and Justinian, who allowed them to live against his palace.

The Chalke attack was abandoned, the mob now swarming toward the Senate. I spotted Lukos up front, his men and Bargas subtly keeping the vanguard herded together. The Senate was empty of senators, and would soon be empty of any valuable item. The archers above the Chalke Gate looked puzzled but held their bows notched and down as they watched the lepers gathering up their wounded. Estrilda gave me a smile behind her dirtied face, and began to lead her beggars back to their home against the south palace wall, where imperial servants would later thank them with food, wine, clothing and coins.

The Senate House looked to be open for business, with hundreds hanging around the stately columns and portico steps, some senselessly chipping off marble for a souvenir they would throw away before the night was done. Men struggled off under heavy loads of ivory benches and thick tapestries. There went the podium, and over there four men were battling each other to carry off a gold secretary's stand. Fire was sending smoke out the top of the main entrance, it would not be long before the heat of combustibles cracked the stone and caught the wooden framing afire.

I saw three of Lukos' men on the Senate steps and thought to take them with me. They were not yet 17 years old though ruthless to the core already and would be excited to torch the most sacred building in the Eastern Roman world. I took a step toward them and stopped. I thought of crying Pawah, his mother's kitchen knife. That vision, the realization of what I was about to do made me shake. I tried to think my way out of it, but could not. There was no way out, and I felt sick, sickened by myself. Why had I ever learned to like this destruction? The frisson of destroying flickering in me at this moment as if to ignite. Maybe I should have been made a eunuch at 10. I would have been free from this awful burden. I left Lukos' three men undisturbed and headed uphill to Hagia Sophia.

I easily broke into the church, which had been abandoned by its caretakers once the rioters swept into the Augusteum. I gathered several oil lamps placed about and set up a pile of benches and drapery at the end of the apse, with the meticulous wood working and carved images of saints and Jesus himself watching me. I set this on fire and got four others started, two more in the main sanctuary and two in outlying rooms. I opened a few doors and broke some high windows with stones for venting and went outside. I pushed a cart against a wooden vestibule that was a service entrance and threw a lit oil lamp onto the cart. I smashed a burning lamp on the old eastern side door, where the wooden staircase and ceiling rafters would catch fire and leap high.

Throwing oil lamps onto the hot spots, it took about half an hour for the fire to really get going. As the flames took hold the rioters at the Senate watched in awe as Hagia Sophia was also claimed in "their" ruin. I had already moved to be part of the awed crowd watching the great church burn, the once-darkened windows under the dome now glowing yellow and orange from within, like the angry eyes of God upon me. Then, with a dutiful moment of silence and respect paid, looters began to run into the church to steal what they could before it was all gone.

The windows glowed brighter, and I felt in me the heat that was in Hagia Sophia. Heat or the Devil, I was not sure which. I began to head off in the direction of The Mese and away from the mob, dazed and shaken. I picked up my pace, but dared not look back. I did not want to see God's fiery eyes glaring at me from the smoky night sky. Heat was escaping from my skin, my head, my nostrils, and I felt it was my soul burning. But I did not look back.

26

Cat Cornered in a Kitchen

A dozen boys were curled up in my bed like a litter of puppies. These sleeping pups – Martial, Titus, Stinky, Alexander and the others – were in part responsible for our success. Pawah had taken the lead position and was snoring in exhausted sleep on my feather pillow at the head of the bed. They were dead tired, so were my troops, about three dozen of them spread out on every chair and spare spot in my apartment, with some in the basement below.

It was early morning, dawn beginning to lighten the dark edge of the horizon. I looked at my sleeping rioters from the couch in the sitting area. I needed to plot our next moves but sat stewing in the phantom heat from Hagia Sophia. It had followed me and burned in me now. I had actually sponge bathed myself with cold water not long ago, but the heat remained. I knew what it was, and it was not going away. Nor did I want it to. I needed this fire with me on the streets in our next action – now with the divine mania from God's burning eyes augmenting my natural store.

I remembered Monaxius and Tedius asking me when I met them back at my home where I had been when they were all destroying the Senate. I lied to them, making sure to not let them see the heat in me, pretending to be very tired and needing sleep. That was only three hours ago, I think. I only slept for a few moments, too anxious to lead these worn-out soldiers around me to a safe end – including the boys in my bed, who might one day tell their children how they helped move a mob, how they stood with the Great Wilder.

No time to sleep, the strange insight that flowed into me from Hagia Sophia's flames seemed to tell me. *Feed on the energy of the streets, don't stop now.* I couldn't, didn't want to stop. *This will be a glorious day! Your day.* This would be a glorious day.

I went into the main room, stepping over my warriors, walking past sleeping Tedius and Monaxius lying almost head-to-head on the dining room floor. I was struck with their appearance, as if it were a sign with a special meaning for me alone. It was the vision, the holy wisdom. Had to be. I went into the street for a breath of fresh air, where I saw Phocas coming toward my place in a hurry – another sign!

"I have only a moment, Gaius Galen, much to do," he said. "Emperor Justinian will give more races today at two hours before midday. Your men are to be there," he offered a grin, adding, "and that Estrilda, too. Ammianus has a special gift for her and her 'lepers.' He is quite pleased." This pleased Phocas as well, and he touched his hand to his helmet in salute, then headed away quickly.

After a breakfast delivered for all of us that Tedius had arranged, we made our way to the Hippodrome, spread out and stationed much as the day before. I was in the Blue section where the 200 or so Green-Blues leaders had taken their headquarters again. I spotted a new face acting familiar with the primary leaders, who weren't returning his friendliness. I had seen him before, a commander in Quintus Cornelius Alban's private army, trying to act at home in this crowd of race fans and failing. I saw other new faces in close contact with faction leaders and fan club representatives. Senators' men and others of the aristocracy seemed eager to get sweaty with these Green Blues.

The Hippodrome was not full, with many tired from yesterday's intense action but more people suspicious of the emperor's motives. Thousands of those loitered outside to see what might happen. The emperor may have called for the races, but he wasn't there in the Kathisma. His mandator announced that the disrupted Ides races of yesterday would continue today, as "true entertainment for the worthy race fans." No mention of riots, hundreds killed, attacking the gate of the palace, or the smoking ruins of Hagia Sophia a few hundred steps to his right. A string of disorganized *Nika!* and *Green-Blues Forever!* chants quickly drowned him out. The Hippodrome was agitated. I felt it, my pulsing agitation in step with the crowd, perhaps leading it. We were one.

The eunuch Chamberlain Narses dropped the white mapa, mimicking the napkin Emperor Nero once tossed out to get the first race going when Roman fans yelled at him to cease his lunch. This Hippodrome crowd began throwing things onto my track. Tankards, pieces of broken benches, stones, clothing, food – it all impeded the charioteers, who stopped. This disruption set the crowd off, and thousands poured out of the stands onto the track. Then they headed out the north entrance, disdaining the emperor's "gift" of races and rejecting his authority with their exit.

They torched the Hippodrome's main entrance gate area and some of the attached buildings on the north side, getting a nice fire going in the bright morning sun. I took my men to go with the crowd, sending a runner to tell Monaxius to stay behind to monitor the Green-Blues plotters who stayed in the stands. I told Monaxius to order the others in our group as he saw fit, as there was no word yet from Flavius on what we should do.

The rioters had moved on to the beautiful Baths of Zeuxippus right next to the Hippodrome, where I had spent many a post-race, with a relaxing bath in the glorious museum Emperor Constantine had fitted out with the most beautiful art in the world. All around and inside the Baths were hundreds of statues amid beautiful architectural details. Inside were gorgeous bathing areas and lounging sections, with colored marble hallways and luxurious pools, accessible for a few coins by everyone in the city. It was like bathing in culture to be around such splendor and the symbols of all that is civilized, inspiring and wise.

But now the revered inhabitants were leaving. There went Homer, horizontal on the shoulders of three robbers. Four men fought over Aphrodite but abandoned her after she crashed to the ground, falling into ugly chunks. Fire was taking hold inside, setting off a rush to get a valuable old sculpture. I saw the Spartan Lysander riding off in an ox cart with Cupid next to him. Achilles was dragged from the great entrance hall of the Baths and toppled down the front portico stairs, a team of Blues and Greens working together to defeat the marble legend and cheering their success.

The many drapes, tapestries and carpets, wooden doors, ornamentation, furniture and wooden structural support beams blazed up. Soon, no more famous men or goddesses came out, nor did looters go back in. The heat from the fire cracked the stone and marble, and it took a while but the walls of Zeuxippus crumbled down to delighted and primal screaming. The fire had already jumped to the portico of the Augusteum. The mob splintered into destructive wings that went off in different directions to destroy something nearby, then they swarmed together again to throw fuel onto the Augusteum fire, heaving in benches, doors, carts, apparently intent on burning the very idea of the old forum. I wanted to throw things onto that big fire myself – for old times and this new one.

Everyone wanted to destroy – and many did. Some people are ready to riot when they see one other person acting up, like throwing a rock at a prefect policeman. Others are slower to act, drawn to toss a stone only after five or six other people around them are doing so. Some need to see a street full of people doing it before they join. Almost everyone has that point where the attraction of anarchy overpowers the sense of responsibility, and core values evaporate.

I already had a foot in anarchy before I set one in the street today, but I couldn't destroy right now. My power was to lead others. I was on the verge of thinking I was the only one who could truly see what was going on, the only one who knew. I could see them, the plotting in the stands, the senators' men. I couldn't quite see where it was all going, but I knew I would soon enough. And it was thrilling to feel it happening in the Hippodrome and in me. At that moment, I knew I was succumbing to the pull, tensing and tightening like a mob knowing that it's about to go off in destructive abandon. Overtaken by self-certainty, all restraint seemed to be fleeing from me. It was right and it was good.

I took 12 of my men, sent the others away to Monaxius, and we struck out on a side street, heading away from the rioting around the Augusteum.

"Why are we leaving?" asked one of my men, looking around in confusion. "Nothing is happening over here."

"You can't see them, but the signs lead us onward!"

"Gaius Galen, I see no signs," said the doubter and he stopped; the other 11 did also. For an instant, I had a doubt. It passed, and I crossed the line, the transition completed with my stepping forward.

"Of course you don't. But don't worry, follow me." They did. I had to be careful, they were reluctant. I still saw the signs – or did I just sense them? No matter, I knew they led us further away from the Hippodrome. I kept us in the shadows when possible and moved us along quickly, now down a narrow quiet lane full of cheap goods for sale. I stopped us to admire a gray fur hat, bought it and presented it to our boy runner, as if I had given him a solid gold crown. The old woman seller, teeth having abandoned her mouth long ago, smiled slyly at me, eying my train of men and nodding her approval. She knew, I sensed. She knew, and I gave her a conspirator's smile.

We continued to switch from one lane, alley and street to another, wherever my instincts pointed me, even if they sometimes pointed me in two directions at once. I chose one, because it must be the way, the way around the mob, around the Hippodrome and to a secret passage into the palace. If I could just kill the emperor myself, this would all end. Ammianus would be irrelevant! Annia, Martha and Elissa would be safe!

In that instant, something happened, my thoughts all left me at once. A sheet of time was ripped away.

Tedius was looking at me, smiling meekly, offering me his hand to get up. I was lying down, my head against a wall. My dozen men were huddled together, looking at me from across the narrow street. "You've been gone from us for a while," said Tedius.

I jumped up so fast it startled him and the others. "Come on men, we've an emperor to dethrone."

Tedius' surprisingly strong grip stopped me. "Gaius Galen, the Green-Blues leaders called for Emperor Justinian to throw Eudae-mon, John of Cappadocia and Tribonian out of their posts and ap-point new men of the Green-Blues approval."

"Folly!" I shouted. "They've overplayed. I must get to them and show them –"

" – the emperor has accepted and promises new ministers," said Tedius, his grip leaving my arm and his arm coming tight around my shoulder. Down the street coming at a brisk trot was Monaxius. Good.

"Friend Monaxius!" I called out. "Come quickly."

He ran and stopped in front of me. He looked into my eyes, then looked at Tedius. The two were conspiring against me! I needed to get to my dagger, but when I inched my hand up to get it, Tedius beat me to it, pulled it out and threw it over to my men. Monaxius had gotten behind me somehow and grabbed me tight at the waist.

Memory fails, but I have visions of some things.

Threatening to kill Tedius with my right index finger.

My 12 men coming at me with arms extended as if cornering a cat in a kitchen.

Tedius lunging, and me poking his cheek with my finger, then closing my eyes and crying.

Monaxius saying I would feel better with the rope tied around my hands.

Tedius' dead hand patting my shoulder.

27

Kicked by a Donkey

I had been kicked senseless, hours ago, maybe days. I remembered that dead Tedius was strong and willful as he and three monks held me down while Monaxius tried to jab a spoon into my mouth, once or twice succeeding. Then I heard the tiny squeal of a rat's flea, an unwavering note carried for an eternity. A black roundish object trimmed by dying embers was the vision that occupied my mind for some time. It was a hoof print … from a donkey's kick.

I have waved off water, wafers, dried fruit, ale, conversation, eye contact – for how long I was not sure. I was in my bed, I think. Once I wondered, out loud apparently, where my pups were. A voice said that was a good sign.

Later I was sucking on a cloth dipped in barely broth, and it tasted sublime. I was lying down (it was my bed, I recognized its solace) and I was listening to what had happened to me, their version. Monaxius was telling someone this was the first manic attack I had had in some time – since the last days of our former rioting. The someone suggested that the rioting and the pressure on me to guide a mob while protecting others from harm had overheated my four humors all at once, causing my mind to separate from reality.

Sounded plausible to me. I also thought that the anguish of burning down a holy place was a considerable contributing factor. I did not say that. Monaxius explained to the someone that in our younger days, my bouts of mania were not frequent but always entertaining, with me wound up to being all controlling and sure I had special powers. That was familiar. The cloth of barely broth was removed from my hand and a warm towel was laid over my closed eyes. I drifted off amid low talking.

The towel was removed from my eyes, where it had been undisturbed for hours, but that was only a guess. Tedius loomed over me holding the towel and a worried look not covered by his false smile. Monaxius sat on the other side of the bed. The light was low. I asked what time it was.

"An hour past midnight, Master."

"So, I did not kill you, Tedius?" I asked, my first words since thinking I had.

"You tried, but your finger was not lethal," and he gave me a real smile then, at my foolishness. That was fair. "How are you feeling?"

I wanted to avoid those loaded words and asked, "More barley broth?" A fresh cloth was dipped and handed over. "Did the Hippodrome burn down?"

"You remember," said Monaxius, brightening.

"Some. Only some."

"It did not burn down, only a small part of the exterior," said Monaxius. He paused then asked, "Can you comprehend what I say?" I shook my head *yes*.

"How many men did you set out with from the Hippodrome this morning, Gaius Galen?"

"A test?" I asked. "Very well, 12 men. Was it *this* morning?"

"Yes, it was."

"Feels like last month. Continue – if I have passed the test," I said, looking over to Monaxius, giving him a slow wink.

Much happened since I was last cognizant.

I was out of control leading my men in circles, following imaginary signs and God knows what twisted logic. The men sent our runner to find Tedius after I pulled my sword on one of them. Later, after Tedius arrived and I failed to kill him, they restrained me. At one point I was tied to a pole like a dead deer and carried through the streets. Once back home, they administered the Donkey Kick potion, but not without a struggle and me nearly tearing off the ear of one of Zazo's monks. That was just about 10 hours ago.

"How do you feel," Tedius asked again.

"Nothing, I feel like nothing," I said after thinking about it for a moment. I was emotionally flat and may as well have been the bed sheet that covered me. But there was a desire in me to be normal. "Tell me of events, Tedius. What have I missed?"

Much. While I wandered all powerful and stupid, the Blues and Greens in the Hippodrome demanded of the absent emperor that he replace three of his ministers: Eudaemon the Prefect, Praetorian Prefect John of Cappadocia and Tribonian, the Quaestor and compiler of the great Law Code of Justinian, also Chrysanthos' employer. Eudaemon was a natural choice, as he started the whole thing with his executions – particularly the botched one making Ovidius and Nikias potent symbols in our control. John of Cappadocia was roundly hated by city and country dwellers alike for being an overly efficient tax collector, though he was a raucous supporter of the Greens and something of an uncouth lout. Race fans cared nothing about laws, but senators and nobles being pinched by the changes these brought about did. As a jurist, Tribonian was said to sell judgment to the highest bidder. And like John of Cappadocia, he was considered one of the most important ministers who had Justinian's ear, making him a popular foil for onerous policies.

Every emperor in recent memory had acquiesced to this type of demand. And Justinian had today, very quickly. He was bent on consolidating power, pulling all patronage under his wing, and stripping the old families of their wealth and civic function. Like other recent emperors, Justinian would like to neuter the factions, the fans, the whole combustible cauldron of the sport. For the emperor, it was a tangled, volatile position. Now for their own benefit, non-racing influences were clearly trying to push the factions and partisans, who pushed the mob, and you never knew where that might go.

"Justinian accepted the demand and said he would do what his people wanted," said Monaxius. "But what they wanted was him. The rioting paused long enough for the streets to celebrate winning these concessions from the emperor, but they only paused. Only recently have they died down, exhausted and needing to rest. Tomorrow will be just as bad. The imperial Scholarian and Excubitor guards are said to be in a state of split loyalty, and are not being sent into the street at all. We hear that they are waiting to see which side will break first and then make their move."

I pulled myself up to lean against the headboard and reached for the cup of broth, sipping at it. "What else," I asked. "Tedius' Adam's apple is jumping around – what else?"

"We've failed in three of the four efforts Flavius has ordered us to carry out today and tonight," said Tedius.

They related that only Zazo and Jacob were successful in a last-minute deflection away from a Rhodes shipping concern. Bargas' troupe and Lukos' failed to move a section of a flowing mob toward the warehouse owned by an old aristocratic family, as ordered, and our men were lucky to escape with most of their lives. Tedius tried to move a crowd of some 400 or so Blues against a popular tavern. He thought this was a personal grudge move by Ammianus of no strategic value. The crowd chased Tedius and his men for several blocks. Monaxius, too, lost one, failing to protect a consortium of blacksmiths in the metal working district. Men were lost in all these, mostly to desertion but several wounded and killed.

"Flavius has been here twice, as has Phocas," said Tedius. "We kept them away, saying you were out rounding up replacements and rallying your troops."

"In Phocas' last visit," said Monaxius, his face cold, "he related that Ammianus will give us until tomorrow to produce you and success, or he'd fetch Annia and my daughters to keep him company. He knows where we moved them to. I am prepared to lead the men tomorrow, perhaps you will be ready to join in by afternoon."

I protested that I was ready right now, bringing a weak laugh from Monaxius.

"We have more medicine for you, Gaius Galen," Tedius said, a thin smile barely creasing his lips.

"Better not be more Donkey Kick," I said as he left the bedroom. "I am flattened from crown to toe already."

In a few moments the door opened, but it wasn't Tedius – it was Messalina! She floated toward me in a white gown with crimson belt, her *Do you want me?* look beaming like a dream. Her hips exaggerated her slow steps toward me and she put her finger to her lips, the same red as her belt.

In the longest moment of my life, she turned slightly and lowered herself to sit on my bed, backing snug against my thigh. She leaned into me, her look teasing me until it became her kiss, two feathery light ones on my cheek, her tensed breath promising more.

"I am your medicine, Gaius," she pulled back slightly. "But the dose must be carefully regulated," her mouth partly open came to mine and the dose was a full kiss, spiritual, beyond passion, igniting my moribund soul. I held her, she moved her kiss to my cheek, my eyes, my chin, back to my open mouth. I laughed gently as she nipped at my lips, then up to my ear. She finally ended it, leaving me to lean my head back on the pillows, feeling rather cured already.

"Yes, the dose is *all* important," came not from Messalina but from the direction of the door. "All important, I have learned," continued Sister Flacilla, following the path my white angel had just blazed to my bed. "We will, of course, carefully regulate the dose of your medicine, Gaius Galen."

Messalina suppressed a laugh as she rose from my bed, Sister Flacilla taking her place – but no bottom snugged against my thigh, no breasts leaning into my chest for a kiss.

Her hand went to my forehead, and she peered into my eyes. "Bring me my case, child. I think I left it on the big table."

Messalina went to get it. Sister brought the oil lamp to my ear to get a better view inside, then she pinched my ear lobe with sharp fingernails.

"Oww!"

"Good, it hurts. Stick out your tongue – my goodness, you're wearing almost all of her lip color. Stick it out, stick it out." Flacilla examined my tongue, then took my hands in hers and squeezed them like

I was her beloved son, a pleasant thought that warmed me.

"My bag is in the carriage, it will take her a moment to go get it," she said, her eyes dancing, her face sly and knowing. "You love her, Gaius Galen, don't you?"

"Yes. Completely."

"How could you not? She adores you, has been sick with worry since these friends of yours," she nodded to Tedius and Monaxius, "told us of your predicament." She put her fingers to the sides of my throat and felt for my humors throbbing along.

"Descent, also more accurately called Donkey Kick, is what you took," she said, a quick glare to Tedius, "rather, that's what they forced into you." I silently agreed as she examined inside my mouth. "My word, did they stab it into you with a knife? The important thing is to get it out of you. Eunuch fools, no wonder half the court is always sick. Tedius, this man is to drink as much water as possible. After three hours, you can begin to add weak wine."

Messalina returned with a tattered leather bag.

"Give me the pearl balm, Dear, and come assist," Flacilla instructed. She dabbed a greasy substance onto her index fingertips and began to massage this into my temples. It burned pleasantly.

"Messalina is what you need, Gaius Galen," Sister said. "We have discussed it this evening at our temporary home during this rioting: Scorpus' estate away from these destroyers – yourself included." Her touch lightened even as she scolded.

"Scorpus?" I looked quickly at Messalina. "Staying with Scorpus? Can you trust that man with your waywards?"

"Quiet," Sister Flacilla snapped. "He's a gentleman, a kitten really, and a fine host. Do you want your mob to pull Messalina out into the street? We are much safer in the suburbs across the Golden Horn – with Scorpus."

I leaned into her circling touch, nodding agreement. Sister rose and indicated Messalina take her place. "You two can hold each other, you both need it – just holding."

Messalina demurely sat down and nestled into my arms.

Sister Flacilla looked around the room, moving to the lounge in the sitting area. "Tonight, I will stay here, we will stay here," she pronounced. "Messalina at your side the rest of the night will do you wonders, Gaius Galen. In the morning we will travel back with the 10 riders Scorpus has sent with us."

My mind considered quiet sex in the dark, but Sister was there first.

"There will be nothing sexual, if indeed your crushed psyche could muster such in your weakened state. Messalina will allow only hugging and kissing, and not too much of that."

She stepped closer to the other side of the bed and pushed down on it a couple of times.

"Oh yes, I could sleep on this bed with you fine – and I will if you show any sign of not behaving, Gaius Galen. Messalina, I trust completely." At this Messalina gave my side a pinch. Flacilla saw me flinch.

"Gaius Galen, this is medicine, even that pinch. I will observe you and give you potions and balms, like the powdered pearl cream to coax your thoughts back to order," she said. "Messalina is love for you, the physical and emotional embodiment of love. And there is no stronger medicine than that. This is medicine we bring to your scattered brain. We are here to pull it together, so you can save that man's family, that man's wife, Messalina's sister and her own chance at happiness. And that will take a strong man, a sharp man, which you are not at the moment."

She pulled pins out of her hair and it fell as a gray-white curtain over her shoulders, a signal that she was comfortable with me, a step of intimacy she must have thought I needed. Flacilla was a beautiful woman and perhaps my Godsend. She laid down on the lounge and pulled a knitted cover over her.

"I sleep with both eyes open, just ask my girls. Tedius, bring the pitcher of water. Monaxius, leave just one candle lit. Awaken us before dawn," ordered Flacilla, though with a bedtime sweetness to her commands. "And see to it that Scorpus' men are well settled and fed."

"Already done, our Sister," said Tedius. "I am eternally grateful for your help, eternally," and he nodded to Flacilla, then to Messalina and gave me a big grin.

"Gaius Galen, get under your covers," said Flacilla, closing her eyes. "Messalina, on top of the covers. Tedius, a blanket for her."

I didn't hear another word from Sister Flacilla the rest of the night. In the spirit of her mission, I only held Messalina, with a few kisses. It was what I needed, what I wanted to have from here on. But later in the night, Messalina's softness backed into me, her sleeping breaths a whispered pace, my spirits did rise. Quite well. And when I could finally get them to pass and I began to drift off, I felt healthy, a young man with a beautiful woman in his bed, my one thought as I fell asleep.

28

Belisarius Attacks

I awoke alone. Sister Flacilla was not on the lounge, and Messalina was gone from my bed. Had I dreamt those visitors, my medicine? I was beginning to worry when the door crashed open and five or six of my pups ran in, jumping on the bed and me.

"Come quickly, Gaius Galen!" said Stinky with urgent tugging. "The Sister is flaying a eunuch at your table!"

Pawah threw me a robe and they led me into my dining room, where several of our men were standing against the wall laughing as Sister Flacilla at my dining table was pouring out the bottle of Donkey Kick into a house plant. Herulian was across from her with a pained look, Agrippa standing behind his chair. Messalina came up from behind to kiss my cheek and handed me hot water and raw vinegar sweetened with her, "Good morning, Gaius."

Herulian stood and greeted me, Agrippa threw a salute.

"Here he is, alive and looking much better," said Sister Flacilla, shaking the last drops of Herulian's medicine into the potted plant. "No thanks to you eunuchs. Poppy poison? For a manic episode? Do you overkill so with all your potions, Herulian?"

"It worked. Look, he is standing, smiling even – at your ridiculous show," he said with a smile.

"We sent for this man-thing last night, Gaius Galen," she said. "He's not so bad a physician, I suppose. We all have our different approaches."

"Yes, one being to call yourself a physician when you are no such thing," said Herulian. "But we really don't have the time for this banter, do we, sister-thing."

"No," said Flacilla, nodding approval at his rejoinder. "We are both busy things. We've been discussing events with these court eunuchs, Gaius Galen, and we've been discussing you. And we have a simple question."

"I am ready," I said, "if that's the question." She nodded it was. I put my cup of posca down on the table and said, "Your two medicines, the Donkey Kick and the angelic caresses of Messalina, have me on my feet and as foolish as ever."

"There will be a relapse, surely," said Herulian, and Sister agreed.

"And I will handle that, with the help of all of you," I said looking around at my runner boys, my best friends Monaxius and Tedius, my crazy monks, wounded actors, eunuchs, Green thugs, saintly Sister, and my Messalina. "All of us."

They all smiled, happy to see me back from my departure with reality.

"Now, what have *we* been discussing as I slept off the kick?"

Herulian related the mood in the palace. Justinian and Theodora had gathered among them senators and noblemen, ostensibly as council, but Herulian was not so sure. The two nephews of former Emperor Anastasius, Hypatius and Pompeius, were there. Their cousin Probus, also a senator and nephew of Anastasius, was not. Monaxius pointed out that these three were the most likely usurpers of the throne.

"We are not sure of that," cautioned Herulian.

"The leaders of the Green-Blues are," said Lukos. "And that alone might make it so. The streets are ready to explode again. They believe, really believe that they can rise from spectator seats and rule!" Lukos said with excitement. "We can take the city and the palace with it."

"Don't forget," I broke in, "we have a job to do – and lives depend on it, lives of people we love."

"That's not a word I would have heard from you before, Wilder," Lukos said with a smirk. "But I know, I know. I am in this to the end.

But I feel the Greens and Blues can carry all, and seat ourselves in the Hippodrome *and* the Senate. And I am not the only one."

I have never seen Lukos so serious, dreaming of order and rule rather than smashing something in the street.

We ate breakfast provided again by the same baker who had served us before, a man Tedius said Flavius had insisted on engaging. After Messalina and I shared an intense and private goodbye, the women and their guards went back to Scorpus' estate in the Sycae suburbs, and Herulian went back to his laboratory. Agrippa was staying with me.

"He is your aide, Gaius Galen," said Herulian. "He is also an excellent soldier. I have helped train him."

"And I imagine he is to monitor my state of mind, as well," I said.

"Sister Flacilla wanted that duty, but she would not do so well in a street fight," Herulian replied. "You are needed by your men – by the city, Gaius Galen. Should you begin to emotionally falter, Agrippa will see it and remove you from harm."

Agrippa tapped the hilt of his sword at his left side to confirm.

The lad was quite good, showing resolve and leadership within the hour when we were ordered in a message from Flavius to rush Senator Probus out of his house before a mob got there, possibly, I thought, to try to proclaim him their new emperor. Flavius' messenger gave me a note to give to Probus that explained why my group was to escort him. I considered that Ammianus' clients must think Probus was the wrong man. Twelve of us arrived on horseback, after passing close to the slow-moving mob, distracted with bouts of destruction. When Probus' doorman tried to shoo us off, Agrippa stepped forward and slapped him hard, telling the man he was an imperial eunuch in the emperor's service and would see Probus or, "I'll see you dead and then see Probus." I was impressed; so was the doorman.

Domestics helped us rouse Probus from his bed, telling him what was headed his way. When he objected, I gave him the note. Whoever it was from – and it could not have been from Flavius – he must have been a powerful person for Probus immediately agreed to come with us.

About a thousand screaming men, many already drunk at this early hour of the morning, were overwhelming streets and smashing houses and people as they moved down the hill to Probus' fine house above the Harbor of Julian. Probus was gone when they arrived. They insulted his wife and burnt down the house of the man they would have made emperor a few moments earlier.

Probus must have been a third choice because he was a monophysite, which would have made him unpopular with the majority of Christians. He was probably only chosen because Hypatius or Pompey weren't available. Rebellion of some sort was definitely the plan, however poorly realized by a thoughtless mob. The senatorial and wealthy backers, the faction professionals and the partisan ringleaders had a hot population on their hands, and if it didn't have some direction and resolution soon, it would combust the entire city, imperial loyalists and rebel alike.

We saw Probus off in a boat that Flavius had arranged. We returned to my building and corralled our horses in the courtyard, the other tenants daring not say a word. I had sent Pawah around yesterday with gifts of wine to the other tenants and my apologies for the inconveniences I had caused the past few days. We divided our forces in half, my half heading up The Mese, the other sticking near the palace and Hippodrome.

It was noon when we made it to the smoking Praetorium ruins, where four men were trying to pry off a jail cell door as a souvenir. I saw three Greens jump a Blue, steal the bag he carried and beat him up. A buzzing ticked up in my head at this, the old rivalry not quite dead yet, the buzz staying with me as we moved on. I was somewhat alarmed that the internal sound had mania behind it. But I kept that to myself: to hell with telling my young eunuch nanny.

We joined a large rumble of rioters heading west along The Mese in my old neighborhood, behind this mob were weaker scavengers, mostly men but some women picking through the wreckage of lives, homes and businesses. Up ahead a fresh billow of black smoke spoke a new fire – and it was my family home!

"All follow me tightly and run!" I yelled, and we closed together, forcing our way through the people and debris.

We crested the rise of the road a block from my house, the area in front choked with 100 or so men, cheering on the last few who braved flames to fetch valuables from inside. I recognized furnishings, silver plate and clothing heading away on men's shoulders. The front entrance way was beginning to collapse and impossible to enter now, the smarter spot for us was a block behind, at the tailor's shop and the tunnel.

Our cohesive group of about 40 men cleared a small perimeter around the tailor's shop, which was ablaze and smoking heavily from the burning cloth inside. I considered the tailor's family and his children I had played with as a child, and could only hope they had made it out.

As I stepped into the short stairwell, the secret door pushed outward from inside, and a couple of slaves I recognized flew past me up the stairs, my former wife, Fulvia, and three other women coming up behind. One was Tedius' wife, Kiya. I rushed them up to the street and told Agrippa to form protection around them. Lukos' man Paul took six others and wrested a wagon away from three men and brought it to the tailor's shop.

Fulvia was crying and babbling, the other women watching her. A few more from the household came out of the tunnel and ran through the corridor we held open to the wagon. We had 12 people in the wagon, when up from the secret tunnel came five angry rioters following those fleeing from the house. I shoved them down the stairs, stabbing at one as he fell backward. Four of Zazo's monks came to my aide and we held them back. More rioters were coming from deeper in the tunnel behind them.

"Mother, Father, Hesiod, Timasius, did they get out?!" I yelled to Fulvia.

"Your father and Hesiod were not here. Your mother and Timasius I did not see once the crowd broke through the vestibule," Fulvia said through sobs, her shoulders heaving. One of Zazo's men next to me was cut in the neck and fell. The crowd liked that and pushed in harder.

"Back men, to the wagon!" I cried. About 20 of our men flanked the wagon as it got underway, Paul's whip cracking the two draft horses on faster. An arrow thudded into his shoulder, but he went on. We all did, Agrippa and I leading a rearguard action to slow the rioters following the wagon. We felled a couple of them, and the rioters began to lose interest, falling away. We kept moving north until we cleared all disturbance.

"When did you last see Mother and Timasius?" I asked Fulvia.

"They were together with a few other servants, and Timasius was moving them toward the kitchen building. That's the last I saw of them," she said. "Can we go back to them, Gaius?"

"It's death to go back now. But it's possible they made it out." I said, wiping someone's blood from my face. I wanted to go back to throw myself into the mob and fight them all! My head was buzzing, so I focused on Fulvia and took her hand. "We may see them yet, take heart. I will get you back with Father, when we find him."

She yanked her hand away and said, "No! No! I can't. I can't do that again!"

"Fulvia, it's where you belong. It's still your family without me."

"He makes me sleep with him sometimes," she spat out, "for years now since you left. I won't live through that again." Anger hardened her eyes. "I want you to kill him – kill him for me."

Fleeing to save my life and others', my mother possibly dead in her blazing home, it is a wonder I did not collapse with this new horror. Without thinking I said, "I can't do that. I can't do one more thing. First, we save ourselves."

I called out to Paul to head to the Golden Horn, we would see these women to safety at Scorpus' house. But Paul could not drive the wagon to the wharf. The arrow was high in his chest, and he was losing much blood. I grasped his hand and praised his bravery. He managed to say that he was, "Proud to die a Green," right before he did. I helped load his body into the back of the wagon along with the fallen monk, so they could be decently buried. Two of Zazo's monks helped, and I realized they were Nikias and Ovidius, the hanged Green and Blue saved by Zazo, now under his mantle.

The wagon and an escort of 10 headed north to the Golden Horn, the rest of us went back toward the Hippodrome. One of Bargas' runners found us and said troops were now out nearby and not sniveling Scholarians but imperial army regulars under General Belisarius, Master of Soldiers in the East, likely called back from fighting the Persians. He was leading his personal troops, almost all Goths. My head buzzing, upset by deaths of my men, Mother's unknown fate and Fulvia's bad news, I stopped us, said I wanted revenge on someone, and for an instant thought Belisarius and his men would do fine.

A hand fell heavily on my arm, Agrippa's.

"Take this, Gaius Galen, breathe it into your nose," and he poured some gray powder from a small vial onto the side of his hand. "Do this now, or the mania will take you completely, and we will all die as you lead us into Belisarius' Goths."

He watched me closely and raised the powder to my nose. I hesitated – then I blew it in his face!

"I'm not your patient, I'm not taking your poison, and I'm not taking us against the Goths," I declared harshly as he coughed away the cloud of powder. "I'm your leader. Now get behind me to help or leave now."

Agrippa straightened up. "Lead, Gaius Galen. But I will try to help if you swerve. It is my charge."

He held his hand out to me. I gripped it, saying, "Now let's go *monitor* Belisarius."

It was not difficult. We moved toward the palace and into a rush of bloodied rioters, some screaming about wicked Goths. We broke into an empty inn and ran to the rooftop three stories up. Two blocks away in an open area between the portico of the silversmiths and the Hippodrome we saw General Belisarius on his grey charger rushing to the front of a disintegrating line of Goths, who held faster with him in their ranks. Other cavalrymen rode into the mob, weapons slashing. Even so, no horse and rider stayed up for long, so they rushed in then back out as fast as possible. Here in the relative open Belisarius had an advantage, and he took it, splitting his men into tight formations, wheeling them around to trap clumps of 20, 30 rioters between them, who were killed by the hardened Goths. But the mob wouldn't have it, and though men died senselessly running against a line of armored professionals, more rioters continued to run against them, sure that the numbers of the mob would triumph.

Tedius and his men joined us on the roof, then Monaxius. Soon nearly all that was left of my forces, now about 100, watched the Blue and Green rioters clash against the empire, well represented by Belisarius' Goths, a group of warriors who cared not for Blue or Green or anyone in Constantinople. They likely relished slaying the citizenry that had locked their ancestors in an Arian church a hundred years ago and killed thousands of them.

The Goths did well in the open, but were easily bested by the rioters who knew the smaller streets, alleyways, twists and dead ends of the city, where they led the aggressive Goths. We watched, almost as if in a theater, our eyes on the stage action. From this vantage point, the battle looked about as chaotic as it did at ground level being part of it. But we could see patterns of action emerge, as well as patterns of defense. As the sun faded, so did the Goths, in as orderly a retreat as could be managed. Wherever the Goths vacated, the mob filled in, cheering *Nika! Nika! Nika!* Belisarius and his men double-timed into the heavily defended side gate of the Great Palace. Though killed 10 to 1 by the soldiers, the rioters still held the ground, blood-soaked and ruined as it was. It appeared that Belisarius had only about 600 men left. In the street, such a force was disadvantaged and could be winnowed to nothing quickly.

Our respite as spectators ended as an arm of the victorious mob turned in our direction. What was before them would probably burn. We planned our evening bivouac and broke up accordingly before heading down into the streets, where darkness was delayed by the flaming city.

29

Zazo's Revenge

My mother, she might have been killed and with me so close by. Had I saved Probus to lose her? If I had come a few moments sooner, the flames would have been passable. Even earlier and I could have escorted the entire household through the tunnel to safety. Now her protection depended on Timasius, a strong tree but an old one.

And Fulvia, raped by my father, and wanting me to kill him. The thought of him going at Fulvia sickened me. More burden. I was already overwhelmed – and with the threat of mania incapacitating me when I didn't even know it. Soon everyone I was trying to protect could be dead. But I was not giving up. Wilder never did.

A few hours ago I met with Flavius, summoned to his home. He looked awful. Even his 10-year-old twins, who were up with the knock of a midnight visitor and jumping around like acrobatic monkeys, couldn't cheer him up. At least I'm not Flavius, with sons and a daughter to fear for. His news was that General Mundus, a Hun in the service of Justinian, and his rapid expedition force of the Illyrian Army were on their way. My men were to avoid all troops, monitor the Green-Blues leaders and await orders that would depend on "developments."

I left him and his jumping twins and walked for a half hour in the freezing early morning cold of January 16, further chilled by the prospect of meeting up with Atakam, though he might not be with

Mundus' troops. I held onto that prospect.

My men – and Estrilda, a true warrior and a truly sweet soul who was now the patron protector of the south palace wall squatters – were battered and tired. Half of those left were staying at my house. Some of our men were dead or wounded, more had given up. Adalwolf had rallied locals from the Gothic Quarter to our cause, most of them Blue or Green partisans. They were angry that their fellow Goths under Belisarius were killing Blues and Greens and were ready to tangle with them. These were not the stable, trained men I had lost but they would have to do. And like the others, many would likely leave after the first engagement.

I don't blame them. It's a contract with lunacy, stepping into the ferocity of the crowd, trying to move it. I would have left too, if I could. But I was feeling resigned more than anything. Physical exhaustion must wear out mania at some point.

Morning was sunny, still cold with a northwestern wind biting through thick wool into my skin. The city was quiet, very quiet. Monaxius and Tedius and their men were monitoring the Green-Blues leaders and those around them. The representatives of the nobles cautiously backing rebellion were unctuous in their attachment to these former sportsmen, who claimed they had their hand on the tiller, though no one can reliably pilot rioters. These were just now coming out of their homes after sleeping off a difficult day of wilding, yelling for hours and engaging imperial Goths. They awoke as we all had, wondering what would happen today.

Some of the guild firefighters were out, the daylight and the lethargy of the mobs encouraging them to put out some fires. We did not see any imperial troops around.

Then word came from Flavius via runner to move as fast as possible to protect a house in the wealthy neighborhood near the imperial wharves and to save the residents at all costs. We took off at a trot and increased speed, Bargas and his remnants with mine and Lukos', plus our 25 Goths. I sent runners to bring Jacob and Zazo who were patrolling near the palace.

Our destination was a group of six houses on an exclusive lane perched on a ridge, with drive entrances in front of the houses and an almost vertical drop off of 20 feet behind them. Five of the houses were already empty of people, with fighting breaking out among looters over such finery as a gold leaf foot stool and casks of expensive wine.

The sixth house, a pink marble beauty with stout outer walls, was under attack by about 70 men. One of them was Zazo – already here before us. Though hooded and with a scarf over his mouth, I could recognize his body. His men and other rioters charged against terrified servants and slaves thrown together as a fighting unit to protect the house. The crowd had dismantled the high gate at the entry drive and was everywhere but inside the house. The servants scattered before the charge, one or two dead, a few of their identically liveried fellows watching from the house's roof. The vestibule was still holding, and the house not yet breached.

I told Bargas and Lukos to start tempting people to another house under pretense of hidden riches and then ran to stop Zazo, my 10 men and Adalwolf's Goths making a decent force.

The tall brother was on his knees drawing a plan of attack in the drive's sand. About 15 of his men were hunched over looking.

"Brother Zazo," I called as I pushed into the circle around him.

"Gaius Galen, we've had God's good fortune again! Do you know who lives here?" He didn't give me a second before saying, "Anthemius, Anthemius of Tralles."

"The architect," I said. "One of the emperor's favorites."

"But more important is his guest, who I saw earlier this morning leaving the faction offices in a litter with a dozen bodyguards." Zazo was excited, and happy. "I followed him here, and I then brought these people here to welcome him – to welcome, Ammianus Dio Verus. I believe that is him peering at us right now." He turned and pointed to an upstairs window.

Zazo waved nicely to what he said was Ammianus, but I could see nothing more than the window.

"Flavius sent us to protect this place at all cost," I objected. "You need to … "

I was stopped by the widening of Zazo's smile. And in an instant, it fell into place perfectly.

"What we need to do is to fail at protecting this house," I said.

"Yes, fail. Go on." The tall one nodded, leaning toward me a bit.

"Say Ammianus dies, and the famous architect, too."

"But he won't. Anthemius has already left. He and a few personal guards rode out of here just before you came." Zazo glanced at the window then said, "I would have given him an escort. He was grateful for my leniency in letting him escape."

"Ammianus dies, and my client must show himself," I calculated. "Perhaps this whole thing will end!" I immediately thought better, out loud, "But not likely. Ammianus is only one horse of a large team, he would be replaced with another."

A crash of iron and a mighty rattle came from the entrance. They were battering the gate to the vestibule.

"Ammianus took Martha, Gaius Gallen," Zazo said, all happiness gone with this thought. "He menaces her still, and her sister and mother. You cannot be implicated in his death brought on by random rioters. That's why I am trying to hide my identity here and having my men lead the others. Monaxius' family will not be harmed."

Commotion came from the entrance. Zazo and I moved over to see Adalwolf's Goths with their backs against the gate, their swords in the faces of the crowd. They had downed two men, fallen over the dropped battering ram. They held tight like a clan of cousins, Adalwolf on the far right, Estrilda far left, snarling.

More people were pushing past us to confront the gatekeepers, and more still filling into the lane, fire from the stables at the back of the house already high enough to attract others.

"Adalwolf!" I screamed out. He looked at me, and I cut my hand back and forth across my neck, "Stand down! Stand down, Estrilda!"

They both lowered their swords at once. Their fellows began to file off behind Adalwolf. Swordsmen now gone, in an instant 30 men were on the gate, hammering at hinges, hacking at the chain and the bars, the large tree-branch ram smashing, rearing back, smashing, finally crashing through.

We moved off to the side, and I sent Pawah to tell Bargas and Lukos to stop trying to lure the rioters away and come to me. I saw Jacob and his men just entering the lane. Zazo next to me pulled the Scholarian's sword Lukos had given him from inside his robe.

"Where are you going?" I asked. But I knew.

"I'm going to make sure our friend Ammianus receives the blessings he deserves." He flicked the edge of his blade with his thumb. "You can't depend on a mob to do anything right, all that rage and excitement blinding them."

He tightened down his hood and made a stooping run into the pack, which was now cramming through the open vestibule door, the house done for. A score at least of his fellow monks in street clothes followed him in, the two hanged Green and Blue men among them. I imagined that the interior of this famous architect's house was exquisitely detailed, the layout a triumph of space, the furnishings and belongings superb and priceless – all being happily destroyed by people who only witnessed such wealthy displays from afar and found great justice in obliterating these symbols whenever possible under the cloak of riot.

Fires were appearing in all the houses on the lane. It wasn't long, maybe a quarter hour, before I saw stooped Zazo coming out from the stable entrance. He must have changed his mind and granted mercy, for his brothers had a man shackled and hooded walking between them.

"Gaius Galen, God's will is truly amazing," said Zazo. "You will be pleased, I hope."

One of his monks pulled off the hood.

"Father! You?" I looked to Zazo, "And Ammianus, is he lost?"

"No Gaius Galen. He is found, but not by his Maker, but by the Devil, I am certain."

"Is he dead? Did you kill him?"

"He is dead. I did not kill him. Others had the pleasure. He died as you might think, groveling, claiming a special bond with 'Wilder' crying and crying as they fell upon him." He looked back at the burning house. "It is a better funeral pyre than he deserves."

I looked to Father in the band of Zazo's men. His clothes were torn, his cheek was sliced slightly. His eye focused scorn on me.

"Put the hood back on him," I said, very calmly. One monk secured it, another punched Father in the stomach for good measure. I knew the hooded head groaning and cursing deserved it.

"He and his slave, who is held safely by some of my men, had with them architectural drawings of a grand domed church like Hagia Sophia, but much, much larger," said Zazo, cutting his eyes to me and away. "Something was up between these three. But whatever it was is over. My men are burning the drawings. God can build a church without this man's help," indicating Father with his thumb. "What should we do with The Elder?"

I thought to take him back into Anthemius' house and let it consume him. I thought to charge him with Mother's death and strangle him to his. Then I thought about my orders to burn Hagia Sophia, and seeing Hesiod's architectural drawings of a large dome the night I visited him in his office when Father attacked me.

"Chain him in my basement," I told Zazo. "Put Nikias and Ovidius in charge of him, and tell them to kill him if he makes a move to escape. They can entertain him with their miraculous tale."

Zazo nodded, and led his monks and Father away. The rest of us moved on as well. We learned from others in the street that Belisarius was out again, had surprised a large gathering of rioters resting in the Forum of Constantine and was running his infantry formations through them like water, hacking down hundreds. The vanguard of Mundus' men had arrived on horseback and were scattering and killing rioters. Flavius' runner came asking for a report. I took Lukos, Jacob and four of his Jews and we followed the runner back to Flavius.

He was in a well-guarded room in the basement of the Church of St. Irene, not far from Hagia Sophia's rubble. Men were coming and going, and Flavius had three secretaries keeping track of it all. His focused expression while he worked darkened the moment he saw me. He stood up straight, the left side of his mouth twitched.

"He did not survive, Flavius," I said. "Ammianus is dead."

His head dropped, then sprang up. "Did you kill him?"

"No, of course not. But we could not keep the crowd from taking the building. They had broken in just before we got there. One of our men saw him at a window in the architect's home. He did not come out, and it is blazing to heaven as we speak. In the stables we found his litter and a couple of porters, who verified his presence."

I let it sink in just a moment before announcing my point.

"Flavius, this could actually help you, but I'm sure that's not easy to see at this instant." His head dejectedly shook that it was not. "Here is what I require, or I take my 200 and we will run the mob into this church and burn all of you down in it. You know I will – I am ready to burn all the churches in Constantinople!"

"You don't need to threaten: I'll arrange it, the meeting you desire with Ammianus' superior, your client," he said, exhaling his body limp. "That's what you want, isn't it?"

"It is what I want, Flavius. I thank you, my friend."

"I may well be your dead friend," he said, "because I am not sure I will be alive after delivering this news."

Lukos, I and our five Jewish mates walked out looking around as if we might come back and burn the place down. Men in the room paused to watch us pass, some of them wore the markings of imperial officials, looking mortified to be among the likes of us street thugs in the process of overthrowing their emperor.

30

My Client Revealed

Like a good commander, I gave my men leave but just for a few hours. They were free to rest, sleep, gamble, anything but fight or loot in the streets. Ammianus was dead, Flavius was momentarily powerless and setting up the long-desired meeting with my real client. So we were free. It felt very good, if even for just a few hours.

By a generous count, we had maybe 100, including the new Goths, who had shown well at following orders, even the conflicting ones at Anthemius' house. And they were overly ready to take on Belisarius' Goths and the Herulian troops Mundus was bringing in. They hated Herules, who were former Goths at some time. Adalwolf said he could keep his men out of trouble, but I was not counting on it.

I rested for just a little on my balcony under furs and next to a nice fire, listening to the distant chaos in several quarters, watching smoke trails rise toward the late afternoon sky. After a half hour of such sweet idleness, I recalled that my father was chained to a wall in my basement! I was laughing for forgetting that pleasantness when Tedius opened the balcony door: it was time to go meet our client. My slave and protector was dressed warm, was armed and he intended to go with me.

"You'll stay here, Tedius." He shook his head that he wouldn't. "You will. I may not come back, you know that."

"Which is exactly why I must go."

"I need you and Monaxius to carry on if I am gone. We have people to protect still," I reminded him, trying to guilt him into taking over my responsibility rather than force him. "I do not know what will happen with Ammianus dead. Maybe our client will just take over Ammianus' threats to Annia and the girls, as well as all of the others Ammianus has threatened, your wife included. Our real client might kill us all anyway."

His Adam's apple wobbled. He stepped to me and gave me his hand to pull me up. "God be with you, Gaius Galen. God be with you."

I took Lukos, Jacob and eight others. Agrippa tried to come but I dismissed that, tiring of his spying eyes. We moved east toward the Hippodrome. We were meeting in Flavius' office, mere steps from mine. Maybe that was to mean something, but I was beyond trying to interpret such signals. It was all action now as far as I was concerned. And there was plenty around us. I saw buildings half burnt days before, burning again. For the past few days, the winds had often pushed the fires in the opposite direction of where the rioters had intended them to burn.

It was almost dark when we entered the stable complex. It was a wreck, having been taken over on a couple of occasions by rioters playing at chariot racing, upending the drivers' personal lounges and tearing up their baths, even though they idolized these men as heroes. An excited man's mind doesn't work well, and the minds of 500 excited men don't work at all.

We made our way to the circular curtain and entered my work area. Dirt samples were all over the floor, the neat wooden boxes smashed and overturned, a large pile of them had been burned, some remnants still had a little heat in the char. It's a wonder the building didn't go with it. The big drapery to Flavius' office was closed, and he was in front of it, along with three armed men.

"Precautions, Gaius Galen. They stay out here with me and your boys as well," said Flavius. He pulled apart an opening for me and said, "Your client awaits," sweeping his arm in for me to enter.

I stepped inside, it was well lit and immaculate, unlike how Flavius usual kept his office. Behind his desk Chrysanthos smiled at me!

Shocked, I could not move for an instant. As I gathered enough composure to nod to Chrysanthos and return his smile as if I was back at his home having dinner, I grabbed onto one thought: no matter my background with this man, no matter how I burned inside at the growing feeling of being used, no matter what he might say, to me he was the same as Ammianus. I could not let my past with Chrysanthos cloud this moment in the least. Or so I desperately hoped.

"Gaius, come. Sit with me over here," and he indicated the comfortable chairs under the high semicircular window. I made myself move in that direction. He joined me, taking my arm and guiding me to a chair. He sat opposite me. I noticed some men against the wall, then others, probably eight.

"Shall I invite my associates, too?" I asked. My head was ringing with surprise and confusion, but I had to cover.

"I can go nowhere these days without escort. I cannot even dismiss them at home," Chrysanthos said, his eyes fluttering slightly and his hand feeling for his long braid on his shoulder. He was nervous, too. "Ammianus is dead, and you finally get to meet your client."

"I doubt it."

He gave a little laugh. "You are perceptive and wise to be distrustful." He leaned forward, could have touched my knee. "I am your client, Ammianus was working for me, and Flavius is still."

I didn't say anything.

Chrysanthos' eyebrows pulled upward as he said, "If you mean that I am not the ultimate force behind these … actions, you are right. I am to your client what Ammianus was to you. Did you kill him, Gaius?"

"I have said I did not, which you should know."

"But did you kill him?"

"No. We arrived too late to protect the house and only found out afterward that he was in there."

"Yes, we have recovered what we believe is his body," said Chrysanthos, showing a bit of distaste for the detail.

There was movement against the wall to my right, and we both turned to see Jacob with a knife to one guard's throat and Lukos with a dagger pointed in the gut of another. I don't know how they snuck in, but was glad they did.

"Keep talking gentlemen," called out Jacob. "We're just getting to know one another."

"Such friends, Gaius. They respect you greatly," said Chrysanthos. "A criminal and a Jew, but they must be handy in a brawl."

"I find them more honorable than eunuchs, as a rule. Lukos, Jacob, leave your friends and join us," I said, turning to Chrysanthos in deference to him as host of this meeting. He nodded consent. They came to me and stood off behind and to the side.

"Speak freely in front of these men, Chrysanthos," I said, thanking the pair with a quick nod. "We'll all likely be dead before this whole affair is over."

"I hope not, Gaius. I truly hope not." His expression softened, he wanted to be honest. "The fact is that nothing has changed. I hold the same cudgel Ammianus did – the wives, the little girls, the sister, Messalina, Sister Flacilla's entire home and all the residents. And your contract is still intact."

"Chrysanthos, it is impossible that nothing has changed, as you know. Things are changing as we speak – in the streets, in the circus."

"Yes, yes. But you must stay on course, Gaius."

He leaned closer, resting his hand on my knee this time.

"Our lives depend on it. You are right, all is changing, it started when the two men failed to hang. We – my client – saw it as an opportunity to push far beyond our original objective, which you were helping with as agreed. But this breaking of a gallows beam – they reported that it had been slowly eaten to weakness from the inside by insects over years – has thrown new plans into motion. Insects, Gaius! Insects! And your Zazo, something of an insect himself, has put an empire in motion."

He leaned back into his chair, more excited than I have ever seen him.

"Insects, men, Gods, who knows which moves what," I said, standing up. "I am now most moved by a chaste prostitute. I have my father in chains. I have 200 men awaiting my orders, and our spies know how the wind will blow as well as anyone. I have a court eunuch and dear friend and mentor twisting me, using me, probably killing me. Who are we fighting for, Chrysanthos? We're not fighting for ourselves and my men and I don't care which insect is emperor."

He frowned at that and said, "I cannot tell you. And you have about 100 men, rather 99, one is a woman." He sighed and rose from his chair. I pulled back a half step.

"Then I assume your client is Quintus Cornelius Alban and other aristocrats anxious to be rid of Justinian's controlling ways," I said. "It is shocking to learn you were Ammianus' patron, but much more so to find that the honorable Chrysanthos I know would turn against his master."

"Hmmm. Would that things were so easy, Gaius." He moved over to Flavius' desk and looked up at us when he was behind it. "Assume what you want, my son. But come, come over here. I'll show you your final task."

Lukos, Jacob and I stood over the desk. Chrysanthos tapped the most beautiful painting of the Hippodrome I have ever seen, covering the whole desk. The artistry with the paint and light was magnificent. The track was run by 12 chariots, the fans were on their feet roaring – you could almost hear it and you could see some detail on tiny faces. The sixth dolphin on the spina was down so it was the final lap.

"Who will win this race, Your Excellence?" asked Jacob.

Chrysanthos chuckled at the question. "I believe this is Jacob, Jacob the Jew as he prefers. I understand he's good with an iron rod and smart as well."

"We all are," I said, "or we would all be dead by now."

"The winning driver of the race is not important. The team color is not important," said Chrysanthos. Waving his hand over the painting he added, "It's the place that is."

He reached out and put his hand on Lukos' shoulder, causing him to flinch.

"The Hippodrome is where this will end. The Hippodrome is where emperors are acclaimed, or reaffirmed, by the people. You are the people, Jacob and your friend Lukos here," he squeezed Lukos' shoulder then dropped his hand away. "Gentlemen, the Hippodrome will be your last destination."

"We will be there when you tell us to be, Chrysanthos," I said. "Ammianus was a pig. You, I used to trust with my life – up until walking in here a moment ago. Now, I'm not so sure. But with the lives of others at stake and in your hands, I will make the same leap of faith I did as a 10-year-old boy. I'm counting on your honor, and if you would do me ill, then life is not worth living I suppose."

"That's a powerful challenge, Gaius," said Chrysanthos, affected by my words. "I swear that you can trust me to do my best to protect you and those you are protecting. With great good fortune and God's blessing, we will talk about this later, in more detail and more comfortable circumstances."

I fastened my over tunic around my neck. "Let's go Jacob, Lukos. I think we can rest tonight, can we not, Chrysanthos? We need it."

"I believe you can, though I am likely to need you early in the morning," he said, and he walked with us to the drapes. "I am in your debt, Gaius Galen. Farewell."

"We will," I said, "depending on what you send us into."

- 31 -

Father in a Bind

"Put his hand on my shoulder," Lukos said as we headed home. "Why did he do that?"

"Probably because he knew it would annoy you."

"I've never touched a eunuch before, much less been touched by one," and he spit on his gloved hand to clean his shoulder.

"You should take an actual bath tonight," I said.

"It won't be in the Baths of Alexander," said Lukos.

"That whole area north of Hagia Sophia is burning," added Jacob. "Imperial buildings, private homes, the hospices of Sampson and Eubulus, the Church of St. Irene."

"St. Irene! I'm glad Flavius made it out beforehand," I said, turning to look in that direction, the evening sky like a sunset of flames.

The mobs may be crazy but not altogether stupid. They usually refrained from burning down neighborhoods in which regular people lived – those in the mob – and tended to burn public places or wealthy homes. The exodus of the well-to-do had begun early on, with the first cheer for "Blues and Greens Together!" in the Hippodrome. Many were already cozy in their summer estates along the Asian shores of the Bosphorus. However, all rumors consistently had the emperor and empress still in the Great Palace.

"Do you believe that eunuch? Do you trust him, Gaius?" Lukos asked.

237

"I believe few people, but I trust Chrysanthos – in some things. Besides, do I have a choice?"

"You can trust him but the emperor cannot? You intimated he was working for Quintus Cornelius Alban," said Jacob.

I stopped. "All I did was formally acknowledge Chrysanthos' honor. Finding out whether or not he is still loyal was not my intention, and I knew he wouldn't tell me anyway. In a way, I was asking him to honor our relationship, be loyal to me as a man. It may help save your lives, too, you Jew, you criminal."

"You've been both yourself," countered Lukos, pushing me onward. "I need wine, food and a woman."

"You'll get two of those," I said.

Once we sighted my house, our minds allowed our unnatural energy to drain, and we trudged up my stairs like over worked oxen stepping into the barn for the evening.

Tedius met me at the top step, putting a mug of warm spiced wine into my hands and warmed me further with his news.

"Your mother and Timasius are safe," he reported, grinning with the good news. "He bribed their way out by revealing a hidden strong box in the stable. They are at the house of your mother's sister in the west side of town. It should be safe there."

I felt palpable relief. "Timasius has come through. Mother is safe." I looked to Tedius and said, "Father is too."

"I stumbled upon him and the hanged pair downstairs," said Tedius. "Zazo's men told me what happened. My father has not yet turned up."

"He will, Zazo said he was alright." I turned to Lukos and Jacob and said, "Ready, men?" They were. "Tedius, where's Agrippa?"

"Out back in the kitchen, helping unload supplies. Why?" he asked.

"Come see," and the three followed me. The lad had a sack of flour on his shoulder and was carrying it into the pantry.

"Gaius Galen, I am glad to see you back, not that I was worried," he said.

"I have news for you from a friend of yours," I said, Agrippa's eyes happy for an instant – then Lukos grabbed his head in a lock and

Jacob disarmed him. Both held him by the arms and faced him to me.

"Chrysanthos sends his greetings, my young spy," I said, playfully pushing him in the chest.

"Chain him in the basement with Father," I told Tedius. "At least we have one thing dear to Chrysanthos. Might help keep him honest. Send word to Chrysanthos that we are holding Agrippa for his own safety from mad men roaming the streets."

Agrippa protested, squirmed and got slapped on the back of his head for it by Lukos, who appeared to feel much better having laid a proper hand on a eunuch. "Gaius Galen, I've only been here to help you!" Agrippa pleaded.

"And I am helping you." I patted his head. "You are much more likely to survive in my basement than you are in the street, spying on me. Away now."

Jacob shoved him forward.

"Easy Jacob," I cautioned. "He may be tough but he has a definite soft side. You can fill Agrippa in on what has just happened at Flavius' office."

Another full house, and I was liking the feeling of this odd family. We ate, drank, talked of the bizarre things, the funny things, the disquieting things we saw, and of those who had left our group, either by death, wound or wisdom. No one wanted to speak out loud of the danger, our bonds being formed against death and through the shared stupidity of sitting on this floor instead of leaving for safety.

Monaxius and Tedius had a productive day. Without question the Green-Blues were now co-opted through their leaders by disaffected nobles and senators. Quintus Cornelius Alban and his son Rufus appeared to be among them, as were other prominent men and families, most of them connected to former Emperor Anastasius, as well as others having ample reason to begrudge wrongs Justinian had done them. Faction leaders were riding high on the largess and fawning these men showered on them. They had the army of Blues and Greens, and boasted that virtually the whole population would follow these factions as loyally as they once did the emperor. I wasn't so sure.

"We've made ourselves visible and our intentions clear, and they know that Wilder's troops are in play – you're something of a phenomenon now, Gaius, not the least because Zazo is working for you," Monaxius said with a laugh. "They will be watching for you, and we have said we will be watching them, as well. So everyone is confused and anxious. But it seems set to erupt, and they'll go for the crown. The disappearance of the Scholarian and Excubitor guards has fortified them, knowing they are waiting on the strongest to rise. Mundus' troops made a late sortie and there were maybe 400 of them. More could be on the way, but for now, with Belisarius down to less than 500, that's not even a thousand men – against a city."

I gave the runner pups my bed again and took the lounge, sleeping deeply until before dawn, when a messenger from Flavius arrived. We were to escort the nephews of former Emperor Anastasius, Hypatius and his brother Pompeius, to their homes – from the Great Palace where they had been staying the past two days. His note explained that he needed street-smart fighters he knew he could count on to carry out this important task.

Before I left I went to the basement, where in one room Agrippa was chained to a bed and Father to a support column across from him. Nikias unlocked the door, kissing my hand in thanks as I passed. A little light from the cracked door showed Father's gruff face, angry even in sleep. I drizzled honey on his sleeves, on the front of his shirt, then on his nose. He woke to a slow stream of cold and sticky, made a face and jerked at his arms to try to free his chains.

"Fulvia sends her sweet love to you, old man," I said, dribbling a little more on his hair. Agrippa was leaning on an elbow watching. "Lick your breakfast from your dirty clothes – you're lucky to get any. She told me about you taking her, crying about it and hating you. She even asked me to kill you!"

I thought about kicking him hard in the throat but didn't. I calmly stepped to Agrippa and put the honey jar by him.

"Father, your plans for the great dome, the ones I saw on Hesiod's desk the last time I visited, they have burned along with Ammianus." His eyes showed surprise. "It's a shame I set fire to Hagia Sophia. Had I known it may have profited you, I wouldn't have."

He looked at me in silence, then licked his arm.

"I don't know what that woman has told you," Father said, "but she's as mad as you. As for the architectural plans, that plumb job has been rumored for about six months now, but with a re-construction date years out. And when it burnt down, everyone who'd been working on proposals rushed to Anthemius to get in at the start. Ammianus and I were in on the deal together. It may yet work out for me," he said, sneering at me as if he would triumph after all. "Thank you for expediting things – and removing a partner to split the revenue with."

Agrippa had stretched himself out and kicked Father in the knee, glaring and saying, "You are like my father – and if I could get my hands on you, I'd stuff this honey jar in your ugly mouth!"

"Oh yes, have you met Agrippa? A promising eunuch of 16, probably looks as I would have, had you had your way. Be nice to Agrippa, and he'll be nice to you."

"Not to this man, ever," Agrippa said, trying to kick Father's ankle.

The satisfaction I got from this taunting encounter was sweet but short, gone before I mounted my horse. Flavius had sent six new ones to add to the 14 we had. Twenty of us rode, the rest of our men were sprinkling out along the route to Hypatius' home, not far from Probus' near the Propontis shore. Adalwolf's Goths were hidden outside Hypatius' estate.

The two brothers and nephews of Anastasius, their two stewards and four bodyguards rode out of a gate in the south wall of the Great Palace. The two were dressed as commoners rather than senators. And they were very nervous. We waited as Flavius had instructed and 10 more horsemen with bows joined our party, wordlessly. No markings to say who they were, no exchange of glances.

On our short journey to Hypatius' home, I overheard the senators' stewards near me talking. I could not catch all they said, but they were not happy to leave the safety of the palace. Justinian had summoned the brothers there before the Ides races and there they stayed, safe and sound. Until now. These men were puzzled why the emperor would first protect these brothers, the most direct descendants of former Emperor Anastasius, then toss them out – after it was known the mobs had unsuccessfully attempted to retrieve Probus, who had disappeared before they arrived. Would this be what was in store for them, too, the stewards wondered? So did I.

Flavius was in my building's courtyard when we returned. We were to stay put and in close contact with him and each other. We received reports throughout the day from our men monitoring events. Mundus' army attempted to smoke rioters out of the Octagon plaza but the fickle wind shifted, setting ablaze the Church of St. Theodore Sphorakios and just about everything around it. The wind turned again, blowing the flames from house to house, shop to shop, the fire splitting into two burning down more homes and imperial offices. At the end of the day, the destruction was greater than that wrought by the rioters the day before – and they hooted and jeered just that at the troops, thanking them for their help.

Smoke rolled over my balcony from the burning city. My men reported utter jubilation in the streets. The forces of Belisarius and Mundus seemed reluctant to engage, not wasting men chasing rioters down side streets.

A note came from Messalina, with one from Scorpus as well. They had intended to come midday and leave Messalina with me overnight, but that turned out to be impossible with the mob, soldiers and fires. Her note was sweet and strong. She wanted to be with me in bed tonight to keep me warm, keep me strong, keep me sane, though she did not write this last one, I read it between her lines. She hoped that another night next to her might make me want that every night, as my wife. That was also not actually written, but I knew it was there.

Scorpus' note lamented that he had not yet turned even one of the wayward women. He said this unnatural failure was primarily because events were distracting, the wills of the waywards were surprisingly strong, and Sister Flacilla hovered inhumanly in three places at once.

"Your former wife, Fulvia, is safe, comfortable and quite lovely," he wrote. "Your future wife, should you still have enough brains to realize this, is the same but more lovely in every way. I will keep her safe for you. Be careful, be courageous."

I kept Messalina's note inside the cover of my pillow. My head wasn't there for more than a couple of hours.

Late in the evening Flavius sent news that our day in the Hippodrome was on us. Tomorrow we were to oppose reconciliation with Justinian and push toward acclamation of Hypatius among the Green-Blues leaders and directly to the crowd. We were to be traitors to Justinian and by extension to God who had ordained him as his representative on earth. Though I expected this to be coming, I still found it almost impossible to believe that Chrysanthos could do this.

Moments after Flavius' messenger left, criers trotted through the streets proclaiming the emperor would be in the Hippodrome to-morrow morning to speak with his people. An army of hired boys and men were making the call in the streets, plastering up declarations. The emperor was calling out the populace to meet him face-to-face to work things out.

I went back to the solitude of my cold balcony, stoked up the brazier and wondered how I could possibly live through this. The end was in sight, once more to the Hippodrome our last task. But would it be? Might there not be another – a counterattack by Justinian and his loyalists, and us sent back out into the mob? The only choice was to do it right, to acclaim Emperor Hypatius as directed. Then we would gather our due from Chrysanthos, gather up Messalina, Annia, Tedius and any others who wanted to come, and flee Constantinople. Perhaps to Britain.

After an hour of such hopefulness, I saw our baker trundling up the street in his old wagon, accompanied by four grubby horsemen, armed and surly. It was halfway between midnight and dawn, and I went down to see why the old man was already here. He showed me.

"Gaius Galen, I bring you the finest bread in the empire," and he threw open the back door of his wagon, pulled off a weathered tarp to reveal the floor covered in bags of flour. He reached in one and pulled out a handful of gold coins, already cut into quarters and eighths.

"Aye Sir, you'll have fine bread with this!" cried the baker, excited as if some were to come to him – or it already had, whether officially or lost in transit. "All from Flavius, with this message: these coins are to seed the crowd today, and make sure they know it is from Hypatius and his backers."

We had much to do, and I roused Tedius, Monaxius, Jacob and Lukos to set our strategy. I shared with them an idea that had been rolling around in my mind since we learned from Chrysanthos we had one more task in the Hippodrome. They liked it.

"Jacob, you get some men going on the coin bags – cut up into small squares every fine garment I own, every drape, bed cover, seat cover, tablecloth. I want them to look handsome. Flavius said Justinian's payouts are already going to subjects with influence and allegiances he needs to weather this. But we'll be passing out money at the track to the lowly fans who know their emperor disdains them. It will make a huge impression. Everyone needs to be on this task now and work fast."

I sent for Zazo and all his men, then got to work in the courtyard gathering materials for the processional display I had in mind. The baker loaned us his wagon, said he'd take Porphyrius' chariot in its stead if I could manage that. We removed the box that was his traveling kitchen so the wagon was an open bed. We erected on the bed a simple beam structure and swapped his oxen for two faction horses. We had it together, for the most part, as the sky began to lighten. Tedius and our men began loading it up with the colorful bags of money, covering the beam and the whole back of the wagon with canvas.

I recognized cloth from my silk sleeping shirt that had last pressed against Messalina, and grabbed three of those bags for myself. I needed a reminder of her.

32

Justinian Offers Truce

Jacob and I drove our wagon to the Hippodrome, with four of Zazo's monks in the back sitting on a bed of bagged coins covered with canvas and straw. I was admitted through the Green faction entrance, and we pulled our wagon into the staging area under the stands by the large entrance to the track. It was barely light out, but some faction employees were about; many more were not. No drivers were around and only a few grooms I recognized. But others wearing faction colors they'd probably never donned before were there trying to look busy. I figured these were imperial agents masquerading as faction men, with the intent to show this was just another day at the races. We put our wagon off to the side, where debris gathered from rioting had been piled. I left the monks with the wagon along with a runner I sent straightaway to tell Flavius to protect the wagon that had his gold in it.

Jacob and I walked around the outside of the Hippodrome. Some people were already showing up, two hours yet before the event was to begin but nothing like on a race day. No sausage vendors would be setting up today, no curse tablets hawked. The scene was somber and eerie. The Hippodrome's northern facade was badly burned, and the Baths of Zeuxippus, Hagia Sophia, and many public and private structures in sight were destroyed. The Octagon directly across from the track's north entrance was covered in blood and still some bodies, one being robbed of a ring as a final indignity. Smoke and ash cast a dismal haze, but was a welcome incense to partially cover the putrefying air from bodies still resting on the Senate steps from days earlier. This could not be a good day.

I put my arm around Jacob's shoulder for some needed connection and said, "Let's go back in. I want to see the place empty and quiet one more time. Like us, it may not be here tomorrow."

Inside, I kicked about the sand on the track, told Jacob how we sold people the honor of adding their blood and other bodily fluids to it, about how Gildo and I lorded over the Green and Blue contractors desperate to get their dirt under the hooves of famous horses and heroic drivers. Jacob showed polite interest then asked me if I was feeling alright. It was touching, in the way I had first seen him calm his daughter.

We started up the steps into the stands at the sphendone curve, Jacob turning it into a race to the top. I won and thought he probably let me. We looked west to the Walls of Theodosius, which now seemed to have been built to keep destruction from spreading out rather than keeping it from getting in. The Great Palace to our right was intact, its huge grounds with buildings and gardens encased pristine behind walls, an island of order in a sea of desolation. I pointed to the flotilla of boats coming out of the Golden Horn heading across the Bosphorus to the Asian side and safety. Full of scared families, household pets and items too valuable to leave behind, these boats dumped their cargo, then hurried back to get another load, charging an exorbitant premium for the ride.

"Why are those coming to the imperial south side?" asked Jacob, pointing to a string of vessels coming from the Asian side, not heading northwest to the mouth of the Golden Horn but straight across to the south part of the peninsula, to the imperial wharves.

"I don't know," I said. "Probably evacuating people from the palace. But look, those are low in the water coming here, while the boats leaving the imperial wharves are high in the water going to the Asian side."

"These are empty, the others are full," said Jacob, "full of supplies, probably. The emperor intends to stay, perhaps."

"Look there – and there, and in that one!" I said pointing. "See where the sun is catching a gleam in those. Could those be metal spear points the sunlight is catching, turned just so as the boat bounces? Spears. And soldiers, Jacob, soldiers! Look – someone must be repositioning his shield, the rising sun had it for an instant!"

My mind was churning, and I didn't think it was with manic imaginings. If they were soldiers, they were reinforcing the Great Palace, not attacking it, because there was no sign of skirmish at the wharves. Reinforcements would not be unusual. But how many, for how long? The line of boats coming to the imperial docks was not being followed by others. Was this the last detachment due to daybreak? And possible discovery?

"Jacob, get down there. You're a sailmaker, you have to have someone you know who can get you in. Find out what you can," I said, digging into a heavy inner pocket and fishing out my three nightshirt bags of coins. "Take these, find out if it is soldiers arriving. And come back to me as soon as possible!"

"Gaius Galen, it will take some time to get there, find out what you ask without being killed and return," Jacob said, nervously gripping his hickory rod.

"So be it, but hurry Jacob, hurry!"

He took the coins and took off from our perch, flying down the big steps.

I passed a fretful two hours before the Hippodrome began filling up slowly, partly due to apprehension and partly to show disdain for the emperor's orders. Tedius, Monaxius and Lukos worked their contacts and confirmed that a play for the throne was indeed in the works. The plan of the Green-Blues leaders was to see what Justinian would say, gauge the crowd's reaction and push for Hypatius if it looked promising.

"They're already maneuvering to claim ministries, prefectures, military offices," said Monaxius. "And it is the weakness of Justinian's military that has them most encouraged – calculations of less than a thousand soldiers between Belisarius and Mundus, the palace Scholarians and Excubitors still sitting on their swords. Quintus

Cornelius' man is acting like these spoils are his to grant."

"And that's not sitting well with many of the neighborhood Color bosses and professional faction men," said Lukos. "If this marriage takes place, it may not last."

I hesitated to tell them, but they had to know.

"The less-than-a-thousand soldiers may be more," I said. "Jacob and I saw what looked like soldiers in boats just after dawn crossing from the Asian side to the palace wharves. Jacob's gone to see what he can find out."

"Probably just some late reinforcements," said Lukos. "The Green-Blues are expecting some of that. Rumors of an Imperial Council meeting last night say that Justinian was ready to flee, but Empress Theodora shamed him into staying, saying her purple robe would make a fine binding sheet for her burial if it came to that."

"They may be determined to fight. But we need to know what Jacob finds out," I said. "It could change our tactics."

We set up our men as before, mostly in the Blue and Green sections where we could monitor the hardcore elements and claquers, who might join or might resist, depending most likely on who had paid them best. Zazo and I positioned ourselves at the track staging entrance. Odd for the Hippodrome to be so quiet, more like the prelude to a church service than a chariot race – or rebellion. Men sat on their hands to keep them warm and to wait and see before committing.

A trumpeted fanfare drew our attention to the Kathisma, where the white-uniformed Excubitors were finally stepping out to show themselves. The fanfare continued as the imperial entourage was on its way across the walkway from the Great Palace, Justinian, Empress Theodora, Chamberlain Narses and other officials. A squad of Scholarian guards brought up the rear, their late presence now drawing laughter and ridicule.

The stands began to chatter, and many hands lifted to point to heaven, a sign that they were loyal to His chosen ruler, Justinian. But more pointed at the man, accusing, jabbing, poking as if into his eyes across the way. A moderate force of Belisarius' Goths appeared outside the north entrance, looking like they did not want to enter, hoping the emperor could quell the disturbance.

The mandator took to his rostrum when the imperial party was seated. A good number hailed the emperor as usual: "Thrice August, most honored Justinian, protector of the Empire, protector of the orthodox, protector of us all!"

These were shouted down by what was shaping up to be a clear majority of angry dissenters. Some of the loyal chanters were pulled down and beaten into silence.

The mandator pointed to the beatings taking place, saying, "So there, and over there, here and there continues the bedlam that is destroying our great city." He paused, and I expected a lengthy speech, but he surprised us all. "Your Emperor, the beneficent Justinian!"

Justinian took the mandator's rostrum and watched as the sections hushed until quiet.

"Zazo, get the men and bring the wagon here but keep it covered!" I urged, sure that the moment was very close.

Justinian picked up a jeweled Bible from the rostrum and held it in both hands at his waist.

"I offer you our Holy word that your grievances are heard," he called out, pausing as the sub-mandators and claquers relayed his words, the stands quiet and still.

"I will redress those grievances," he said, then raised his voice louder. "I will comply with your demands and there will be amnesty for all!"

Justinian's words spread around the stands. Cheers rose up, then grumbling, more cheers, then calls of *Nooo!* Justinian raised the Bible high and level to his forehead, and he touched it to the crown he was wearing.

"I wear my crown because I am your Emperor. Emperor Anastasius once offered you his in this very spot, and you would not take it." As this was relayed around in the stands, cries in support and cries against clashed, the balance shifting.

"I give not my crown, but Holy Justice!" Justinian said with force, and he lifted the Bible over his crown. "I give you my word that no man will be punished and that all are forgiven!" He shook the Bible, arms stiff and locked in place. Inflexible.

"*And Who Will Forgive You?!*" came from the Blue section, a timed chant of at least 200 that Bargas lifted up, with Adalwolf helping him lead it on. "*And Who Will Forgive You?*" roared three times louder as others picked it up.

"*You Perjure Yourself!*" rang from another section, and not from one of my men. Another prepared line simultaneously called out. "*You Perjure Yourself!*" again.

Zazo had the wagon pulled up to the track's entrance just steps behind me, as I stood out at the track's edge watching the emperor.

A group of some 200 standing together in the Green section pointed their fingers to heaven, a show of support for Justinian. A crackling of cheers broke out, until men attacked the 200 pulling their hands down. Hundreds of others piled on the group of heaven pointers.

I grabbed the bridle of the left horse ready to lead the wagon out onto the track. No one was sitting, I glanced up and saw Excubitors around the Kathisma cross lances and tighten their formation. The crowd hissed, some throwing objects at the Excubitors in the imperial box.

"Now Zazo!" I yelled as I began leading the horses out.

Zazo pulled his hood off, his coiled hair springing out. From everywhere came cries like, "It's Brother Zazo!" "Zazo The Holy Uniter!"

I looked up from my vantage between the horses to see Zazo standing taller than life, nodding acknowledgment to the crowd. I looked to the Kathisma and saw that Emperor Justinian – like everyone else – had his eyes on Zazo.

He turned and yanked off the cloth over the wagon revealing a replica of the broken gallows, with a beam angling down from a high support to the wagon's floor, Nikias and Ovidius standing beside it with nooses around their necks. The circus erupted, men leaping for joy, screaming – and touched to see these miracle men who had not been seen since the gallows broke at the Praetorium annex. At a nod from Zazo, Nikias and Ovidius threw their nooses toward Justinian and pointed at him, indicating he was the one who should be hanged.

Cries of *"Green and Blue Forever! Green and Blue Forever!"* rose up, coming together as one. Even the earlier loyalists joined in, realizing that not doing so might be their end.

"Green and Blue Forever! Green and Blue Forever!" The force of the voices seemed to clear the air of smoke. It may have gone on all day, but Zazo held up his long arms, eventually silencing the entire Hippodrome. All eyes were fixed on the tall brother, who at that moment appeared to command more authority than his emperor looking down on him.

"Blues, Greens, Reds and Whites – All Men of God," cried out Zazo, his voice superhumanly loud and carrying over all. He turned and swept his right arm toward Nikias and Ovidius, then said, "These Are the Very Men – Hanged Yet Alive!" Zazo patted his outstretched hands downward to quiet the crowd.

He looked at the hanged men, arms still out. He looked at the opposite side to the Green-Blues area, then he turned to the Kathisma, which was emptying fast, the imperial couple moving inside a phalanx of Scholarians toward the palace. *"Blues And Greens, Men of God!"* boomed Zazo. *"Long Live Hypatius! Long Live Hypatius!"*

Led by our men, with Blue and Green claquers jumping in, the crowd picked up *"Long Live Hypatius! Long Live Hypatius!"* Zazo got the horses going, wrong way around the track for a race, with four of his monks hopping on the wagon with the hanged men, and they all began throwing out colorful bags of money into the stands yelling, *"Long Live Hypatius! Long Live Hypatius!"* Hypatius may as well have been in the wagon tossing out the bribes.

Men were already clawing at the Kathisma, pulling down hanging drapes and imperial banners, climbing on top of one another to get a piece of the shutters or of anything. Belisarius' troops at the Hippodrome front entrance were already in retreat. Money bags flew from the wagon, then groups of our men began to throw them down into the stands from the top rows, with shouts of *"Long Live Hypatius! Long Live Hypatius!"*

Men had jumped the track and were climbing into the spina, running gleefully like children in a first snowfall. And the pretty little bags of money fell out of the sky, thrown by our men walking the top rows, more tossed up from the wagon and from 10 of our other men on horseback dispensing money bags around the track – always with the cry of *"Long Live Hypatius!"* We had to dump the bags fast to prevent being mauled.

A new cheer started from the area of the Green-Blues leaders, claquers quickly getting it in one rhythm: *"To Hypatius, To Hypatius – With a Crown!" "To Hypatius, To Hypatius – With a Crown!"*

Those leading the chant jumped onto the track and headed toward the north exit. Most of the others in the Hippodrome began to flow out, to Hypatius' house not far away. Bargas, Adalwolf, Lukos, Monaxius, Tedius, and all their men and Jacob's came together at Zazo's wagon. A stream of people came by to thank him, asking his blessing, touching his foot as they went out to find a new emperor.

"We've done it, Wilder! We've done it!" cried out Lukos, he and his boys dancing, horsing around, throwing money bags at each other.

"Nothing is done, it is only started," I said, feeling certain of my control and not due to manic delusion. "Go with the crowd – Zazo, be conspicuous, everyone else, don't be. Monaxius and Lukos, stay with the Green-Blues leaders and their backers; dog them, remind them that it was you – us – who rolled out Zazo, the hanged men and the money. Tell them to keep pushing, keep pushing Greens and Blues together. I will stay here with a few men and some runners. You should all be coming back here with Hypatius soon."

"Are you waiting here for Jacob?" asked Monaxius.

"Yes. But keep me in touch if anything starts happening," I told them. "You've done extraordinarily well, all of you. But we will lose all if we lose our focus now. Go quickly!"

They ran off like proper traitors, howling for Hypatius.

33

Purple Birds of Prey

I went up into the stands to watch the mob make its way to Hypatius' house. After they spent a few moments there, apparently with Hypatius in hand, the crowd had headed uphill, turned eastward on The Mese and came to a halt in the Forum of Constantine. No troops had tried to stop them – not a sortie of Belisarius' Goths or Mundus' Herules to even harass them. I had seen no movement from the palace. Some men were beginning to enter the Hippodrome ahead of the stalled mob with Hypatius.

"Gaius Galen! Down here. Help!" Jacob was kneeling on the track below, clutching his side. I ran down the circus steps, almost twisting my ankle once, but my sturdy boots with the Green chariot wheels kept it from turning.

Our runner Titus was with Jacob by the time I made it down, trying to get Jacob to drink some water, but he turned his mouth away. He was bleeding from his side.

"Stabbed, on my way here," he got out, breathing very hard.

"By imperial troops?"

He tried to laugh but pain wouldn't let him and said, "Drunken Greens, three of them. They got your money – I didn't have to spend any at the wharf."

I took the water from Titus, and Jacob cooperated with me to drink some. Men continued to arrive, many on the track around us.

"What about the boats?" I asked.

"You were right, Gaius. Full of soldiers!" he wheezed out, then gasped when I felt at his side, wet with blood. "Mundus, most of his men came across over the last three days, in the boats – " He winced as I cleaned at the stab wound with my sleeve and water. "Thousands crossed, only at night, all night."

"Thousands, Jacob?"

"Yes," he huffed for breath, "a linesman on the wharf guessed two thousand, maybe more. He said they'd been coming across in boats for three nights at least. Once the arrivals began, no one working there was allowed to leave."

It suddenly became very important for me to pour an exact amount of the water in Jacob's mouth and I held his head to do so, saying, "This will fix everything – if I don't spill any …" and I focused on the dribble of water about to come out of the skin.

As I poured a gentle stream of water into his open mouth, I realized my intent focus on this simple act – with all that was happening around me I had to deal with – was the mania trying to detach me from reality again. I violently shook my head to fend that off, water splattering across Jacob's face.

He gave me an odd look, as if he might have known, then asked, "What's happened since I left?"

"Justinian offered forgiveness and reform, but they rejected him. Hypatius, they went to get Hypatius and are now returning." I shook my head again to make the mania stay away.

"So, only a few troops in the streets," I said, thinking out loud. "But two thousand or more Illyrian Army regulars in the bowels of the Great Palace."

"Yes," said Jacob, looking closely at my face, gauging that I was in control. "A trap is surely about to be sprung. Here."

"Then Chrysanthos *was* loyal to the emperor," I said. "All along. Justinian hiding the troops, holding them back."

"Until the Greens and Blues are together," Jacob finished, "cramming themselves into this bowl."

I rose from kneeling by Jacob, the rebels already flowing onto the track. "Titus, take him out of here as fast as possible. Get him help in the nearest church – the one just east of here. Both of you stay in there. Do not come out until the Hippodrome and the streets are quiet."

"But I need to stay with you, to help," Jacob said, getting up with Titus' help.

"No, I order you to do as I say, Jacob. Your daughter needs you. I know your good intentions, and mine now is to get every one of us away from here. Now let's go!"

I helped Titus get him outside, and they moved off toward the church. I saw Estrilda approaching the south gate with more than a hundred beggars.

"Take them back!" I called out. "Take them away, Estrilda! You're in danger!"

"Why, Gaius Galen? We are here to help – they want to help the new emperor."

"It's a trap. Troops hidden in the palace. A trap!"

"I go to Adalwolf inside!" she said, frantic.

I saw her tell the beggars to leave before I ducked into the Green faction entrance and ran to the track. It was almost covered in people now, tens of thousands on the track like it was a big party. Several wagons stacked with wine barrels were up against the spina, lines of men flowing past and filling cups, goblets, cupped hands, mouths, the spilled wine looking like blood in my track mix. The stands were not half full, most of the people were on the track, and more were coming in through the north entrance.

Up in the Kathisma, Hypatius wore a crown improvised from gold chains. Guards were around him, made up mostly of Blue and Green faction men and groups of private troops, including Quintus Cornelius Alban's. A man nearby called out to no one in particular, "Emperor Justinian has flown away – taken a ship already loaded with gold. It's Emperor Hypatius' day. Long live Hypatius!"

Bodies continued to push in on me. We were packed in, and still more came from the street, the stands filling higher, the track compacting with men and even some women.

I yelled out, "Monaxius! Tedius! Lukos! Bargas!" I yelled it again, then moved on, checking the faces I saw, no one I knew. But then, there was Gildo, with wine cups in each hand. He toasted them together then at me.

"Gaius Galen, the Green Sandman, the Blue Sandman salutes you!" He started to drink from one and I knocked it out of his hand.

"It's a trap, Gildo! Get out, it's a trap!"

"It's not a trap, it's a coronation!"

He wheeled off and ignored my yells, "It's a trap, Gildo, a trap! Get out!" People around me gave me mean looks, one threw wine on me and told me to shut my mouth. I knew, and they didn't. But no one would listen to me. This time, I really did know. It was not mania, it was worse: horrible truth.

Pawah tugged on my leg. I picked him up and started to carry him to safety but I didn't know where that was. He talked into my ear as I carried him, winding between bodies heading toward the north exit.

"Most of our men are over near the Green-Blues section," he said. I put him down.

"Go tell them I said it's a trap. Thousands of Mundus' troops are going to pin us in here. Tell them to go to the faction staging area and go out that way. Hurry!"

His eyes wide and mouth open in shock, Pawah took off dodging around legs and disappeared.

I was in a sudden commotion of men turning to look up, several crying out, "They're trying to break into the Kathisma! Imperial troops!"

The walkway from the Great Palace was filled with imperial troops, not Scholarian guards. But they were bottled up at the door of the Kathisma. Some tried to breach the interior door, while others who had broken through the outside stairway door hacked into the men blocking their path. It had begun.

Around me I could see it worry some faces, while others considered it amusement. The men on the Kathisma steps fought back with success, pushing the troops back up the stairway and onto the walkway. That brought a cheer from many – but it brought others to their senses and they realized what was happening. Justinian was not folding up his tent after all. He was fighting for his crown. Hypatius in his borrowed Kathisma looked white as imperial troopers fought to get at him. And for a few more moments, he was almost emperor.

But then Belisarius appeared at the north entrance to the Hippodrome on his grey charger, and a host of Goths and army regulars flowed around him pushing into the Hippodrome. In reaction to their thrust, the crowd at the north end of the track began to force itself back on us in the middle on both sides of the spina. From the north gate flew a flock of arrows into the stands, dropping more than a hundred men in an instant. Right behind that came another volley, many found the backs of men who had turned to flee. But there was nowhere to go. Three more volleys aimed into the Green and Blue sections filled them with dead and wounded men. In less than two minutes, probably a thousand of the mighty Green-Blues were felled by imperial arrows, without ever getting in a blow, their cause dying before it ever really lived.

As survivors began scrambling out of the stands, Belisarius' Goths chased them down and started cutting them to pieces. On each soldier's arm was a streamer of purple cloth, flapping like thousands of imperial banners as they sliced into Green and Blue traitors. More arrows were decimating sections of fans, volleys efficiently planned to fall in particular sections.

I turned to try to make it to the opening of the staging area, an idea at least 10,000 others had. We clogged together, some men turning on their fellows, stabbing another for his space ahead of them desperate to escape. About all I could see was panicking race fans, wishing they'd never come to stomp their feet in the glorious Hippodrome track. A sickening wail came from behind us, and I turned to see that the south entrance gates had swung open, Mundus bringing in his Herules and Illyrian Army regulars. I recognized the crimson cloak worn by some of the officers, and could make out furious grimaces on the faces of the Herule soldiers as they stabbed into the crowd of traitors, streamers whipping around like purple birds of prey in a feeding frenzy.

On the track the troops were using a simple maneuver to kill us by the score. A force would approach the section of the mob straight on, but the soldiers' center would suddenly fall back as if in panicked retreat. But then their flanks swung out wide creating a semicircle the traitors fell into, sealing them off when the flanks came together, turning inward and cutting down 50 traitors in a moment. I was pushed against my will toward the spina almost at the south end, the statue of Hercules towering above me fearless. I was not.

An instant later I realized troops were flanking around me, closing in on a section of 100 or so of us. We helplessly watched as ordered forces on both sides squeezed in on us. Just as I raised my short sword, intent on taking a few Herules with me, I was upended, pushed backward on a pile of people.

I couldn't get up, couldn't move, except to be buried further into the pile as more were heaped on top of me. I could hear blades slicing skin and cutting into bone, some petrified fan's urine was flowing over me. Men gasped for air, and everyone was screaming, troops too, only now it was their turn to cry out, *"Nika! Nika! Nika!"* Sadistic cackling mixed in their cry of victory, mocking their stupid enemy.

I was completely pinned, couldn't move my arms. Weight was bearing down on me, swords and spears stabbing into the body pile. I was struggling to breathe, my face jammed into a man's stomach, his fat suffocating me. A lance caught my right forearm, another my left leg. The noise was beginning to muffle. I wanted to think of Messalina, see her image before I went, but couldn't. Only her name came to mind. Men were vomiting up the wine they had happily gulped only moments before. I took a breath and decided to hold it, see if I could make it my last.

But someone grabbed hold of my beautiful boots! Some bastard was trying to get them before they were buried in a pile of gore. A jerk, and the right boot almost came off. Hands grabbed not my boot but deeper, getting a hold of my knee and yanked me up an inch. A pocket of air opened and I sucked it in off the dead man's stomach. Someone grabbed my left knee and pulled – I was being pulled out, not just my boots! My left arm caught on a bone, a head, something, and I was hung up, but the men pulled hard, freeing me from the pile. I was tossed on my back, looking through soldiers' legs at a patch of sky with clouds streaking it. I sucked in a big breath, then into the patch of sky came Atakam's head. He was grinning his sarcastic smile, appearing upside down to me.

"Good thing you wore those ugly boots today," he said, as if he was in my sitting room commenting on my wardrobe selection. But a nightmare of screaming was all around us. Horrible cries of pain and terror shrieking from a head bashed in, an arm lopped off.

Atakam and someone else righted me, so I was standing upright next to the squirming pile of bodies I had been extracted from by my Hun friend, his fellows diligently stabbing into the bodies as if it was a practiced maneuver.

"Take him to the wagon with the others," Atakam told the soldier who had pulled up my right leg. "And Gaius, make no mistake, it's over. You can do no more. You should be safe with my officer here, but only with him."

I stared at Atakam for a moment, feeling like a spirit plucked from death. "I'm going to live?" I asked. Atakam looked into my eyes, his hand on my shoulder, and nodded that I was.

"Go with him, Gaius. Your wounds are slight, your blind good fortune and ridiculous boots have saved you. We will finish your work for the emperor," and with that, Atakam stabbed twice into the pile – a gesture I will never forget – before heading away, a squad of men following him.

I was walked back – limped back – through a secured corridor of troops, like a protected lane through a garden of killing. And that killing was unending. The Blues, the Greens the neighborhood race fans, the traitors fought hard, but not well. The toughest street fighters were no game for the troops' pincer movements and coordinated thrusting into the prey with deadly practiced spear and sword work. I saw men jump off the top row of the Hippodrome to their death below rather than be slaughtered by soldiers chasing them.

Once in the faction staging gate, the officer put me on our baker's wagon, its replica gallows structure removed. Tedius was in it, his eye swollen shut, his face bloodied and he was unconscious, but breathing. Lukos and one of his men were sitting on the driver's bench, silent and bloody. The screaming, the killing continued for some time. Weakened from loss of blood or courage one, I passed out at some point. And I am glad I did.

-34-

Spies Among Us

I wasn't out long, because when the wagon moved and jolted me awake, the screaming was still intense, though muted in the area where we were under the stands, troops five deep blocking the entrance way from the track. Over their heads I could see scattered killing in the stands across the track. I looked away.

Monaxius was lying in the wagon bed with a head wound one of Zazo's monks was tending. I brushed his white streak of hair matted with blood from his forehead, we shared a flickered gleam of wonder at still being alive. A soldier drove us toward the faction exit, which was blocked by troops, but they let us pass and we picked up a bodyguard of about 20 men. We were taken to Chrysanthos' house, and all along the way was thick with troops on guard, including Excubitors and Scholarians manning their normal posts around the Great Palace. Emperor Justinian was in complete control. In the passing of perhaps three hours, he had gone from almost vanquished to victor, Nika unquestionably his.

We were offloaded by servants who took us to Herulian's sprawling laboratory, which had several beds set up for us. Agrippa, Iovita and two others tended to our wounds. I wondered why Agrippa was not still chained in my basement but that was not worth thinking about at this point. The doors were closed by troops and locked. It was clear we were not guests. Herulian entered about an hour later and approved of the treatment we had been given. None of our men spoke much at all, silenced by the enormity of the slaughter, the entrapment we now knew we should have seen coming, and the vague certainty that our lives – and the city itself – had changed forever.

After a while they brought us food and drink, and we talked some then. Tedius related the destruction of Adalwolf, Estrilda and their Goths, lit into by Mundus' Herules. Lukos saw Bargas die and most of his men.

"Some might have gotten away," Lukos added, "I just didn't see all of them be killed." He was drained and dejected. "I don't want to be here, I want to be dead with my Greens in the Hippodrome. Would have been, too. I was just about to leave this world by lunging into a large group of soldiers when two others grabbed me from behind. I thought they were going to slit my throat but they started dragging me away, and I saw Atakam grinning at me."

"His men pulled me out, as well," said Monaxius. "And they asked me where Gaius was and others with us. They had orders to save us. They showed me a sketch of myself Atakam had done and given them. They had sketches of all our leaders."

Monaxius started to run his hand through his hair, but his head wound stopped him.

"What happened, Gaius?" he asked, hurt showing in his eyes. "Pawah reached me just as the second force came through the south entrance. He told us you said it was a trap and to leave. But it was too late. What happened?"

I took a deep breath, which awakened the pain in my stabbed leg. "They wanted all of the traitors in the Hippodrome acclaiming Hypatius."

"Who?" asked Lukos, "who wanted us there?"

"Emperor Justinian, our client. We have been working for him all along."

"Justinian!?" Lukos stood up and glared. "Why didn't you tell us!"

"I've always told you everything I know," I insisted. "I only figured it out as the mob returned with Hypatius, which is when Jacob – who ran with a stab wound to find me – confirmed that imperial troops had been coming into the palace complex by boats for the past three or so nights, staying out of sight while everyone thought the imperial forces were too small to fight against the Green-Blues and the mob of supporters. But the easiest place to put down the rebellion was to move it from the streets to the Hippodrome, which we did for them. We were deceived and out maneuvered – all of us."

I told them about what Jacob found out at the imperial wharves. It all made Lukos more certain than ever that he wanted to be dead on the track. Instead, he'd helped kill thousands of Greens – and Blues. He had thought he was part of a historic moment when the factions united and the fans came together to create a new political power. But he was just a stupid tool of a ruthless emperor. He drank himself to sleep. The rest of us had hot baths and massages arranged for us, which seemed ridiculous, as if we were spa patrons relaxing after a vigorous game of ball.

A little before midnight, the guards opened the door and Herulian entered. I was in a comfortable chair with my bandaged leg up, talking to Tedius and Monaxius.

"Gaius Galen, Chrysanthos has returned. He wants to see you right away," Herulian held out his hand to help me up.

I stood without his help and stiffly followed him out.

Chrysanthos' study was warmly lit by several small lamps and the yellow glow of the fireplace. He was sprawled out on a long couch but gathered himself up when I entered.

"I am so tired, but that's meaningless to a man who has been through what you have this day – these past several days," this Chrysanthos said with a faint smile. "But you are safe now, Gaius Galen."

"I don't think I am." I wanted to show my anger but did not have such energy. "I have been duped. I have led friends and innocents to their deaths, came a breath away from it myself. And I was not safe at all – you knew it was more likely than not that I would die in there. And I doubt I will ever be safe again. How many men would want to kill me now for helping you – even unwittingly – slaughter their friends?"

"We had a plan to pull you and your men out of the crowd before it reached the Hippodrome, but you were not there," Chrysanthos explained. "Things got confusing, the soldiers had unexpected troubles and, and …" He stopped a long moment before continuing. "Yes, Gaius. Your life was always at risk. Always. But it could not be helped. You were picked out months ago by a special council the emperor started when he decided that the factions and partisans had to be stopped. The empire could not be at the mercy of mobs that had become more frequent, more powerful. The sport of racing had become a civil poison."

He seemed truly distressed that I had almost died. But I wasn't sure at all that he was concerned about my men who did. I felt for the first time that I was his equal, if not his better.

"In the end, Gaius, what Emperor Justinian wants, he will get," he said, as if this would be comforting. "I was helpless to do any more than I have to try to keep you from harm. I've been working closely with Chamberlain Narses on this plan and have reported many times to the emperor and empress on our progress. Almost a year ago after the last conflagration caused by the race supporters, Justinian declared that the days of providing bread and circuses to keep the people happy were going to end. Soon, it would be bread only."

"That's hard to believe," I said. "How were you going to do that? If you ended the races, the Colors and the city would eat itself and its emperor."

"True, and we did not know that we could actually do it. Our plan with you and others was to provoke the Greens by showing more favoritism to the Blues. And when the next rioting came, we would seek to crush the Greens while mostly leaving the Blues alone. The idea was that one Color would cause a lot less trouble."

He looked upward, shaking his head, perhaps at their naiveite, then continued.

"But then, the Blue and the Green hanging failed – a true act of God through his diligent insects. Very shortly after Brother Zazo had instantly, and brilliantly, called for the Colors to join and spirited away the miracle survivors to the church for sanctuary, the emperor, several ministers and our special faction council met," said Chrysanthos.

"Seeing how quickly support built for the Blues and Greens to come together, we determined to take advantage of the unprecedented opportunity to push them together against us – to encourage a coup that the senatorial enemies of our reforms would likely join. Then we might be able to crush both together, as we have done today. The alternative was likely Justinian's fall and the destruction of the empire."

"So you purposefully pulled the Excubitors and Scholarians back?" I slowly asked, piecing that rationale and my words together. "Rumors we heard were that they were waiting to see which side prevailed."

"Rumor is a wonderful weapon. If that had been the case, the first order for Belisarius and Mundus – both of whom we summoned before the volitivity of the Ides race day – would have been to cut both guards down, then go after the factions," Chrysanthos explained, seeming amused at the gullibility of the people, and of me. "And yesterday we intentionally started the rumor that Justinian wanted to flee, holding a fake council meeting where Empress Theodora employed her considerable acting skills. We made sure Belisarius' meddlesome secretary Procopius was there, knowing he would help spread our rumor, as did others."

He laughed to himself, enjoying their trickery. And at that moment I had to admit that it was brilliant, making fools of just about everyone.

"And rumor again fooled Hypatius sitting in the Kathisma," he continued. "He was led to believe that Justinian had fled the palace, and he thought he really was Emperor Hypatius."

"His secretaries the other morning," I recalled, "they did not want to leave the Palace. Was he pushed out? He was, wasn't he – you needed him available, and you didn't think the monophysite nephew Probus was suitable."

"Correct, Gaius. Hypatius was going along with our scheme, though he was very uncomfortable to even pretend to rebel," a worried look crossed Chrysanthos' face, his age showing with the concern. "I imagine he will be executed tomorrow. They are talking about that now."

"And the others, the senators and noblemen who pushed themselves onto the Green-Blues and supported Hypatius? Will they be executed as well?" I asked, wondering where my men and I might fit in this citywide cleansing.

"It is more likely that they will be banished and their estates confiscated. The emperor tends to think that forgiveness at that level provides a great return by instilling loyalty in the rest of the nobility. It is the factions and their uncontrollable rioters we wanted to punish most," he said, tilting his head down to look at me, one of the uncontrollables. "They're calculating that upward of 25,000 were killed today in the Hippodrome and streets, the flower of the factions exterminated along with many of the vermin that follow them – and the traitorous senators who would lead them. Perhaps we can have some peace without the infernal fighting of the Blues and the Greens."

His servant entered and whispered to Chrysanthos, who nodded his approval, and the servant left.

"Gaius, Chamberlain Narses thinks I am making a mistake in what I am about to do, but I told him it is what I owe you. And I owe you as much honesty as I can afford to reveal."

He motioned to the door and the servant opened it, and I sensed it must be for Atakam and Scorpus. And they did enter – along with Brother Zazo.

"Spies," I said, giving Scorpus a sporting salute. "I knew Ammianus had to have spies on me, I just didn't know who."

"How's the leg?" asked Atakam, his tone sincere but not worried.

"I thought you were a possible, and was almost certain of Scorpus, particularly after he visited me in the tavern and warned me about Ammianus. How long, Atakam?" I asked tiredly, my foolishness weighing heavier and heavier.

"First day. Me under attack, you to my rescue. Ten of my men planted in the crowd around us should anything have gone amiss," Atakam was smiling at how he had tricked me. "We had to see if you were capable of following through. From what I know now, I would follow you as my commander any day, Gaius."

"I, as well, Gaius Galen," said Scorpus. "And I might have to, because it looks like there won't be much chariot racing for some time."

"Let's hope chariot racing is on the same path as gladiators and bear fighting," said Chrysanthos. He brightened and said, "When the city began to burn up, I needed to put the most valuable thing to you in a safe place. So, Messalina went to Scorpus, along with Flacilla and her girls. I knew that if you could, you would eventually show up there, for her."

I didn't want to ask, so said it instead, "And Messalina, she was one of your spies, too." I looked to Chrysanthos.

"No, Gaius," he said, his eyes twinkling with pleasantry. "She was not. But two of her fellow repenting ladies are."

"Sister Flacilla?" I asked, not wanting to hear a *yes*.

"No, though I tried," Chrysanthos said. "Sister Flacilla is," he chose his word slowly, "uncorruptible – and before you ask, we did not even consider approaching Tedius. That man would die for you, and not because he is your slave."

"I know this, and owe him my life – several times over," I said, then turned to Zazo. "And you, Brother? From the day I met you at Monaxius' door?"

"Before, Gaius Galen. I was told to strike a relationship with Monaxius, who would lead me to you," he said unhappily.

"But," Chrysanthos interjected, "we lost him. When Ammianus kidnapped Martha, Brother Zazo came to me to quit. He would have nothing to do with Ammianus from that point on, even if I threatened to have him killed."

Zazo nodded proudly and said, "Chrysanthos was gracious – and wise – allowing me to continue on as I saw fit without reporting on you. Gaius, I always wanted to protect you, your friends and Monaxius' family. You all put your trust and faith in me."

"These three were selected not just to inform us," said Chrysanthos, "but to protect you, my child – and you are that, since we met under troubling circumstances those many years ago. When your name came up as a resource for the emperor's needs, I was shocked, but not in a position to override it. Your mental issues were disconcerting, but Atakam insisted that he knew you would be fine. I admit that Herulian's medication was not the answer – and I was actually glad to hear that you rejected it when Agrippa tried to get you to take it again."

"Messalina," said Scorpus. "It was Messalina's visit that saved you. Don't look at me like that, Gaius. I never touched her or *tried* to. In fact, we have become good friends. Confidants, I would say."

I stepped over to him and shook his hand. "Thank you for watching over her. It was a great relief for me to know she was safe, if not from you at least from the riots."

I looked to the tall one. "Brother Zazo, I can't call you a traitor for spying on me, because you have helped us so much. I depended on you, at times more than I did on myself."

"And was he not fantastic grabbing the hanged men and realizing their potential to bring the partisans together?" announced Chrysanthos, beaming. "Absolutely brilliant, Brother Zazo. Would you like to be a bishop?"

"No, Sir. Never," he said. "I would rather Gaius Galen know the truth about Hagia Sophia."

"Of course, of course," said Chrysanthos. "Justinian was going to make substantial improvements to the church, but that was years off. Ammianus, who had family relations with Anthemius and was already in league with your father to get part of that lucrative contract, decided to take advantage of the rioters' destruction and have you burn it down to speed up that process. I was not aware of that plan. Zazo allowing Ammianus to perish saved us from executing him for his unholy, selfish scheme."

This brought me some relief, though not much, for even though God would punish Ammianus for this, He still knew who kindled the fire.

"It was just a building, Gaius Galen," said Zazo, sensing my thoughts. "God knows that and knows your heart. He forgives you, as you must yourself."

I hugged Brother Zazo, and in that moment with my face tickled by his curls, I gathered composure. "I owe you my life, Brother Zazo, perhaps my soul."

I moved to Atakam, and gave him my hand. "I owe you my life as well, soldier. Of course, you could have told me what was going on and I would have never been in the Hippodrome, but you were faithful to your orders. I understand."

"I was frantic looking for you in the Hippodrome after they told me you were not pulled from the earlier crowds around Hypatius because they couldn't find you." He looked at my feet, in a pair of silk slippers Agrippa had given me. "Your boots, those awful boots, stuck out to me, and I could not believe my luck."

He hugged me, kissing my head before letting me go.

"There is one other thing we need to address, Gaius Galen," said Chrysanthos. He took a large swallow of warm wine and said, "Your father."

"What about him? He's chained in my basement."

"So was Agrippa, but you see he's not there," said Chrysanthos. "We knew he was there. In addition to these spies, that boy they call Stinky serving as your runner was very helpful. We knew everything that was going on around your home. But back to your father. What do you want us to do with him?"

I shook my head. "I don't want that responsibility, Chrysanthos."

He seemed to be debating something then said, "Gaius, months ago when we had Ammianus identify people who had the credibility to push our agenda in the street, your father gave him your name, relating your lucrative past."

I was almost not surprised to find this out, but it made my decision easy.

"Banish him," I said. "Make him work in one of his mines until some later date, perhaps his death. Divide his estate among Mother, me and Fulvia."

"We can banish him. And the emperor can confiscate his estate, then give it to you and you can divide it as you please," said Chrysanthos. "Is that acceptable?"

"Yes."

"Do you wish to see your father? He is here."

"No, I do not."

Obscured by Clouds

Three weeks later we were to meet with the Chamberlain Narses. *We* meaning as many of our group as were still alive. And in the past days many of ours had turned up, most happily for me was Estrilda. Her husband had died, and she should have, but some of Belisarius' Goths found her on the ground, severely wounded but still alive, and took her to safety.

The Hippodrome's Gate of Death, where an occasional charioteer or horse was carted off previously, proved well named, as thousands of bodies were taken out through it for more than a week in cleaning up the slaughter. A heavy snow and hard freeze suspended work for a day. The people of the city seemed buried alive. Mute, vacant-eyed, treading lightly, fearful of any sound and of each other. Everyone was a mourner.

And who was a traitor? Who had been a Green? A Blue? All the faces said, *Not I.* The winners were busy appropriating from the losers. Estates, businesses, offices, patronages, all forms of contact and authority had to be re-established, reformed, and the missing had to be replaced. The beggars and unfortunates from the countryside who lived through the catastrophe were winners in the aftermath of the ruined city, for there was opportunity for anyone still standing. And though I and all of my survivors were technically winners, it did not sit well at all, with any of us.

The past three weeks I spent with Messalina lounging around Scorpus' estate. I mourned my deceased companions, the effective death of the Blues, the Greens and the races, though Scorpus thought they would return, or wished it. Annia, Martha and Elissa were united with Monaxius before he left Chrysanthos' home the day after the slaughter. But we could get no word on Arbella. Chrysanthos was trying but he thought perhaps Ammianus had moved them right before his death, and it was possible that Kyros and his troupe might remain a mystery for a while. Messalina had Tedius and all the waywards working on it.

She and I recuperated together. I did not want to be at my home, not near the memory of the fallen members of my strange family of followers, sleeping head-to-toe on my floor, the pups pillow fighting in my bed, orthodox monks and Jews in harmony together, laughing at an awkward escape. The ghosts of the fallen would make sleep impossible, at least for a while still. Sister Flacilla left Messalina and me alone for the most part.

"Are you still my Gaius?" Messalina asked, her head against my hip, both of us stretched out on a couch that would have accommodated eight. "Or are you also Wilder still?"

She slid her warm hand up my side under my tunic, causing my skin to shiver. Still such a tease. Sister would not have approved of that or of other things she has done to me in the past days, though always short of being enough.

"Yes, I am still your Gaius. Wilder is gone," I said, flinching as her fingers twirled my chest hair. I tried to push her hand away to stop the tickling.

She lifted her head up and danced her brown eyes at me, saying, "Are you moving my hand down or away?"

"Down?"

"Not yet down. Away for now. But in a month – "

" – That's 30 days. 30!" I complained.

"Yes, well in a month Sister Flacilla's home will be all repaired and fit to host our wedding."

The fingers were at my chest hair. I called it torture, she called it play.

"And after that day – in fact before the day is done – I am going to treat you, completely. And treat you," she plucked a hair out! "and treat you," there went another! "and treat you, so good," this last was whispered as she raised up, and we kissed for some time.

That evening we were guests of Chamberlain Narses, the 51 of us who could be found. We sat at a huge table that could have held 30 more people easily, and we dined on some of the finest food I had ever tasted. Chrysanthos sat next to Narses, one of the least eunuch-acting of the eunuchs I now knew. Singers and musicians entertained us, as did Scorpus, who was on a tear of joke telling, laughing hard at every one he told.

After dinner, while we had little sweets served to us on silver trays and sipped on a sweet wine from Macedonia, Narses, who seemed to be a man of extreme composure and natural kindness, addressed us.

"Emperor Justinian sends his best wishes to each of you. He knows your names and includes them in his prayers." Jacob almost choked. "And talking of names – Estrilda where are you? Oh there. The daughter of Emperor Justinian's cousin gave birth to a girl in the palace during the rebellion, and he has given his permission for the girl to be named after you, Estrilda."

This made her cry. And she thanked Narses, though overcome with tears and emotions. She held up her glass and said, "Adalwolf would be proud," struggling to hold her chin from shaking. "Your Excellence, please convey my pride to the emperor and his cousin's daughter."

"Of course," said Narses with a smile. "And the empress especially sends her thanks to each one of you, calling you the empire's bravest warriors." He was not expecting our silence at this, but then seemed to understand. "I know you did not choose to be imperial warriors, but you are, and I would wear it with pride. Your efforts have enabled us to end, for some time at least, the continuous troubles, disturbances, disorders – whatever they should be called – that have weakened our state."

Narses searched out and found Lukos, and held his eye.

"And it does not escape me that this was not your intention. But how much of life's course do we ever get to choose?" he asked, still watching Lukos.

"But you didn't have to kill them all!" Lukos challenged. Narses pushed back in his seat at the verbal assault, a bemused smile granting this unusual license. Lukos couldn't help himself, saying, "No emperor has ever done that – I sang the man's praises in a Green choir often and properly revered Justinian. But not now. How could I? How could I revere any man who has me murder my friends, kill my Color?"

Lukos looked at Narses as he might a Blue he had caught out in an alley.

The Chamberlain nodded, gave a quick wave as if at a fly, and spoke to Lukos.

"Why, if the emperor saw that look on your face now, he would know for certain that he has done the right thing, Lukos," Narses said, and narrowed his eyes at him. "You are consumed with this grief, young man, and I thoroughly understand, which is why I have waved off my guards over there from taking you out for a beating or execution – they've never heard such words spoken to me. I agree with you in part, and forgive your insolence."

"Say, *Thank you*, Lukos," advised Atakam before I could.

"I apologize to you Chamberlain – and to Emperor Justinian," Lukos managed, glancing quickly at the guards against the wall who were visibly tense to have at his throat.

"Thank you, young man," Narses accepted. "I feel for your loss, truly. And I advise that you fear your emperor as well as revere him. As should others. For he has asked me to tell you all that your actions have helped free him of a tremendous burden, and he is now ready to set an even more ambitious course than anyone has dared to imagine. These details will be revealed in time, but I will tell you simply that the Roman Empire of the East will unite with the Empire of the West once again."

I had heard rumors that Justinian's forces were being readied for an attack on the Vandals in North Africa, but not that it was then to be on to Rome. Atakam was just about bouncing in his seat at this from Narses, ready to get going after dinner. Lukos looked as if he was realizing how close he had just come to death, saved only by a eunuch's grace.

"Now I must excuse myself, friends. There is much work to do in rebuilding and reuniting Constantinople," this Narses said with a flourish, and downed his wine, the rest of us following suit. "But I almost forgot. Gaius Galen Licinius, rise, Sir."

He snapped a finger and walked to me, his servant handing him a crimson bundle. He shook it out and unfurled it around me – the crimson cloak of an Illyrian Army officer.

"General Mundus awards you the honor of being admitted to his most trusted guard," and he pinned the cloak together with the silver spearman emblem, though no sliver of ruby on the spear tip. "The emperor – and Atakam – say it is an honor well earned."

Narses took both my hands in his and bowed his head to me for a silent moment. I was proud for so many reasons and for perhaps the first time ever, honestly proud of myself. I gave the chamberlain a stoic smile and squeezed his hands tight in thanks.

"I've arranged a special performance for you tonight in the private theater of the emperor over in the Great Palace," Narses said. "Chrysanthos will tell you of your rewards, and will field any requests you have of your 'client,' Emperor Justinian," this he said to me. "For example, Jacob here will now be a premier sailmaker of the imperial fleet."

"Good God!" blurted out Jacob, his head knocked back against his chair with the surprise.

"Yes. And you'll do a fine job. You'd have the official title but for the Jewishness, you understand," said Narses, dismissing the detail as a nuisance. "Flavius, you'll take Ammianus' job, but there will be little to do with no races for the time being, perhaps a very long time. Lukos, we have not overlooked you. You and your … associates can move into your new home: the one Anthemius left, which we will refurbish from its fire damage. We will also provide you with reputable employment – should you be ready for that." Lukos, shocked into a humility I have never seen, bowed his head with hands pressed together as if in prayer to the eunuch chamberlain. "And the rest of you," said Narses, "will be suitably attended to as you wish. Good night to you all."

He turned to me and again shook my hand. As he straightened from bending to me he looked at Messalina, and without taking his eyes off her said, "Gaius Galen, I wish I could be as lucky a man as you."

Could I receive a better compliment? From a more unlikely source?

I really didn't want to go to a theater performance but did. Besides slighting the emperor, Messalina would have killed me had I not allowed her to be entertained in the Great Palace.

Each person had a very comfortable seat, and on the arm of each seat was carved a small actor's mask with diamonds for eyes. Lukos was in front of me, trying to pry a diamond out with his fingernail until I stopped him with a push. We were seated in the chairs with our names on a card in the seat. Messalina was by me, there was an empty chair, then Atakam, Monaxius and Annia. Tedius and his wife, Kiya, were in front of us next to Lukos and four of his boys.

The seating section lamps were extinguished, and the dramatic stage lighting narrowed the focus of our attention. This was no low-brow pantomime but a proper Greek comedy. Two houses were in the background of the stage set. A woman came down from an upper row behind us moving slowly in the dark and began to enter our aisle. She stepped right in front of me, moved across Messalina, then bent down and asked her, "May I sit with you, Sister?"

"Aay!" Messalina screamed then jumped up and grabbed Arbella. They sobbed, laughed, hugged, kissed, somehow managed to sit down while holding one another close. Messalina reached over to squeeze my knee to tell me how happy she was.

The chorus on stage, dressed as clouds, was murmuring its song in spite of the sisters' sobbing disturbance.

But that stopped abruptly when a loud voice from the stage called out, "Quiet, quiet! Goodness, we're in the Great Palace and you don't know how to act any better than that?"

It was Kyros and he was shaking his head at us.

"I'm to play the lead in a stuffy comedy I haven't had to perform since I was 12, and the audience is worse than one in a cheap faction house." The light reflected from a mirror held by a stage hand followed him as he wandered and talked.

"It hasn't been a good day at all, no. I was awakened – before noon – by an official who informed me that I was privileged to have my most talented and prettiest slave, Arbella, purchased by one Chrysanthos, who immediately freed her. Just as young Gaius – or is it still Wilder? – has freed his man Tedius. These people are addled. And this city? What is going on here? Give me Jerusalem over this trash heap of corpses any day."

I laughed then shed tears the next instant. How could I possibly laugh at 25,000 dead? Yet I had reflexively. Surely a comedy would be good for us. We had seen enough tragedy.

Kyros went right into the play he hadn't performed since he was a boy, "The Clouds" by Aristophanes. The sleeping character Pheidippides was tossing and turning, speaking of driving his chariot straight, and, "How many times round the track is the race for the chariots of war?" Then Kyros, as his father, chastised the dreaming sleeper, "It's your own father you are driving to death … to ruin."

Chrysanthos was behind me, leaning down to whisper in my ear, "The play was chosen not to taunt, but to help you heal – help all of you heal." He rested his hand on my shoulder then let it trail off to return to his seat.

Throughout the performance, Messalina continued to squeeze my knee every now and then, though she never let go of Arbella. At the end of the play, the actors burnt Socrates out of his house, none of it striking me as being very comedic or curative. Lukos agreed, with his snoring.

Later, Messalina, Arbella and I bundled up in the covered cabin of the long boat rowed by six men who whisked us over the calm water of the Golden Horn back to Scorpus' estate. Messalina and Arbella hardly stopped talking, except when Messalina remembered me and turned to give me a kiss and a smile. I excused myself and stepped out of the cabin.

I turned to face the city we were leaving behind. The wind was blowing from the south pushing the smell of smoke across the Golden Horn. The fires had all been extinguished some time ago but the flavor of smoke still hung on, and onto every half-standing wall, every wooden door, every man's tunic, every woman's hair. This vantage point north of the city did not show the areas burnt out and destroyed. Those were on the other side of the hills I was seeing, the lights in homes speaking of civilization, a great city built by determined people, almost destroyed by deranged ones. Constantinople looked like a body huddled up into a ball against the cold. I looked deeper at the body under the cloudy sky, deeper until my eyes stopped seeing the lights as I stared. I saw my legs sticking out of a pile of bodies, I saw the first trail of smoke that rose over Hagia Sophia, I saw blood in my sand. The city was colorless, no Green, no Blue. Only black, tinged in purple.

About the Author

Richard Wall is a creative writer living in Atlantic Beach, Florida. He graduated from the University of Tennessee with a BA in history. His background includes newspaper reporter, magazine editor, TV producer, freelance writer and medical content editor. He is a lifetime sports participant and fan, who considers himself to be a Blue as a supporter of Manchester City Football Club in the English Premier League, whose team color is light blue. Richard enjoys reading history and fiction, surfing, paddleboarding, swimming, playing golf, and taking bike rides with his wife. He will soon publish his novel "Drive Nice" about an eco-vigilante group that tries to enforce driving civility in San Francisco. Contact him at 1AtlanticEditorial@gmail.com or visit RichardWall.net.